FOREVER AND A DOOMSDAY

ALSO BY LAURENCE MACNAUGHTON

It Happened One Doomsday

A Kiss Before Doomsday

No Sleep till Doomsday

LAURENCE MacNAUGHTON

FOREVER AND A DOOMSDAY

A Dru Jasper Novel

Published 2019 by Pyr®

Cover image by Shutterstock
Cover design by Jennifer Do
Cover design © Start Science Fiction

This is a work of fiction. Characters, organizations, products, locales, and events portrayed in this novel either are products of the author's imagination or are used fictitiously.

Inquiries should be addressed to:
Start Science Fiction
101 Hudson Street
37th Floor, Suite 3705
Jersey City, New Jersey 07302
PHONE: 212-431-5455
WWW.PYRSF.COM

ISBN: 978-1-63388-556-1 (paperback) | ISBN: 978-1-63388-557-8 (eBook)

Printed in the United States of America

For Cyndi

CONTENTS

1   The Night Before Doomsday   1
2   Burning Salem   9
3   Nothing Is All Right   17
4   Inside These Walls   24
5   Field Guide to the Undead   32
6   Moon Dust   41
7   Those Who Want to Use You   51
8   Other People's Drama   58
9   Fashion Secrets of the Sorcerers   66
10 Get Swole   75
11 Gazing Into the Dark   87
12 Just Out of Reach   94
13 Body and Soul   100
14 The Evil Within   108
15 Send Me an Angel   115
16 Before It's Too Late   125
17 Run Away With You   132
18 Driving Rane   141
19 Forbidden Places   148
20 The Darkest Sky   155
21 Hard Hat Area   162
22 Behind These Walls   169
23 The Things We Hide   178
24 Don't Scry for Me   184
25 Of Roman Descent   192
26 Evil Rides With You   199
27 Immortal Cravings   207
28 The Dark Unknown   214
29 The Shining City   225
30 Under a Hollow Sky   233
31 Hell to Pay   241
32 Soul of Sin and Steel   250
33 The Darkness Within Us   256

34 All That's Left Is You   262
35 All in a Doomsday's Work   270

1

THE NIGHT BEFORE DOOMSDAY

If the world was going to end in flames, there was one person Dru desperately wanted at her side. Whenever an apocalyptic menace threatened, he was always there for her, just when she needed him most. No matter how many sorcerers Dru had met, how many monsters she had fought, or how many curses she had broken, she had never dreamed that there could be anyone as courageous and loyal as Greyson.

Or anything as dark and dangerous as his demon-possessed car, Hellbringer.

The heat of the vanished summer sun still radiated up from the empty road long after dark, baking the parched blades of grass and shriveled weeds on either side. A glimmer of headlights spread across the black asphalt, bleaching it silver, illuminating the pitted double-yellow lines that stretched into the distance. The long, black muscle car roared past, burning-hot exhaust pipes cackling as Hellbringer kicked up a haze of dust. Darkness instantly returned to the road, except for the lava-red slits of taillights dwindling into the darkness, like the eyes of a demon descending into the abyss.

In the passenger seat, Dru shifted beneath the weight of the warm white plastic bag in her lap. For a sorceress who spent a distressing amount of her time getting splashed by magical potions, blasted by fiery spells, and slobbered on by foul creatures, even a single quiet, romantic evening like this was a blessing.

So she had made the most of it. Gotten her hair done. Spent extra time on her makeup. Picked up a brand-new blue dress with short sleeves and a nice V-neck. Let Greyson take her out to dinner at her favorite neighborhood Chinese place. Laughed and talked about everything except doomsday until the sun sank below the mountains and the stars came out.

Now, the quiet calm of this deserted road made her feel like the two of them were the last people on Earth, and she couldn't be happier about that. She wished this rare moment alone with Greyson would never end.

As if sensing her thoughts, he lifted his palm from the gear shift and took her hand, holding it tight. Then they hit a bump in the road that nearly toppled the contents of the steamy plastic bag. She let go of his hand to catch the bundle and make sure it stayed upright.

Just like that, the moment was gone. She could almost see the gears shifting in Greyson's head as he looked at the bag. As desperately as she wanted to hold onto this dreamy evening, to make it last, she felt it slipping away. And it was all her fault.

His eyebrow quirked up. "Are you sure about the chicken soup?"

She sighed and pushed her glasses back up her nose, mentally cursing her own overextended sense of professional responsibility. It had kept twinging in the back of her mind all through dinner, and just before they had left, she had made a split-second decision that she now realized was in danger of ruining their date.

"I just want Salem to get better," Dru said, hoping that she wasn't making a mistake. "He may be one of the most powerful sorcerers around, but he's still human. And he's kind of a friend. Sort of."

Greyson's leather jacket creaked as he turned toward her. The dashboard lights illuminated the stubble on his chiseled jaw and cast his broad chest into shadow. "The fact that he's injured could make him dangerous."

"I think the word I would choose is *crabby*. He did almost get crushed to death beneath a rockslide. That would put anybody in a bad mood, right?"

Greyson grunted. "Not just anybody in a bad mood can flick his wrist and flip a car over."

"He's not going to flip the car over," Dru said with a confidence she didn't entirely feel. Quietly, she added, "I hope."

Greyson turned the steering wheel. Hellbringer's headlight beams swept across a desolate parking lot, briefly illuminating glimpses of tall dead grass, windblown candy bar wrappers, and the sparkling scattered glass of broken bottles.

Like everything else around here, the parking lot was deserted. The only car actually parked there, in the exact center of practically an acre of abandoned asphalt, was an old black hearse. All the long bits of its chrome trim shone for a moment in the passing headlight beams, like shooting stars streaking across a night sky. Creepy as that particular vehicle was in the daytime, it was downright spooky at night. Especially since the layer of tan dust coating it indicated that the hearse hadn't been driven in a while.

"Well, Salem's home," Dru said brightly. "That's good news."

The look on Greyson's face said that he didn't agree. "Hope he likes soup."

Hellbringer drove across the cracked asphalt, crushing dead grass and weeds beneath the tires. Ahead loomed a sprawling industrial building, the entire ground floor covered in graffiti. Empty holes gaped where windows had been smashed out long ago. Under ordinary circumstances, Dru would have been scared to set foot anywhere near this place. But more than anything, she wanted to help Salem recover from his injuries. She was pretty sure he wouldn't appreciate it, but she had to try. In a way, she felt responsible.

From the driver's seat, Greyson cast a sidelong glance at the bag.

"We'll just drop it off and go. I promise." Dru pulled the knot tighter at the top of the white plastic bag, hoping that would prevent anything from spilling out. The old demon car filled with the mouth-watering aromas of chicken broth, green onions, fresh cilantro, and spicy garlic.

At the top of the bag, wax paper crinkled under the pressure. "Ooh, look at that! Mrs. Xin slipped in some bonus egg rolls. She's been extra nice ever since we saved her from those nasty spirit-possessed *shi shis.*"

But Greyson wasn't listening. He suddenly sat up straighter in the driver's seat, frowning, and his chest swelled with an intake of breath. His blue eyes scanned the darkness outside. All at once, swarms of tiny sparks flared to life in his irises, as if a raging fire had been struck inside him. His eyes began to glow a hellish red.

He was sensing danger. "Something's out there."

Eyes wide behind her glasses, Dru turned to follow his gaze. Greyson's danger sense had never been wrong before, but she didn't see anything out of the ordinary. Just graffiti, trash, weeds, and some broken bits of concrete. Still, she turned and pushed down the little chrome knob in the door, locking it.

"Let's take a look around." Greyson turned the big steering wheel and slowly circled the building. The headlights played off of the crumbling concrete walls festooned with indecipherable spray paint. To the casual observer, the place looked dead and abandoned. But Dru knew firsthand that the entire top floor of the old building was Salem's personal lair. As a sorcerer, he was probably second to none. But when it came to his curb appeal, he had plenty of room for improvement.

The steady rumble of Hellbringer's engine thudded off of the grimy walls and reflected back at them. If there was somebody—or some*thing*— out there in the darkness, they had to know exactly where Hellbringer was. The demon car was as subtle as dropping a ton of bricks. About as quiet, too.

Dru leaned forward in the seat, staring out through the windshield, scanning the night. She saw a flicker of movement and pointed. "There!"

Greyson turned Hellbringer toward it and goosed the gas, making the engine bark with barely contained menace. But the headlight beams revealed nothing. Just an expanse of broken, windblown asphalt. Greyson turned his burning red gaze toward Dru with an unspoken question.

Her heart beat faster. She shook her head, worried. "There was something moving out there. I know it."

He nodded grimly. "Maybe we should get out of here."

"Not if there's any chance Salem is in danger." Fighting down the clammy fear that threatened to paralyze her, Dru set the bag of soup and egg rolls down between her feet, and quickly dug into the cluttered depths of her purse. Beneath a thick wad of expired coupons, some little pencils from IKEA, and a snarl of headphones currently wrapped boa constrictor-like around a necklace she hadn't seen in six months, she found what she was looking for. It was a rectangular crystal about the size of a Tic Tac box, with rounded edges.

Dru pulled out the ulexite crystal, which resembled a frosted piece of sea glass, and pressed it to her forehead. Instantly, her vision swam as her magical energy flowed through the crystal.

Outside the car, the black of night grew deeper. Yet at the same time, the air filled with a luminous glow, making her feel as if everything had suddenly plunged underwater. The world around her lit with an eerie inner light. Using the ulexite, Dru could pick up ethereal auras that were invisible to the naked eye. She could also spot magical spells, invisible lurkers, and most supernatural creatures. All of the horrifying, sanity-stealing things normal people weren't meant to see.

She swiveled her head left and right. There was nothing immediately in front of them, as far she could tell. Then she turned around to look behind them.

A slender, luminous figure slipped through the night. It didn't walk so much as *glide* through the darkness, and the eerie movement made her skin crawl.

As if sensing her gaze, it jerked its head to look straight at her. But its face was hideously wrong. It had no eyes. Nothing but twin pools of impenetrable blackness.

For a moment, Dru couldn't get any words out. In her admittedly brief career as a sorceress, she had faced down all manner of disturbing creatures: demons, shape changers, web-spinning undead, and on one particularly disturbing occasion, a colossal evil clown statue. But those staring pools of darkness left her struggling to breathe through her tightening throat.

The thing disappeared into the gloom of the ground floor just before Hellbringer turned the corner, circling the building.

Dru pointed and forced the words out: "It's back there!"

Greyson slowed the car. "*It?*"

She struggled to put what she'd seen into words. "Some kind of . . . ghost?"

Greyson studied the look on her face, and nodded slightly, as if making a decision. Instead of turning the car around, he nailed the gas. The tires chirped, and the sudden acceleration nearly toppled the bag of Chinese chicken soup onto Dru's feet.

"Salem's ladder is on the other side of the building," Greyson said, referring to the only way up to the sorcerer's top-floor lair. "We'll go in that way. Get to Salem first, make sure he's okay."

"We need to call him." Dru was already fumbling in her purse for her phone. She tried ringing Salem. But as many years as she had known him, he had never once answered the phone. And he didn't answer now.

Resisting the urge to start cursing, she then tried her friend Rane, who was also Salem's on-again, off-again girlfriend. Currently on-again.

The phone was still ringing as Hellbringer screeched to a halt at the base of the bare metal ladder. It stretched up the side of the concrete building to the roof, looking dangerously rickety and exposed. Dru swung the door open and got out just as Rane answered.

"What up, D?" Rane puffed. From the sound of it, she was running. But not in an emergency, run-for-your-life kind of way. More like the measured, steady strides of training. But just behind her pounding footsteps came the distinctive snuffling and panting of what sounded like a very large canine. Which was particularly worrisome, because Rane didn't have a dog.

Dru couldn't keep the panic out of her voice. "Are you *okay?*" she practically screamed. "Where *are* you?"

"Dude, I'm getting my cardio on," Rane's husky voice snapped. "What's your problem?"

"There's a ghost at Salem's! Hurry!"

To Rane's credit, she didn't waste any time asking for details. There was a scuffling sound, like running shoes skidding through dirt as they changed direction. Her footsteps pounded faster. She swore under her breath. "I'm like twenty minutes out. Twenty-five tops."

Rane was the strongest ally they could have at their side right now, but she was too far away to help. A hard knot formed in Dru's stomach as she realized what that meant.

"D, listen. Whatever's about to happen, it's probably gonna happen before I get there," Rane said steadily. "You have to hold out. No matter what."

"I know." Dru focused on keeping her voice from quavering. She suddenly felt the night closing in around her. "We'll handle this." Though she had no idea how. Or what *this* was, exactly. She only knew that whatever she had seen a minute before, it definitely wasn't friendly. And it was already inside the building.

A few paces away, Greyson stood at the base of the ladder, red eyes glaring left and right, watching for danger. The metal snaps on his leather motorcycle jacket glinted in the glare of Hellbringer's headlights. He caught Dru's gaze and nodded his chin toward the ladder.

Dru nodded. "Okay. We're going in. You'll call Salem?"

"Just tried. Dude's not answering." Rane didn't often sound worried. When she did, it sent shivers down Dru's spine. "And D?"

"Yeah?"

Rane panted. "Be careful, cowgirl. When I get there, you better still be in one piece."

Dru hung up without saying another word. Her knees were reduced to jelly, and it took a moment to force her legs to move. But if that thing was coming after Salem, she had to try to stop it somehow.

She crossed to the ladder and put a hand on the rungs.

Greyson stopped her with a puzzled look. "You're really bringing the chicken soup?"

Dru looked down at the heavy plastic bag hanging from her hand. She had meant to leave it in the car, but she had grabbed it automatically as she was on the phone, and now its weight comforted her like a security blanket. A savory, garlicky, chicken security blanket. She didn't want to let it go.

Dru cleared her throat. "Well, in case this thing is carnivorous. Maybe I can distract it."

"By throwing chicken soup at it." Greyson did not sound convinced.

"You should see some of the things I've fought monsters with. Light bulbs. Fire extinguishers. Air compressors. That kitty litter stuff in your garage."

"Point taken." He looked back over his shoulder at Hellbringer and made a circling motion with his finger. "PATROL," he told the car in a commanding voice. His eyes blazed brighter red.

Immediately, Hellbringer's engine roared to life. With a deafening howl, its rear tires spun, spewing out white smoke. The demon car shot backward, headlight beams burning brightly through the choking clouds of burned rubber left behind. With a squeal, the car's long nose whipped around to face the opposite direction. Immediately, Hellbringer shot away down the length of the building, the slits of its red taillights staring back at them with barely restrained aggression.

Dru would have felt safer if she'd been able to stay inside the car. Hellbringer knew how to fight and was a formidable ally. For perhaps the hundredth time, Dru was thankful that the car was on their side.

But a nagging voice in the back of her mind made her wonder if relying on the car so much was wise. Though it generally obeyed Greyson, it was still, at its core, a demon. What would happen if she trusted it one too many times?

She pushed those thoughts aside. Now was not the time or the place. They had to get upstairs and protect Salem before that ghost—or whatever it was—got to him first. As Dru put one foot on the ladder, the heart-stopping sound of breaking glass cut through the night, coming from somewhere above.

Were they already too late?

2

BURNING SALEM

Dru climbed the ladder as fast as her feet would carry her. Her purse, heavy with crystals and the assorted accoutrements of a highly disorganized sorceress, banged steadily against her side, threatening to knock her off-balance. It didn't help that she was hauling a heavy plastic bag full of chicken soup and egg rolls, too.

When they reached the roof, Greyson put a cautionary hand on her arm. "That thing is getting closer," he growled. "I can feel it."

Despite the moonlight, the flat roof stretched out before them like a river of darkness. At the far end, the roof ran right up to the adjoining building, which stood at least two stories taller. The only entrance was Salem's door, currently wide open. A rectangle of warm candlelight spilled out, at once welcoming and eerie.

Dru squinted through her glasses. She was too far away to see if there was any movement inside. She cupped her free hand around her mouth. "Salem!" Cold fear tightened her throat, constricting her shout to more of an agonized stage whisper. But still, the sound split the night. "Salem!"

Greyson took the heavy plastic bag from Dru and grabbed her hand. "Come on!" He pulled her along, and together they ran across the roof toward Salem's door.

Intellectually, Dru wanted to get inside and find Salem—or, in a worst-case scenario, what was left of him—as quickly as possible. But no matter how hard she tried, she couldn't just ignore the fear that threatened to hold her back.

The idea of that ghostly eyeless thing, gliding through the darkness, made her desperate to turn around. Deep down inside, every instinct told her to run the other way.

She refused to give in to that feeling, because there was no way she would leave Salem to fend for himself. In the end, her intellectual side finally won out, and she charged onward.

The smelly still-warm roof tar sucked at the soles of her shoes. At least she had worn flats, she reassured herself, trying to focus on her footwear instead of the supernatural evil that was almost certainly lying in wait for them. If she needed to run away, she didn't want to do it in heels. Fancy shoes were Opal's specialty. If Dru tried to dress like that, she would probably trip and go flying over the edge of the roof.

They reached Salem's scratched, black-painted metal door. It stood all the way open, propped by a pop-eyed gargoyle statue with a hooked beak. Someone, presumably Rane, had crowned the statue with a pair of fuzzy pink bunny ears.

Inside, the cavernous building stretched away into the gloom, cluttered with antique chairs, old clocks, odd sculptures, and glass-fronted bookcases packed with primitive artifacts. An unlit crystal chandelier the size of a small fountain hung from the broad wood-timber roof. Here and there, flickering candles and antique lamps broke up the darkness of the museum-like maze.

Greyson, his entire body tense, scanned the shadows with his burning red gaze before he silently stepped inside. His nostrils flared, as if he could pick up the scent of danger.

Dru took a tentative step after him, wrinkling her nose at the smoky, musty interior. How Salem could live like this every day, she had no idea. No wonder Rane got outside every chance she could, day or night.

Dru pressed her ulexite crystal to her forehead again, looking for any sign of life. Or *unlife*, which at this point was far more likely. The crystal warped her sight, making the room seem to stretch away into a vast canyon. All around, on shelves high and low, Salem's collection of magical artifacts lit up in her vision like a swarm of fireflies. Nearly everything in here had a magical purpose, or retained at least a trace of some long-vanished spell.

A human figure slowly approached out of the darkness. Even through the distortion of the ulexite crystal, Dru recognized him instantly. Salem was a constant, and constantly obnoxious, presence in her life. His protective powers largely obscured his aura from her view, leaving him in shadow. Still, a few tantalizing flashes of color slipped through the cracks in his defenses.

The majority of his aura was dark violet, hinting at high-level thinking, but it was split by a seething peppery orange-red that represented barely contained annoyance. Everything she could see revealed the exact opposite of optimism, peace, or happiness. In other words, Salem was being his usual prickly self.

Still standing just inside the doorway, Dru lowered the crystal and tried to blink away the momentary wooziness that swept over her. She smiled with relief. "Salem! I'm really glad you're still alive."

"Amazingly enough. Despite your best efforts." Salem limped toward them, leaning his weight on a glossy black cane topped with a miniature brass skull. It was gripped tight between his spindly fingers, as if his black-painted fingertips were trying to crush its shining grin. Salem probably wasn't a day older than Dru, but because of his injuries, he moved like a creaky grandpa.

In place of his usual black silk top hat, his head was wrapped in bandages. His ruffled black shirt was unbuttoned nearly down to his metal-studded belt, and bandages were wrapped around his chest. His angular face, normally rock-star handsome, was set in a deep frown. His gray eyes, rimmed with thick dark eyeliner, held a look that was at least half crazy. Probably more.

Dru had all kinds of things she really needed to say to him, starting with thanking him yet again for saving her life. But there was no time for that. "We have to get out of here. Your life is in danger."

He rolled his eyes. Without a word, he turned and hobbled back into the depths of his lair, leaving Dru with her mouth gaping open in surprise.

A moment later, his voice drifted out of the shadows. "Good night."

Dru turned to Greyson, who looked just as puzzled as she felt. He held up one empty hand palm-up in the universal sign of *I don't know*. Then he lifted the soup bag in an unspoken question.

Shaking her head in disbelief, Dru hurried to follow the rhythmic tap of Salem's skull cane. Considering how heavily he leaned on it, he was actually fairly nimble.

"Salem. Salem!" She caught up with him. "There's some kind of ghost downstairs. I saw it enter the building."

He just grunted and kept hobbling along.

Seeing him limping like that, Dru couldn't help but feel bad for him. And she also felt a twinge of guilt, even though his injuries weren't technically her fault. "Look, I'm really sorry about your cracked ribs. And . . . everything else." When he didn't answer or even look her way, she added, "But I like the cane. It gives you a nice retro vibe. In a megalomaniacal, *mu-ha-ha* sort of way."

His heavily lined eyes slid over to meet hers, and then away again just as she smiled.

She turned serious. "I heard breaking glass."

He made a mocking gasp and touched his free hand to his throat. "Scandalous!"

As Dru opened her mouth to reply, he made a flicking motion with his long fingers. "I don't want to hear about whatever *danger* you think is headed this way. No hysterics allowed. This is my private sanctum. It's completely secure."

"Really?" She glanced back over her shoulder. "Because we just pretty much walked right in."

"That's because I *let* you."

As they wended their way through his maze of magical junk, she got out in front of him and stopped him. "Listen, I'm not kidding. There's a ghost, or an evil spirit, or something nasty. And it's headed closer."

He leaned heavily on his cane. "Believe it or not, the ground floor is chock full of nasty surprises. I recommend not going down there after dark. It's thoroughly unpleasant."

Greyson, who had been following a few steps behind, folded his muscled arms. He had a dark smudge of engine oil on his wrist that Dru had been trying to ignore all through dinner.

"Why do you let this building get so trashed?" Greyson said. "Why not clean it up?"

Salem turned to Greyson as if seeing him for the first time. "Camou-flage. Obviously. In case you hadn't noticed, those of us who operate at the pinnacle of the food chain find that too much attention from the outside world tends to make things obnoxiously complicated." His tone turned sharp. "We don't all tear up the city streets in the most conspicuous way possible."

Greyson regarded him levelly. "You drive a *hearse.*"

Eyes slitted, Salem turned and led them to an abrupt clearing in the middle of the huge room. The scarred wood-plank floor was swept spot-lessly clean. In the very center lay a six-foot-diameter ring of carefully arranged artifacts.

There were engraved clay tablets covered in ancient writing. Ceremo-nial masks, propped up and grinning. Brass bowls full of burning incense. Elaborate curved daggers jammed tip-first into the floor. Glittering crys-tals Dru recognized from her store, the Crystal Connection. Smoky hand-dipped candles, plus several jar candles full of herb-filled wax.

One of those alchemical jar candles had burned all the way down to empty, and was now a sooty broken ruin. So that explained the sound of breaking glass.

All of the objects were arranged in a donut shape, each one meticu-lously placed in relation to the others. And they all surrounded an object Dru instantly recognized. It was a slim roll of time-stained parchment, untold millennia old, wrapped around a silver rod with wicked-looking spiked tips. It had originally been sealed with seven wax seals the color of dried blood. Six of those seals were broken, leaving jagged edges behind. Only the seventh seal remained whole and intact.

Dru took a sharp breath. It was the most dangerous artifact in the world.

It was the apocalypse scroll.

And it was just lying out there in the open, in the middle of Salem's floor. Seeing it there made Dru's stomach flop over. "Oh, my God. What are you *doing?* You can't just leave that thing unprotected!"

"You call this 'unprotected?'" With a groan, Salem seated himself on an ornately sculpted wooden armchair with royal purple velvet cushions.

It looked pretty much exactly like a throne, which made Dru wonder whether it had at one point actually been the resting place of somebody's royal butt.

"That little art assemblage in front of you represents the combined knowledge of six hundred years of sorcery," Salem said. "It's an airtight ward. A nuclear bomb couldn't get through it."

"You said you were going to keep this thing in a safe." Dru jabbed an accusatory finger toward the scroll. "I thought you had some kind of a vault or something."

"I said I would *keep it safe*," Salem snapped. "Which is more than you can say. Am I the only one here who remembers the Amulet of Decimus the Accursed? You were keeping it in a Tutti Frutti candy box."

"No," Dru insisted. "Well, it was an Atomic Fire Ball box. But that's not the point."

His eye twitched. "You still allowed it to be stolen from you. By one of the Harbingers, the most dangerous sorcerers who ever existed. And *that* little boo-boo, darling, nearly led to doomsday."

"That's not—" She glanced at Greyson, who was busy glaring at Salem, who was in turn ignoring him. "That's not exactly how it happened," she finished lamely. She hated to concede that Salem could have a point. But all the same, her cheeks burned with heat.

Still. If anyone could just walk in here and grab the scroll, that would put the entire world in danger. She took a step closer to the ring of creepy-looking artifacts, and then another, intending to reach out and grab the scroll. But as she moved in closer, she felt a distinct change in the air.

An unseen pressure built around her, crushing against her eardrums. A deep vibrating hum resonated through her bones, warning her back. She tried to swallow down the uneasiness she felt, but it stuck like a lump in her throat, making her queasy. She forced herself to take another step.

A snarl of invisible magical energies surrounded the ring of artifacts, making her skin itch, bodily pushing her back. With a little squeak, her shoes slid a half-step back along the wooden floorboards.

Obviously, the defensive spell was working, and she got the feeling that it would get even more dangerous the harder she pushed. But she could sense a weakness in the spell.

Through all of the magical noise, Dru detected the ringing tones of nine crystals spread evenly around the ring. Because Salem didn't know crystal sorcery like Dru did, he hadn't charged up the crystals he had woven into his protective spell. They served merely as anchor points for the other artifacts. If the crystals were destroyed or moved out of position, the entire spell could fail.

Dru closed her eyes for a moment, sifting through the vibrations she felt in the air, isolating the crystals. She could charge them up, strengthening the defenses of the spell. But considering that it was composed of a tangled nest of ancient artifacts, she wasn't sure how to do it safely. Charging the crystals would affect the balance of the rest of the spell. The ring looked intensely complicated, and that meant she would have to work together with Salem to make sure everything went safely.

She definitely wasn't ready to jump into any kind of spell-casting partnership with Salem. Not when he was in this kind of mood. In fact, probably not ever.

Plus, there was a ghost wandering around downstairs. Which apparently didn't concern him in the slightest. Sometimes, she wondered about Salem's sanity.

Slowly, she backed away from the circle of artifacts, relieved when the pressure eased up. Seconds later, she felt completely normal again. She waved her hand toward the circle. "All right, so you do have a pretty nifty protective spell in place. I'll give you that. But it's not airtight. There are weaknesses. I could help you with them."

His eyes flashed dangerously.

Before he could argue with her, she pressed her point. "Regardless, having it out in the open like this is too dangerous. If anyone or anything gets a hold of the scroll and breaks the seventh seal, you know what that means." She didn't want to say it out loud, but she forced herself to, just to be crystal clear. "It means *doomsday*."

Salem sighed. "See, this is what I love to hear. Vague threats, ominous dangers, mass hysteria. What *exactly* did you see downstairs that has you so spooked, darling?"

Dru started to explain, and then changed her mind. She'd had enough sass out of Salem. Rane would be there soon enough. Dru decided to let her deal with this nonsense. It was time to go. "You know what? No soup for you!" She snatched the heavy plastic bag out of Greyson's hand and started for the exit.

Greyson's arm came down in front of her like a gate at a railroad crossing, stopping her. "Wait," he warned her. He glared in the direction of the door.

Instantly, a creepy feeling crawled up Dru's spine. Her voice dropped to a whisper. "What is it?"

As if in answer, a lamp at the far end of the room winked out, allowing the shadows around it to spread. Then another lamp went dark. One by one, the candles and antique lamps lighting the room were snuffed, except for those in the ring of artifacts. Darkness spread toward them like a flood.

Dru took an involuntary step backward. "Salem?"

"It's not me." Salem's sharp voice took on a worried edge, which frightened Dru even more than the rapidly encroaching blackness. He struggled to his feet. "Dru. What *exactly* did you see down there? Because this is no ghost."

Before she could answer, a pale shape swam through the darkness toward them. At first, it was nothing more than a faint flicker, maybe just a trick of the light. Then, impossibly, Dru found herself staring into a pale eyeless face as it glided toward them, its gaping mouth nothing more than a dark hole.

With long shadowy arms, it reached out for her.

3

NOTHING IS ALL RIGHT

Dru liked to believe in the fundamental rightness of the world around her. She earnestly looked for the good in all people, the bright side of every situation, even the questionable nutritional benefit of the bag of Spicy Queso Chee-Z Puffs that Opal had shared with her the day before. But every once in a while, something came at her that was just fundamentally *wrong*.

This was the worst of those times.

As the unspeakable phantom rushed toward her, Dru's hand shot into her purse, searching for a crystal. Any crystal. Her fingers closed around the smooth curve of a polished sunstone. Immediately, her magical power flowed into it, propelled by the urgent desire to not let a horrendous apparition from beyond the grave devour her face.

The sunstone lit up the inside of her purse with a pure honey-gold brilliance. When she yanked the crystal out, it painted Salem's drab lair with a blast of summery sunshine. The effect on the creature was instantaneous.

With an eardrum-scraping screech, the thing pulled back. The dark pits of its eyes hid behind its long arms, and it shrank back beyond the edge of the light. But it didn't flee. With an eerie motion, the ghost glided back and forth along the edge of the light, like a predatory deep-sea creature penned in by aquarium glass.

Dru blinked at the oval sunstone-shaped spots that pulsed in her vision, trying to see past them to the horror that lurked in the darkness beyond. "Jeez Louise. Sure looks like a ghost to me."

With a *thunk-thunk* of his cane, Salem stepped up beside her. As he gazed into the shadows, his dark-lined eyes narrowed. "What do you want me to say, it's an adorable little puppy? No, it may look like a ghost. But it's not behaving like one."

At her other shoulder, Greyson hefted Salem's throne-chair in both hands, like a weapon, ready to crush the thing if it came any closer. Seeing the chair held out like an extremely ornate Gothic baseball bat, Dru did a double-take.

So did Salem. He let out a heavy sigh. "Even *you* can't possibly think that would work."

Greyson's red gaze ticked from Salem back to Dru. One eyebrow quirked up.

Dru shuffled her feet uncertainly. She had to admit that she had no idea how to fight this thing off. She had powered up the sunstone crystal partly on instinct, and partly by accident. In ancient times, people had believed that a sunstone's radiance could cure lunacy, which they also believed was caused by the full moon. They were pretty much wrong on both accounts, but the sunny crystal did seem to hold the ghost back. For the moment, anyway.

The shadowy figure slipped around to the side, disappearing for a moment behind a row of Salem's glass-fronted artifact cabinets. Dru moved to intercept it. She had to keep it from circling around behind them.

She caught a momentary glimpse of the thing's non-face in the darkness. Pinpoints of light ignited in the depths of its eye sockets. But instead of coming after her again, it lifted its arms in a particularly sorcerer-like gesture. That gave Dru pause. Before she could figure out what it meant, the darkness around her suddenly came alive.

The shadows on all sides of her deepened and took on physical form, as if made of thick black oil. Tendrils of swirling darkness stretched toward her from every direction, churning in the air like tentacles.

Instantly, Greyson moved to defend her. "Get back!" He swung the heavy antique chair at the living darkness. It *whooshed* through the air once, then twice, as the black tentacles snaked out of the way.

On the third swing, Greyson made contact. With a sharp crack, the chair struck a mass of tentacles and shattered. The tentacles swiftly recoiled, driven back by the impact. Jagged chunks of dark painted wood, now sporting pale, raw wood edges, scattered across the floor. Greyson glanced at the purple velvet cushion he was left holding, and threw that, too.

A rare look of wide-eyed surprise passed over Salem's features. "That chair was two centuries old!" As he spoke, a tangle of shadow tentacles rose up behind him.

"Look out!" Dru yelled.

Pivoting on the cane, Salem raised his free hand. White-hot sparks of magic crackled between his fingers as the shadows snaked toward Dru.

She retreated, holding up the glowing sunstone even higher, as if that would somehow make it brighter. But although the light kept the phantom itself at bay, it had no effect on the writhing tentacles of darkness.

A swirl of shadow slapped across her palm so hard that it felt like her small bones were broken. The sunstone flew out of her numb fingers, extinguished.

They were plunged into near darkness. The only light came from the burning candles in the circle.

The black tendrils swarmed around the protective artifacts, trying to worm their way through its magic defenses. A horrible realization dawned on Dru.

"It's not after us! It's after the scroll!" Her heart hammered in her chest, and her knees nearly knocked together. But she knew what she had to do next. She had no choice.

She had to get the scroll first, before those tentacles did.

Fearing she was about to die, Dru dove for the ring of artifacts. She badly misjudged the distance and fell short, landing painfully. Her glasses flew off and skittered away across the floor, leaving her nearly blind.

Ignoring the teeth-aching pressure of the warding spell, she elbow-crawled forward, not daring to lift her head. Shadowy tendrils hissed back and forth, just inches above her skull.

Summoning up all of her courage, Dru reached one shaking hand toward the ring of artifacts, fearing it would be crushed by a grasping tentacle, or worse.

The humming vibration of the defensive spell started up again as she reached toward it. The sensation was not unlike sticking her hand outside a car window at highway speeds. Even though there was no wind, the air itself took on an invisible force, trying to push her away. The teeth-aching pressure came back, pressing painfully against her eardrums.

Currently, that magical pressure was the only thing keeping the dark tendrils at bay. But in the feeble light of the guttering candles, Dru could clearly see the swarming darkness inching down, like a tornado descending from storm clouds to wreak destruction.

She had to get to the scroll first. But no matter how hard she pushed, she couldn't get her fingers past the creepy ring of artifacts. The invisible force was too strong for her to get through.

But the tentacles were stronger. Slowly but surely, they drilled downward. Now they were only inches from the scroll.

Despite the fact that she had lost her glasses and had only a few candles to see by, Dru was still close enough to spot a crystal among the artifacts. It was a forearm-sized amethyst crystal, dark purple at the blunt end, fading to a pale rose pink at its narrow tip. Amethyst was one of the most powerful protective crystals, especially against any kind of non-physical attack. Immediately, she dropped her hand to it, and felt it tingle her skin with its vibrations.

She didn't necessarily have to reach the scroll, she realized. She just had to prevent the shadows from getting it. That meant she had to bolster the defenses of the circle. And that would require powering up the nine crystals Salem had placed around the circle. But was she powerful enough?

"*Dru!*" Greyson called from the darkness somewhere behind her.

Where was the ghost? It could be on them in an instant. "Stay back!" she shouted. "Protect Salem!"

Salem, meanwhile, thrust out his free hand, now crackling with jagged arcs bright enough to sear her retinas. A glimmer of magic suffused the air around him, silhouetting him in a luminous haze as he tried to force the tentacles back with waves of invisible force. The wash of his magic rustled Dru's hair like a silent wind.

Clearly, it was a strain for Salem to operate at full strength. He pushed out harder with his incandescent hands, and his lips drew back from his teeth in a desperate snarl. The air around him shimmered like heat waves on a desert highway.

The floorboards hummed. Every small object nearby went airborne, as if blown away in a storm wind. Books flapped their pages, flipped over, and hurtled up into the air. Lampshades tilted and tumbled over Dru's head like kites. The glass fronts of the display cases around her cracked, then shattered. Bits of broken glass sprayed overhead, glinting in the faint candlelight like distant stars.

Dru's new blue-framed glasses came skittering across the scratched wooden floorboards toward her. She snatched them up and settled them on her nose.

As she did, the white plastic bag of Chinese takeout tumbled end over end, as if kicked. It came open, and Dru was instantly soaked head to foot in a particularly aromatic garlic chicken broth, along with chunks of luke-warm chicken, gobs of squiggly noodles, and chopped carrots the size of silver dollars. Tiny diced green scallions peppered the lenses of her glasses.

Gasping in surprise, she nearly lost her grip on the amethyst crystal. But she held on tight. Blotting out the chaos around her, Dru focused all of her attention on charging up the crystal. She willed it to become an extension of her body, her thoughts, her force of will. She pushed her magic into it, and it started to give off a cool gleam, like summer twilight.

As she charged up the amethyst, its protective energies flowed around the ring of artifacts, strengthening its defenses. For a moment, the thrill of success made Dru giddy. But it evaporated as she watched the black tentacles continue to corkscrew downward. Now they were barely an inch away from the scroll. Salem wasn't slowing them down at all.

In moments, the living shadows would be able to touch the scroll's last remaining wax seal, the only thing holding off doomsday.

Frustration burned inside her. The amethyst crystal wasn't enough. Dru was powerless to stop the tentacles. Even Salem couldn't help.

And then Greyson was there at her side. He held out his hand, and she gladly took it.

Greyson was more than just the greatest guy she'd ever kissed. He was also an *arcana rasa*, a natural-born sorcerer who had never developed any spell-casting powers of his own. As a result, his body was like a furnace of magical strength that he himself couldn't burn. But he could give it to her.

As she tightened her grip on his broad palm, she felt the familiar jolt of his magical power mingling with hers. For the briefest of moments, it felt like the two of them had become one. She could draw on his energy as well as her own, doubling her power. A tremendous rush came with it, and she gave in to the wild flow of power as she sent it shooting into the ring of artifacts.

She reached out to not only the amethyst but all nine of the crystals carefully arranged around the circle. All at once, they lit up, radiating different colors of light from where they were nestled among the various creepy artifacts. They flared red and blue like a fire engine, silvery white, bottle green, sunrise orange. A faint ringing sound pierced the air, growing louder and shriller as the crystals grew brighter.

Their combined light, pure white in the center of the circle, slowed the dark tentacles to a stop, and then gradually drove them back. No matter how much they writhed and thrashed, the crystals pushed them further away. Six inches away. A foot. A yard.

Despite the fact that Dru was terrified out of her mind, aching from head to toe, and dripping with soup, she found herself grinning ear to ear. They were doing it. Together, they were protecting the apocalypse scroll.

The tentacles pulled back, as if the hands that controlled them had been yanked away. They had already expended so much of their power that Salem had been able to sneak in from the side. With a blast of force, he flattened the tentacles into a writhing wall of solid darkness.

Though he leaned heavily on his cane, his other trembling arm was deeply engaged in powerful sorcery. His spidery fingers were nearly consumed in a crackling hot vortex of magic.

As he slowly crossed this clearing in his cluttered loft, closing in on the apparition, the wooden floor around him was swept clean of every speck of dust by the force of his spell. At the periphery, a massive whirlwind of debris roared around, orbiting him and the ghost.

Salem lifted his brilliant hand higher. His magic threw the shadowy creature against the brick wall and pinned it there. With its long bony arms splayed out to either side, the thing squirmed and struggled, unable to break free. Under the constant onslaught of Salem's unrestrained power, the ghost shriveled to no more than a skeletal wisp of a thing, shrieking with an inhuman keening cry that chilled Dru's blood. As she watched, the thing became thinner and thinner.

It dwindled until it was nothing more than a wrinkle of shadow, easily mistaken for a jagged crack in the wall. In moments, it would be completely destroyed.

Despite the fact that Salem was possibly the most obnoxious sorcerer Dru had ever had to deal with, it was impossible not to feel awe at the sheer magnitude of his power. When he completely cut loose like this, he was seemingly unstoppable. It was easy to see why Rane was so drawn to him.

But just when Dru was starting to think Salem had saved the day, his knees buckled. His trembling arm drooped, and the blinding light of his spell began to flicker and fade. Dru knew what was about to happen, but she was powerless to stop it.

The problem was that Salem didn't do anything in moderation.

Even on the best of days, he had the tendency to overtax his own powers to the point where he ran himself into the ground. And right now was anything but the best of days. Being injured, he'd had little enough stamina to begin with. And now he looked like he was about to pass out.

Before his spell had completely done its work, it abruptly died away. The roar of magic dwindled to a whisper, and then nothing at all. Airborne debris clattered to the floor. Papers fluttered down out of the air like a flock of birds. Smaller objects pelted the room, like heavy raindrops, some of them breaking on impact.

The ghost, withered to no more than a jagged fissure of darkness, began to pulse and swell. As Dru watched, strength came surging back to the nearly destroyed creature. With a soul-chilling cry, it regained its humanoid form. Its long arms reached out, ghostly fingers grasping, as it broke loose from Salem's spell.

Salem's head lolled. As he toppled to the floor, unconscious, Dru came to the cold realization that there was no way to stop the ghost now. They were all as good as dead.

4
INSIDE THESE WALLS

Dru had never felt particularly comfortable in the candle lit expanse of Salem's enormous lair. It was smelly, gloomy, and surprisingly claustrophobic for being the approximate size of a Romanesque cathedral. But her discomfort stemmed mostly from Salem's snarky presence and unpredictable behavior.

He, however, was now silently sprawled in an undignified black-clad heap on the wooden floor a few feet away. Meanwhile, she was lying on her belly, grasping Greyson's hand, the fingers of her other hand shoved into the circle of creepy-looking artifacts and wrapped around the big amethyst crystal. She was still charging up the defensive ring, but in a minute that wouldn't make any difference. She was a sitting duck.

The ghost surged back to full strength. Its night-black tentacles grew thicker and twitchier. The dark pits of its eyes turned toward her, full of malice.

Dru swallowed. "We can't fight that thing."

"And we're fresh out of chairs." Greyson's red gaze scanned left and right. "Nothing left to hit it with. Salem's spell pretty much cleared the place out."

Every option looked bad. If she stayed here, the tentacles were sure to get her. If she let go of the crystals and fled, the protective circle of artifacts would eventually fail, and the ghost would break through. That would almost certainly mean the end of the world.

Dru hesitated, uncertain what to do even as the ghost peeled itself off the wall and bore down on them. But she was flat out of alternatives, except for one.

Grab the apocalypse scroll and run.

Not a great plan, but it was the only one she had.

She looked up into the heat of Greyson's glowing eyes. "When I say 'Go,' grab Salem and follow me. Okay?"

He nodded once. No hesitation. But as the ghost's shadow tentacles convulsed and swelled overhead, Greyson's clenched jaw told her what he thought of their chances.

Dru had no time to worry about letting him down. She turned her attention to the amethyst crystal in her grip. Magical power hummed down her arm and into the nine crystals arranged around the circle, reinforcing the invisible defensive shield woven by the artifacts. Salem had obviously put a ton of work into carefully arranging each one of them to maximize their effectiveness. As far as sorcery went, it was a kind of poetry, or sculpture.

To get the scroll, she had to knock all of it down like a line of dominoes.

With a groan of effort, she struggled to reverse the direction of the flow of power through the crystals. It was like trying to push a parked car. It didn't budge. She fought against the circle, driven harder by the terror of the eyeless ghost and its grasping tentacles. But the magic in the circle was meticulously crafted and solid. Even with help from Greyson's power flowing through her other hand, she felt like she was accomplishing nothing.

Just when she could push no harder, she broke through. An invisible shudder ran through the circle, and the floor trembled under her feet. A dangerous whining sound whipped around the circle, making Dru's hair stand on end. The air wavered.

One by one, the crystals around the circle went up in a blinding flash and exploded. Hot chunks of rock, sizzling with foul smoke, shot in every direction. The artifacts in the circle—ugly masks, wickedly curved daggers, brass figurines in distorted poses—all shook and tipped over, each one colliding with the next. Crackling magic crawled over them, sending up fountains of sparks along with plumes of toxic green and yellow smoke. With sharp pops and sizzles, the magic spell disintegrated.

Dru reached into the campfire-hot air inside the circle and plucked out the scroll. Oddly, it was icy cold and smooth in her hand.

About twenty feet beyond, a small oval crystal lay on the floorboards, glinting in the lights of the dying spell. It was her golden sunstone. If she could get to it, she could use it against the ghost again. It wasn't much, but it was all they had.

She glanced at Greyson. "Get Salem! Go!"

He leaped into motion. The moment he let go of her hand, the spark of magic between them broke, and she suddenly felt alone again. She turned and leaped for the sunstone crystal, overwhelmed by the feeling that she was about to lose Greyson forever.

But she couldn't stop. She couldn't look back to make sure he was safe. Because he wasn't. None of them were.

The artifacts in the circle behind her died in spasms of multicolored light, illuminating the cracked wooden floorboards in disorienting flashes. But the sunstone gleamed. *Right there.*

She stooped and snatched it up, willing it to life in her palm. Hot sunshine spread out between her fingers, lighting her skin red. Somewhere behind her, the ghost screeched in dismay.

Greyson ran past her with Salem thrown over his shoulder like a sack of lawn clippings. He snatched her hand and pulled her along. The crystal's glare surrounded them, illuminating the tumbled debris that had landed along the periphery of Salem's powerful spell. Beyond lay the back end of his cluttered apartment.

"Come on!" Greyson said, climbing over debris. "The front door's blocked. We have to go out the back."

"There is no back!" Dru struggled to keep up with him. "There's only one way in or out!"

Greyson dodged around a bookcase packed with curiously orderly rows of matching black and tan books, perhaps an old legal library. His red gaze cast about. "There has to be a fire exit or something."

"Oh, sure. Does Salem strike you as the fire-code-abiding type? No!" Dru gestured at the unconscious bundle slung over Greyson's shoulder. Distantly, though, she did recall Rane once telling her that Salem had a secret door. At the time, Dru had thought it was a joke.

But that unusually tidy bookcase caught her eye. It was the only clean, orderly thing in this entire maze.

Before she could inspect it closely, the wailing ghost reached the edge of the sunstone's light. Pinpoints of fire burned in the hollow pits of darkness where its eyes should have been. With a howl, it raised its long arms, fingers clawed, and again Dru got the distinct impression that in a previous life, it had been a sorcerer.

But ghosts couldn't use sorcery in the afterlife, could they?

She had no time to analyze the situation. As dark tentacles flashed out toward them, she threw all of her weight against the bookcase, silently praying her hunch was right.

To her surprise, the bookcase came loose with a screech of old rusty hinges. It swung away from her into darkness, trailing cobwebs from its edge. Beyond lay a dusty, narrow spiral staircase leading down.

Greyson didn't miss a beat. He pushed Dru inside as the tentacles whipped toward her. He tried to shove the heavy bookcase back into place, but a half-dozen of the tentacles had already wormed through the gap.

"*Run!*" he shouted.

Dru had no idea where the stairway led, except down. And Salem, being unconscious, couldn't tell them anything. But still, it had to be better than here. She fled down the tight spiral stairs, following the golden light of the sunstone, her chicken-soup-soaked shoes squishing on the rusty metal steps.

Above her, Greyson put his shoulder into the bookcase and slammed it hard enough to make the wall shake. The tentacles recoiled for just a moment. He stormed down the steps after her.

At the bottom, the secret passage ended in a narrow, cobweb-covered door roughly assembled from stained plywood and two-by-fours. There was no handle.

Dru's panic was nearly matched by her unwillingness to touch the web-covered, splintery wood. She summed up the courage to plant a soggy shoe against it. It didn't budge. Just then, Greyson barreled down the tight stairwell and plowed shoulder-first into the door. With a crackle of fossil-ized dirt, it swung open.

Together, they rushed out onto the filthy ground floor of the aban-doned building, which had apparently been some kind of factory in the distant past. Rows of rusty, riveted metal tanks stretched along one wall. Each tank was roughly the shape of a grain silo, and probably ten feet tall, built to hold hundreds of gallons of liquid. A tangle of valves and pipes connected them, tented with spiderwebs.

From the ceiling hung a cluster of rusty chains with links thicker than her thumb. They terminated in a wicked-looking metal hook big enough to hoist a whale.

Everything below head height, all the way down to the floor, was coated with indecipherable spray-painted graffiti and an offensively deep layer of grime. Even in the daytime, this place would have been nothing short of creepy. In the middle of the night, it was downright terrifying.

The nearest exit she could see was a side-by-side pair of doors, once painted a depressing green, now chalky and streaked with rust. Clutching the cold apocalypse scroll to her chest, Dru ran for the door. Above and behind them, the wailing ghost's shadow tentacles obliterated the stair-well. Broken lumber, torn metal treads, and choking dust exploded from the opening.

Dru crashed into the big outside door and tried the knob. It wouldn't budge. It was locked.

Greyson dumped Salem's unconscious form onto the floor next to her and kicked the door. It rang out with a clash of metal against solid metal.

It didn't give an inch.

Tentacles of darkness, each as thick as Dru's leg, wormed their way out through the remains of the staircase and wriggled toward them. They were cornered. Greyson gave up on the door and picked up a length of rusty iron pipe, raising it like a baseball bat.

At that moment, Dru's phone rang with a pounding hip hop beat, an instant reminder to never let Rane play with the settings on her phone. But all the same, right now, that ringtone was the most beautiful sound in the world.

"*Rane!*" Dru screamed into the phone. "*Help!*"

Rane was breathing hard, her breaths blowing into the phone. "The hell are you, cowgirl?"

"Downstairs! Somewhere! There's a bunch of tanks!"

"Tanks?" Rane sounded flabbergasted. "Like . . . the *army?*"

"No! We're by the green door!"

"Which *one?* They're all green!"

Frustration burned through Dru like a physical pain. She didn't know where she was. But there was a good reason she'd never been in this part of the abandoned building before. She had always wanted to stay out of trouble—which was exactly what she had found here.

"Talk to me, D!"

But Dru was busy charging up the sunstone, lighting up the basement as bright as day. The tentacles struck at them like a nest of vipers. Greyson sidestepped and swung the pipe. It connected with a tentacle, knocking it back hard enough to fly back and dent one of the empty tanks. The impact boomed like a gigantic drum.

"Heard that," Rane puffed. "Got eyes on the door. Stay back. *Way* back."

"Why? What are you—" But the call ended, beeping twice. Dru stared at the phone, quietly finishing: "—going to do?"

A moment later, she had her answer. The double doors shook with a deep metallic *BOOM* that rang through the building, as if the mass of a dinosaur-killing asteroid had plowed into them. A cloud of dust burst into the air, peppered with flakes of paint and rusty bits of metal.

Greyson glanced back over his shoulder, looking worried. Even the tentacles paused for a heartbeat.

Another *BOOM* shook the building. The deafening noise echoed back and forth through the midnight-black depths of the abandoned factory. This time, the impact deformed the door as something outside hit it hard enough to punch a shape into the metal.

Dru adjusted her glasses and squinted. That shape looked an awful lot like the sole of a very large running shoe.

Remembering Salem, Dru grabbed him under the warm armpits of his black silk shirt and dragged him back as far away from the door as she could.

Greyson grunted as he fended off the tentacles. Mercilessly, they drove him back. More tentacles swarmed down the spiral staircase and joined the rest. Too many to fight at once.

A rapid clanging sound approached outside, like running footsteps, but metallic. With another earth-shaking *BOOM*, the battered doors flew open, now almost bent in half. They shrieked on tortured hinges and clanged off the wall on either side, gouging chunks out of the concrete.

Through the door marched Rane. Six feet tall and bulging with muscle, Rane's entire body was composed of gleaming raw steel. With every powerful stride, the air rang with the sound of a sledgehammer striking concrete.

Rane bunched her fists and nodded her chin to Greyson. "Hey. 'Sup?" Then, without breaking stride, Rane marched up to the slithering tentacles and threw a devastating punch into the center of their mass.

The blow sent some of them flying back, while the rest whipped around her so fast they whistled through the air. Her forearms and waist were instantly wrapped in darkness.

"Rane! No!" Dru stepped forward, brandishing the sunstone. But it did nothing to drive off the tentacles. Instead, she could only watch in horror as Rane was bodily lifted up off the ground.

Behind Dru, through the open door, rolled a rumble like thunder, louder by the moment. Headlights washed across the run-down parking lot, briefly lighting up clusters of scraggly dead weeds. Hellbringer's tires screamed with white smoke as the demon car slid to a halt. Its doors swung open.

Greyson had already picked up Salem, but he hesitated when he saw Rane in trouble.

Her metal body flashed in the light of Dru's crystal. She scissored her legs up and clamped them around the rusted chain that dangled from the high ceiling. Twirling in the air, Rane swiftly wrapped the tentacles in the thick chain.

Then she dropped to the floor, heels banging on the concrete, and pulled at the tangled tentacles with both hands until they were stretched taut. Teeth bared, biceps bulging, she leaned back against the quivering tentacles until they snapped in half. The severed ends dissolved into boiling smoke.

She staggered back, thrown off-balance, and was about to jump back into the fight when Dru yelled, "Rane, no!"

"Don't worry. I can take this thing!"

"First, help Salem!"

Rane glanced over, and her gaze lingered on Salem's unconscious body. With obvious reluctance, she retreated to the door.

Worryingly, Salem didn't stir when they flung him into the back seat. Rane ducked in next to him, making Hellbringer's suspension creak in protest, and cradled Salem to her steel chest.

Right behind them, the ghost boiled out through the twisted metal of the double doors. Beneath the distant city lights, the thing glittered like moonlight rippling across dark water. All around it, the darkness writhed to life and came after them.

Dru jumped into the front seat. "Get us out of here!"

Greyson yanked the shift knob, dropping Hellbringer into gear. The engine roared like a beast unchained from the pits of Hell. The sudden acceleration crushed Dru into the seat.

As they roared away across the empty parking lot and down the road, the thing followed, slowly falling behind. The pit of its mouth opened wide and released a skin-crawling wail into the night.

It quickly dropped out of sight behind them. But it was still back there, somewhere. Dru had the sickening feeling that it wasn't finished with them. If it was after the power of the apocalypse scroll, it would never give up, she was sure. She felt it to the core of her being. This thing would pursue them to the end of the earth.

Perhaps literally.

5

FIELD GUIDE TO THE UNDEAD

Clutching the slim, cold weight of the apocalypse scroll, Dru took deep breaths, trying to force herself to calm down. Every instinct told her to flee, run for her life, find someplace to hide. But even though her body was physically moving far in excess of the speed limit, she still felt like a target as long as she sat there in the passenger seat.

She couldn't blot the horrifying sight of the ghost from her mind. The hollow pits of its eyes would haunt her for the rest of her life, she knew. What she didn't know was how they could stand up to that thing. How long did they have before it caught up to them? Was there any way to stop it?

She couldn't stop looking back over her shoulder at the impenetrable blackness behind them. Along this little-used road that shot straight through the industrial part of the city, streetlights were few and far between. There was nothing but ugly factory buildings and warehouses lit only by occasional yellow security lights, surrounded by chain-link fences. Everything else was darkness.

In the back seat, Rane had turned human again. Tanned and bulging with muscle, she wore hot pink running shorts and a camouflage sports bra. At a full six feet tall, her blonde ponytail nearly brushed the car's headliner. She cradled Salem to her chest, smoothing back his long hair. He was still unconscious, and possibly drooling a little bit.

"What the hell? I only left him alone for an hour." Rane sounded perplexed. "I figured, how much trouble could he get into?"

Dru turned around in the seat. The low seat backs and complete lack of headrests in the old car gave her room to reach out a comforting hand. "It's not your fault. That creature could have shown up at any time."

"I guess so. P.S., what the hell was that, anyway?" Rane said it like it was somehow Dru's fault. Her fierce gaze traveled up and down Dru's body, uncomfortably intense. "Dude, you have noodles on your head."

"Oh. Ugh. Sorry."

"You're making me hungry."

Dru tried to finger-comb the gooey chicken noodles out of her hair, intending to throw them out the window. But they were too slippery to grasp.

"Here. Got it." Rane reached up and swiftly plucked them out one by one, amassing a mashed handful that looked nauseatingly like a glistening gray brain. Before Dru could roll down the window, Rane sniffed the noodles hungrily, then stuffed them in her mouth.

Dru couldn't hide her horrified expression. Her hand flew to her lips.

"What?" Rane demanded, her cheeks bulging as she chewed. "You saw me give that tentacle thing the smackdown, right? Now I'm in calorie debt." She chewed and smacked her lips. "Not bad. Is that from the Chinese place we saved?"

With an effort, Dru pretended that it was perfectly normal to eat noodles off of someone else's head. Because being friends with Rane required that sort of pretending on a daily basis. She held up the heavy and strangely cold apocalypse scroll, careful not to get any soup on its wrinkled parchment. The silver tines on each end glittered in Hellbringer's dashboard lights. "That thing was an apparition of some kind. And it was after this."

Rane looked like she wanted to crush the scroll in her bare hands. "Why? What for?"

"I'm going to go out on a limb and say its intentions are not wholesome."

Rane turned around and looked past Hellbringer's towering back wing. "That thing still chasing us?"

Greyson glanced up in the rearview mirror. "I can feel it. Still back there somewhere, following us. Doesn't seem to be fast enough to catch us. As long as we keep moving."

"We need to figure out how to stop it," Dru said. "Not just its squiggly shadow tentacles. The thing itself. Whatever it is."

She had seen plenty of weirdness in her brief career as a sorceress. The one thing she had learned above all else was not to jump to conclusions about what they were up against. The slim margin between life and death often depended on the difference between being mostly right versus being exactly right.

She had to be exactly right.

"I need to get to my books, do some research, figure this thing out." Dru peered out the window as another nondescript brick industrial building slid past in the night. She didn't recognize it. "Where are we? How far are we from the shop?"

Greyson grunted. "We're taking the scenic route. Are you sure you want to go back to the shop? If that thing follows you home . . ." He didn't finish, but the menacing implication was clear. At the shop, they would be sitting ducks. But at least they would have magical defenses.

"The shop is protected by the crystal grid," she assured him. She and Opal had painstakingly constructed a network of powerful crystals just inside the walls of the old brick building. It wasn't one hundred percent impregnable, but it was the best she had. "That's the safest place we can go right now. By the way, how's Salem doing back there?"

Half-awake now, Salem stirred. One bloodshot eye fixed Dru with a murderous glare. "*Salem* is just as pleased to see you as he always is." His eyebrow kinked, accentuating the sarcasm.

Rane picked flakes of rust and grime off of her shirt. "Meh, he's fine."

"At least he's awake." Dru decided to leave him alone for the moment and focus on getting more help. She set the scroll down between her feet and got out her phone. Opal answered on the second ring.

"Hello there," Opal sang out. "You remember that fabulous new peaches-and-cream outfit I got with the fuzzy skirt and the sparkly low-cut top? With the matching cork wedge shoes? And the earrings, of course. The ones that you said looked like disco balls with comet-tail tassels?"

The unexpected question caught Dru completely off guard. It took her a moment to collect her thoughts.

Opal was a full-figured black woman blessed—or cursed, depending on your particular tastes—with an outrageous fashion sense. But her designer appetites were constrained by the meager income that came from the crystal shop's admittedly limited cash flow. Yet somehow, Opal always managed to look marvelous enough to practically be chased across the red carpet by hordes of paparazzi.

After considerable mental digging, Dru did, in fact, remember that particular outfit. Specifically, she remembered asking: *Where on earth are you going to wear that?*

Dru cleared her throat. "Um, yes. Very nice. So anyway, I need you to—"

"Very *nice?*" Opal sounded insulted. "And by the way, I *am* having a lovely evening, thanks for asking. Dinner was spectacular. I'll tell you all about it later. How are you?"

Dru took off her glasses and pinched the skin above her nose, feeling a headache coming on. "Look, Opal, I don't have time to—"

"I'm just making you aware of the fact that I *am* wearing my brand-new peaches-and-cream outfit, and it *is* absolutely fabulous, thank you." Opal's voice took on a harder edge. "And I do not have any intention of doing anything crazy that's going to ruin my clothes. *Again.*"

"No, I promise, I'm not—"

"Because every time you call me this late, it's never like, 'Oh, hey, hi, how're you doing? How was your date with Ruiz?' Instead, it's like, 'Hey, how about we go dig up some moldy old *graveyard?*'"

Dru felt the last shreds of her patience evaporate. She bit off what she was about to say next, knowing she would have regretted it, and squeezed her eyes shut. She wished she could block out the endless growl of Hellbringer's engine or the cloying smell of Chinese chicken soup drying in her hair. "How. Was. Your date. With Ruiz?"

"Terrible. I mean, dinner itself was absolutely amazing. He wanted to eat there, but I said, let's take it to go. Because between you and me, I've got to work tomorrow, so I've got to move this thing along. So I get him back to my place, and just when things are getting all hot and heavy, guess what?" Opal paused, as if pretending to give Dru the opportunity to answer before she plowed on ahead. "Work calls Ruiz. Somebody apparently tried to stuff an entire bucket of KFC down the garbage disposal, and guess how that turned out? Nasty, that's how. Now their sink is overflowing with puked-up week-old fried chicken and gravy, and the boss says my man needs to drop everything he's doing and go fix their garbage disposal, *right this second*, because now it's dripping down into the downstairs neighbor's kitchen and now they've got *two* angry customers. So where does that leave me?"

This time, the pause was longer.

"Where *does* that leave you?" Dru asked, with great reluctance.

"Back at the shop, trying to research a good date spell. Or at least a good plumbing spell, so I don't get interrupted again just when we get to the good part."

"Oh, good!" Dru instantly brightened. "You're at the shop!"

There was an awkward pause. *"That's* what you got out of all that?"

Quickly, Dru related the night's events, culminating in their current flight through the deserted back streets of the industrial district. "So I need you to do some research. We have to identify that ghost, or whatever it was, so we can figure out how to stop it. Do we still have *The Libram of Lost Souls* in the back room?"

"Yeah . . ." Opal's heavy sigh was completely devoid of any enthusiasm. "Of course we still have it. Hang on."

Rane tapped her on the shoulder. "See if she's got any more of that fizzy orange potion. The one that smells like mouthwash."

"Fizzy . . . what?" Dru struggled to think of a single potion that matched that description. "We don't have anything like that."

"Sure as hell do, dude. Opal gave him one last time he was like this. Fixed him right up."

"Um, okay." Dru raised the phone back to her ear. "Opal?"

"Yeah, I heard. It's a top secret recipe." Opal chuckled. "I'll tell you when you get here. Had that boy bouncing off the walls inside of five minutes."

Dru frowned. "Is it safe?"

"Safe?" Opal let out a low laugh that sounded like she was getting some kind of revenge. Dru didn't dare ask why.

Very deliberately, she turned and gave Rane a thumbs-up. "Don't worry. Opal will make him another potion."

"Sweet." Rane smiled.

"Oh, I will, will I?" With a dejected grunt, Opal sat down heavily, probably in one of the ugly plaid armchairs in the back of the shop. The crinkling of ancient paper carried through the phone as Opal flipped through the old book's handwritten pages. *The Libram of Lost Souls.* Would've been nice to have this book back when we were fighting those web-spewing slime zombies."

Dru would never forget facing off against those horrible things, the web-wrapped undead creatures conjured up by a former friend of hers. He was a sorcerer whose powers had led him down the dark path of necromancy, and ultimately his own doom. That happened far too often to powerful sorcerers. "Technically, those weren't zombies."

"Oh, so you're the expert now?" Opal said. "Just don't forget who's got the book. All right. Let me see here . . . Hmm . . . That thing you saw tonight, does it have a basic form?"

"What does that mean, 'basic' form? Like a triangle?"

"I don't know. That's what it says here in the book. I assume they mean like a basic human form. Arms, legs, all the right parts."

"I would call that a humanoid form," Dru said.

"Honey, I'm not the one who wrote this thing. If you got a problem with the technical language, you can take it up with the crazy-ass German monster catcher who wrote this thing."

"Dutch."

"What?"

"He was a crazy-ass *Dutch* monster catcher. Although he did write it in German. *Der Foliant der verlorenen Seelen.* But we have the English translation, *The Libram of Lost Souls.* By the way, did you know that 'libram' isn't really a word?"

Opal sighed again. "Look. I don't have all night. Did this ghost have a basic form or not?"

"Well, it definitely had arms, because it reached out for me." Dru put her hand over the phone and turned to Greyson. "Did the ghost have legs?"

His glowing gaze didn't waver from the road. He nodded once.

"Let's say yes on the basic form."

"Hmm." Opal turned a few more pages. "Was any part of it invisible?"

"In direct light, it was invisible. You can only see it in the dark."

Opal made a frustrated noise. "How are you supposed to see it if it's dark?"

"Is that one of the questions?"

"One of *my* questions," Opal muttered. "Right behind: Why do I have to be a part of this conversation . . ." Her voice trailed off as she flipped more pages, humming to herself. "Huh. That's a weird one. Does it have a definite mouth?"

Dru remembered the dark pit of the thing's mouth growing inhumanly wide, as if it intended to swallow her soul. The idea made her skin crawl. "Definitely."

"That's actually a good sign," Opal said. "Means it's not some kind of formless apparition. Or worse, like an Elder God."

"Yay," Dru said, without enthusiasm.

Opal flipped another page. "Is it elephantine or larger?"

"'Elephantine?'"

"Or larger."

"No."

Another page. "Does it have a head?"

"Doesn't everything?"

Opal huffed out a breath. "Headless horseman doesn't have a head."

"True. But this one has a head. And no horse."

"Answers my next question. How about moldering bones, festering wounds, or putrefying flesh?"

"Eww! Definitely not."

"Well, that's something." Opal turned the page.

"Thanks. I feel so much better now," Dru muttered.

"I should've asked this earlier. Is it harmed by sunlight?"

"Maybe. I'd have to wait until tomorrow morning to find out for sure. I lit up a sunstone crystal and that held the ghost off, but I don't think it harmed it. And it didn't protect us at all against the thing's spells."

"Spells? Hmm." Opal went silent for a long moment, flipping pages back and forth, as if in frustration. Finally, she set down the ancient book with a heavy *thump*. "Honey, I don't think this thing is a ghost at all. Sounds to me like it's a wraith."

Dru scratched her scalp, which was getting itchy as the chicken soup dried. "How is that different, exactly?"

"It's like a ghost, except that the person's body didn't die first. The soul came from a still-living body, and now it's outside on its own, running around causing trouble."

"So its body is still alive?"

"Or in some kind of suspended animation."

"So, hmm." Dru thought about it. "If it's the roaming soul of a sorcerer, that would explain the shadow magic. Wouldn't be a big jump from shadow magic to astral projection."

"No, this isn't astral projection. This is different," Opal said. "With astral projection, you're planning on coming back to your body pretty soon. But with a wraith, there is no going back. It's a one-way trip out of the body, never to return. We're not talking about slipping into a pleasant trance or meditation. We're talking the darkest kind of magic, probably ceremonial, definitely primordial. The kind one single sorcerer couldn't pull off alone. Wraiths can only be created by a group of the most powerful evil sorcerers. And the whole thing is freaky as all get-out, I'll be the first one to tell you. A wraith has their soul ripped right out of their body. They become dispossessed."

Dispossessed. That word sounded familiar. Where had she heard it before? She had to think about it for a second. "We have a book somewhere back there, I think Tristram wrote it, about the dispossessed."

"You're thinking of Ursula K. LeGuin," Opal said.

"No, it was an eldritch manuscript. Something about the kingdom and the key. Listen, does it say anything in the *Libram* about how to fight wraiths?"

"It basically says to run away, as fast as you can. Wraiths are seriously bad news. In order to exist, they have to keep feeding. So don't get too close."

Dru turned around and looked past Rane and Salem into the darkness behind them. She hesitated to ask her next question, but she had to know. "What exactly do wraiths feed on?"

"Human souls," Opal said quietly, and the hushed tone in her voice sent a chill down Dru's spine. "Honey, what have you gotten us into?"

Dru traded silent looks with Greyson. "Find that book by Tristram. It might be the only way to defeat this thing. If you're correct, and this wraith was dispossessed by a group of evil sorcerers who are after the apocalypse scroll . . ." Dru thought through the possible implications. "This is only going to get worse. Either they will send more wraiths, or they will come themselves. Or both. No matter what, they're coming after us."

"But who are 'they'?" Opal said.

"Like it or not, we're going to find out. Lock the doors. Get out your protective amulets. We're on our way back to the shop now."

Beside her, Greyson put his foot down on the gas, and Hellbringer sped into the night, leaving behind only a rush of hot wind and the fiery red gleam of its taillights.

6
MOON DUST

Dru raced through the front door of the Crystal Connection, intending to put about six things into motion at once. As she came down the main aisle, she plucked crystals and potion ingredients off the shelves, gathering up an armful of ideas that just might help defend them against the wraith.

Rane marched along behind her, slowing down only barely enough to help Salem limp along. Outside, Greyson issued a command to Hellbringer. "Patrol," he said, in a deep voice that would make anyone jump to attention. Engine growling, Hellbringer swung away from the curb and prowled down the street.

Dru headed into the back room, worrying with every step that she was about to lose her balance and send her load of magical ingredients crashing to the floor. With her luck, all of the little clinking glass containers she was carrying would shatter, and the wrong essential oils would mix with the wrong crystals, and probably set fire to half her shop.

She *hated* it when things got set on fire. Especially since it happened all the time.

Opal was waiting for her in the back room, leaning over a leather-bound book bigger than a jumbo pizza box and twice as thick. She looked up, horrified. *"That's* your date outfit? Honey, have you listened to nothing I've ever told you?"

Dru stopped short. "What? What's wrong with it? The blue stripes match my new glasses."

Opal sighed. She put a warm arm on Dru's shoulders and looked deep into her eyes. "Listen, sweetie. You need to come by my place and borrow some clothes. Normally I don't say that to anyone. But right now I am begging you, for your own good." She sniffed the air. "What is that?"

"I smell like chicken soup," Dru said in a small voice, and clutched the armload of jars and crystals closer. "It's not my fault."

Opal was kind enough not to ask any more questions. "I know. It's all right."

Salem limped past them, leaning heavily on Rane's arm. With a pained groan, he sank down into one of the ugly plaid armchairs wedged between dusty stacks of books and cardboard boxes of crystals.

Rane regarded him with a mixture of worry and impatience, then glanced at Dru. "D, do you have a spare cane or a crutch or something?"

"I don't *need* a crutch," Salem snapped.

"Fine," Rane said. "Haul your own cranky ass around, then."

Opal, with a wicked smile, crossed the room and held out a tapered glass bottle to Salem, filled with a fizzy orange potion exactly the color of smoked salmon.

His gaze fastened greedily onto it. Wordlessly, he took it and held it in his lap for a moment, as if steeling himself to drink it.

"You're welcome," Opal said, and crossed the room back to the giant book.

Dru set down her armload of stuff, and carefully set down the icy cold apocalypse scroll. So much depended on this one ancient artifact. But she couldn't carry it around forever. It would be safe for the moment on her workbench. She pushed her glasses back up into place and came over to lean close to Opal.

"What's in that potion?" Dru whispered.

Opal flashed her a mischievous smile. "Just between you and me? It goes like this: one vanilla protein drink, a packet of orange vitamin powder, a Red Bull, two splashes of margarita mix, and a can of salmon. Blend and serve."

Dru couldn't keep the revulsion off of her face. "Oh, my God."

"I've been telling that boy for years that he needs to eat properly. Rane kept going on and on about protein and vitamins one time, and I thought, you know what? He'll drink this if he thinks it's magical."

Dru glanced back over her shoulder. Salem had just finished chugging down the frothy orange concoction. He made a gagging face, and then nodded to himself in satisfaction. He belched. Rane retreated, waving her hand in the air.

"Five minutes from now, he'll be back to his sunny old self," Opal assured her.

"But why *salmon?*"

Opal gave her a no-nonsense look. "The day he starts talking to me respectfully, I'll stop putting fish in his energy potion. Till then?" Her stern expression made it clear what would happen until then.

"Ick." Dru regarded the book Opal had been studying. "Hey, this isn't the Tristram book."

"Do I look like a reference librarian?" Opal said. "This is the best I can do on short notice. You do realize we have over a thousand books back here? And half of them aren't even logged into inventory, much less alphabetized. The word 'disorganized' doesn't even begin to cover it."

"I just bought all those books about getting organized." Dru looked around the mess for the brightly covered paperbacks she'd forgotten about. "Where did I put them?"

Opal snapped her fingers and pointed at the wrinkled old pages spread wide before her, easily the size of a newspaper. "Take a look at this. Wraiths can't be out in the sunlight."

"Oh. Goody. So if we can make it through the night, we'll be safe."

"Safe?" Opal said.

"Well, *safer*, anyway. Until tomorrow night."

Opal shook her head. "Not according to what I'm seeing. All a wraith has to do is come into physical contact with you, and that's all she wrote. Its touch can drain your life force in seconds. *Bam*, like that. You're dead."

"Bam?" Dru bent down and squinted at the heavy, dense columns of handwriting. "This doesn't sound good."

"No. I have to agree with you on that one."

"But look at this here." Dru skimmed over the giant pages, growing more excited as she went along. "It says here that dust can render the wraith corporeal. Right now, it's ghostly, and that makes it nearly impossible to defeat. But dust can make it solid again. That means we can physically fight it, and maybe even win. That's what we need to know. What is this book, anyway?" Dru struggled to lift its heavy front cover and read it. "Is it a reputable source?"

"It's the Codex of Gormsley Manor," Opal said with finality. "That's as real as it gets."

The name carried chilling connotations. "Gormsley Manor. Didn't those guys all drop dead on New Year's Day in, what, 1564?"

"Their bodies were *found* on New Year's Day," Opal said ominously. "After that, the manor was wall-to-wall haunted by wraiths for about eighty years, until Orlo the Elder dug up the bodies and found out they hadn't decayed one bit. Then he destroyed the bodies and burned the manor down. He documented pretty much the whole thing in this Codex."

"Yikes. Good for Orlo." With some effort, Dru managed to lift the left-hand pages enough to read the title page aloud. "A Boke or Counseill Against the Un-Dead Soule, Commonly Called the Shade, or Spirrite." She settled the heavy old pages down again. "'Spirrite?'"

"Spirit," Opal said. "They didn't have spell check."

At that moment, Greyson entered from the front of the shop. His glowing eyes scanned every corner, every shadow, as if watching for threats. Only when he was satisfied did he turn to Dru. "I don't see anything outside. I've got Hellbringer patrolling the neighborhood, looking for that thing."

She studied the set of his stubbled jaw, trying to glean his thoughts. Just his presence comforted her, but at the same time the thought of a wraith coming after Greyson made her throat tighten in fear. "Can you sense any danger? Anything coming our way?"

He stared off into the distance. "It's out there. I can't tell how close it is."

"But it is coming," she said, hoping she was wrong.

He took her shoulders in his strong hands. "I'm going to keep you safe. No matter what happens. We all will."

She nodded. Part of her knew that it was more likely she'd be the one keeping *him* safe. But another part of her needed to hear that from him, and welcomed the strength that his presence gave her. Together, they could take on so much more than they ever could separately. "Listen. I need you to check all the doors, all the windows. Make sure everything is locked up tight. We don't want even a draft getting in here."

He nodded once and gave her a quick kiss before he strode away. The heat of his lips lingered after he was gone, and she found herself unconsciously touching her mouth. The warm feeling vanished as soon as she felt Salem's twitchy gaze studying her with almost scientific scrutiny, as if she were some kind of exotic insect. His long fingers toyed with the empty potion bottle.

"Are you honestly considering making some sort of remember-the-Alamo last stand here, in the back of your little crystal shop?" He said it as if only an idiot would consider a plan so monumentally stupid.

Apparently, the fish potion had worked.

Dru squared her shoulders. "Well, things didn't work out so well at your place." She took a moment to compose herself and use her well-honed customer service voice to carefully ask, "Why, do you have a better idea?"

Mild annoyance flashed over his features. "Haven't you been paying attention? I *always* have a better idea. Let's start with handing over the scroll to the most qualified person in the room." He held out one long-fingered hand.

Opal put one hand on her hip, obviously puzzled. "Scroll?"

Dru went over to her workbench and picked up the ice-cold apocalypse scroll. As she held it up, an electric charge seemed to suffuse the room, tickling her hair. Somehow, the ancient artifact made the air feel thicker, and the light in the room seem dimmer, as if the world itself was warped by its very presence.

"*This*," Dru said quietly.

Opal's eyes nearly popped out of her head. "I thought Salem was going to lock that away in a vault." She gave him an accusing look.

"We already had that conversation," Dru said, as Salem's eyes flashed with irritation. "He insists there was a misunderstanding."

"I bet he does," Opal said out of the side of her mouth.

"And no, I don't want to give it back to you, sorry," Dru told him.

"Oh, my mistake," Salem said. "I must have given you the impression that I care what you *want*."

"I have a plan." Carefully, Dru set down the scroll again, clearing the clutter away so that nothing else was touching it. "You tried to build a protective circle, and hey, it really was an A-plus effort. But the wraith's spells were about to go right through it. So, obviously, we don't want to repeat that experience. Instead, let's draw the wraith straight to us, and fight it on our own terms."

Salem's eyes widened. "Using the apocalypse scroll as *bait?*"

"It can't actually come inside and get it. The crystal grid will stop it at the door. Right now, it's ghostly, and that makes it nearly invincible. But once we know where it is, we can turn it corporeal, and once it becomes solid, we can focus all of our efforts on destroying it. I'll use my sunstone crystal, you use your powers, and Rane, you hit it as hard as you can."

Rane folded her arms. "I'm good with that."

Salem clearly wasn't buying it. "And how exactly do you intend to render it corporeal?"

"We sprinkle it with dust." Dru turned to Opal. "Am I wrong about this?"

With an uncertain sigh, Opal turned the giant crackling pages, shooting a couple of worried looks at Dru while she found what she was looking for. Her perfectly manicured finger slid down a faded column of handwritten text. "According to this, you can make a wraith corporeal for a few moments by throwing dust on it." Then she shook her head and straightened up. "Oh, nope. You can forget about that angle. It has to be *moon* dust."

"Moon dust? You're kidding." Dru felt an uneasy quiver in her stomach. Nothing was ever easy.

Salem flung up his hands. "Using the scroll as *bait*. Do you actually need me to tell you how insane that sounds?"

Rane sat down on the arm of the chair next to him, making it creak dangerously. "Yo, somebody want to fill me in? What the hell is moon dust? Some kind of herb?" She mimed smoking.

Salem patted her bare thigh. "It's dust, darling. From the moon."

"Unfortunately, he's right," Dru said.

Salem gave her a sour look. "Unfortunately?"

Dru ignored him. "Opal, do you remember the time we busted the poltergeist that was bugging the professor? Remember that thank-you gift he gave us?"

Opal looked nonplussed. "You're talking about Professor Harvey, the man with the plaid patches on his elbows? Yeah, we've still got that box around here somewhere. Why?"

"Because inside that box is the tiny little lunar meteorite he gave us. It's a chunk of actual moon rock. If we grind up that bad boy, *voila*, instant moon dust."

"This night just keeps getting weirder," Opal said, but she was already digging through the shelves.

Dru turned to Salem and Rane to explain. "Harvey didn't work for NASA, but he worked for the Colorado School of Mines. Which, per capita, is probably at least as IQ-dense as the rocket scientists at Cape Canaveral."

"Not Cape Canaveral," Opal pointed out, her voice muffled by the shelf. "NASA is actually in Washington, DC."

"Yes, thank you, Carmen Sandiego," Salem snapped. Wincing in pain, he rose out of his seat. "This whole defend-the-scroll strategy is all well and good in theory, and I'm saying that with as much generosity as I can possibly muster. But has it occurred to you that the best way to take this thing out is to simply"—his voice dropped to a whisper—"go take it out?"

Dru traded curious looks with Rane. "What do you mean?"

"Just a little while ago, I had this wraith ninety-nine percent destroyed. All I need to do is find it, squeeze in an extra one percent, and it's a done deal."

"Except for the part where you fell over like an empty beer bottle," Rane said, elbowing him.

"Easy, Buttercup. There were extenuating circumstances." With a swish of his hand, Salem indicated the bandages on his head and chest. "On any other given day, that wraith wouldn't have even made me late for dinner. Even you have to admit that." This last part was directed at Dru.

"Okay, maybe," Dru said. "But we all have to work together to—"

"No." Salem leaned closer. "Not together. And definitely not *here*."

"Well . . ." Dru looked to Rane for support.

But Rane nodded toward Salem. "Well, I *did* kick ass on those tentacles. Once I take them out, he can blast the thing, and then it's Miller time."

"I'm going to hunt this thing down," Salem said, showing teeth. "Destroy it. Lay it to rest. Then I can get back to more important things." His gaze darted over to Rane, watching her closely. "Are you ready?"

She tossed her head to the side, making her blonde ponytail bounce. "Hells, yeah. Let's bust this thing."

"Excuse me," Opal said loudly, as she pulled the little white box of lunar meteorite off the shelf. "Did nobody else hear the part about where the wraith touches you and you *die?*"

"It will never get that chance," Salem said with finality. "We're leaving. *With* the scroll." He motioned for Rane to get it.

Dru put a protective hand on it. "No. The crystal grid in this shop is the only thing securing the scroll right now. I can't let you leave with it."

"Oh, come on," Rane said.

"No! You saw what happened at Salem's place. That was too close. We need to do this here, at the shop. I'm dead serious."

Rane turned from Dru to Salem. "Dude, she has a point."

"And she has the unfailing habit of being *wrong*," he snapped.

"Hey," Dru said. "I'm standing right here."

"Let's just leave that thing here with Dru," Rane said. "You and me can go."

"Not empty-handed." There was a dangerous edge in his voice.

A tense silence fell over the room as Salem glared at Rane, and she glared right back. "Don't push this," she said. "When it comes to doomsday stuff, I'm on Team D. You should be, too. Don't get all so wrapped up in your own head. She knows what she's talking about."

"Except when she doesn't." Salem's black-outlined eyes twitched. "This is exactly the sort of overconfidence and blind faith that almost got me crushed beneath those rocks."

"Well, maybe if you hadn't been running around with that tramp Ember—"

"She at least has self-control!" His voice rose. "And a healthy dose of skepticism where amateur sorceresses are concerned."

Dru frowned. "Again, standing right here."

Opal fluttered a hand in her direction. "He can't possibly mean you."

"*Both* of you!" Salem roared, earning a venomous look from Opal.

Rane jabbed a finger at him. "Hey! Hey! Don't be such a buzzkill! You don't know everything. You don't know how to kick this thing's ass."

He bristled. "I know *exactly* how."

"Bull," Rane spat. "You can't. If you could, we wouldn't have had to carry your candy ass out of there."

Salem's fingers spasmed, making sorcerer-ish clawing motions at his sides.

Dru realized the two of them were dangerously close to activating their powers and having an actual fight. It had happened before. She stepped in between them, arms out like a referee. "That's it! No more! Not in my shop!" She glared at both of them, but mostly at Salem. "We can't fight amongst ourselves. This is too important. We all need to work together."

"That's never going to happen, so you can just save your breath." Salem paced in a quick circle and motioned to Rane. "Let's go."

Rane folded her arms. "I'm staying right here, dude."

His nose wrinkled. "You're choosing *her?*"

"You don't like it, then don't make me choose," Rane said flatly.

An unspoken ultimatum passed between Salem and Rane, and seeing it made Dru ache inside. An invisible crack had appeared in the tenuous power balance that bound them together, and she knew it would only spread wider, until it split them apart. She had seen this happen before, more than once, and she wished that there was something she could do to stop it from happening again.

Salem's darkly lined gaze held Rane's. "I have better things to do," he ground out through his teeth.

"Better go do it, then," Rane said, with steel in her voice.

He stared her down a moment longer, and then he abruptly turned away and limped toward the back door.

Rane didn't move to follow. Her hands curled into fists, as if she wanted to break something. "D. Maybe we should give it to him, so—"

"No," Dru insisted. It broke her heart to say it, but she couldn't let Salem's arrogance land the apocalypse scroll in the wraith's clutches. "The scroll stays here."

Rane shot her a hurt look, then turned and stomped into the front of the shop, heading in the opposite direction from Salem. Dru watched her go as Salem shuffled out the back door into the night, alone. The door slammed.

Dru exchanged worried glances with Opal, who flung up her hands as if to say, *None of my business.*

As much as it hurt to see her friends fighting, that wasn't the worst part. It made her guilty to think in purely pragmatic terms, but regardless of Rane's feelings, the truth was that Dru didn't know how they could possibly defeat the wraith without Salem.

7

THOSE WHO WANT TO USE YOU

Thunder cracked and rolled slowly across the city, though the air was dry and uncomfortably warm. Lightning flickered far to the northeast, away from the tall downtown buildings, over the suburb of Aurora. Jagged bolts electrified the clouds from within, revealing their dark bulk. The fleeting glimpses Salem caught in the clouds reminded him of monstrous faces, creatures, bodies writhing in agony before they faded away.

He ignored all that as he limped angrily across the flat gravel-covered roof. Gritting his teeth against the pounding pains in his leg, his ribs, and his skull, he leaned briefly against the throbbing metal bulk of a rooftop swamp cooler. It smelled of rust, mildew, and old machinery.

With a grunt, Salem pushed off of it and made his way to the waist-high concrete wall that ran along the front of the building. Here, three stories up, he had an unobstructed view across the street to Dru's quaint little shop. Warm golden light spilled out of the scratched front windows, faintly bouncing off the glossy hand-painted sign that spelled out "The Crystal Connection" in obnoxiously elaborate script.

There was no movement inside the front of the shop. From this angle, he could see the ends of the rows of shelves packed full of crystals, old statues, jars of dried herbs, and other assorted sorcery components. But everyone was apparently in back, out of his line of sight.

Wincing, he leaned against the short wall so that he could take the weight off of his bad leg. And then he just watched. And waited. Fuming the whole time.

As much as he wanted to leave Dru and her entourage to stew in their own troubles, he couldn't just wash his hands of the whole situation. There was too much at stake. And it wasn't just that a rank amateur like Dru was now holding an artifact capable of destroying the entire world. It was mostly that Rane was caught up in all of this. And he couldn't just leave her on her own. He would rather die.

He almost had, in fact. Several times, recently.

And the singular common denominator in all of those painful fiascoes was Dru. Every time she showed up in another hair-raising panic, it never took long for things to jump from bad to worse. Instead of taking the necessary time to observe, and study, and then formulate and execute a flawless strategy, he always found himself chasing after Dru and getting caught directly in the line of fire. Which was exactly the problem he was determined to avoid this time around.

Unfortunately, he didn't heal as fast as Rane did. Or Greyson, for that matter, who drew his power from some infernal depths that no one really understood. And for some inexplicable reason, nobody had a problem with that. They all seemed to think Greyson was just an ordinary guy with a conveniently self-driving car. Never mind that Hellbringer was an evil speed demon literally summoned to Earth to destroy the world.

The fact that he was the only one bothered by this made his head feel like it was going to explode. The sky crashed and groaned, echoing his pain.

As if summoned by his thoughts, the old black Charger came rumbling down the street, headlights burning like the eyes of a predatory animal. It slowed down and crept past the front of the shop, as if the driver was peering in through the front windows. But as it passed beneath a streetlight, pale light fell across the driver's seat, which was clearly empty.

Salem watched Hellbringer prowl down to the end of the block and turn right. The red slits of taillights disappeared around the corner, carrying the thudding sound of exhaust with it. A few minutes later, it reemerged at the other end of the block and repeated its route, crawling past the shop again.

So the car had learned a new trick, Salem thought. Was it patrolling like a loyal guard dog? Or circling like a hungry shark?

Would it turn against them sooner or later? Had it already? Was it leading darker forces straight to the apocalypse scroll?

No one else seemed to find Hellbringer suspicious. But Salem had seen too many sorcerous catastrophes over the years to let himself get lulled into a false sense of security.

He watched the sword-like silhouette of the car slice through the night, circling the shop. He had tried to warn Rane, but no. She insisted on remaining oblivious to the danger. The thought of her choosing to embrace Dru's rose-tinted view of the world made him choke.

He tried to channel his anger in a more productive direction. His angry gaze bore into every shadow along the street, scrutinizing every movement. He watched a lone figure with a backpack and flip-flops scrape his way down the street and slump onto the graffiti-covered bus stop bench.

Salem's fingers itched with unspent magic. He wanted the man with the backpack to start acting furtive and suspicious. He needed an excuse to do *something*. But a few minutes later, a tired-looking bus hissed and clanked to a stop, blocking his view. When it left again, the man was gone. The street was empty.

A tiny voice inside Salem told him that it wasn't really Dru and Hellbringer that were making him mad. Rane had been acting differently lately. Ever since the night he had nearly died in that valley fighting Lucretia, the connection between them had changed.

She didn't look at him the same way anymore. Once, she had been in awe of his magic. A certain spark had lit her up every time he cast a spell. But after the valley, she didn't look up to him anymore. Now, she saw him as broken. Weak. Someone to be taken care of.

That had never happened before. He didn't like it. Not one bit.

And just lately, her habit of going for runs at night had taken her further and further away. Longer runs. And she had come back more flushed with excitement than tired. Like she couldn't wait to get out again. That was new.

The same tiny voice inside him implied that maybe she'd met someone else.

But he squelched that thought instantly. Obliterated it from his mind. Because it was impossible. Her raw physical strength was a perfect complement to his powers of sorcery. Together, they made an unstoppable duo.

Rane had always been drawn to him because of his sorcery. And no one else was more powerful. Who else could possibly compete with him?

No, she couldn't have met someone else. There had to be another explanation.

Fuming, he watched Hellbringer prowl down the dark street again. The next time it came around, it paused in the midst of turning the corner, even though there was no other traffic on the road. The car just sat there at an angle, engine rumbling, facing his direction.

As if its headlights were watching him.

That was interesting.

Salem stared back, hard. He channeled all of his frustration, his pain, his cold fury into his stare. He knew from experience that his direct gaze unsettled most people. He liked to give them a glimpse of just how far he was willing to go to prove his point.

Which was always, inflexibly, all the way.

He stared down the possessed car, and it stared back. Challenging him. Studying him. Evaluating him. Perhaps trying to find his weaknesses.

His long fingers twitched at his sides. He knew that thing was evil, deep down inside. It had nearly killed Rane once, nearly crushed her against the wall of Greyson's garage, with its sharp front end pressed tightly against her throat. Salem would never allow that to happen again. He would annihilate Hellbringer first.

Dru might have tamed it on the surface, but it was still a demon. It would still turn on them the moment they let down their guard.

He knew what he could do to the infernal thing. All he needed was an excuse.

Slowly, as if by their own volition, his hands rose above the waist-high wall. His fingers spread out wide, flexing. He could feel the hot sizzle of magic humming across his skin. Just waiting to be unleashed.

Abruptly, Hellbringer's headlights clicked off. The flip-up covers closed, and the car backed away, slipping into the darkness around the corner. It didn't come back.

Slowly, Salem breathed out, and all the aches and pains in his battered body returned. He sagged against the short wall. He desperately wished he could sit down, rest, at least for a little while. He was so damnably tired. He even wished he had another one of Opal's curiously refreshing potions, even though they did taste like they had been used to decontaminate scuba gear.

He spied the empty bench three stories below, across the street. With a chop of his hand, he let loose a torrent of nearly invisible magic. The air shimmered around the bus stop, and the thick steel bolts popped off the concrete like bottle caps, one after another. Metal groaned as he ripped the bench from its moorings.

With a flick of his wrist, it tumbled skyward, as if sucked up into a tornado. He twirled his fingers and gently settled it onto the gravel-covered roof beside him, its back to the wall.

With a thankful sigh, he took a seat, one arm sprawled along the top of the wall. After a long, contented minute, he lifted his bad leg and propped it up in front of him. Much more comfortable that way. Looking out across the scattered lights of the city, he smiled for the first time he could remember.

Tonight was turning out to be not so terrible after all. He had forced the demon car to submit. He had discovered that he could walk without his cane if he had to. And now he had a cozy place to sit. Albeit one that stank of old cigarette smoke and rank body odor. But that didn't matter. He had kept watch over Rane in much worse places.

This was ridiculous, he realized after a while, sitting up here all alone. On impulse, he took out his phone, intending to text Rane.

But then he thought again about the look she had in her eyes these days. *Maybe she met someone else.*

No. Impossible.

Still. His fingers hesitated over the screen. Agonized.

She would tell him he was being stupid. She would tell him to come down from the roof. Hang out with the rest of them. Get all cozy with the evil car.

He couldn't do that. He needed someone clear-headed to watch his back. He needed an outside perspective. Another pair of eyes. He needed backup.

He scrolled through his admittedly short list of contacts until he found what he was looking for.

I need your help, he typed. But then he hesitated again. That sounded too needy. Needy wasn't his thing.

He deleted the last few letters.

I need you.

Good enough. He sent it. And waited. And watched the street below. Hellbringer stayed hidden. Perhaps scared off. Perhaps plotting its next move.

He kept checking his phone, waiting for her answer. When none came, he idly wondered if she had misinterpreted his message as something more personal. There had always been that unspoken tension between them, but so far everything had stayed strictly professional. He intended to keep it that way, whether she knew it or not.

But she hadn't spoken to him since she lost her powers. She had disappeared. Holed up somewhere. Refused to come out. That was an amateur move. Not like a professional at all. A professional always showed up when there was trouble, and dealt with it, no matter what.

Watching the street, he had plenty of time to think, and grudgingly had to admit that he had done the same thing. Holed up. It was a natural instinct for sorcerers, or anyone really. But now it was time to come out. Holing up was no longer an option, now that they were only one step away from doomsday. Now was the time for action.

His phone buzzed in his hand.

I can't help you, her text read. *I can't help anyone.*

A moment later, she added: *I'm done.*

He rolled his eyes at all of her drama. Ridiculous. Even he knew that she was far from done. There were always options. Some more unpleasant than others, perhaps. But options always existed.

His thumbs tapped out a quick message: *What are you doing right now?*

She didn't answer. She probably wasn't doing anything.

That's what I thought, he texted. *Get over to the shop girl's place. Tout de suite. Help me keep watch for undead.*

He kept one eye on the phone, one on the empty street below.

What's in it for me? she texted.

He nodded to himself. Now he had her right where he wanted her. Because now that the door was open, even a crack, all he had to do was push it a little wider.

Do you want your powers back? he texted. And then he deliberately waited a long moment before he added: *Because I can make that happen.*

Lightning flashed again over the distant reaches of the city, but this time it was silent.

The phone buzzed with her reply. *Yes.*

He smiled with satisfaction. Finally, things were headed in the right direction again.

8

OTHER PEOPLE'S DRAMA

The last thing Opal needed was to get caught up in any kind of sorcerer drama, because that never ended well. If Salem wanted to go home and pout, she was fine with that. The less he was around, the better, as far as she was concerned. Besides, they could find a way to fight the wraith without him.

Or so she thought at first. But as the night wore on, and she helped Dru dig deeper into research, she became less and less sure. No matter how many dusty books they flipped through, no matter how much cramped, faded handwriting they deciphered, they couldn't turn up any more advice about fighting wraiths. They couldn't find the elusive Tristram book, either.

Meanwhile, Rane transformed into solid rock and used her magically enhanced muscles to grind up the golf-ball-sized lunar meteorite with her stone hands, like a mortar and pestle, until she had reduced it to a chalky gray powder.

Dru poured it into an old faceted glass salt shaker. If everything went according to plan, Dru would sprinkle the moon dust on the wraith to make it solid, and then Rane would pound it into oblivion.

Sounded like a pretty terrible plan to Opal, but nobody paid her any attention when she pointed that out.

They spent the rest of the night standing an uneasy watch, as Greyson paced back and forth along the length of the shop, searching for any hint of trouble.

Finally, by the early light of dawn, Opal dared to hope that the wraith was gone for good. As the sky grew brighter and the sun finally emerged, that slim hope turned into a full-blown conviction. They had made it through the night. They were safe.

At least until tomorrow night.

Eyes gritty with lack of sleep, Opal stood in the open back door of the shop, watching across the alley as the first rays of sunshine kissed the tops of the surrounding buildings with gold. She could never remember another time in her life when she had been so happy to be up all night and discover that absolutely nothing had happened.

Dru joined her, blinking owlishly as she cleaned her glasses. "I can't believe it. We got stood up."

Opal nodded. "You know, I'm okay with that. Hey, maybe Rane really did clean that thing's clock. Maybe it's gone for good. Just took off."

"Sure," Dru said slowly. "That could happen." The disbelief on her face clearly mirrored what Opal was thinking. Nothing was ever that easy. The wraith would come back, and Opal just knew that when it did, everything would go horribly wrong.

A chugging engine wheezed its way down the alley toward them. Definitely not Hellbringer. Tires squelched across scattered gravel, and Ruiz's white work van rolled up behind the shop, ladders on top shining in the morning light.

With a broad smile, Ruiz climbed down out of the van, leaving the engine running. He was still wearing his dumpy stained work coveralls, presumably having resolved the fried chicken fiasco. With the air of a champion returning triumphant, he held up a flat box of donuts in one hand and a cardboard holder full of steaming coffee cups in the other. "Hey, check it out!" he said brightly. "I got the hookups!"

Opal leaned close to Dru's ear. "I may just have to marry that man," she murmured.

Dru eyed the donuts. "I might just beat you to it, if there's any Boston cream in that box."

Ruiz handed off the goodies to Dru and gave Opal a warm kiss. "I hate to say this, baby, but I gotta get back to work. Good news, I'm getting paid crazy overtime."

"But you were up all night." She ran her fingers back through his messy hair, trying to figure out exactly how tired she really was. Narrowly avoiding death at the ghostly claws of a soul-devouring wraith made her reevaluate what she wanted to do with the rest of her day. "Maybe you could call in sick. Take today off." She looked deep into his eyes. "You know, we could've died last night."

"No way," he said excitedly, clearly oblivious to her intentions. "You're gonna take that thing down, baby. I know it. But first, you know, I gotta be at the job site by nine. That electrical's not gonna run itself."

Opal sighed and ran her hands across the chest of his coveralls, her fingers lingering on his name patch. "You get off work early today. I don't care how. Make it happen. And come over to my place. That's an order, soldier."

He grinned, planted a lingering kiss on her lips, and hopped back into his van. She watched him drive off and sighed. "You know, that man's the only person around here with a real job," she said to Dru, who had disappeared inside and now emerged chewing on a donut.

"What about us?" Dru said around the mouthful of donut. "We have real jobs."

"I need to go home and get a shower." Opal headed inside for her purse. "And no, this is not a real job."

Dru followed after her, looking forlorn. "Then how come I have to pay so much taxes?"

* * *

At home, Opal slept a few hours, then made an effort to clean up and hide the ravages of the all-nighter. She'd had so many of those lately that she had her morning emergency routine down to a science. With enough vitamins and skin products, she could work miracles. Despite the grittiness in her eyes and the constant ache in the back of her head, she managed to pamper herself just enough to feel like a human being again.

She decided to go with a vintage look. She had on a new petunia-purple knit top, accented by a braided gold belt, over buttery-soft leggings the color of gingerbread. And, of course, brand-new shoes. Rhinestone-encrusted heels with open toes wrapped in satiny lavender ribbons, to showcase her fresh teal pedicure. Just looking at those shoes made her feel amazing enough to almost forget that an evil wraith could show up and devour their souls the moment the sun went down.

No time to worry about what might happen. She just had to get back to the shop and do whatever needed to be done. She was on the case.

She had her car keys in one hand, her empty latte mug in the other, and her favorite Miami Sound Machine song playing in her head. She stopped at the hall mirror and checked her hair. She looked spectacular. She felt amazing. She was ready to conquer the day. Then she opened up the front door.

And screamed.

Salem leaned against the door frame, arms folded, his scowling crazy eyes level with hers. For a heart-stopping moment, Opal was certain those cold gray eyes would be the last thing she would ever see before she met a dark and grim end. To drive the point home, Salem's old hearse with chrome-tipped fins was parked at the curb in front of her house.

Hyperventilating, Opal stiffened, waiting for her life to flash before her. That was what was supposed to happen to people right before they died. When no touching childhood memories popped into her mind, she wondered if maybe there was hope yet for a long and healthy life.

Salem rolled his eyes, as if he could read her thoughts and found them obnoxiously boring. "Darling, when you're done being shocked and apoplectic, a friend of mine needs your help."

"*You* have friends?"

"You wound me." He rolled a long, bony finger vaguely in her direction. "You do still do that whole 'helping other people' thing, don't you? I need a favor."

With an effort, Opal got her breathing under control and stuck out her chin in defiance. "Don't look to me for favors, Salem. I wouldn't help you if you paid me."

He considered that, his eyeliner-darkened gaze ticking back and forth above her head, as if doing mental arithmetic. "I do pay Dru for her admittedly somewhat useful services—"

"Definitely don't pay her enough," Opal muttered.

"And Dru does pay your salary. So technically, in fact, I do pay you to help me." With a smirk, he cocked his head, making his silk top hat shine in the morning sun. It was perched at a strange angle atop his head bandages, but that only served to make him look even more unhinged than usual.

Opal spotted motion behind him, lurking near the bushes that bordered her front walk. She sidestepped and peered over Salem's shoulder. Behind him, a young woman with inky lipstick and eyebrow piercings was trying to blend into the scenery and failing completely.

She was Ember, a sorceress Opal hadn't seen since the infamous night in the canyon where Salem had nearly been crushed to death by a rockslide. That partially excused his bratty behavior, Opal supposed. But only partially. And come to think of it, Ember had been pretty badly injured in the same battle, and she wasn't laying any hassle on Opal's doorstep. Yet.

Opal caught Ember's gaze and tried to hold it. But Ember quickly looked away. She backed up a step and turned as if she was about to bolt.

Opal immediately noticed three important things about her.

First, the sorceress was out and about in the daytime, which wasn't her style at all. With her midnight-black clothes, ripped fishnet tights and knee-high leather boots edged with metal spikes, she looked incongruously exposed in the daylight. Her face still showed a few lingering scabs from the canyon battle, inexpertly covered with makeup.

Second, Ember's usual bravado was completely gone. The woman usually had an attitude a mile high, looking down her long nose at anyone beneath her, and refusing to even speak to those she deemed unworthy. Her painted lips had only two expressions: displeasure and superiority. But now, all of that was gone, and Ember looked like she was frightened of her own shadow. More particularly, she looked like she was afraid Opal would hurt *her*, instead of the other way around.

Third, Ember wasn't wearing her long, raven-black coat. The voluminous trench coat had always hung from her shoulders like a gloomy curtain, walling her off from the rest of the world. But now it was gone, and Ember's dark mystique had gone with it. Now, she just looked like a refugee from a Slayer concert who had made questionable choices the night before.

Thinking back, Opal remembered that Ember's coat had been torn apart in the battle in the canyon. Without her coat, she hadn't been able to use her power of teleportation that night, which was her main—possibly her only—magical ability. Now, without the coat, she was left simultaneously stranded, defenseless, and powerless.

Not a great place to be. But more importantly, why was she here on Opal's doorstep?

Opal pushed past Salem. The strike of her heels on the front walk was the only sound in the quiet neighborhood.

From the doorway, Salem piped up. "Let me connect the dots for you. Without her coat, she can't teleport. Hence, why I brought her here. To get a new one."

Opal stopped and put one hand on her hip, temper flaring. "Oh, so you think I'll just hand over a brand-new magic teleporting coat? Just like that? Because it doesn't work that way."

Salem's eyes glittered.

"You can forget it. Because my fashion collection is part of my own private life. Everything having to do with magic stays at work. Speaking of work . . ." Opal made a shooing-away motion at him, jangling her car keys.

When he didn't budge, she pulled the door shut, locked it, and left him there. As she walked on down the walk toward her car, she said to Ember, "I'm sorry, honey. You need a ride?"

No response.

Opal kept walking. Considering how badly Ember had treated her, and Dru, and everyone else in recent memory, it pretty much served her right to lose her powers. Opal had no intention of forgiving Ember for kidnapping her and locking her in a file closet in a radioactive ghost town. There was just no excuse. Who would do that?

Without her teleportation powers, Ember couldn't cause any more trouble, and Opal was just fine with that.

She got as far as unlocking the door to her long purple Lincoln before she took another glance at Ember standing there forlornly.

Opal had never had magic powers of her own, so it was tough to imagine. Or have a ton of sympathy. But the poor girl had been a sorceress, and now she wasn't. Probably felt like she had lost her identity. She didn't know what to do with herself. Felt like the whole purpose of her life had been ripped away. That was a terrible way to be.

Opal stood there with her hand on the car door handle, conflicted. She wanted more than anything to get in her car and drive away. But the truth was that Ember had lost her coat, and her powers, while she was trying to do the right thing. Trying to save the world.

No matter what else Ember had said or done, she had stepped up when it counted. She had risked her own life, and got knocked down because of it. She wouldn't be the first sad case to come to Opal for help, and she wouldn't be the last.

Besides, even if Ember came down to the shop looking for crystals or potions or anything else, it wouldn't help. What this girl needed, apparently, was a new coat. Opal was her only hope.

Against her better judgment, Opal trudged back up the front walk, sighing all the way. She stood in front of Ember until the girl finally looked up at her.

"Are you going to apologize for locking me in a file closet?" Opal crossed her arms and waited.

Still leaning against the doorway, Salem said, "You can't possibly still be hung up on that."

Without even bothering to turn around, Opal held up a finger to silence him. Her keys clattered against her empty travel mug, which she desperately wished was full of coffee. "I didn't ask you," she called, and then dropped her voice to address Ember again. "Well?"

"Why?" Ember said after a moment. When she finally lifted her gaze, her heavily lined eyes were suspicious. "Would that make you do something for me?" Her Arabic accent was faint, her words controlled and precise.

"Honey, you can't *make* me do *anything* for you."

Ember visibly swallowed. The silence grew between them.

"I am very sorry," she said finally. Her gaze was clear and direct.

Opal slowly nodded. "Okay, then."

"Salem said that you would know where to find a new coat."

"Well." Opal took a deep breath. "That right there is an understatement."

Her instincts told her that if she led the way, Ember would follow.

So she went back and unlocked the door, stepped past Salem, and headed back inside. She put down her car keys and her latte mug, which at this rate wouldn't be filled by the friendly local barista anytime soon. But as much as Opal desperately wanted her coffee, it would have to wait. There was a vulnerable sorceress in need.

And what she needed was fashion.

9
FASHION SECRETS OF
THE SORCERERS

Salem followed them inside and slammed the front door with a wave of his hand. "As much as I adore the idea of trying on all of your clothes, we need to make this quick. Only so many hours in the day, and when night falls, it's wraith time."

As sweetly as Opal could manage, she said, "Oh, no, Salem, honey. You don't get to come in. You need to go get us some lattes."

A sardonic smile twitched at the corner of his mouth. "That's an amusing idea, but no."

Opal put her hands on her hips. "I'm sorry, do you know anyone else who can help your friend here? No. Now, you may not think fashion is serious business, but I'm here to tell you. We are going to need some caffeine."

Judging by Salem's narrow glare, it took him a moment to realize that she was utterly serious.

"Biggest cups they have. Extra whipped cream." Opal silently checked with Ember for verification, who shot an unreadable look at Salem before nodding to Opal. "And," Opal added, "get us some of those little pastries, too. Good ones, with chocolate chips and everything."

Salem looked at her as if she had completely lost her mind. One of his eyes twitched.

Opal folded her arms. "Don't make us wait. That would be a mistake."

Without another word, Salem slowly turned and stalked, stiff-legged, out the front door. A minute later, his old hearse coughed to life and drove away.

Relieved, she turned to Ember, who looked ready to flee this place and run after Salem. "Come on upstairs, honey. These clothes aren't going to try on themselves."

The entire upstairs of Opal's house was given over to her fashion collection. Who needed extra bedrooms when you could turn them into giant walk-in closets? Freestanding clothing racks ran the length of each room, dividing it into aisles like an extremely exclusive clothing boutique. Which had always been Opal's career plan B, in case the whole Crystal Connection thing fell apart, a possibility that grew even more likely every time some ultimate evil came blasting through town.

Nothing calmed Opal's nerves more than collecting vintage clothing. Unless it was combing through the racks looking for the perfect new look for her friends.

Thing was, this girl with the chunky boots and face piercings was anything but a friend. Ordinarily, Opal wouldn't let someone like Ember anywhere near her collection. She had to remind herself that Ember was a sorceress in need. Besides, a little voice inside Opal insisted that she had some kind of obligation to use her spectacular fashion sense for good.

That didn't mean she had to let Ember run wild, though. The first thing she did was tell Ember where she couldn't look. "This rack here? And that one? Off limits."

Ember wordlessly pointed to a different rack, full of Opal's favorite disco dance floor fashions, including draped one-shoulder dresses and jersey halters.

The thought of giving any of those to Ember nearly gave Opal a heart attack. "Not on your life, honey. That's all Halston right there. And don't even *think* about trying on any of those shoes."

But from the blank look on Ember's face as she went around the room, clearly she couldn't tell a Missoni from a Mizrahi. Poor thing.

They awkwardly sorted through the racks together, looking at long and short coats from the nineties, eighties, seventies, all the way back to the forties. It took several attempts to get Ember talking, haltingly, about how her powers worked.

Ember's story was sad one, marked more by the things she omitted than the things she said out loud. She was a loner, a worldwide wanderer.

Opal suspected she'd been to more countries than Opal had ever even heard of. And from the sound of it, she survived by her wits alone.

She traveled by wrapping a coat around herself, and somehow disappearing into another realm, an astral plane she traveled through until she emerged somewhere far away. She didn't describe this ethereal realm, but Opal had experienced it once. An airless, endless nothingness, shot through with cold streaks of light that whispered as they rushed past. Opal had rarely been so terrified as the one time she had fallen through that realm for long, agonizing minutes. She couldn't imagine entering that place willingly.

"But it cannot be just any coat," Ember explained. "It must be one with a history. One that has traveled. Everything picks up traces, from one place to another. It builds up, like layers. And that is where the power comes from, by digging down through those layers. Making connections." Ember looked away, suddenly self-aware. "Never mind. I'm just babbling."

Opal wasn't sure how to respond. Talking to a former enemy like this, they were in uncharted territory. "No, I get it. That's why you need a vintage coat. And you know what else you need? Color. Everything you're wearing is so dark. There's a whole rainbow out there, sweetie." With a twinge of possessiveness, she held up a long red nylon trench coat from the eighties. "See?"

Ember shook her head, looking disgusted.

"That's Chanel, honey. Show a little respect." Opal put it back on the rack with a certain amount of reverence. "All I'm saying is, you don't have to wear just black all the time."

"Well. I prefer to."

"Just drags you down, is all it does. Look at Salem. That boy's all monochrome, too. It may look dramatic for a minute, but after that it just gets boring." Opal stole a sidelong glance at Ember. "So what's the story with you and Salem, anyway?"

Ember continued sorting through the clothes, sliding one hanger aside at a time, each one squeaking against the rod. She took a long time to answer, and when she did, she didn't look up. "He has a girlfriend. She is beautiful. So strong."

"Mmm-hmm."

"Are they close?" Ember said. The anguish was plaintive in her voice. "Of course they are. I am being ridiculous."

"Yeah, they're real close." Opal watched her for another long minute, hoping Ember would elaborate. She didn't. The unspoken words hung heavy in the air.

"You're too good for Salem, anyway," Opal said carefully.

Ember shook her head. A quick, decisive refusal. "I am no good to anyone anymore. Not without my powers."

That was just sad to hear. Opal shook her head. "All you need is a new coat. Right? Then you're back in action."

Ember's darkly lined eyes finally lifted. Her gaze looked haunted. "Not just any coat. It has to be the *right* one. I can't explain it."

"No, I get you." Opal spied a delightful eighties coat covered in electric blue sequins, with gauzy blue sleeves, from a boutique designer she couldn't remember. "Look at these amazing shoulder pads. Here."

Ember's inky lips turned down in disgust. "*No.*"

"Just try it. Just once."

Ember shook her head.

"You want to get your powers back? You're going to have to step outside your comfort zone, sweetie." Opal came around the end of the rack, brandishing the blue coat like a weapon.

She almost needed to use physical force to get Ember into the coat. She frowned into the mirror.

"You look . . . radiant," Opal said. That much was literally true. Put a spotlight on that girl, and she would turn the room into an instant discotheque. "Go on, give it a whirl."

After a long hesitation, Ember grabbed the lapels of the coat and wrapped it tighter around herself. She disappeared into a swirl of blazing blue smoke and an explosion of sapphire sequins. Instantly, she reappeared a few feet away, coughing and gagging.

"No," Ember croaked, stripping off the coat and shoving it into Opal's hands. It looked more than a little worse for wear.

Furious, Opal straightened it out as best as she could and put it back on the rack. She wanted to kick Ember out right then and there. But she couldn't. It took her a minute to get her frustration under control. "Well. Look at the bright side. Now we know you got your power back, right?"

Ember held her arms out to either side. "I could only go this far. How does that help anything?"

"All right, all right. We'll get this. Don't give up hope yet."

The next candidate was a vintage bolero jacket from the 1940s covered with puffy pink ostrich feathers. Opal pulled it out proudly. "You just know this thing has been all over the place. Probably Hollywood. In the glory days."

Ember didn't look impressed. "I will look like . . . what do you call it? The cotton candy."

Still, at Opal's insistence, she tried it on. That teleportation experiment got her as far as the next room, in an explosion of pink fluffy feathers that drifted every which way. Opal waved her hands through the air, uselessly.

This wasn't going to work, she realized. They needed to try something that didn't involve actually blowing up her clothes. But what?

It took Opal a minute to realize that she had lost track of Ember. She looked up and down the narrow aisles between freestanding racks of jackets, dresses, and wraps. No sign of her. Maybe she had stormed out in a rage. Well, that would simplify things.

But she hadn't heard the front door. Worried, Opal tried the next room. No sign of Ember.

Opal felt a terrible sinking feeling inside. Had Ember really just given up and slipped away? Had she taken any of Opal's jewelry with her? That wouldn't be a surprise, but just the thought of it made Opal mad enough that she couldn't see straight.

Opal circled around the top of the stairs and tried the last room. At first, she thought it was empty, aside from the long racks of clothes and ceiling-high shoe racks. But the light was on in the closet at the far end of the room. Opal never used that closet anymore.

Carefully, she squeezed down the aisle, making hangers scrape. She found Ember hunkered down on the floor of the stuffy closet, surrounded by racks of zipped-up garment bags. The light of a single bare bulb with a pull string shone down, highlighting dust motes in the air and flashing off of Ember's piercings. She was on her knees in front of an old iron-banded wooden trunk. She had the lid open, revealing stacks of carefully folded clothes at least a century old. They were wrinkled and discolored by age, as if gravity had somehow drained the dye from the high spots in the fabric.

Still on her knees, Ember bent closer to the trunk. "What is all of this?" she asked softly.

"That all's too vintage even for me. The whole trunk should go to a museum, but it used to belong to a sorceress back in the frontier days. Might be something dangerous in one of the pockets, I don't know. Probably best not to mess with it. Unless you want something terrible to happen."

"Something terrible has already happened to me." Ember's voice was barely above a whisper. She closed her heavily lined eyes for a moment, then opened them wide and slipped her hands down into the trunk, feeling through the clothes.

Opal's mouth went dry. What if there really was some dark artifact hidden down in there? One time, she'd found an old pocket watch in a trunk like this, and it had nearly stolen Dru's soul. It was only luck that had saved them. That, and an epic all-night potion brewing session that had given Opal serious indigestion for a week and made Dru burp like a trucker. She wasn't eager to repeat that experience.

Ember sucked in a surprised breath. Opal slowly backed away from the closet doorway. If anything blew up, she wanted to have the option to duck. Because things like that happened to her more often than she would like.

Out of the depths of the trunk, Ember carefully pulled a burgundy velvet bundle. Excitedly, she rose to her feet and turned to Opal, who sighed in relief that nothing catastrophic had happened.

"All right. Bring it on out here. But if it's cursed or whatever, I'm not taking any responsibility. You just need to know that up front."

Ember stepped out of the closet and shook out the bundle. It was a coat, all right, dusty and stiff with age. The color was a deep and rich red, like aged wine. Elaborate lace, thin with age but not torn, shrouded the upturned sleeve cuffs. Charcoal-gray and gold embroidery swirled around the wide lapels and down the long double-breasted front, highlighting its twin rows of heavy brass buttons.

The high waist was cinched in so narrowly that Opal was sure it wouldn't fit. Ember was smaller than Opal, but she wasn't Victorian-skinny by any stretch of the imagination. Still, when she slipped her arms into the sleeves and snugged the high-shouldered coat up around her neck, it molded perfectly to her body. The brass buttons ran in parallel rows down the front of her rib cage, and below that it flared out into dramatic folds that swirled as she spun around in front of a full-length mirror.

Opal had to admit that on Ember, it looked good. More than that, it looked magnificent. Sumptuous. Majestic, even.

Before, Ember's coat had hung on her like a shapeless shadow, wrapping her up and hiding her from the world. But this coat, as big as it was, had the opposite effect. It made Ember stand out, gave her silhouette structure and power. It caught the eye and held it. The difference was nothing short of a transformation.

"Fits you just right. What about the magic vibe?" Opal was so busy admiring the surprisingly perfect fit of the antique coat that she was startled by the expression on Ember's face.

For the first time ever, Ember was smiling. Widely. Incandescently. Her white teeth shone, practically lighting up the room. It was the most pure expression of childlike joy Opal had ever seen. It changed Ember's face from a dark storm cloud into a beam of sunshine. She didn't even look like the same person anymore.

The effect was breathtaking. At first, Opal worried there was some kind of mood-changing magic involved. But when Ember unexpectedly swept her into a warm hug, she realized the only magic involved was the kind that came from fashion.

"Thank you," Ember said in her ear. There was a hitch in her voice. Opal realized at that moment that Ember probably didn't have many friends. Maybe none. It made this moment feel even more precious.

Ember stepped back, blinking rapidly, and admired herself again, turning left and right.

"Go on, try it out." Opal waved her hands, encouraging her.

Ember took a deep breath, and let it out, shaky. Her smile dimmed. "I am afraid to discover it won't work."

"It'll work," Opal said, with absolute certainty.

Ember met her gaze, clearly nervous, and nodded. Taking another deep breath, she turned back to the mirror, her expression serious. Unlike before, she didn't wrap the coat tighter around herself or try to disappear into it. Her arms stayed straight down by her sides, and her fingertips lifted up as if she was about to take flight. Her dark eyelids fluttered.

Instantly, she was gone, leaving behind only a silent waviness in the air, like the heat ripple above a candle flame.

Opal waited for a full minute, but Ember didn't return. Apparently, the coat had worked. With a heavy sigh, Opal went back into the closet and regarded the open trunk. What else could be hiding in there? What other secrets had been locked away in that iron and wood box for the last hundred years or so?

Nothing that would fit her, obviously. She shut the lid, turned out the light, and closed the closet door.

Just as she was leaving the room, Ember reappeared in a breath of sultry air, inexplicably carrying the scent of the ocean with her. Grinning, she held out a long green stem topped by brightly colored fuchsia and yellow flowers. Exotic, and undoubtedly tropical. A tiny bead of sap glistened beneath the broken tip of the stem. It had just been picked. "Here. For you."

Stunned, Opal reached out and took the flower. It was still warm from the tropical sun. "How far did you . . ."

"Thank you. I will never forget this." With that, Ember vanished again in a gentle puff of wind. She didn't come back.

Opal looked around. "Huh."

Her phone chimed with a message about a crystal delivery from UPS. She realized she should probably get to work.

The flower was very nice, though. Opal put it in a vase on her table and took a picture of it as proof, wondering what it was, exactly. And what tropical island it had come from. She'd have to decide whether to explain to Ruiz that it hadn't been from some other guy, or whether she should let him wonder.

Happy at doing her good deed for the day, Opal grabbed her purse and car keys just as she heard Salem's old hearse grumble and creak its way up to the curb. She opened the door and smiled at Salem's sour expression as he grudgingly held out two giant paper coffee cups with steaming plastic lids.

"You just missed her," Opal said as she took the cups. "But that's okay. More coffee for me."

10

GET SWOLE

After finally showering off the chicken soup, Dru had been much too stressed out to sleep. She was desperate to find any books by the elusive scholar Tristram, who she was absolutely sure had written a world-class treatise on dispossessed spirits. The caffeine and sugar jolt from Ruiz's coffee and donuts had sent her into a brief overdrive, so she had impetuously worked her way through all of her stacks of books, searching.

But some of her books were unaccountably missing.

For all of her efforts, her caffeinated hyper-focus didn't turn up anything she was looking for. She was left sure of only one thing: the Tristram book was not anywhere in her shop.

Which meant someone had taken it. But who?

As always, Salem was her first suspect. On more than one occasion, he had lifted important magical things right out from under her nose. But even if she could find him and confront him, he would deny everything.

She sat down in one of her ugly plaid armchairs, trying to think of her next move. Immediately, her head lolled back and she fell fast asleep.

She woke up with a snort a few hours later, disoriented and intensely hungry. She blinked in the bright sunlight streaming in through the shop windows. Her glasses had gone crooked on her nose, and her entire body ached from sleeping in the chair. Someone had covered her with a light blanket and carefully tucked it up over her shoulders.

She turned her head. Greyson sat in another chair, reading silently.

He was motionless, patiently quiet and unobtrusive, and yet his presence filled the room. Everything about him radiated strength and capability. His hair was slightly mussed up from the long night before, and his stubble cast a darker shadow along his jawline. But that just made her want to reach out and touch the lean contours of his cheek. He was like a rock, keeping her firmly anchored when everything else felt like it was going to pieces.

She looked him up and down, wondering for the hundredth time how they had ever found one another. A guy who didn't believe in magic, wasn't a sorcerer, and hadn't grown up surrounded by the supernatural, the way she had. They moved in completely different circles. Had entirely different interests. He was a wrench-turning car guy, a mechanic and erstwhile muscle car restorer. She was a clumsy crystal sorceress with social anxiety. There was no way they should have ever even met.

Except that a bizarre twist of fate had inflicted a curse on him, dooming him to become one of the Four Horsemen of the Apocalypse. She still wasn't exactly sure what he was. Mostly human, part demon, possessed of magical powers that neither of them fully understood.

Once, he had been a monster, threatening to destroy the world in a fiery apocalypse. But Dru's magic had saved him, brought him back from the brink, turned him human again with the most passionate kiss of her life.

He was dangerous, that much was clear. She wanted to believe that it was a good kind of dangerous, the kind that would keep her safe and protected. But what if she was wrong? What if Salem was right, and Greyson had a hidden dark side that no one had seen yet?

And even if Greyson was a good guy all the way through, as she so badly wanted to believe, how would the two of them ever make their relationship work in the long run? Did they even have a relationship, technically? So far, they had shared only a few dinner dates—most of which ended in some kind of supernatural disaster—and several extremely hot kisses.

That, to her, constituted the start of a relationship with serious possibilities. Especially since every time she was near Greyson, she just wanted to be lost in his warm embrace. It wasn't just his brawny good looks, either. He always seemed to know what she was feeling before she felt it herself. Even in the heat of battle against the forces of darkness, he was always there for her. They made a great team.

But she still had to admit that on the surface, it seemed the two of them were completely incompatible. No matter how safe and protected she felt around him, she still had to wonder how he really felt about her. She also couldn't ignore the nagging worry that the same twists of fate that had brought them together could someday tear them apart.

But even after a sleepless night, the guy still looked amazingly handsome, and that right there was almost too good to be true. She didn't want to do anything dumb to jeopardize this blossoming relationship.

Dru surreptitiously checked to make sure she hadn't drooled on herself, then sat up and fixed her glasses, making the room zoom out of focus and back in again.

"Morning." Greyson smiled bemusedly and held up his heavy brown leather-bound book. "I don't know how you read these things."

She cleared her throat and made a twirling motion with her finger. "You have to turn it over." Too late, she realized that maybe she shouldn't have pointed that out.

One eyebrow went up, but he didn't seem offended. Carefully, he turned the old book right side up and stared at it some more, then flipped the page. "Huh. How can you tell?"

Dru leaned forward and squinted at the book. Greyson held it up again, so she could see the pages.

"Oh, don't worry about that book. That's nothing." She waved it off. "It's a pharmacopeia written in transliterated Nahuatl. Actually, it's not even that. It's a seventeenth-century forgery. I was just using it as a doorstop."

Greyson nodded slowly. His expression clearly indicated that he wasn't following.

"Nahuatl. It's the language of the Aztecs," she explained, which probably didn't help at all. She wanted to smack herself in the forehead.

He nodded again as if he understood and carefully set the book down. "Well, the pictures are interesting, anyway."

As soon as the words left his mouth, Dru felt a sudden flash of déjà vu. She remembered Rane sitting in that exact chair the previous winter, while snow piled up against the windows, guffawing with laughter as she flipped through the pages of a similar book, looking at the pictures. *Oh, my God, look at this poky thing. Tell me that's not what I think it is.*

Dru had never really wanted to talk about what Rane apparently thought "it" was, but she did remember Rane cackling and insisting she had to take the book home to show Salem. Which Dru had immediately vetoed, or so she remembered.

The book Rane had been reading was the Tristram book. About dispossessed souls. And come to think of it, Dru hadn't seen it since that day.

As if sensing Dru's chain of thoughts, Greyson straightened up. "Everything all right?"

"Maybe. Are you up for a drive? Because we need to go to Rane's place. She might have exactly the book I need to stop the wraith."

"Rane? A book?" Greyson was clearly skeptical. "She's a big reader, huh?"

Dru tried to keep a straight face. "Not exactly."

* * *

After a quick bite at Denver's famous sandwich shop, Snarf's, Dru directed Greyson to the little-used frontage road that led to a sparsely populated area near the river. Calling it a neighborhood was too much of a stretch. It was more like a no-man's-land between several blocks of working-class apartments and an industrial zone of endless concrete warehouses and smoke-belching factories. In between stretched a lightly wooded area that bordered the river, scattered with random storage yards and empty old houses. It appeared that no one quite knew what to do with the land, and had given up worrying about it decades ago.

An unmarked gravel road bumped and turned through the trees, leading to a squat brick building that looked like it had been hastily abandoned years before.

Piles of weathered lumber sat under threadbare tarps that did nothing to shield them from the elements. Two burly dump trucks, spotted with rust, sat abandoned in the weeds beside an old pickup with broken windows. To one side of the building, a tall chain-link fence completely enclosed a paved lot. The fence was run through with strips of weathered plastic that blocked out the view and rendered its contents a mystery.

Which made it the perfect place for a sorceress like Rane to hide out from the world.

Forehead furrowed in thought, Greyson shut off the engine and regarded the brick building. "Maybe I should wait here."

Dru almost told him to come on in, but then she thought better of it. After the brief but painful argument last night that had precipitated Salem's sudden departure, Rane had been left fuming. Dru had no idea what sort of frame of mind she would be in now.

Dru had texted her before heading over, but Rane's response had been unusually short and delayed. *Getting a pump*, she had texted enigmatically.

But maybe that was a good thing. For Rane, lifting weights was a form of mindful meditation. Then again, so was pulverizing brick walls with her metal fists. With her, you never could tell what would come next.

Dru laid her fingers on Greyson's arm. "If I'm not back in five minutes, come after me."

He checked his battered metal watch and nodded, looking unusually serious.

She wanted to kiss him and tell him that she was actually joking. Kind of. But she hesitated just a bit too long, and the moment was lost.

Feeling awkward, she got out of Hellbringer and followed the rhythmic thumping of dubstep music around the chain-link fence to the side gate. The air was clammy and thick with the earthy smell of the weed-choked river that ran nearby.

Dru slipped in through the gate, as she had done many times before. The fenced blacktop back lot was a maze of industrial junk. Bundles of rusted steel rebar lay near a giant black tractor tire. Wooden wire spools were piled up in a far corner, and beside that sat several lengths of concrete pipe big enough to crawl through.

Rane lay atop one of the huge concrete pipes, all six feet of her stretched out, blonde ponytail damp with sweat, muscles glistening in the sunlight. Grimacing, she pushed her palms straight toward the sky. Balanced on her hands, much to Dru's disbelief, was the biggest wolf she had ever seen.

Dru took her glasses off, blinked, and then slipped them back on again. The wolf was still there, tongue hanging out, panting happily as Rane bench-pressed its furry bulk into the air. It turned its big shaggy head Dru's way, and its fierce golden eyes stared directly into hers.

Dru backed up a step, feeling trapped in the cluttered yard. She was used to encountering constant weirdness, but the last thing she expected was a giant gray wolf standing in for a dumbbell.

Rane finished counting out her reps and grunted something to the wolf. With a *whuff* of breath, it bounded easily to the ground, its intense gaze still locked on Dru. It was an impressive animal, easily the size of a person. But for all its massive bulk, it moved with sleek grace.

Rane sat up and swiped a pink towel across the sweat pouring down her body. "Yo, D! What's shaking?" Before Dru could answer, Rane turned and yelled after the wolf. "If you're going to change, dude, go change over there. And put on some pants!" She pointed to a pile of broken cinder blocks in the corner of the yard. Tail wagging, the wolf trotted off in that direction.

Dru watched it go, her lips pursed in thought. "So, when exactly did you get a dog?"

Right at that moment, Rane was chugging water from a plastic sport bottle. At Dru's words, she spit out a spray of droplets that shimmered in the bright sunlight. Alternately laughing and choking, she croaked, "Hear that, Feral? Even *she* says you're a dog."

Through the gaps in the pile of cinder blocks, Dru caught a glimpse of the wolf shimmering with unearthly green light. The tan and silver fur shrank away, revealing dark brown human skin rippling with muscles. A protean sorcerer, Dru realized, a human who could transform into an animal.

Not too long ago, a group of proteans had teamed up with an evil crystal sorceress named Lucretia in an attempt to destroy the world. The secrets of shape-shifting sorcery had been lost for more than a thousand years, but Lucretia had somehow brought the lost magic back with a vengeance. As a result, Dru and her friends had been forced to fight countless sorcerers who transformed into giant animals, including a bat, a snake, a panther, and a particularly huge tarantula that still gave her the heebie-jeebies. The idea that Rane was casually hanging out with one of them was absolutely inconceivable. And yet, here he was.

From behind the concrete pile, a thick, brown arm reached up and grabbed a bright pink piece of clothing. A few seconds later, a tall, well-built guy strode out from behind the jumble of broken concrete. Tribal-looking tattoos twined up the bulging muscles of his bare arms and scrolled across his well-defined chest. He was completely naked, except for a pair of bright pink shorts that exactly matched Rane's.

In fact, they *were* Rane's shorts. Dru's jaw dropped open, and it took a concentrated effort to shut it. As he walked up to her, smiling broadly, she managed a faint, "Hi."

"He*llo*," he boomed, squeezing her hand. "I'm Feral." His grip was unbreakable.

"Dru." This close, she was very aware of the fact that he was dotted with sweat and possessed pecs nearly the size of her face. Awkwardly, she leaned to the side and peered past him to make eye contact with Rane, who was loudly unwrapping a protein bar.

Rane glanced up. "We met at a party," she explained, even though that didn't really answer any of the questions that were pinballing around Dru's brain. "You were there. The Volvo party. Under the mountain."

"You mean the *volvajo*," Dru said, remembering the masquerade ball full of costumed sorcerers all competing with one another in spectacular displays of magic. That night had been so crazy that it had literally almost destroyed the world.

Feral cocked his head at Dru. "You were there that night?"

"Mmm-hmm." Dru nodded, trying to maintain eye contact with him and not get distracted by the naked man chest standing right at eye level.

He shook his head, smiling. "I doubt that. Definitely would have remembered you."

Rane bit off half the protein bar and chewed. "Remember the evil mastermind red skull dude?" she said, her mouth full. "Dru danced with him."

"Oh, so you're *that* sorceress." His smile grew even brighter and more friendly. Too friendly for comfort. "Heard a lot about you."

"Oh . . . kay," Dru said quietly, feeling more than a little overwhelmed at Feral's near-nudity. An awkward silence descended between them. Before Feral could fill it, Dru hesitantly pointed to Rane. "Can we just . . . Um, we really need to . . ."

Rane chewed for a long moment, looking puzzled, before she finally understood. "Oh. Yeah. Hey, Feral. Get lost for a minute, will you? Go take a run or whatever."

He gave her a look that said, *You must be joking.* And then he winked at Dru as if they were sharing a private joke. "Actually, I'm feeling the need to stay hydrated," he said a little too loudly. "Being a wolf makes me thirsty." He picked up Rane's big water bottle and shook it. It was nearly empty. "Be right back." He headed inside with long, slow strides.

Still chewing, Rane watched him walk away. Dru wasn't sure if she was checking him out, or just checking his muscle tone. Or both.

Dru rushed over, close enough to smell Rane's sweat, and whispered, "Is he wearing your shorts?"

Rane glanced down at her own pink shorts and nodded. "Yeah, dude. I can't focus on my reps if he's walking around wagging his junk."

Momentarily speechless, Dru pointed in the direction Feral had just disappeared. "What? Why is he wearing *your* shorts?" She studied Rane's flushed cheeks and slowly added, "So . . . what's going on with you two, exactly?"

"Nothing." Rane crammed the rest of the protein bar in her mouth and crumpled the foil wrapper. "Feral lives in the woods, dude. He doesn't have any pants." She stated it like an obvious fact.

Dru made a very deliberate decision not to try to unpack the logic of that particular statement. "Never mind. Listen. Do you remember borrowing a book from me last winter? A book by Tristram, about the kingdom and the key? About dispossessed spirits? Does any of this ring a bell?"

Rane shook her head. "Why would I want a spirit book?"

"You said the pictures were hilarious."

"*Oh.* Yeah." She chuckled. "Did you see the one with that thing poking up?"

Dru waved for her to stop talking. "I just need the book back. It's urgent."

"Yeah, I got it inside. You want it?"

"Yes!"

Rane looked over her shoulder as Feral came strolling out with the newly refilled water bottle, still dripping from the faucet. "Hey!" she called. "There's a big old book underneath the microwave. Grab that for me?"

"Grab anything you want," he said with a sly smile, and headed back inside.

Frowning, Dru watched him go. "So . . . are you sure there's nothing, um, extracurricular going on? I'm asking as a friend. Because I have to know."

"Maybe just stop asking questions, okay?" Rane snapped. "Maybe I'm just sick and tired of being cooped up with Mr. Mopey Face and his freakin' moods. So maybe I'm just out here in the sunshine, getting a pump, getting a tan, getting some R and R. That all right with you?"

Dru held up one finger. "And by *pump*, you mean . . . ?"

Rane shot her a long, annoyed look. Then she lifted her arms and flexed them, pointing her fists at her head and making her biceps swell up like inflatable lawn ornaments. It was moments like this, when Rane got a steely gleam in her eye and showed off her bulging muscles, that made Dru just the slightest bit afraid of her.

Feral came strolling outside, still wearing only the pink shorts, carrying a sizable brown leather-bound book embossed with an elaborate pattern of cryptic symbols. The edges of the covers were scuffed, and a round dimple was depressed into each corner. From the microwave's rubber feet, presumably.

Feral held out Tristram's thick book as if it weighed nothing.

"Um, thanks." Dru took it. To Rane, she said, "So why was this under the microwave?"

"So that it can hold it up," Rane said slowly, as if there could be nothing more obvious in the world. "See how thick that thing is? Oh, hey, there's a little cheese on there." She reached out and scraped at a waxy orange blob with her fingernail. "There you go." She turned to Feral, eagerly. "Okay, let me see 'em. Do it."

Feral widened his stance, shifting his weight side to side as if trying to find perfectly level ground. Then he slowly brought his fists together near his belly button, as if he was hugging a huge barrel. Two by two, muscles popped out all the way up his tattooed arms and down his chest. His pecs ballooned out at the top of a tall V-shape that led down into so many little abs that Dru lost count.

"Yeah, that's it. Work it." Rane appreciatively patted his pecs with both hands, making loud slapping sounds. "Check you out. Getting all swole."

He grinned right back at her, showing all of his teeth, looking like he wanted to devour her. Then he turned to Dru, apparently for her approval. "That's what I'm talking about. Right? Here, feel these."

She took an involuntary step back. "Actually, no. I just washed my hands."

He looked a little wounded.

Rane chuckled and spanked him. He didn't even seem to notice. He just grabbed the plastic bottle and strutted away through the yard, squirting a stream of water into his own mouth. Some of it missed and ran down his chest.

Dru stood there clasping the Tristram book tightly, feeling like now was a good time to leave. But her gaze kept ticking back and forth between Feral and Rane, as if her eyes had a life of their own, trying to read the situation.

Rane caught the look, and was obviously annoyed by it. *"What?"*

"Nothing." Dru knew the best thing to do was go, right now, and say nothing at all. But some sort of weird friendship gravity anchored her to the spot, and she couldn't help blurting out, "Did you just spank him?"

Rane waved off Dru's concerns. "Dude, it's not a thing. I'd spank anybody." Then, with lightning reflexes, she reached out one long arm and soundly spanked Dru.

"Hey!" Dru backed away.

Rane looked around. *"Aaaand* where's Greyson?"

Dru pointed an imperative finger at her. "No! You will *not* spank Greyson!"

At that exact moment, Greyson walked in through the open gate in the chain-link fence, eyeing the two of them warily. One of his eyebrows lifted up.

Dru struggled to come up with some sort of intelligent explanation, which wasn't immediately forthcoming. Her mouth worked, but nothing came out. Luckily, Rane just stayed where she was and stretched her arms behind her back, making no sudden moves to spank anyone.

Feral came strutting through the yard toward them, shimmering with sweat. He stopped between Dru and Rane, subtly creating the impression that the three of them were all together. Which was exactly the sort of message Dru did not want to send.

Her discomfort level, already sky-high, shot into orbit as Greyson's expression darkened. Facing Feral, he seemed to puff up. Something unspoken passed between the two men, primal and dangerous.

"Hey, you know what? Got the book right here!" Dru said with forced cheer. She held up the heavy leather-bound book. "All done here. Now we can head back to the shop. Ready?" She hustled toward Greyson, hoping to steer him right back outside, but his flinty gaze was still locked on Feral.

Rane called after her. "You need a hand at the shop, D?"

Dru hesitated. The only thing keeping them safe from the wraith right now was daylight. And that wouldn't last forever. Come nightfall, she would need all the help she could get.

Before she could answer, Feral started to follow her, his bare skin glistening in the sun. "Maybe I'll come on down to the shop with you, give you a hand."

"No," Greyson said firmly. It came out like a command. "We're good."

Feral stopped where he was and nodded curtly, barely even lifting his chin. The muscles tightened in his neck as he stared back at Greyson.

No one spoke. The tension in the air was so electric that it felt like it was about to spark a fire.

Dru suddenly had visions of two of them coming to blows, with her caught in the middle. She didn't like that idea one bit.

Meanwhile, Rane's head kept turning from one guy to the other, as if she was watching an invisible tennis match. An eager smile lit up the corners of her mouth. Clearly, she couldn't wait for their next move.

Dru didn't waste any time. She took Greyson's broad hand in hers, feeling the subtle tingle of the magical connection that bound them together. "Hey," she said softly but firmly, getting his attention. "There are only so many hours until sunset. We need to get this back to the shop. Fast as we can."

He nodded. With one last hard look at Feral, he let her lead him outside. She had the book she needed, but it didn't make her feel any better. She couldn't shake the sneaking suspicion that the wraith wasn't the only dangerous problem headed their way.

11

GAZING INTO THE DARK

The old book contained nothing but bad news. In archaic English, Tristram spelled out all of the different ways that Dru and her friends were screwed. It turned out that wraiths grew stronger the more souls they fed on. A medieval-looking illustration showed a faceless black-robed wraith wrapping its bony fingers around the throat of a hapless victim, whose eyes were rolled back and arms flung out in abject agony. Lifeless corpses lay heaped at their feet. Just seeing that made Dru nervously rub her own neck.

The book painted a bleak picture of any attempt to combat a wraith. Even if it could be temporarily made corporeal with moon dust or blasted with a magic spell, it would eventually just re-form itself. That meant the wraith would keep coming back, no matter what anyone did. Unless the wraith was itself consumed by an even greater evil, the only way to stop it was to find its physical body and break the dispossession spell.

Unfortunately, Tristram was a little vague on how to accomplish that last part.

Frustrated, Dru shoved the old book across her workbench and sagged back in her chair, rubbing her temples. The more she learned, the worse things got. The only crumb of hope Tristram's book offered her was a diagram of a magical circle that contained three interlocking triangles. Supposedly, if a wraith stepped into that circle, it could get trapped inside. At least then they would know where it was, and stay back far enough to elude its deadly grasp.

There had to be a way to defeat it. She was busy contemplating various crystals and their chemical properties, tapping a pencil against her teeth, when Opal and Ruiz came in, giggling.

"That reminds me," Dru began the moment she saw them, realizing too late that she was once again beginning a conversation in the middle of her own thoughts. She had a bad habit of doing that. "Did we ever order another fire extinguisher?"

"Another?" Opal asked, unfazed by the random question. She put her purse down.

"We used ours when we had that magic carpet problem." Dru stopped just short of saying it was Opal who had used it on Ruiz, who had been on fire at the time. But since Opal had been the one carried away screaming by the magic carpet, Dru was willing to forget it.

"I got a fire extinguisher in the van," Ruiz piped up. His usual cheer was dimmed with worry. "Where's the fire?"

"We're not there just yet. What kind of fire extinguisher is it?"

His gaze rapidly darted around the room, as if the correct answer was hiding just out of sight. Slowly, he said, "The kind that . . . puts out fires?"

"Right. Do me a favor. Look at the label, see what it shoots. Foam, chemicals, or pure CO_2, which is carbon dioxide. If it shoots carbon dioxide, I need it."

"Okay, cool. You got it." He turned to go, but Dru held up her pencil like an orchestra conductor.

"Wait, wait," she added. "Do you have any paint?"

"Paint?" He scratched his head. "What kind?"

"Any kind. I need to paint the floor."

Ruiz looked uncomfortable. "I don't mean to be critical or anything, you know? But, I'm thinking, maybe right now is not really a good time for home improvement. Next weekend, though, I got some free time on Saturday." He held up his hands disarmingly, as if to say, *Just my opinion.*

"Right. Well, I need to paint a magic circle on the ground." She crossed over to the back door and drew an imaginary circle around her feet, which made her glasses slide down her nose. She pushed them back up. "I think we may be able to trap the wraith in a circle. So any color is fine. And if you have a brush or maybe—"

"Oh, don't worry, I got brushes. What kind? Flat brush, angle brush? I got rollers too. Anything you need."

After a brief discussion, Ruiz enlisted Greyson's help and tromped in with paint brushes, rollers on sticks, paint trays, folded drop cloths, white coveralls, rolls of blue tape, and several gallon-size buckets of paint streaked with dried drips in different colors.

Ruiz poked his chin up over the mound of stuff in his arms. "I got my paint sprayer in the van too, if you need it."

Dru glanced up from her circle calculations. "How about the fire extinguisher?"

Ruiz, looking apologetic, shifted under the weight of his burden and held out a thick red fire extinguisher to Dru. "It's the dry chemical type, not the carbon dioxide type. Real sorry about that."

She shook her head. "That's okay. Don't worry about it."

Opal patted his arm. "Keep that thing handy, honey. You never know when we might need to put out a fire around here."

Dru had Ruiz paint the ground just outside the back door with fine lines of leftover white house paint. They stood out starkly against the concrete. What began as a simple circle about four feet in diameter became much more complex as Dru kept refining her calculations. Inside the circle, three interlocking triangles swept around one another, their outer points all meeting the circumference of the circle. Dru and Opal flipped back and forth through various magical texts, finding more powerful details to add to the circle. Tiny swirls, swooping arrows, and angular glyphs painstakingly spelled out the circle's protections in *sorcio*, the symbol-language of magic.

While Dru gathered up more crystals, Opal supervised Ruiz painting an identical circle in front of the front door. Apparently, in Opal's mind, the word "supervising" was synonymous with giggling and flirting.

They had the doors propped open, letting in the hot summer air as the circles dried, filling the shop with paint fumes. Dru was feeling pretty good about their progress until Greyson took her aside.

"We should paint one around that thing too." He nodded his square chin toward her workbench, where the apocalypse scroll sat.

"On the floor? The wraith shouldn't be able to get inside the shop. And even if it could, I'm not sure I want to trap it in the same place *with* the scroll."

"Better than letting it get away with it." He considered the work-bench. "You know I keep a spare tool kit in Hellbringer's trunk."

She wasn't sure what that had to do with anything. "Right. Which seems a little bit unnecessary, seeing as how Hellbringer can fix itself."

"You just never know when you're going to be broken down on the side of the road in the rain." He gave her a wry smile. "Sometimes, things don't go as planned."

He had a point, she realized. She took his hand and gave it a squeeze. "I'll ask Ruiz to paint one more circle in here."

"He's busy. I'll handle this one for you."

With a measuring tape, masking tape, and Dru's directions, Greyson carefully painted a third circle around the workbench. It was a laborious process, getting all of the little symbols and glyphs just right, but he painted exactly what she asked for, often finishing her sentences for her.

The fact that the two of them were so different, yet they worked so flawlessly together, always gave her a warm feeling. If only the threat of the wraith wasn't hanging over them, it would have been the perfect summer afternoon.

But still, something was obviously bothering Greyson. Ordinarily, he had total faith in her and her magical plans, which she so often desperately needed. But this time, he seemed less sure.

She studied his expression, wondering what was on his mind, until she finally just came out and asked him. "What's wrong?"

He shook his head. It took him a minute to reply. "I don't like this. It feels like we're just sitting ducks. There has to be a better way than holing up here."

She followed his gaze to the apocalypse scroll sitting on top of the workbench and shook her head. "There is no better way."

"There is. We take the scroll, we hop into Hellbringer, and we go."

"Where?"

"Anywhere." Finished with the circle, he straightened up and carefully avoided stepping on the drying paint. He set down his paintbrush and wiped ineffectively at the paint streaks on his well-defined forearms. There was something about his efforts that she found endlessly endearing.

"I wish we could." She laid a hand on his now-clean arm. "If this thing was an ordinary ghost, you'd be right. We could leave it in the dust. Ghosts generally manifest around a specific geographic area. A mansion, a river bank, a basement, whatever. But wraiths don't have any boundaries. They can roam at will. No matter where we go, this thing will catch up to us eventually. And if we leave now, we won't know when to expect it. It could catch us just when we let down our guard."

His jaw set. "Where is the wraith now?"

Dru crossed her arms. "Your guess is as good as mine. It's daytime. They can't be out and about in the daylight. Beyond that? We don't know."

"But it has to be somewhere." His gaze was steady. Not judgmental, but persistent. He pointed at the Tristram book. "It say anything in there about how to go looking for them?"

"Historically, I don't think people actually went looking for wraiths. They ran the other direction as fast as they could. Then again, if we did know exactly where it was, maybe . . ." She chewed on her lip, thinking back over the massive amount of information she had just uploaded into her brain from the smelly old book. "Well, there was this one case where a wraith was stalking a fishing village in the Balkans somewhere, and they weren't sure if the wraith was coming from upriver or downriver, so they didn't know which way to flee. Tristram figured out how to build a compass of sorts using hammered copper and cat's eye."

Greyson's eyes narrowed, which was as close as he ever got to a wince. "I feel bad for the cat."

"No, no, not an actual eyeball from a cat. *Eww.* No. Cat's eye is a crystal. It's a form of chrysoberyl. Here, I'll show you." She led him up to the front room of the store and down one of the long, narrow aisles. Wooden shelves rose almost to the ceiling on either side, packed with dusty cardboard trays full of thousands of different crystals of all colors, shapes, and sizes. As she went down the aisle, she ran her finger along the hand-lettered labels.

"Let's see. Peridot . . . alexandrite . . . cymophane. Here we go." She pulled out the narrow white tray, just a few inches wide, and was disappointed to see that she had only a single polished cat's eye in inventory. It rolled to the front of the tray like a large marble. She picked it up and held it out on her palm. It shimmered like translucent gold, split by a narrow band of bright white reflected light, like a slitted eye staring back at her. "See?"

Carefully, he picked up the cat's eye crystal with his thumb and forefinger and held it at eye level, staring deeply into it. Then his gaze ticked back to her. "So you're saying you can use this to find the wraith."

"Well, I don't know about that. I mean, theoretically. Assuming Tristram didn't leave out any important details, and the spell doesn't backfire and burn my eyelashes off." Dru regarded the crystal thoughtfully.

Rane stomped up the aisle toward them, hefting a huge sledgehammer with a long black handle and a traffic-cone-orange steel head the size of a brick. "Hey, check this out! New toy."

Dru pointed frantically. "Careful! Fragile!"

Rane eyeballed the shelves to her left and right. "What is?"

"*Everything.*"

"Listen. You know that strength tester at the carnival where you ring the bell?" She let out an evil chuckle. "Dude, you should see the look on Salem's face every time I score him a big stuffed bunny."

"So, that's your plan to win him back? With a stuffed animal?"

"What? No way. Screw that." Rane shifted her grip on the hammer. "Point is, I'm going to take out the wraith with this. Before he gets close enough to grab me."

The thought of Rane swinging that enormous hammer around the shop was enough to give Dru nightmares. "Where did you even get that thing?"

Rane jerked a thumb over her shoulder. "Out of the back of Ruiz's van. Dude has *everything* in there. You should see his power tools."

"Let's not go all the way to power tools yet," Dru muttered. "First, we need to—"

"Wait! That's not all." Rane set the hammer down on the floor with a metal *clank*, then held up a black metal wrecking bar the length of her leg. She hefted it and held out the hook-shaped end to Greyson. "Merry Christmas."

He regarded it seriously, then reached past Dru and took it. The four-foot bar curved at the end into a sharp forked tip, and it made a hearty *clang* when he rested the tip on the floor.

Rane jerked her chin at the cat's eye crystal. "What's with the freaky eyeball thing?"

Greyson pressed it back into Dru's palm. "She found a way to track down the wraith."

"Sweet. We're gonna go kick its ass?"

Dru shook her head. "That's not exactly what I—"

"No, that's *awesome*." Rane's face lit up with savage glee, and she clapped a heavy hand on Dru's shoulder. "Beats sitting around here. Come on, don't be a wuss. I got the sledgehammer. You find that wraith, give it a *shake shake shake* of moon dust, and I'll hammer its ghostly ass clear into next week."

A nagging worry settled in Dru's stomach as she looked down at the crystal and it stared back at her. Would she really be able to cast a medieval undead-finding spell and go poking around in dark places looking for a soul-sucking wraith? What could possibly go wrong?

Everything.

12
JUST OUT OF REACH

Dru spent the rest of the afternoon researching, cross-referencing, and building a little handheld wraith-finder that she was pretty sure had zero chance of working. For one thing, Tristram didn't exactly provide detailed step-by-step instructions. He sketched out his invention only in the broadest strokes.

At some point in the intervening centuries, someone with horrible handwriting had doodled a spiral in the margin, and beneath that appended a list of various herbs and spell components. Which was great, except for one tiny detail: they didn't bother to note the proportions. So she had no idea how much of each ingredient to use.

Dru was forced to improvise as best she could, based on other contemporary sources and her own personal experience. It was like trying to re-create a graduate-level chemistry experiment using a stranger's grocery list and an IKEA booklet.

In other words, it didn't go so well.

After stinging her fingertips in acid, sneezing on ground-up herbs, and nearly singeing her hair off in a startling burst of flame, she was about ready to scream. Until she finally figured out what the crudely hand-drawn spiral meant.

It was supposed to represent a chambered nautilus shell. That was shorthand for the Fibonacci sequence, which was still a pretty revolutionary mathematical concept at the time Tristram wrote his book.

Every number in a Fibonacci sequence was the sum of the two preceding numbers: 0, 1, 1, 2, 3, 5, 8, 13, and so on.

So what she needed to do was ignore the first ingredient, then mix together one part each of the second and third ingredients, two parts of the next one, three parts of the one after that, and so on. Once she finally figured that out, it made sense. But it would've been so much nicer to know that up front.

Cursing the dyed-in-the-wool paranoia that made sorcerers the worst communicators in the world, she started over from the beginning and remeasured the proportions of ingredients according to the Fibonacci sequence. This time, she was able to avoid any bodily injury as she assembled Tristram's wraith finding device. Or at least a crude reproduction of it.

When finished, it looked like a tiny bird's nest made of crumpled raw copper, half-full of a tarry licorice-smelling substance that glued the cat's eye crystal in place. The whole thing fit awkwardly in the palm of her hand. It didn't win any points for aesthetics. But it was done.

"Ta da!" she sang proudly when Rane walked up. "It's like a tiny piece of postmodern sculpture, don't you think?"

Rane frowned and poked it with one chipped fingernail. "How do you turn this thing on?"

"It *is* on."

Rane cocked her head. "Doesn't *look* on. Shouldn't it light up or something?"

"No. It'll move in the presence of a wraith. The eye will turn toward it. So if it's just sitting there doing nothing, it means we're safe."

"Or it's broken."

Dru sighed in frustration. "Well, we'll just have to wait until nightfall to find out."

Rane glanced at the fitness monitor strapped to her wrist. "Should be like, five minutes."

"What? No, no, no!" Dru's anxiety level shot through the roof as she realized she had spent hours more than she meant to, and the day was almost over. She rushed to the front of the shop and watched the descending sun slip down below the rooftops across the street. There was no time to go test Tristram's device. Night was almost here.

She felt like her life was perched precipitously on some kind of cosmic scales, and they were tipping further and further out of balance no matter what she did.

Arms folded tightly across her chest, she stood at the front windows and chewed her nails, watching the white clouds above turn brass, then light afire in the copper sky. Ever so slowly, the encroaching night shaded them black against the deep blue twilight, as if the sky itself was silently burning out.

Some kind of primal instinct urged her to go outside, find a clear view of the sunset, and drink in every last minute of it, because it could be her last. But she resisted the urge. She had to stay here, inside the grid of crystals that protected the shop. The crystals silently hummed away in the background, their magic barely perceptible even to her, generating an invisible shield against magical intruders. If the wraith tried to cross the invisible border line, it would be in for a nasty surprise.

As long as the crystal grid held up, the wraith could do nothing but circle around the outside, frustrated, until it tried one of the doors or wandered into one of the additional circle traps they had painted around the outside of the shop.

Dru wanted to tell herself that nothing bad was going to happen tonight, but deep down she didn't believe it. The wraith couldn't have just disappeared, of that she was sure. Nothing was ever that easy.

Through her many years assisting the sorcerers that came into her shop looking for various enchanted ingredients to solve their magical problems, she had learned a few hard truths. One of them was that problems that went away on their own tended to come back on their own.

As she brooded by the front windows, Rane came up to stand next to her with arms folded, mirroring her pose. Together, they surveyed the street outside. Traffic was light. Only a few cars were parked nearby. Nobody waited at the bus stop, which was curiously missing its bench.

"Where's Opal?" Dru said.

"Went with Ruiz to get more paint."

"Yeah, but that was hours ago. What have they been doing all this time?" Dru checked her phone. There was a text from Opal saying that they were on their way back. And then another one saying that they were *really* leaving now. And then, apparently, they had a flat tire.

Dru shook her head. "What about Greyson?"

"Just went out back to send Hellbringer on patrol again." Rane made a dinosaur-ish sound of frustration and drummed the heels of her hands on a bookshelf. "I hate all this standing around. When do you think the party is going to start?"

"Hopefully never." Dru pushed her glasses back up her nose. "Tonight could go one of three ways. One, the wraith could come back, and hopefully now we're prepared to beat it this time. Two, it could bring reinforcements, either in the form of additional wraiths, or the evil sorcerers who created it. That's the worst-case scenario. Or three, nothing might happen at all, and we'll just end up sitting here all night, bored out of our skulls."

"*That's* the worst-case scenario."

"But the good news is, I do have popcorn." Dru raised one finger when Rane made a face. "And I promise I won't burn it this time."

"Whatever. I'm going to go see if the G-man has spotted anything out back." Rane walked away. "By the way, why can't you just make popcorn in the microwave like everyone else?"

"The Bunsen burner is more fun! It's like popcorn, plus science!"

* * *

On the rooftop across the street, Salem slouched on the grimy bench he had borrowed from the bus stop and drummed his long fingers on the still-warm brick wall. Throughout the day, he had watched Dru's endless preparations with teeth-grinding annoyance. The lengthy stakeout gave him a dizzying amount of time to think the situation over. Eventually, he decided that when he got right down to the essence of it, he was there to observe, not interfere. Like a scientist studying monkeys.

He wasn't all that concerned with what ultimately happened to Dru. She tended to bring her troubles on herself, having the consistently obnoxious habit of jumping into the deep end of the pool, no matter how many times he warned her away from it. So ultimately, when she got in too far over her head, that was on her.

Salem's only concern, besides getting the apocalypse scroll back, was minimizing the collateral damage, specifically surrounding Rane. To the casual observer, she might seem invincible. After all, she could turn into solid metal or rock at a moment's notice. Dangers that would utterly anni-hilate most people usually left her without a scratch.

Usually. But not always. He knew Rane well enough to gauge her overconfidence and try to compensate for it when needed.

Together, they made a nearly unstoppable team. By combining her brute strength with his ethereal magic, they had defeated more opponents than he could count. But sooner or later, the two of them were bound to come up against a vastly superior foe.

Worse, he was the only person who recognized that fact.

So, he kept watch, waiting for the inevitable moment when things tilted from ordinary strangeness all the way down to sheer madness. Which could happen at any time. Even left to her own devices, Rane never took long to start causing mass destruction. Teaming her up with the omnipresent crystal shopkeeper Dru was a surefire recipe for mayhem on a colossal scale.

Hence, the rooftop perch, which he did on a fairly regular basis. And so far no one else had caught on, which was a mind-boggling oversight in and of itself.

He sniffed. *Amateurs.*

He would never admit it, but he still wasn't quite back in top fighting form. Accordingly, he'd been banking his strength all day long. None of his usual magical flourishes. Nothing wasteful. No idle toying with the unsuspecting passersby on the street below. Much as he was tempted.

Instead, he just rested, and occasionally napped. He even choked down a handful of Rane's protein bars and energy gels, which wasn't actu-ally food at all. How she could nourish her long, lean, endlessly fascinating body on this sticky mush was a mystery to him.

As the sun sank down into the mountains west of the city, and the angular blue shadows crept across the street and climbed the buildings, Salem tried not to think about Rane. But he couldn't stop.

It had only been a day since their last tiff. But already, he was feeling her absence as acutely as the ache in his injured ribs. He missed the raw, physical power she plowed into everything she did. He missed being the focus of that power. From the hot rooftop across the street, he caught only occasional sight of her, mostly her muscular legs, through the front windows of the Crystal Connection. Each glimpse was like a soothing sip of cold water that only left him thirsting for more.

He sighed. With her, nothing could ever be easy. Being this close to her, and still so far away, was torture. For reasons that constantly eluded him, she derived some kind of perverse pleasure from making everything difficult. He didn't know how he could win her back this time, but he swore he would.

Nothing—and no one—would stand in his way.

13

BODY AND SOUL

On the other side of town, Feral loped along the riverbank on four silent paws, led more by his keen wolf nose than by the last traces of twilight. The gurgling eddies of water that slopped through the reeds exhaled the froggy smells of algae and mud, tainted by the reek of car exhaust and motor oil from the teeming human population that sprawled out around him. Feral wasn't particularly fond of this stretch of the river, but it allowed him to move unseen through the outskirts of the city.

He needed to stay hidden. Easier that way.

Nose to the ground, Feral followed the scent trail over the hard-packed earth of the unofficial walking path, sniffing past wildflowers, dead branches, bugs, discarded paper cups. Beside him, the water frothed between a pair of protruding boulders that broke the surface of the river.

She had come running through here earlier in the day, sweating, moving fast. Long strides. Not panicked. Measured. Steady. Just working out.

In the distance, tires shrieked. He lifted his furry head, ears turning to catch the echoes of cars on a nearby road.

But it was nothing. No danger.

He sprang back into motion, tongue lolling. He knew where she'd gone. Home. And he knew the way.

By the time he got there, the night was completely dark. But he could tell right away she wasn't there. The tumbledown brick building was too dark, too still. But he sniffed around it all the same, just following her trail. Around the chain-link fence that left an unpleasant metallic tang in the back of his throat, and into the workout yard, all chalky-smelling broken concrete and sweat-stained iron dumbbells.

She'd come through here earlier, sweaty and spent from her run, and headed inside. But the candle-smoke-and-patchouli scent of the skinny little sorcerer she called her boyfriend, Salem, was nowhere to be found. So when she left here, she had left alone.

Good.

Feral left the yard behind and trotted downhill through the darkness, toward the river. Just out of sight of the house, there stood a cluster of short bristlecone pine trees, leaning together like gossipers. Their bushy dark green needles scratched along his fur, not unpleasantly, as he pushed his way into the hollow center.

Surrounded by fresh-smelling tree trunks, he sank down onto the soft bed of fallen needles and finally let go of his wolf form. Waves of emerald-green light rippled up his legs and over the length of his body. With it came the queasy disorientation of becoming human again. He waited it out. Breathing in, breathing out. Getting used to the change.

Now human, he no longer had his fur to keep him warm against the river's chilly breeze. But for now, it felt refreshing.

He dug under the pine needles and pulled out his bag, a dirty black ballistic nylon carryall he'd had for years. Here in the city, he couldn't go completely wild, like he could in the mountains. In this bag, he kept the absolute minimum number of possessions necessary to interact with the human world.

A shirt. Pants. Shoes. Toothbrush. And a phone.

Remembering once more how useful it was to have fingers, he turned on the phone, and a minute later, he texted Rane.

Hey. You busy?

Her reply was almost immediate: *Working.*

Not too busy to text him back, then. Good.

Smiling, he typed: *Go for a night run?*

It was deliberately vague. It could be interpreted either as a question (Did you?) or an invitation (Want to?).

The type of woman he usually went for would think that over, look at it from all angles. Try to pick apart the different layers of subtext. Try to glean exactly what he was saying.

But Rane was different. She didn't get tripped up by subtleties. She simply reacted, on instinct. Said whatever was on her mind. Some people might call that impulsive. He called it instinct, and he admired that. He felt like they clicked, the two of them.

He was just waiting for her to figure that out, too. Maybe she would never get that far.

In that case, her friend Dru presented interesting possibilities. Definitely a lot going on behind those glasses, even more than she let on. Thing was, she already had a man. Greyson, that was his name. Feral got a dangerous vibe from him, a whiff of something dark and primordial. On one level, Feral was always up for a challenge. But on the other hand, Greyson struck him as the sort of guy you didn't mess with. Not the type he'd expect a smart girl like Dru to hang around with. But people made all kinds of crazy choices in life.

Lord knew he'd made plenty of crazy choices of his own. Definitely the craziest one was Lucretia. She was one of the Harbingers, a tight-knit group of the most powerful sorcerers in the world. Most of them had vanished decades ago, leaving her solo. Lucretia had been practically twice his age, but for some reason that didn't matter. Not with her.

She'd been the one who taught him the protean magic that made him a wolf. Unlocking those secrets had changed everything in his life. That kind of freedom had made her irresistible.

But it wasn't just her insanely powerful magic that had attracted him. It wasn't her looks or her no-nonsense command of every situation. The truth was that it was her eyes.

Haunted. Knowing. Obsessed. The kind of eyes that, in a single look, told him all about wounds that ran so deep inside her they would never heal.

He was always drawn to the troubled ones like her. He knew that, and he knew it was bad. For some reason, he wanted to take care of them. He had the feeling Dru was like that, with her demon-haunted Greyson. But that was her business.

Rane was different.

She wasn't troubled by anything, not even after all she had seen. She didn't play games. Didn't try to manipulate him with that killer body of hers. Didn't say the things she thought he wanted to hear.

She just spoke the truth, right off the top of her head, without any agenda. He had to respect that.

She lived in the moment, just like he did. She always threw herself into action at every opportunity. She never backed down. Same as him. And he had never met anyone else like that.

That was why he had no intention of letting her slip away, like Lucretia had. Rane was a keeper.

The phone chirped in his hand and lit up, startlingly loud and bright against the dark murmur of the river.

Dude, I'm WORKING.

He frowned at the phone. At first, her words sounded like a brush-off. But the one thing she had never pointed out, and still wasn't saying now, was that she already had a man. Maybe because that man was a ticking time bomb, and had the bad habit of treating her like he didn't care.

Bad for him, anyway. Good for Feral.

Right now, he was content to bide his time. He'd just be the workout buddy. The guy next door. The shoulder to cry on.

Sooner or later, it would dawn on her that he was always right there for her, and Salem wasn't. He had a hunch that that day wasn't far off. And his hunches were usually right.

Where you at? he texted.

This time, she replied right away. *At the shop. Waiting for a stupid wraith. Sucks.*

Time to be the shoulder to cry on. *I bet. Want some help?*

No, she texted.

He frowned. Not the answer he was hoping for. As he debated his next move, she texted again.

You ever fight a wraith?

He didn't have anywhere near as much experience as she did with this type of thing. He was fairly new to the whole sorcerer world. But the more he learned about it, the more he wanted to go back to the mountains and run free.

Still. A man had to try.

He thought back to the many things Lucretia had told him in those long nights in the ghost town. Most of them had gone over his head, but he did remember something about wraiths.

You don't want a wraith to touch you, he texted. *Bad news.*

Seriously. A long moment went by. *Worse thing is this one casts magic.*

He nodded, wondering if he should just call her. Maybe she could talk. He could let her hear just how much he wanted to see her.

Freaky, he wrote.

Sorcerer wraith? ??? D calls it Dispossessed.

Alarm bells went off in Feral's head. He had heard the word *dispossessed* only once before, from Lucretia's lips. Under the stars late one night, in one of those rare moments when she had let him in, really showed him a glimpse of the terrifying darkness that haunted her every waking moment.

She had whispered to him the truth about the other Harbingers. He had assumed they were all long dead, done in by their own dark magic or some ancient evil they had unearthed in the depths of the netherworld. But that wasn't what had happened at all.

The Harbingers hadn't died. But they weren't exactly alive, either.

All of the Harbingers except for Lucretia had left their bodies in the netherworld, in a place called the Shining City. They had kept their magic powers and let their souls roam free through the darkness. They had become dispossessed, and that made them even more powerful than ever before.

And if Rane was facing one of them now, the rest of the Harbingers wouldn't be far behind.

* * *

As the sky deepened into ever-darker shades of blue, Dru picked up the salt shaker full of moon dust and gripped it tightly, feeling the faceted glass sides warm against her skin. It didn't seem like a formidable weapon against a dispossessed evil spirit that could drain your soul. It was too little and ordinary-looking to inspire confidence.

What if the books were wrong? What if moon dust didn't even work on wraiths? What would they do then?

She tried to push those negative thoughts aside. They'd been through much tougher scrapes than this, and successfully fought the forces of darkness with much less.

Besides, with every passing minute, she became less certain that the wraith would even show up at all. Maybe Salem really had beaten that thing the night before, and it was gone for good. What a welcome surprise that would be.

Where was Salem, anyway? She wished he would just come back. But he had never been a team player, and he certainly wasn't likely to become one now.

Eventually, darkness swallowed the world outside. It was officially nighttime. But the scariest thing she saw outside was a dirty brown camping van with a tire strapped to the roof and a grungy window-unit air conditioner poking out the back. She watched it creep past, one taillight dim and purplish because it was mostly made out of tape. It turned the corner, and the street was empty.

She waited.

Nothing was happening. At all.

Daring to breathe a sigh of relief, Dru strolled through the shop, trying to shake off the tension that had gripped her for the last twenty-four hours. She found Greyson peering out the back windows, but apparently he hadn't seen anything either.

Rane was busy texting on her phone.

Dru clapped her hands together. "Okay, people. We can all relax. There's nothing—"

An uncomfortable vibration suddenly buzzed through her skull, stopping her short. It set her teeth on edge and filled her mouth with a harsh metallic taste. She tried to pin down exactly what it was, but it was like nothing she had ever experienced before. "What *is* that?"

Rane traded glances with Greyson. "What is what?"

"You guys don't hear that? It's like the whine of an old-style TV. But louder." The vibration pounded up the back of her skull, like the first terrifying throbs of a migraine. But it wasn't inside her body, she realized, it was somewhere inside the shop. But what was it?

Quickly, she headed up front and checked the golden cat's eye crystal in its smelly little copper nest. It stared right back at her, a burning white slit that didn't waver. It wasn't reading anything. Or else it didn't work after all.

Heartbeat racing, she set it down by the cash register and looked out the windows again, watching for any sign of movement, magical or otherwise. The street was empty. The neon sign of the twenty-four-hour liquor store next door lit up the front of the building in blue and red. A discarded fast-food cup lay on its side in the gutter.

The high-pitched vibration grew even sharper. Outwardly, everything looked perfectly normal, but it didn't feel that way. The night air had shifted. It was nothing she could see or explain, but she could certainly feel it.

Greyson moved until he stood in front of her, putting himself between her and the front windows, as if to physically block any frontal assault from the street. His eyes burned like coals in a hot furnace as he scanned left and right. "Something dangerous is headed this way. Fast. We need to go."

Dru's blood ran cold. Somehow, the fact that everything looked so normal made this even more frightening. "Is it the wraith?"

"It's different from last night." He gave her a sharp look. "This is bigger."

Rane marched past them, carrying her bright orange sledgehammer. "All right, it's go time." With one finger, she touched its shiny steel tip. With a scraping sound like a sword being drawn from the sheath, a metallic sheen spread down the length of her arm and across her entire body. A moment later, her entire body had transformed into shining steel. She hefted the hammer. "Just tell me where this thing is. I'm gonna crush it." Her words echoed.

Greyson shook his head and looked straight at Dru. "We need to go. *Right* now."

The forcefulness in his voice got through to her on an emotional level, and she felt herself nodding in agreement. Theoretically, the crystal shop was the safest place they could be. The store shelves were piled high with powerful crystals, magic potions, and protective charms. She had everything on hand she needed to handle any eventuality.

In addition, they had put several specifically anti-wraith defenses in place. In the back room, the apocalypse scroll was wrapped in a protective circle. They had more wraith-trapping circles painted around the front and back doors. Best of all, they were surrounded by a powerful crystal grid that protected them with an invisible magic shield. Short of someone dropping a bomb on the building, they were safe.

This was the absolute best place to be, she told herself. It had to be.

Just then, the air in the room rippled around her, like sunlight sparkling off of a windswept lake. An uncomfortable pressure filled the shop. Dru's ears felt like they were about to pop.

A high keening sound came from all directions at once, so painfully loud that Dru had to press the heels of her hands into her ears. She struggled to find the cause. At first, she had no idea where it was coming from.

Then, as the noise grew deafening, she knew.

It was the protective crystal grid that surrounded the shop. An outside force was pressing against it from every direction. Squeezing it. Constricting it. Crushing it. Trying to break through.

14
THE EVIL WITHIN

The grid around the shop was formed of specially chosen crystals placed at strategic intervals along every wall, and even in the ceiling. Now they wailed in protest, as if they were under tremendous pressure from all directions at once. That had never happened before.

As the pressure built, it pounded on Dru's skull. She had to blink to clear her vision. "We have to bolster the strength of the grid," she yelled over the noise, motioning to Greyson. "I need your help!"

She led him to a knee-high mountain of smoky quartz in the corner, the biggest crystal she had. She put her palm flat against its cold, rough-hewn point. Immediately, she felt its protective frequency humming against her skin. She pushed as much of her own magic into the crystal as she could, making it light up from within.

She held out her other hand to Greyson, and he took it. Immediately, their fingertips sparked as his *arcana rasa* power flowed into her, doubling her efforts. It should have been enough. She felt the quartz tremble as it was pinned between their combined power and whatever was assaulting it from outside.

But no matter how hard she pushed, she kept losing ground. The crystalline shriek grew deafening. The overhead lights flickered. The air itself trembled. With a shock that jolted her whole body, the invisible field that surrounded them shattered.

The force of its destruction flung her away from the massive quartz crystal. Magical sparks danced around it, scorching her sleeve, filling the sudden silence with the foul smell of singed rock.

Greyson caught her before she fell, and she clung to him, pulse pounding in her ears.

"D!" Rane's metallic voice rang out as she took Dru's free arm, steadying her. "What happened?"

Dru shook her head. Her throat was suddenly dry, and she had trouble forming words. "That's not supposed to happen."

Then the power went out. All at once, the lights flickered and died, leaving them in darkness. The faint background hum of nearby electrical devices faded away into a stifling silence. Dru could hear the sound of her own rushed breathing, and her own quickening pulse. "There are flashlights under the cash register."

Greyson's boots scraped across the floor, and he dug under the cash register. There was a rapid clicking sound, but no light. He slammed things down on the counter. The landline phone clattered. "Everything's dead."

Rane felt her way toward the front end of the store, metal feet clanging, making the inventory rattle on the shelves. "It's a blackout. The whole block is dark!"

Even as the oncoming rush of fear paralyzed Dru to the spot, the detached analytical part of her was grudgingly impressed. The crystal grid she had painstakingly assembled around the perimeter of the shop was formed of the strongest crystals she could find, carefully matched to multiply their protective powers.

For someone—or some*thing*—to overpower the entire grid at once and shut it all down required more than just a colossal amount of sheer might. It also required a coordinated effort from multiple fronts, simultaneously. A group of some kind. Not only powerful but also highly intelligent, magically literate, and working together.

They had to be, in order to find enough weaknesses in her defenses to exploit them all at once. In other words, whoever or whatever was out there, they were a terrifyingly powerful team.

They. Wraiths, *plural.*

Her stomach knotted up. Things were rapidly spinning out of control. The crystal grid was their key defense. They couldn't last without it. Was it already too late to run?

She reached out for Greyson, but couldn't find him in the dark. She fumbled her phone out of her pocket and tried to turn on its flashlight. But the phone was dead in her hand, as if its battery had been completely drained.

Abandoning the phone, she pulled out her sunstone and willed it to life. The low angle of its hot light threw long, sharp shadows in strange directions, transforming the shop from a familiar sanctuary into an eerie tangle of shadows. She turned to Greyson. "You were right. We need to get out of here. Before they get inside."

Rane's metal face shimmered with disbelief. "*They?* I thought there was just the one wraith."

"So did I. But one entity couldn't do it alone. Their magic had to come from at least four different directions at once. Maybe more. We're outnumbered." She touched the knee-high quartz crystal in the corner, trying to light it up, but it responded with only a faint watery flicker within its depths. A chill shivered through her. "They didn't just take the grid down. They drained it. They consumed the energy, somehow. It's gone. Same with the elecricity. Like they're feeding on it."

Greyson glanced in the direction of the front door, then the back door. "Which way do we go?"

Rane pointed at the front counter and raised her sledgehammer. "*D!* It's moving!"

On the cluttered countertop, next to a beat-up calculator and a secondhand stapler, sat the golden cat's eye crystal. Before, it had been so utterly inert and useless that Dru had convinced herself it didn't work. But now, it twitched inside its nest of crumpled copper.

Dru felt her hair stand up. Heart pounding, she forced herself to take one wary step closer, and then another, watching the white-hot slit of the cat's eye flicker toward her and then turn away, like a frightened animal looking for an escape route.

She bent over it, her mouth dry, her palms growing damp. The cat's eye shivered and rattled inside its base. The bright slit looked left, right, then behind her.

Carefully, she picked it up. The crudely shaped metal base felt uncomfortably warm in her hand, and it smelled of pungent herbs. She held it out at arm's length and aimed it at the front door. The eye fixed in that direction, trembling in its base.

Then she turned to check the back door.

The eye changed directions.

Dru's heart thudded faster. "They're out front *and* out back." She tried to keep her voice steady, but it still trembled with fear. In her hand, the cat's eye likewise picked up speed, vibrating faster. Dru turned around in a slow circle. The eye locked in not only on the front door and the back door but also at several points along each wall. It didn't make sense.

"Where the hell are they?" Rane spun on her heel, her head swiveling in all directions. "I can't see them. How can I hit them?"

Greyson shook his head suddenly, as if a swarm of insects was buzzing around him. He picked up his crowbar and turned grimly to Dru. "They're here. Now."

"The front door's clear," Rane called, and then ran past them toward the back door, lugging the sledgehammer. "Back door's clear. Where *are* they?"

"Come on." Greyson took Dru's arm and steered her toward the back. "Get the scroll. We just need to run for it."

She resisted. "What if they're invisible? They could be anywhere. We could run right into them." Which would be fatal. The thought made Dru's blood run cold.

Greyson hesitated.

In her palm, the cat's eye spun in all directions, throbbing faster. "This thing is acting like they have us surrounded."

Rane came back to join them, breathing heavily. Every steel muscle in her body was bunched with tension. "Where?" The word rang out as if she had shouted it through a megaphone.

Dru tried to gauge the vibration of the frantic cat's eye. It sped up to a constant, unsettling buzz in her palm. "They're getting closer."

"How close? Inside the shop?"

Dru had the irresistible urge to swallow, but her throat was too tight. "I don't know."

She looked from Greyson to Rane and back, and saw her confusion mirrored on their faces. And then, at last, she knew what the cat's eye was trying to tell her.

She looked up.

* * *

In the woods, Feral waited for Rane's reply, but it never came. His thumbs flew across the keyboard, trying again and again.

He sat in total silence, his muscles aching with tension. There was no reply.

He tried again. Still no answer.

She had gone silent. That wasn't like her.

He tried calling her instead. Immediately, her voicemail greeting spilled out into his ear: "Yo, my phone's off, so—"

He hung up. Her phone wasn't off. Something was wrong.

He shut off his phone, stuffed it back in the bag, and buried it under the pine needles. Gritting his teeth, he brought on the change. His vision flickered with a brilliant green light as the wolf took over.

In a blur of gray and tan fur, he exploded out of his hiding place, teeth bared. He charged through the woods on four swift paws, following the winding riverbank. He had to get to the shop and find Rane. As tough as she was, there was no way she could take on the Harbingers and live to tell about it.

He had to warn her. Unless it was already too late.

* * *

By the time night blissfully blanketed the street and the temperature on the sweltering rooftop dropped down to tolerable levels again, Salem was done with waiting and watching. He wanted to saunter right into the shop, take back the apocalypse scroll with his usual flair, and win Rane back to his side of the table.

He knew he could seize the scroll by force. But he was still no closer to figuring out how he would regain Rane's sympathies. Being injured didn't carry the same weight it once did. Pure logic had failed miserably. Perhaps an overwhelming display of power would catch her attention. It had worked before.

He felt the bandages around his aching ribs and grimaced, thinking hard and getting nowhere.

Then the lights went out. Everywhere.

The friendly golden glow in the windows that lined both sides of the street winked out instantly. The streetlights above them lingered on a moment longer until they, too, died. The only holdouts were the blue and red neon lights of the liquor store next door, which fizzled and held onto their ghostly luster briefly before succumbing.

The street below became a pit of darkness beneath a sky still lit to an insubstantial non-color by the surrounding city. So presumably, the blackout was localized around Dru's shop. Maybe a truly unfortunate coincidence.

But Salem didn't put much stock in coincidences.

Wincing, he got up off the bench and stood, leaning on the waist-high brick wall. He flexed his hands, limbering up his long fingers, feeling the knuckles pop. The hot hum of magic raced across his palms, itching to be released.

Something was coming. He could almost taste it.

He didn't have to wait long. On the street below, a vaguely predatory shape glided through the incomplete darkness toward the blocky shape of Dru's building. Just a flutter of motion, nothing more.

Something fluttered against the back of Salem's neck. Fearing the worst, he snatched at it, but it was just the dangling end of the bandages wrapped around his head. They were coming loose. With grim determination, he pulled them off and tossed them aside, then carefully nestled his silk top hat in place and tapped it down.

It was time to destroy that wraith, once and for all. This time, he wouldn't let it get the best of him. He was ready to finish this.

Sparks sizzled and crackled between his eager fingers.

Then he saw more motion on the far side of Dru's shop, coming around the corner. And even more slipping up over the roof, converging from different directions. A cluster of wraiths, faintly phosphorescent, twisting and twining in the darkness, each one more than a match for any of those inside.

Salem could practically feel the blood draining from his face. One wraith, he could handle. But there were too many. Three, four, maybe even half a dozen of them. He couldn't be sure. All he knew for certain was that suddenly the situation had reversed. Instead of teaming up against a single wraith, now they were the ones who were badly outnumbered.

And Rane was down there, surrounded.

He pulled out his phone to call Ember, intending to use her teleportation powers for a lightning-fast rescue. But he realized with a stab of fear that the phone was drained of power. Dead. Just as the rest of them would be as soon as those wraiths entered the shop.

15
SEND ME AN ANGEL

Dru realized too late that she'd been preparing their defenses all wrong. She'd been expecting an intruder to come in through the front door, possibly the back door. Maybe, at the worst, try to sneak in through a window.

But a wraith was no ordinary intruder. It wasn't bound by the usual laws of physics. Gravity, for example, meant nothing to a spirit. That meant wraiths didn't have to come in on the ground floor.

That cold realization dawned on her as she stared up at the shadowy ceiling of her shop and watched with growing horror as a writhing mass of pure blackness gathered there. In undulating waves, it spread across the ceiling as if it had come oozing down through her roof, slipping through every tiny crack, like smoke. But it was like no smoke she had ever seen. Opaque black, churning and twisting in unnatural ways. Surrounded by a faint bluish-purple glow that shed no real light.

It was only when the faint outlines of fingers and faces started to emerge from the mass that Dru realized she was looking at more than just a single wraith. One after another, vaguely humanoid shapes peeled themselves out of the mass. Pairs of luminous slits blinked open and stared down at her with ferocious intensity. Like a pack of hungry predators.

But not any ordinary predators.

They were undead, and quite possibly insane. And also, sorcerers.

They untangled themselves. Six of them. She barely had time to count them all before they split apart and flew in different directions. They streaked across the ceiling and came down the walls all around the shop, grasping hands outstretched, cold eyes burning in the darkened depths of their faces. Their insubstantial bodies crackled with flickering arcs and blooming orbs of magic as they powered up their spells.

They hesitated at the edges of the sunstone's light, held at bay like the wraith from the night before. But only temporarily.

On instinct, Dru took a step back and found herself pressed up against the cash register counter, accidentally knocking over the pencil jar. Its contents scattered as she set down the spastic cat's eye and snatched up the salt shaker full of moon dust. Its glass sides were slick in her damp grip.

She held it out before her like a weapon, but even to her it looked ridiculously unimpressive. Looking back into those ghostly gazes, she realized her original plan was a colossal failure. There was no way she could sprinkle this dust on even one of the wraiths, much less reach all of them.

On either side of her, Rane and Greyson tensed for a fight that they were certain to lose. She wanted to tell them to run, but her tongue seemed to swell up inside her dry mouth, rendering her incapable of speech. She wanted to flee out the back door and snatch up the apocalypse scroll on the way out. But the door might as well have been miles away, with these wraiths circling around them.

Rane's long steel hair glinted in the golden light of the sunstone crystal as she swiveled her metal head to frown at Dru. "D?"

At that moment, Greyson's red-hot eyes also glanced her way, holding the same question: what was she going to do next? Because now they were out of time.

The moment froze solid as Dru's mind raced. On the inside, part of her was screaming with abject, wordless terror. Every instinct told her to duck and run away from these dark bodiless things as fast as her feet would carry her. But there was nowhere to run, and giving in to that raw animal instinct would surely get them all killed.

Meanwhile, the rational part of her brain knew that she had to do something with the moon dust in her hand. It was their only weapon against the undead. Without it, Rane and Greyson had no way to fight the insubstantial creatures. Her sunstone would hold them back for only so long, and it wouldn't stop their magic powers.

As one, the wraiths surrounding them raised their hands. The flickering outlines of their fingers kneaded the air, conjuring up dark magic. Each of the creatures apparently had unique powers, because they all manifested differently: green crackling flames, blinding blue zigzags of lightning, vortexes of swirling pinpoint coppery-orange lights.

Somehow, that particular combination of powers tugged at Dru's memory. It lined up with something she had read once, long ago, but in her fear, she couldn't place it.

She tore her gaze away from her impending doom and looked all around for anything that could help them. But there was nothing. Just ordinary clutter. Cash register. Landline phone. Spilled pencil jar. Ruiz's fire extinguisher.

Her gaze locked onto it. *Fire extinguisher.*

A crazy idea popped into her head. She moved the sunstone crystal between two fingers and held tight as she grabbed the fire extinguisher. Unhooked the black spray tube from its side. Twisted the cap off the salt shaker. Dumped the moon dust down the barrel.

As crackling magic filled the air around her, she leveled the fire extinguisher at the nearest wraith. "Hey, you! *Get out of my shop!*"

She squeezed the handle, and the fire extinguisher kicked in her hands. With a deafening hiss, it spewed out a choking white cloud of chemicals and pressurized gas. She spun in a circle. With startling quickness, the fire extinguisher flooded the entire room in an acrid fog, dispersing its contents evenly across all of the wraiths. Dru swept the blast all around, high and low, coating everything in sight in a grainy layer of government-approved chemicals and moon dust.

She coughed. The light of the sunstone crystal glared through the swirling cloud. A wraith emerged from the white fog, flying straight at her. At the last moment, the protective light of the sunstone made it turn aside, giving Dru a clear look at a face that was nothing but a featureless pale expanse between a gaping mouth and the black pits of eyes. Those evil pits flared with icy blue light as the undead sorceress raised her twisted fingers and cast a spell at Dru.

Thick streams of crackling green flame shot out. They would have burned Dru to a cinder if Greyson hadn't yanked her down in time. She let out an involuntary yelp as the roaring green flames scorched through the air where she had stood.

The next thing she knew, she was in Greyson's arms behind the cash wrap, staring up into his handsome face at extremely close range. Beside them, the spent red fire extinguisher fell over with a hollow clank.

Greyson spared it only a glance. "Pretty impressive." She could feel the heat of his breath on her neck.

"Thanks." Her glasses had gone askew, but she didn't care. Despite the fact that they were surrounded by half a dozen evil, soul-sucking sorcerer wraiths, she still had the irrepressible urge to kiss him.

A bookshelf toppled over and crashed into the counter, sending a cascade of receipts falling down around them like snow. Along with them came a hard rain of miscellaneous pencils and ballpoint pens, which were decidedly more pointy.

"Ow." Dru stood up, rubbing her head, but stayed crouched behind the counter. Holding onto Greyson's hand, she willed the sunstone to burn brighter, using her own power as well as Greyson's to brighten it to the heat of the noonday sun. Cupped in her hand, it felt like a searchlight, and it was just as blinding. Especially since the fog was slow to settle, and it reflected the light right back into her dust-speckled glasses, making her squint.

In the middle of the shop, Rane single-handedly took on the wraiths as they emerged from the glare of the swirling dust. The bright light prevented them from getting close enough to Rane to drain her soul, the way it had been illustrated in the old books. But she was far from safe.

In life, the wraiths had all been sorcerers. One after another, they streaked toward Rane, their twisted legs dangling inches above the floor as they flew past her and thrust out their ghostly fingers, unleashing the fury of their dark magic.

Jagged bolts of lightning, geysers of burning sparks, and whip-cracking black tentacles all tore up the floor and shelves around Rane, obliterating everything around her as she ducked and dodged the attacks. Shelves toppled over one after another, like giant dominoes. Their fragile contents dumped out with a dull roar pierced by the sharp punctuations of shattering glass and breaking crystals.

Weaving through the hail of spells, Rane disappeared for a moment behind the debris and then came leaping over the top. Her steel sledgehammer flashed in the light as she brought it down in a deadly arc, driving it into the center mass of a circling wraith.

Any living being would have been crushed by the force of the blow. But the wraith, being the opposite of alive, was merely stunned. The dark pit of its enormous mouth let out an inhuman wail that chilled Dru's blood as the wraith spun away through the air, scattering bright pinpoints of moon dust.

Despite the overwhelming danger, Dru felt the briefest flash of hope. The moon dust worked. It *was* possible to fight back against the wraiths.

That tiny candle of hope was instantly snuffed when the other wraiths clustered directly over Rane, hurling down their magic in blinding flashes. She tried to use a toppled bookcase for cover, but it was blasted to pieces.

Dru's heart leaped into her throat. She shouted out a wordless cry of warning, but it was no use.

Up ahead, glass exploded as something big crashed in through the front windows. It burst right through the cluster of dust-covered wraiths, scattering them in all directions. The large object, smoking from the impact, tumbled end over end across the debris-covered floor and clattered to a stop near the cash register. It stood precariously on one end for a moment, legs bent, and then toppled onto the floor.

Inexplicably, it was the missing bench from the bus stop outside.

* * *

Sorely missing his cane, Salem staggered across the street, hands out before him, fingers spread wide. Between his fingertips, blinding sparks of magic sizzled and snapped, each one burning and sharp. But he had learned to ignore that distraction years ago, and instead channel it into crushing his enemies.

The problem, in this case, was getting a clear shot at them.

As he hobbled toward the fight, he tried to see through the window shattered by the flying bench. Inside, the white dusty fog was lit from within by one of Dru's crystals, causing a complete whiteout. He could spot the wraiths only as glimpses of flickering darkness streaking through the luminous fog, punctuated by multicolored flashes of magic as a fight raged on inside.

Beside him, the front door of the liquor store swung open. Its scratched glass reflected the flashes of magical light from the battle next door. Salem wheeled around, fingers crackling, ready to blast this new threat to bits.

But it was only a wrinkled old Asian man, presumably the liquor store proprietor. He blinked at Salem with the sort of wary resignation likely reserved for inebriated customers and government officials. He glanced up at the nonfunctional streetlight overhead and then at Salem's sparking fingers. "You're not from the power company."

"No," Salem snapped. "Get back inside."

"No air conditioning inside."

"I don't *care*. Out here, you'll get killed. Almost certainly. But if you get back inside? Mmm, I'd say fifty-fifty." Salem gave him a full-intensity glare. "I'd take those odds if I were you."

With an irritated flinging-away motion, the proprietor turned and headed back inside. Salem ignored him and limped toward the crystal shop as fast as he could.

Not knowing exactly how many wraiths there were, or what powers they possessed, meant he was stumbling headlong into incalculable danger. But even if he'd had time to gather all the information he needed, he still would have charged in after Rane.

Because she was Rane. And she meant everything.

His boots scraped across the pavement. His lungs burned. The stabbing ache in his ribs slowed him down, as did the misery of his injured knee. But he couldn't afford to pay them even the slightest attention. He was completely focused on the nightmarish wraiths inside the shop. He reached out with his mind, trying to sense their exact location. But everything was a confusing jumble.

The sparkling remnants of broken glass crashed down around the hole left by the flying bench, releasing clouds of white dust and mist out onto the street, blocking his view even more. There would be no way to find Rane in all of that. And there was no time to wait for the dust to settle. By then, she would be dead, if she wasn't already.

He had to clear the air. Literally.

Salem's palms sizzled white-hot as he reached out with both hands, pouring every ounce of his fury and desperation into his magic. Violent torrents of energy ran down his arms, snapping at the long sleeves of his black silk shirt. His fingertips burned until they lost all sensation. The air around him shuddered with compression waves.

Even when the spell was ready to strike, he held on a second longer, building the intensity, until it reached the jagged far edge of his control. Only when he could take no more did he release it, and even then it was nearly too late. The recoil knocked him back on his heels. He staggered.

An invisible implosion of force practically ripped the front off the building. With a roar, the glass in the windows exploded outward into millions of diamond-like fragments, salting the sidewalk around his feet. The blast knocked his top hat flying and whipped his long hair back. The building's telephone lines and power wires whipped and snapped loose, slicing through the air around him before they chopped deep gouges into the telephone pole.

The hand-painted Crystal Connection sign broke away on one end and swung loose, groaning in the tornado-like blast of wind. Unidentifiable fragments of metal and wood cartwheeled through the air, smashing into the street. The white fog blew in all directions, thinning to nothingness, revealing the wreckage inside the shop.

Along with all of the flying rubble came two of the wraiths, one inhumanly tall and bony, the other hunchbacked and lumpy, with a mop of ghostly hair that swirled as if drowning in clear water. The mismatched orbs of their blank eyes burned with an eerie inner fire as they swooped toward him.

Doubtless, these undead creatures would have been terrifying to the uninitiated. But two-to-one odds didn't bother Salem overly much.

Then a third wraith joined them, and the odds suddenly became much slimmer. It was the wispy, gaping-mouthed thing from the night before. The one with the shadow magic.

The burning outlines of the first two wraiths' fingers clutched at the air, conjuring up roaring green fire and swirling white sparks. But Salem kept his eye on the wraith in back, as it sent spidery shadows lashing out toward him like writhing tentacles the thickness of his leg.

This was no place for a three-on-one fight. He was caught out in the open, standing flat-footed on the sidewalk between the Crystal Connection and the now-dark façade of the liquor store next door. Luckily, the street was empty of distracting bystanders. But he wouldn't have minded flipping over a parked car to use for cover.

No such luck. The curb was empty. And he had already used up the bench.

With nothing to use as cover, no backup, and really no tactical advantages at all on his side, he had to resort to a move that Rane had once eloquently but aptly christened "Smack Their Heads Together."

The wraiths were too insubstantial and moved too fast to grab with a spell, but there was a chance he could still push their magic around. With a twist of his fingers and a snap of his wrist, he sent out a rippling wave of invisible force. At first, he was too slow, and a tentacle drove into the concrete next to him, cracking it in all directions.

Sidestepping, Salem swept his spell sideways and just barely managed to ensnare the shadow wraith's tentacles. On his other side, another bony wraith's skeletal hands disappeared inside raging green fireballs that left streaks in his vision. As twin blasts of green fire shot toward him, Salem shoved the shadow tentacles into the line of fire.

He expected the two sorcerer wraith's spells to interfere with one another, and maybe buy him a few extra seconds to deal with the third wraith. But he didn't expect the spells to react so explosively. Fountains of hissing sparks arced off in all directions, leaving trails of smoke. When they reached some kind of critical mass, all of those individual sparks reacted with one another and the spells that spawned them. He dodged back as the shadow tentacles and green fire exploded into a violent inferno that left his ears ringing.

As those two wraiths were flung apart, Salem pivoted toward the third, ready to dodge an incoming attack.

But that wraith faced back into the shop, swirling up a glittering vortex with one ghostly arm. He followed the creature's gaze toward its target.

Rane.

With a furious roar, she charged out of the shop, her muscular body made of shining steel, swinging a sledgehammer high overhead. As the hammer swung in a long arc toward the wraith, its vortex stretched out in a long cone toward Rane.

The swirling blizzard of magic dissolved everything it touched: the broken window frame, the wall, the edge of one of Dru's bookshelves. All of them disappeared into sizzling nothingness, instantly eaten away by the all-consuming entropy of the wraith's spell. It devoured the air itself, leaving only darkness in its wake.

Salem instinctively thrust out his fingers, firing a shuddering blast of invisible force at the empty space just beyond the wraith's outstretched hand. A fraction of a second later, the heavy metal head of Rane's hammer dissolved into shining mist, as did half the handle, all the way down toward her fingertips.

If that spell reached Rane's body . . .

It took nothing more than the span of a single heartbeat, but for Salem it felt like a lifetime of agony, seeing the worst of all possible outcomes unfolding before him. In the blink of an eye, the moment was over.

There wasn't enough time or strength in his force blast to stop the wraith's spell completely, but he was able to deflect it. The shimmering vortex of entropy shunted to one side, just barely missing Rane.

The wraith, clearly enraged, started to turn its head toward Salem, already lifting its other arm to send a whirlwind of entropy his way.

But it never got the chance, because Rane's thick metal fist punched right into the center of its torso, scattering pinpoints of burning moon dust like falling rain. That was immediately followed by the impact of Rane's steel body slamming into the wraith and then passing completely through it, like an unstoppable freight train. The remnants of the wraith scattered in all directions, like smoke swept away in a gust of wind.

Rane halted her charge, muscular legs planted wide on the sidewalk outside the shop as she looked left and right at the other two wraiths, which had recovered from the explosion and were both swooping back toward them again.

Rane's wild gaze caught Salem's. Her face lit up with a savage grin.

Its effect was intoxicating. She tilted her head to either side. Her unspoken question was crystal clear.

Which one do you want?

He bared his teeth in a fierce smile, mirroring hers. He thought she'd never ask.

16

BEFORE IT'S TOO LATE

There was only so much mindless terror Dru's brain could take before her cerebral side took control and analyzed the situation. Realistically, from where she hid behind the cash register, things looked pretty darn bleak.

The shop was essentially destroyed. Large pieces of the front of the building were entirely missing. Her protective crystal grid was drained. The whole block was blacked out. Most worrisome of all, she and Greyson were trapped inside with any number of soul-sucking wraiths.

The only thing keeping her from running away screaming, besides the mortal fear of imminent death by wraith-touch, was the fact that she had to protect the apocalypse scroll at all costs. Right this moment, some of the wraiths were swarming just outside the remnants of the front windows, engaged in a fierce battle with Rane and Salem. But she wasn't sure exactly where the other creatures were, or even exactly how many there were.

If even one of those wraiths headed into the back room and got its ghostly clutches on the most powerful object in existence, it would be her fault.

She coughed on the toxic combination of chemical mist and roiling dust that coated the inside of her throat. Even though Salem's spell had swept through the air, she felt like her lungs were being scrubbed out with sandpaper.

She raised the brilliant sunstone above her head and risked a glance up over the cash register counter. Despite the all-encompassing destruction, there were no signs of movement. From outside came the sizzling and crashing of magic spells as Salem and Rane fought the wraiths. Buying her time.

"We have to make a run for it," she managed.

Greyson nodded. "Ready?"

She took a deep breath. "Go!" Before she could talk herself out of it, she darted around the counter and headed for the back room. Her heart-beat pounded. A cold sweat broke out on her skin. At any moment, she expected cold ghostly fingers to close around her throat and squeeze out her soul.

It was only a few yards to the doorway that led to the back room, but it felt like a mile of night-darkened battlefield. By the light of her crystal, she ran into the back room, with Greyson right behind her.

Back here, even by the eerily beautiful crystal light, everything looked remarkably normal: tall shelves of brown leather-bound books, ratty old plaid armchairs, an empty Yummy's Donuts box sticking out of the trash can. Everything looked peaceful and familiar.

Except for the hideous wraith floating in the center of the room.

It was taller and bonier then the others, with a thicket of shimmering white hair that swirled around its skull-like head. Its entire body rippled in a way that reminded Dru of diving deep underwater and looking up toward the sun. It made her feel like she was drowning.

Pinpoints of white light flared to life in the deep black pits of its eyes when it spotted Dru, and its hungry mouth opened wide. With a bone-chilling moan, it lunged at her, ghostly arms outstretched. Its clawed fingers snatched at her throat. She stumbled back.

"Look out!" With strong arms, Greyson swept her back off her feet and out of the thing's reach—but only barely. She felt the cold radiating from its ghostly fingers as they scraped past her, inches from her skin.

The wraith flailed its long skeletal arm in their direction, but it couldn't leave the circle they'd painted around the workbench. It was trapped inside.

Seeing that, Dru felt a tiny thrill of triumph. *It worked!* That was the only thing so far tonight that had gone according to plan.

But that sunshiny, satisfied feeling was immediately snuffed out when she saw what the wraith gripped in its other hand, cradling it tight against its ghostly body like a baby.

The brittle-looking scroll's spiked silver tips gleamed in the bright light of her sunstone crystal. Six of the crimson wax seals had been previously broken, leaving ragged red edges along the length of the roll of time-stained parchment. The final wax seal, no bigger than her thumbprint, glistened like blood.

Dru froze. "Greyson—"

"I see it."

"I don't know how long that moon dust will keep it corporeal. We have to move fast." She looked around for something to help her fight the wraith. Anything. But aside from a ton of books and maybe some stale donuts, all she had was the sunstone.

Greyson nodded grimly, reading the frustration on her face. "We'll have to do this the hard way." He raised the crowbar in both hands and flexed his fingers to tighten his grip. "You play a lot of baseball in school?"

"Um, no. Softball, one time. Broke my glasses, got a bloody nose, accidentally dumped my Gatorade all over the coach. So after that I switched to mahjong. And I'm not afraid to tell you, I was a mahjong champion. Why?"

He hefted the crowbar. "How about you circle around on the other side of this thing? Catch the scroll when I knock it out of there."

"Hmm." She eyed the scroll's spiky silver tips and delicate-looking ancient parchment, and pictured that thing flying at her face at ninety miles an hour. With a grimace, she pushed her glasses back up her nose. "Not really loving that plan."

"I'm open to suggestions." He circled a couple of steps to the side, and the wraith's burning gaze hungrily followed him.

Dru held the sunstone high, eliciting a soulless screech from the wraith and sending it cringing back against the narrow confines of the circle trap. With her free hand, she riffled through a pile of invoices, assorted notebooks, and a six-pack of clear packing tape she'd forgotten to put away. Underneath it all, she found a shimmering golden disk of iron pyrite, also known as fool's gold, which could be energized to create a protective shield.

As she debated whether that would protect her against the wraith's touch, it lifted its free hand and clamped its fingers together in a way that only sorcerers did. It was about to cast a spell.

As Dru lifted the pyrite disk, the air prickled and warped around her, as if reality itself was being pierced by countless needles. They jabbed at Dru's outstretched arm.

She held up the pyrite like a miniature shield and poured all of her power into it. At once, her magic radiated out through the golden disk, making the air around her waver. With a flash of light and a shattering crash, the wraith's spell blasted off the invisible shield and spread in all directions, scorching the floor and ceiling until they started to smoke and burn.

Her arm trembled under the onslaught of the wraith's spell. Struggling to catch her breath, Dru leaned against Greyson and gained strength from his touch. She pushed that extra power into the pyrite, making it shine even brighter in her hand.

But it wasn't enough.

* * *

For a long, delectable moment, Salem had thought they were winning. Then everything went horribly wrong.

Fast-approaching sirens wailed in the distance, the inevitable result of a public brawl with the supernatural. It didn't concern Salem much, but it distracted Rane for just a moment too long. Maybe it was the strange way the sound reflected in the near-total darkness. Maybe she was trying to gauge how far away the police cruisers and fire trucks were. But whatever the reason, it caused her to turn her steel head and look back over her shoulder at exactly the wrong moment.

The same wraith she had destroyed just a minute before now materialized through the brick wall on the other side of her. The purple-tinged outlines of its fingers spread wide, reaching for her throat. Its jaws stretched wide open with an unholy hunger.

"*Behind you!*" Salem shouted, but his warning came too late.

Rane's face showed more anger than fear as she realized her mistake. She sidestepped, instantly turning to face the wraith, and fired one powerful steel fist into its body. It should have destroyed the thing.

But her fist passed straight through it without effect, cratering the brick wall behind it with a deep boom of fracturing stone. Too late, Salem realized that their advantage was gone. Whatever kind of dust Dru had flung at these wraiths, apparently it had been knocked off when Rane had smashed the wraith to pieces a minute before. Now, it was non-corporeal again, like a ghost.

And that made it invulnerable.

Salem spread his fingers wide and fired a quick, invisible burst of force. The wraith was quicker. Salem's force wave rippled through the air and punched a head-sized hole through the weakened brick wall. But the wraith wasn't there anymore. It was already on Rane.

She tried to dodge back, but the thing's ghostly fingers latched around her throat. She froze. Her mouth convulsed, but no sound came out.

The wraith's own mouth gaped even wider, as if mocking her. The pitch-black pit grew bigger than any human mouth could. The thing's warped face elongated to accommodate it, stretching out its hungry maw the way a snake dislocates its jaw to swallow its prey whole.

Instantly, Salem forgot about the other wraiths swirling around him. Forgot about the apocalypse scroll. Forgot everything that wasn't Rane.

His entire world shrank down to the square of stained pavement where she stood choking, her empty hands trying in vain to grasp at the ghostly being that was devouring her soul.

Faint vapors swirled off her body and up into the thing's gaping mouth. The metal sheen on her body flickered and faded, revealing goose-pimpled skin growing sickly and pale.

A wordless roar of rage ripped loose from Salem. He lost all sense of reason. He no longer cared about anything except destroying this unholy thing, utterly and completely. To save her.

Unbidden, a rare spell popped into Salem's mind, crystalline in its clarity, terrifying in its power. It was the darkest and most powerful spell he had ever learned, one he had carefully lifted from the bloodstained pages of a book that he never should have opened. He had cast the spell only once, long before, in a moment of desperation, to save Rane's life from a bloodthirsty horde of specters aboard a ghost ship.

She had lived then, but the spell had broken something inside him that never quite healed. The aftereffects had driven a wedge deeply between them. She'd told him he had changed. He thought he had lost her forever.

Now, it was his only hope. His usual magic, as powerful as it was, wasn't enough against these things. If he didn't cast that spell again, now, the wraith would almost certainly devour her soul. If it hadn't already. She could already be dead, and her body just hadn't hit the ground yet.

He cast the spell.

It took no time at all, once the decision was made. He had the awful sensation that something dark and irredeemable cracked open inside him. There was a terrifying jolt to the constant hum of magic that coursed through his body. He felt like every bit of his body had been set on fire. Every nerve burned and sang.

Salem wasn't conscious of crossing the distance between him and Rane. But the next moment he was at her side, one arm curling around her waist as his other hand came up in a fist wrapped in white-hot brilliance.

He thrust that radiant fist right into the wraith's gaping mouth. A shock of cold froze his skin, as if he had plunged his hand into a pool of liquid nitrogen, perhaps, or the deepest recesses of the netherworld. Pins and needles ran up his arm. The only thing that kept it from going numb was the hideous torrent of magic now pounding through his veins.

The thing's shimmering round eyes showed no fear. No surprise. Only insatiable hunger.

Salem opened his fist and released his magic.

The blast was bright enough to turn the night into day. For a moment, the wraith was lit from the inside out. The outlines of dark bones flickered inside its ghostly body, along with hundreds of jagged black shapes. They were sorcio signs, cryptic magic glyphs that floated inside the thing, as if they had been tattooed onto the skin of its original body and were then absorbed deep within.

All of this flickered past too quickly to take in. As the spell went off, a shuddering blast of cold knocked Salem back off his feet. The deafening roar rolled across the city like a thunderclap. He landed hard enough that it should have sent jagged spears of pain through his injured ribs, but he could feel nothing. His breath steamed in the suddenly frosty air.

Rane collapsed next to him. She was completely human now, all trace of metal gone. Her tanned skin had gone bloodless and pale. Her blonde hair was flung limply across her face.

With an effort, he rolled her onto her back. "Buttercup?"

She didn't stir. He wanted to say more, but the words caught in his throat. His heart felt like it stopped. His lungs couldn't catch the air. Every part of him had gone numb.

The wraith he had blasted was nowhere to be seen. Nothing remained of it, not even vapor. But the rest of the wraiths swirled around, screeching, their own fiery spells sizzling through the night toward him.

Salem rose to his feet and faced them. They streaked closer, wide eyes gleaming, dark mouths ravenous. With a wordless roar, he raised his still-burning fist and unleashed its searing power.

17

RUN AWAY WITH YOU

On very rare occasions, Opal sometimes turned out to be wrong. But in almost every case, it wasn't her fault. That was her official position on the matter, case closed.

In this particular instance, Opal had promised Dru that they would be back from Home Depot before dark. And then she had promised that the flat tire would take them only a minute to fix. Turned out she was wrong on both counts.

But again, not her fault. First off, there hadn't been enough shoulder on the highway to safely change the tire without getting flattened by the torrential river of passing traffic. So they'd had to limp along to the next exit with their hazard lights blinking, a hulking semi breathing down their neck, and crazy drivers constantly whipping around them like a demolition derby on diet pills.

Eventually, sweat running down his face, hands clamped on the wheel, Ruiz had nursed the van safely off the highway without completely tearing the rubber tire off the rim. But then it had turned out that a couple of lug nuts were stuck in place. That was no real surprise, considering that half of this rattling old van was basically a giant cheese grater of rust held together by chunks of body putty that had been cracking apart since the last Bush administration.

So there they were, broken down on the side of the road, in the dark, completely unable to help Dru with her wraith problem. Which she had more or less brought on herself, in Opal's opinion, but then again no one had asked her.

She told all this to Ruiz, who nodded and made sympathetic noises at all the right times, while he grunted and struggled with the rust-seized lug nuts. She watched him work, first with annoyance at being stuck here, then with growing respect as he quietly got one tool after another out of the back of the van. Like the serious professional that he was.

He sprayed the offending lug nuts with foul-smelling penetrating oil. Heated them up with a little pocket blowtorch that was no bigger than a can of soda. It shot out a sharp hissing blue flame that made Opal sure to keep her sequined and probably flammable skirt far back out of the line of fire. Then he brought out his heavy-duty battery-powered impact wrench. When that didn't work, he fired up the noisy, clackety air compressor bolted to the rusted floor in the back of the van, unspooled a length of orange rubber hose, and attacked the seized nuts with a pneumatic air tool that looked like it could bring down small aircraft. And the whole time, he listened to her complain and just nodded right along.

She had to admit, there was really something about watching a man in uniform do his work. Capable, good-looking, and one hundred percent agreeable to boot. Now *that* was a man worth keeping.

Once the tire was changed and they were comfortably cruising down the road again, with the offending wheel tossed unceremoniously in the back of the van, Opal got to thinking about Ruiz and how good he was with his hands. And all the different ways she could put those hands to good use later.

She tried calling Dru to let her know they were on their way back, but there was no answer. Tried the shop phone too, but that didn't work either. Nobody answered their phone when they were supposed to. Without her there at the shop, nothing got done.

It was only when Opal looked up from her phone with a heavy sigh that she realized that the highway outside had been somehow replaced with a narrow weed-lined frontage road she didn't recognize. It was barely even a street, really. Just a long, potholed strip of asphalt that led across the river on a crumbling concrete bridge. On the other side, the pavement bumped to an abrupt end and the tires rasped onto a rough dirt track. Small rocks pinged the underside of the van like hail. Undoubtedly, some of them were likely to come up through the rust holes.

She turned to Ruiz. "I'm sorry, I hate to say this, but . . . where in the hell are we?"

Slouched back in the seat, not a care in the world, Ruiz grinned widely. "I know a shortcut, baby."

"To where? Kansas? Better turn around and get us back on the highway."

His smile didn't dim. "No, this is better. The highway's all backed up with traffic. Must've been a crash up ahead."

"You're taking us the long way around!"

"If you're talking miles, yeah, maybe. But distance isn't everything. I'm saving us time, see?"

She gave him her no-nonsense look. The one that always worked on difficult customers. Except for Salem. But Salem didn't count, because nothing worked on him anyway. "Honey. It's already dark. We have to get back to the shop. So the best thing to do? You need to turn around, and get us back on the highway, right this minute."

He shook his head. "No, the highway is crazy with traffic. But, hey, check it out!" With a broad sweep of his hand, he indicated the pitch-black darkness outside. Their headlights illuminated the rough dirt track stretching out before them, walled in on both sides by dry shoulder-high weeds. "There's no traffic out here."

"That's because this isn't a road," Opal said.

"Sure it's a road. We're driving on it, right? That makes it a road."

"People drive up on the sidewalk all the time. That doesn't make it a freeway."

He glanced across at her, and his bright smile finally faltered. "Don't worry. We'll get back to the shop, ten minutes tops. There's no traffic or nothing out here to slow us down."

As he spoke, a flash of movement crossed through their headlight beams. Opal caught just the briefest glimpse of tan and gray fur. An unmistakably canine shape moving at top speed.

Ruiz went rigid in the seat, bracing hard against the steering wheel as he stomped on the brakes. Tools pitched forward and clattered behind them. A gut-clenching *thump* echoed from the front of the van.

Opal screamed at the top of her lungs.

The van slid to a hard stop. Road dust billowed into their headlights like a desert sandstorm.

Opal, still screaming, turned to Ruiz and saw that he was screaming, too.

"You hit a dog!" she yelled, waving her hands in the air as if she could somehow rewind the last few seconds and do them over again. Only without any dog casualties.

"That was no dog!" His eyes were practically as round as pie plates. "That was some kinda creature!"

"Stop screaming!" Opal screamed.

He did. With an effort, she clamped her mouth shut, too.

The sudden silence was deafening.

Ruiz got out of the van before Opal could stop him.

"No, don't leave me here!" After a moment of panic, Opal got out on the passenger side onto the dark dirt road and immediately wanted to jump back inside. At least in there, she was surrounded by tools and things she could use as a weapon if she had to. Or she could hide in the back and make Ruiz fight this thing off.

Assuming it wasn't really a harmless, cuddly little dog. That they hadn't just hit with their big, ugly van.

Which she was pretty sure it was, and she was absolutely sure they had.

Besides choruses of crickets, and Opal's desperately fast breathing, the only sound was gravel crunching under Ruiz's work boots as he edged into the headlight beams and looked around. He held a thick metal flashlight the length of his forearm. But instead of turning it on, he wielded it like a baseball bat, and clicked on a tiny penlight he pulled out of the pocket of his coveralls.

Opal put her hands on her hips. "What are you going to do, club it over the head? You already ran it over. Poor thing."

"I didn't run it over, babe. Just a little tap, that's all."

"Mmm-hmm."

A low moaning sound came from the side of the road. Not a dog's whine or whimper. Definitely a man, who sounded like he was having a particularly bad day.

After trading glances with Ruiz, she joined him in hustling over to the side of the road, where the tall, dry grass was smashed flat.

Ruiz swallowed hard and raised his tiny penlight.

Down at the bottom of an incline, a well-muscled black man with tribal-looking tattoos up and down his arms lay sprawled across the grass, gingerly touching the top of his head.

"That man is naked," Opal pointed out unnecessarily.

Frowning, Ruiz nodded sagely, as if this was important information that merited serious consideration. "Yes, he is." Then he added, "And also, definitely not a dog."

"Oh, thank God we didn't hit a dog." A flood of relief washed over Opal, and she clung to Ruiz for support. "You okay down there?" she called.

The man blinked up against the light, giving her an angry glare.

"Uh oh," she muttered, then shouted, "Sorry we hit you!" She pointed at Ruiz. "He's a very bad driver!"

"At least I'm wearing pants." Ruiz cocked his head. "You don't think he's one of them shape-changer sorcerers, do you?"

"Protean sorcerer?" Opal was still shaking with panic. "I can't handle any more craziness tonight. Long as he's not a dog, we're okay."

"But he is running around butt-naked."

"Honey, everybody's got issues. Let's just take him to the hospital, or at least give him a ride home."

Ruiz shook his head vigorously. "No way. Nuh uh. My van nearly got destroyed last time we picked up a naked protean sorcerer, thanks to Rane."

At the sound of Rane's name, the man's head snapped up. But judging from the way he immediately winced, he wished he hadn't done that. "You all know Rane?" he called up to Opal. His deep voice was urgent.

Opal just looked back at the naked man, trying to decide whether to answer.

Slowly, he stood up to his full height. "We need to warn her."

Opal glanced at Ruiz, then back down the hill. "Warn her about what?"

* * *

In the back of the shop, Dru circled the trapped wraith, deflecting the fiery blasts of its spells with the shimmering golden disk of iron pyrite in her outstretched hand. The flat, saucer-shaped crystal smoked, burning her fingertips. But she couldn't set it down, or she would lose her only protection against certain death from this thing's magical onslaught.

Greyson moved alongside her, his crowbar raised high. But as long as this thing kept throwing one powerful spell after another at them, there was no opportunity for him to strike. The clock was ticking until the moon dust wore off and the wraith became invulnerable again.

Whoever this dispossessed spirit had been in life, he or she had to have been one of the most powerful sorcerers around. The mighty barrage of spells it flung at Dru nearly blinded and deafened her. Her knees buckled with the effort of warding them off. She couldn't take much more of this.

Dru had faced magic this powerful only once before. That was the night she had fought Lucretia, the only other living crystal sorceress, who had decades more experience than Dru, and all-consuming anger that made her even more relentless. Lucretia was one of the band of elite evil sorcerers known as the Harbingers, arguably the most powerful magic wielders of the twentieth century.

They had started out innocently enough as a radical group in the 1960s, protesting war, nuclear proliferation, environmental destruction, and other mid-century injustices. Being sorcerers, they had used magic to achieve their political ends. But as they grew more powerful and more radical, they had pursued darker and darker forms of magic in their efforts to set the world right again.

Eventually, they had gotten it into their heads that the world was too sick to survive. It was up to them, they believed, to remake the world into their idea of a paradise. They wanted a clean start. A fresh slate. And that meant destroying the world in a fiery doomsday, so that they could create a new world in their own image.

So, after a monumental effort, they had unearthed the apocalypse scroll and used their eldritch powers to break its seven wax seals, one by one. Each broken seal had summoned up a new calamity to threaten the world. So far, Dru and her friends had stopped them all. But there was only one seal left, and if it broke, there was nothing Dru or anyone else could do to stop doomsday.

She had to find a way to get the scroll back from the skeletal clutches of this soul-devouring wraith, a spectral creature of darkness that had potentially unlimited power at its disposal.

The wraith fluttered its bony fingers like the legs of a pale spider, and a shimmering web whirled straight at Dru, casting off eerie beams of sickly green light in all directions.

Dru braced herself for another fiery blast. But instead of trying to burst directly through her shield, the spell spread out like a giant radioactive spiderweb. It clung to her invisible shield and began to burn through it, releasing crackles of eerie purplish light.

The black hole of the wraith's mouth widened with a cry of triumph, and a light shone in the dark pits of its eyes.

Heart pounding, Dru backed up a step, but the spell had latched onto hers. Her adrenaline spiked as she realized she couldn't shake it loose. She had only seconds until it ate its way through her shield. And then her body.

Greyson put his strong hand on her upraised arm. The moment he touched her, his energy flowed into her hand. She could feel the invisible shield grow stronger, fighting back the wraith's magic. But it only delayed the inevitable, buying them another minute at most. The warm flush of reassurance she felt vanished.

His voice was low but firm in her ear. "We have to push in. Go on the offense."

She shook her head. This thing was too powerful. Even if they turned tail and ran for it now, she didn't know if they would make it. "There's no way we can take this thing."

"We can. Trust me."

As much as she trusted him, she knew he didn't have anywhere near as much experience fighting the supernatural as she did. Everything she knew told her that pressing the attack was a terrible idea.

And yet, what choice did they have?

She felt Greyson tense beside her, ready to attack. The muscles bunched in his arm as he raised the crowbar. Its hooked end nearly scraped the ceiling. And that gave her an idea.

But how could she tell him without tipping off the wraith? Could it understand the spoken word? She had to assume so.

She glanced his way and caught his eye. *"Ix-nay* on the *attack-yay."*

One of his eyebrows went up sharply.

"Ig-pay atin-lay," she explained, enunciating carefully.

He shook his head. He was not, apparently, terribly fluent in pig Latin.

Switching tactics, she instead glanced pointedly up at the hooked end of his crowbar, then pointed with her chin at the scroll still clutched tightly to the wraith's bony torso. If they pushed forward, there was a chance he could reach into the circle with his crowbar and yank the scroll out of the thing's hands.

But they had to do it fast, before the radioactive purple spiderweb spell finished burning through her invisible shield.

Greyson shook his head slightly. He still wasn't getting the message.

Dru tried again, with more pronounced eyeballing and chin pointing.

His red eyes narrowed. His lips moved, silently trying to form words out of her gestures. And failing. He did the eyebrow thing again.

"Oh, for Pete's sake!" she blurted. "Just get the scroll with the crowbar!"

He nodded curtly. "Good plan."

"Go!"

Together, they pushed forward. Dru's rapidly dissolving energy shield shoved the hovering wraith back against the far side of the circle, pinning it. On Dru's side of the shield, she felt like she'd run into a wall, and it knocked her off balance.

At the same instant, Greyson dodged to the side and swung the crowbar underhanded with surprising accuracy. The hooked end of it, originally designed to pry boards and nails off of wooden crates, jabbed up right beneath the thing's bony arm. With a metallic *tink*, the very tip of the crowbar struck the scroll, which popped up into the air, eliciting a surprised screech from the wraith.

Dru watched, frozen in horror, as the scroll flew in a high arc toward her. As it tumbled, the spiked silver tips at its ends glittered in the pure light from her sunstone crystal. The broken wax seals along the edge of the stained parchment flapped at her. The single intact seal, a spot of bloodred wax, glared at her like an angry eye, daring her to catch it.

Every sport Dru had tried in school had ended in miserable failure.

Her brain reminded her of this unfortunate fact by filling her memory with a flickering reel of spectacular fumbles, falls, and face-plants.

But this wasn't just any old ball flying directly toward her. It was the most dangerous artifact in the world. And here she was, with her hands full. Sunstone in one hand, pyrite disk in the other. No way to even push her glasses back up her nose, much less catch the scroll.

She couldn't afford to face-plant this time.

She breathed out, and the world seemed to stop. There was nothing but her and the scroll, and the unseen arc of its trajectory that connected them. She pictured the invisible parabola of its travel, pulled to Earth by the laws of physics. The acceleration of gravity. Feet per second squared.

She took one careful step back. Raised her hands. Dropped the crystals.

As the light of the sunstone faded, they were plunged into darkness lit only by the swirling purple fire of the wraith's spell devouring the last traces of her fading shield.

In that moment, the apocalypse scroll smacked into her outstretched palms. Her glasses went flying off her face. But she caught the scroll.

Grinning widely despite the fact that she could barely see anything, Dru turned and dashed in the direction of the back door, which now was only a shadowy rectangular blur against the darkness. "Go! Go! *Go!*"

In a heartbeat, Greyson was right behind her. They burst through the door into the alley outside just as the wraith sent a flaming blast of rippling blue fire after them. Greyson yanked Dru to one side, flattening her against the brick wall as the unearthly flames roared past them, obliterating the door.

Huddled there between his hard body and the harder wall, unable to see anything, shrinking away from the torrent of magical flames that tried to incinerate them, Dru clutched the scroll tight.

Together, they'd done it. They had the scroll back in their possession. Now, she just needed to find Rane and Salem, and get everyone the heck out of there before it was too late.

18

DRIVING RANE

Dru huddled behind Greyson's body as he pushed her away from the roaring blue flames and toward Hellbringer. The long, black demon car waited in the tiny alley lot behind the shop, engine revving with impatience. She could hear it, but she couldn't see it.

Without her glasses, everything more than an arm's length away was a threatening blur in the night. The wraith-induced power blackout had darkened the entire block. The only source of light was the crackling magical flames behind them. They lit the narrow space between buildings with an unearthly flicker and threw jumping shadows in every direction.

Greyson's strong hands guided her, and she stumbled along.

"Are you okay?" he said.

Dru coughed and waved ineffectively at the smoky air. "Think so. Except I can't see a thing."

His hand swam into focus, holding a gratifyingly familiar object: her glasses.

Thankfully, she slipped them back onto her face and was rewarded with Greyson's lopsided smile. "How did you—?"

"I can see in the dark." His fiery eyes swiveled toward Hellbringer. "Come on!"

The speed demon's doors were already swinging open. Dru jumped into the passenger seat of the old black car. Greyson slid into the driver's seat beside her and shoved the chrome lever into gear. With a peal of screaming tires, they launched down the alley.

Clutching the scroll tight against her chest, Dru stared out the window at the total darkness and wondered if this is what the end of the world would look like.

They reached the end of the alley, and Greyson spun the wheel. Hellbringer's long tail, with its tall wing, slewed around with a howl of tortured tires. They swung around the corner, circling toward the front of the shop.

She gripped the armrest so tightly that it hurt. But despite the fear pounding through her, the analytical part of her brain realized that the end of the world would actually be much hotter than this. Towering flames. Boiling oceans. Stars falling.

She knew, because she had combed through every book she could find containing the lore of the apocalypse, and taken copious notes—filed under "E" for *Eschatology*—but there was more to it than that. She hadn't just studied the end times. She had seen the opening volleys of it firsthand.

On three separate occasions, three different threats had pushed the world right up to the edge of doomsday. First came the Four Horsemen. Then, legions of the dead had risen from the grave. And after that, everything was nearly destroyed by an all-consuming earthquake.

Three doomsdays averted so far, and each one had come closer than the last. Sooner or later, their luck would run out. She was starting to think that had already happened. Especially when she saw Rane lying in the rubble of her destroyed shop.

At the sight of her, Dru's heart leaped into her throat. Rane was physically the toughest and strongest person Dru had ever known. To see her sprawled out on the ground, her towering body tossed aside like a broken toy, was almost too jarring to comprehend. It froze Dru in her seat.

Hellbringer skidded to a hard stop, landing at an angle so that the bright headlight beams spilled across Rane's motionless form. There was no sign of Salem, except for his black silk top hat lying dusty and alone in the middle of the sidewalk, abandoned.

Was he still alive? Were either of them?

Knowing even seconds could make the difference between life and death, Dru forced herself out of the car. She left the door open behind her as she sprinted on shaky legs toward Rane. She wanted to shout her name, but her voice couldn't escape past the choking lump in her throat. She dropped to her knees in the rubble and swept the blonde hair back from Rane's face.

Since Rane spent nearly all of her time outside, especially during the warmer months, the intense Colorado sun tanned her skin bronze. But right now, she looked unnaturally pale. Bruise-like smudges spread out above her cheeks. Her lips were bloodless. Angry red stripes marred her throat, and Dru realized with a start what they were. The imprint of long, bony, undead fingers.

Dru fought down her panic and focused. Rane's skin was cold and clammy to the touch. Fearing the worst, Dru checked for a pulse. At first, she couldn't find it. But there it was. Faint and slow, still beating beneath Rane's chilly skin.

Dru nearly sobbed with relief. She pushed her curly hair aside and lowered her ear to Rane's lips. Still breathing.

Boots crunched on the rubble as Greyson raced to her side. He knelt down next to Rane. "Is she—?"

While Dru struggled to get any words out, Rane's eyes flew open. Unfocused, they looked around wildly until they latched onto Dru.

"I love you, dude." Rane's voice came out rough and slurred.

That brought a teary smile to Dru's face. "Yeah, I love you too, sweetie." A flood of happiness washed over Dru. She gently patted Rane's shoulder.

With a fumbling hand, Rane tugged at Greyson's leg. "I love *you*, too."

At Greyson's curious look, Dru explained. "She lost a lot of magical power. She might act a little loopy."

Blue and red lights flickered across Greyson's back, and the night was split by the wail of approaching sirens. He glanced back over his shoulder. "Maybe we can get her into an ambulance. Or drive her straight to the hospital."

"No. An undead wraith did this. The doctors won't know how to help her. Traditional medicine will only make this worse."

Rane tugged hard enough at Greyson's leg that the fabric of his jeans threatened to rip. "She didn't want me to spank you. But I would. I *would*."

He looked uneasily at Dru. "This could get worse?"

"We need to help her." Dru looked forlornly at the gaping ruin that used to be the front of her shop. Healing Rane would require a long list of crystals. But even if they could avoid the dangerous wraith trapped inside, she would have little chance of finding what she needed in all of that wreckage.

"Opal," Dru realized out loud. "We need to get to her place. She might have the stuff we need. But we have to move fast. Can you carry Rane?"

Rane giggled as Greyson scooped her up. "Tickles."

"What about him?" Greyson pointed his chin down the street, in the opposite direction of the approaching sirens. Dru followed the line of his gaze and saw the spindly figure of Salem charging down the street for all he was worth, one outstretched arm bright with blistering cold white fire. The wraiths swirled before him, hissing and screeching as they fled his spell.

Dru blinked. Salem was actually driving the wraiths down the street. Chasing them away.

"Looks like he's got that in hand," Greyson said. With a grunt, he carried Rane to the car and, with some difficulty, squeezed her into the back seat. As Dru tried to force her giant size 12 running shoes into the car, the front door of the liquor store next door opened and the wrinkled little proprietor stepped out, eyeing them suspiciously.

"Everything okay?" he called.

Dru waved and smiled with forced cheer. "We're fine, thanks, Mr. Chen! We're all good here! Um, how are you?"

In reply, he silently regarded the demolished front of her shop, and then turned back to her. As usual, his expression was entirely unreadable. But it certainly wasn't friendly. "Your shop?"

"Yeah, no, it's . . . It's fine. Really." The scope of the destruction made her want to crumple to the ground and curl up into a tiny ball. "This sort of thing happens all the time, honestly." Which was unfortunately true, she realized. As a career choice, sorceress was the worst.

Some deep and dysfunctional part of her brain immediately coughed up several alternative careers: pet food quality taster, sewer blockage worker, professional armpit sniffer—which was, at least according to one of Opal's magazines, a real thing.

No, sorceress was definitely not the worst job in the world. But it was possibly the weirdest.

"How about your friend?" Mr. Chen pointed one knobby finger at Rane's giant feet. "Not looking so good. Need the police?"

"Me? Nope." Dru tried to act casual as she pushed on Rane's enormous feet, trying to picture what this probably looked like to an outside observer. She didn't come up with anything good. Besides, judging by the volume of the sirens and the blue and red lights bouncing all around them, the police would be there any moment. And Dru had absolutely no intention of sticking around to answer well-intentioned but ultimately pointless questions. So instead, she just shoved Rane's feet behind the passenger seat.

"Ow," Rane complained.

"Sorry." Dru climbed into the front, giving a friendly wave to Mr. Chen. "Well, gotta run. Bye!"

Two police cars and a long red fire truck pulled up behind them as Hellbringer rocketed away down the street. A block later, their headlights illuminated Salem's running feet.

"Slow down!" Dru told Greyson. She rolled down the window as they pulled up alongside Salem.

Dru had no idea how someone as injured and generally unhealthy as Salem could possibly run so fast, but she suspected it had something to do with the spell engulfing his right hand. It was alight with a roaring magical fire so bright and icy blue that it looked nuclear.

Unfortunately, she happened to know firsthand exactly what a nuclear Cherenkov effect looked like, again thanks to having one of the weirdest jobs in the world. Salem's shiny new spell, whatever it was, didn't have exactly that same spooky electric blue spark of radioactivity. But it definitely looked unhealthy.

Keeping one eye on the ghostly wraiths swirling and fleeing a dozen yards ahead of them, Dru leaned out the window. "Salem! Get in the car!"

With an electrifying sizzle, Salem raised his flaming arm and released a blinding bolt of magic at the wraiths, driving them further into the darkness ahead.

Dru flinched back. "Salem!"

He was obviously breathing too hard to answer. His pale face was slick with a sickly sheen of sweat, making his angular cheekbones look even more gaunt. He was so totally focused on the wraiths that he didn't even glance her way.

Something bumped against her shoulder. Greyson, keeping one hand on the steering wheel, held up Salem's dusty black top hat. He must have grabbed it, and she was thankful for that fact. Maybe it would shake the sorcerer loose from his berserk rage. She took it and waved it out the window at him. "Salem! Your hat!"

He spared her only a cold glare. The normally snarky, sarcastic look on his face was gone, replaced by a chilling fury she had never seen. It was so disturbing, so dark and hideous, that it made her pause.

Behind her, Rane struggled and flailed in the back seat. With a deep, heartfelt groan, she flopped over and pushed herself up until her face squeezed out the angular gap at the back corner of the window.

"Dude," she croaked.

That grabbed Salem's attention, snapping his head toward her. He stopped in his tracks, making the car overshoot him. Greyson hit the brakes, stopping with a quick chirp of the tires.

The unholy flames around Salem's arm went out instantly, as if dunked in water, leaving his arm steaming and smoking in a way that Dru found truly alarming. He staggered toward Rane, and all of the vitality drained out of him at once. He tottered, and suddenly it didn't look like he could even make it past the curb.

Dru darted out of the car and got an arm around him, careful not to touch his smoking hand, which looked and smelled like a high school science experiment gone horribly wrong. "Get in the car. Fast."

At the end of the block, the wraiths had apparently realized they were no longer being chased by Salem's atomic zappy fist of death. One by one, the burning outlines of their ghostly bodies wheeled around and flew back toward them, long arms outstretched.

Heart pounding, Dru tilted the front passenger seat forward and half-helped, half-shoved Salem into the back seat next to Rane. The two of them collapsed into a sad, wounded heap as she pushed the seat back into place, slid inside and slammed the door. "Okay, let's—" She was about to say more, but it was drowned out by the thunderous roar of Hellbringer's engine and the warbling of smoking tires.

Greyson swung them around in a tight knot of burning rubber and launched them away down a pitch-black alley, hurling old newspapers and empty fast-food cups into the air behind them. The cackle of Hellbringer's exhaust reverberated off the narrow brick walls, nearly deafening Dru.

"Which way?" Greyson yelled over the noise.

But she didn't have an answer for him. They had the apocalypse scroll, but they were in no condition to defend it. And the wraiths knew that. There was nowhere they could go. No way to escape.

19
FORBIDDEN PLACES

A flare of headlights split the night, and Hellbringer shot out of the alley, leaving behind only a blast of swirling wind and exhaust, and the angry red gleam of its taillights. The demon car skidded onto a nearly deserted side street. The screeching tires left curving black trails of rubber on the pavement as the muscle car straightened out and streaked away down the dark street.

At the wheel, Greyson glanced up in the rearview mirror. Flickers of golden light from passing windows reflected on his grim expression. "Lost sight of them. But I know they're back there. Somewhere. Following us." His jaw worked. "I can feel it."

Dru glanced around at the sleepy city street. Behind these closed doors, innocent people went about their nightly routines, unsuspecting of the soul-draining evil that hunted the streets tonight. As a sorceress, it was Dru's responsibility to find a way to stop the wraiths. But how?

Outside the speeding car, the blue light of television screens flickered in apartment windows. Streetlights zipped past. Tiny pools of light broke up the darkness of the night. A thought struck Dru. "The power is on in this neighborhood. We must be putting some distance between us and the wraiths." She mulled that over. "I wonder what the range is on their electricity-draining power? And can they control that consciously, or does it just happen spontaneously? Is it a result of their undead presence disrupting the natural laws of physics? Or do they feed on the electricity? I mean, do they cluster around power stations and get charged up?" She realized she was babbling only when Greyson gave her a worried look, his forehead wrinkling.

"Sorry," she said. "Sometimes when I get freaked out, I tend to overanalyze."

He nodded once, more in encouragement than agreement. "Right now, we need it to survive. All the analysis we can get. Question is, how fast are these things?"

"Hopefully, not as fast as Hellbringer."

"And hopefully we don't run into any traffic." The road took a sharp turn, and the bright lights of the highway swung into view downhill from them. Lines of slow red taillights ran on the right, matched by motionless headlights pointing the opposite direction.

Dru's stomach, already tight with fear, clenched into a hard knot at the thought of all those innocent lives at stake. "Don't take the highway! Stay on the streets. Too many people could get hurt if anything goes wrong."

Her own words echoed around inside her brain: *If anything goes wrong.* She shook her head. *Everything* was going wrong.

Greyson turned onto the frontage road and accelerated, hurtling past a trailer park, a junkyard, and then a brightly lit gas station. Dru watched the fluorescent lights nervously as they drove past, expecting them to wink out at the worst possible moment. If the wraiths were fast enough to catch up to them, and they had another magical battle in front of the gas station, sparks would fly, literally. She could only imagine all of the horrible incendiary things that could go wrong.

As if reading her nervous thoughts, Greyson glanced up into the mirror again. He shifted slightly in the seat, and she realized he wasn't looking at the road behind them. He was checking on their passengers in the back seat.

Dru turned and looked back over her shoulder at Rane and Salem huddled close together. Salem sat behind Dru, holding his arm down out of sight. Rane, sitting behind Greyson, gripped her fist so tightly around a small chunk of rock that beads of sweat broke out across her forehead. It wasn't clear what she was doing, but Dru didn't want to interrupt her concentration.

"Salem," Dru said, speaking only barely louder than the engine noise. "Let me see your arm. What did you do to it?"

He just shot her a warning glare and said nothing. His attention was focused on Rane.

She let out a pained breath and relaxed her grip on the rock. "It's not working. I can't transform." Her face scrunched up with frustration, and she looked like she wanted to hit something.

"That's because the wraith almost got you for good," Dru explained, as gently as she could. "You're wounded, spiritually, and you've been drained of almost all of your energy. Don't try to transform. Conserve your strength."

Rane scrubbed her fingers into her hair and let out an uncharacteristic whine. "I feel so messed up."

Salem put a comforting hand on hers, but unfortunately he chose to use the arm that had been warped by his dark magic spell. In the gloom, Dru caught only a glimpse of glistening skin that looked plump and shiny, almost reptilian. At his touch, Rane jerked away, as if he had just put a large iguana on her wrist. "Dude! Why is that all *sticky?*"

Salem, pale-faced, muttered something Dru couldn't catch. He stretched out his arm, holding it down low, below Dru's line of sight.

Rane peered closer, with a kind of horrified fascination. "That's *so* nasty. Does that hurt?"

The squinty-eyed expression on Salem's face plainly answered that question.

Salem did something Dru couldn't see, and suddenly Rane looked ill. "Ulp." Her throat worked. She touched her lips.

Worried, Dru turned to Greyson. "Better open the window."

"*Huuhh . . .*" Rane let out a noxious-sounding burp. "*Huuuunnhh . . .*"

Hellbringer abruptly spun the steering wheel out of Greyson's grip and pulled over to the curb. The driver's door swung open.

"Rane! Listen to me!" Dru tried not to let the panic show in her voice. "Hellbringer is a world-destroying speed demon from the deepest pits of the abyss. This car is not known for being merciful. You know this. Whatever you do, do *not* puke in this car."

Rane nodded. A cool wind through the open door tussled her blonde hair. It didn't make her look any less green. "I'm good," she managed, swallowing down hard between the words. It didn't exactly inspire confidence. "Best part of my day."

"Salem," Dru said sharply, earning a venomous look from him. "You have to let me look at your arm. We have to figure out how to treat it."

"With what?" he snapped. "Positive affirmations? Last I checked, this demon car of yours doesn't feature a laboratory or a library of arcane lore. There's nothing we can do right now." He turned to Greyson. "Take me home. I'll tend to myself."

Greyson glanced at Dru, seeking confirmation.

She was determined to help Salem with his arm whether he liked it or not, but he did have a point. There wasn't much they could do until they got off the road. And his place wasn't a bad choice of destinations. "Rane? You okay to go?"

Rane sagged back against the seat, head lolling. "Rock and roll."

"Good." Dru nodded to Greyson, who got the car moving again.

Seeing Rane and Salem like this—injured, exhausted, defeated— frightened Dru nearly as much as the wraiths pursuing them through the darkness. How could the two most powerful sorcerers she knew get knocked down so quickly? If the wraiths could do that to Rane and Salem, what chance did she stand? And what would they do to someone who didn't even have powers, like Opal?

"Oh, my God. Opal." Dru's hands flew to her mouth. She caught Greyson's eye. "She was headed back to the shop."

Hellbringer's engine abruptly dropped in pitch as Greyson took his foot off the gas. "We need to go back."

"No! No. We can't stop. We have to keep going. The wraiths must have some way of tracking the scroll. As long as we have it, they will never give up. They will keep following us. And we can't risk leading them back to Opal." Her mind raced, trying to come up with a plan. "That being said, I don't know if maybe one of them is still lurking around the shop. I have to warn her, just in case." She dug through her purse, pulling out her keys, some Tic Tacs, and a ballpoint pen from the corner bowling alley.

She finally found her phone, only to remember too late why the screen stayed obstinately dark. "Oh, dump cakes! The wraiths drained the battery. This night just keeps getting better and better." She thrust her fingers deep into the debris at the bottom of her purse until they found the wiry pigtail of her emergency car charger.

"Aha!" She straightened up, fiddled with the stubby pigtail cord until she had it plugged into her phone, and then looked around in vain for a power socket. She surveyed Hellbringer's wide black dashboard with its chrome rocker switches and deep-set analog gauges. "Wow. I count exactly zero charging ports in this car."

"No cup holders, either. Welcome to 1969." Greyson took a corner at dangerously fast speed.

"Shoot." Dru stared dejectedly at her phone.

Greyson reached down in front of the gearshift and yanked open a little steel drawer. "Good news, though. There is an ashtray." He popped out the stumpy metal lighter, nearly the size of his thumb, and plugged her phone charger into the socket. "Give that a shot."

Thankfully, the phone's screen lit up. As Dru was about to text Opal, the phone rang.

It was Opal.

Dru hunched over in the seat, hampered by the charger's obnoxiously short cord. "Opal! Don't go back to the shop!"

"Tell me something I don't know," Opal said, sounding miffed. "Why is it that you never answer your phone when everything blows up? What did you do?" Before Dru could answer, Opal plowed on ahead. "Ruiz hit a giant wolf with his van, turns out he's trying to warn Rane."

"Ruiz is? Or the van?"

"No. The wolf is. His name's Feral. And he says he has to tell you about the wraiths."

It took Dru a moment to place the name Feral. He was the protean sorcerer that Rane had been bench-pressing in her backyard. Which was highly inappropriate in so many ways. "What about the wraiths?"

The phone rustled, and in the background, Opal said, "Here. Tell her what you told me."

"Hello?" A deep, breathy voice burst out of the phone, loud enough to be heard clearly over Hellbringer's raucous engine. Greyson glanced at the phone. But more importantly, so did Rane, who perked up in the back seat. Next to her, Salem's crazy eyes narrowed dangerously, and Dru had to wonder how much he knew. Or what there even was to know. The tension level in the car suddenly cranked up.

Cringing under the sudden scrutiny, Dru spoke as neutrally as she could. "Hey, Feral. It's Dru."

He grunted. "Is Rane there?"

Salem's slitted eyes slid straight over to Rane.

She moistened her lips and pushed her windblown hair out of her face. "Yeah," she said slowly. "I'm here."

"We're all here," Dru said, and gritted her teeth. Her finger hovered over the screen, ready to terminate the call the instant things went over a cliff. Which could happen with a single wrong word. The last thing she needed was Salem, in his condition, to freak out and blow a hole in Hellbringer's roof.

Luckily, Feral didn't head down that particularly thorny path. But what he said next worried her even more.

"This wraith you all have been dealing with. Is there more than one?"

She wondered how he knew about that, but decided not to ask. "Yes. Why?"

"How many? Are there six of them?"

Dru looked to Rane, trying to ask what she had been saying to him. But as usual, Rane didn't get the hint.

"These wraiths," Feral continued. "They're dispossessed. Dispossessed sorcerers."

"How do you know?" Dru said.

"Because I know Lucretia. These wraiths, there's no way to stop them. There's no way to fight them."

To Dru, the mention of Lucretia's name was like dropping a bomb on the conversation. The tendons in her neck clenched up, and the muscles in her legs quivered with the sudden urge to flee. It didn't matter that she was already belted into a demonic muscle car doing twice the speed limit, fleeing the undead creatures that swooped through the darkness somewhere behind them.

Lucretia had all of Dru's magical powers, and more, made even stronger by decades of experience. She was the most vicious, cunning, and insanely powerful sorceress Dru had ever tangled with. And before Lucretia had fled into the netherworld, she had tried to destroy the entire world with a cataclysmic earthquake. Dru and her friends had only barely managed to stop doomsday by the skin of their teeth.

The mention of Lucretia's name changed everything. Mentally, Dru disassembled everything she knew so far about the wraiths, their abilities, and their single-minded obsession with the scroll. Then she pieced it all back together in an entirely new and far more disturbing combination. In a blinding flash, all of these disconnected fragments of the puzzle fit together. And the picture that emerged quite frankly terrified her.

She drew in a deep breath. "These wraiths are the Harbingers."

20

THE DARKEST SKY

At the mention of the Harbingers, there was a moment of shocked silence inside Hellbringer broken only by the constant rumble of the demon car's powerful engine. Dru stared wide-eyed through the windshield, into the distance, not really seeing the asphalt rippling beneath their headlight beams. The same thought kept echoing around and around inside her brain.

These wraiths are *the Harbingers.*

Then everyone started talking at once. Feral was trying to explain how he used to know Lucretia, but had severed ties with her once he realized she was up to no good. In the background, Opal worked herself into hysterics about how they were all going to die. Or possibly have their souls devoured first, and then get reduced to mindless, gibbering victims of the undead creatures. And *then* die.

Rane started to say how she was going to kick somebody's ass, and Greyson held up his hand, saying that everyone should give Dru a chance to talk.

But the loudest of all, by far, was Salem, whose voice rang out with enough ferocity to make any ordinary mortal run for cover and cower in fear.

"Who the hell is Feral?"

After that, everyone fell silent. Salem's words virtually sizzled in the dark confines of the car, electrifying the air with a dangerous spark. Ever so slowly, Dru turned her head and looked back over her shoulder, risking a peek at Salem's wide-eyed fury. But he was glaring at Rane, which filled Dru with a relief that was admittedly tinged with guilt.

Rane, pretending she hadn't heard the white-hot anger in his voice, chewed on her lip and looked past Dru, as if she saw something incredibly interesting in the far distance ahead. Salem seethed, facial muscles twitching rapidly, as Rane turned slightly toward him.

With exaggerated nonchalance, she raised her palms. "We work out together. No big."

One of Salem's eyes twitched dangerously. "What does that mean, *exactly?*"

A cough came out of the phone, which Dru now held out at arm's length, as if it was a venomous serpent that she wished she could fling away. Through the phone, Feral's deep voice said, "Look, man—"

Dru's thumb, with absolutely zero conscious volition on her part, mashed down on the red button with nearly enough force to crack the screen.

"Oh, look at that," she said quietly. "We lost him." Sensing what was coming next, Dru unbuckled her seatbelt and turned around to face Salem. The last thing she needed right at this moment, while they were fleeing certain death, was any of his dramatics amplified by magic, in a tight, confined space. At sixty miles an hour.

Time to change the subject.

"Before Lucretia escaped into the netherworld, she said that her friends were waiting for her there. After her earthquake failed to destroy the world, could she have somehow sent the other Harbingers back here from the netherworld to get the scroll?"

He gave her a half-crazy stare, made even bolder by the black eyeliner around his eyes. The anger burning in his gaze made her want to shrink away, but she stayed put, staring right back at him.

After a tense moment, he ignored her and turned to Rane. Her gaze went steely, and her jaw sat in a hard line. Even in her condition, she was clearly anticipating a fight.

Dru nearly climbed over the seat in an effort to keep her face in front of Salem's. She held up a finger to silence Rane before she said anything else, praying that, for once, Rane would keep quiet.

To Salem, Dru said, "Nobody has studied the Harbingers as diligently as you have. Except maybe me. But you have the advantage. You've studied not only your own source materials, but also the ones you stole from me, so you've seen probably twice as much as I have. *And* you're the only other person I know who is willing to lock themselves up in a room for days on end studying the twisted ravings of lunatics bent on destroying the world. In other words, the entire universe of Harbingers geeks consists of pretty much just you and me. And I'm fresh out of ideas. So I need your expertise."

He studied her with an oddly apprehensive fascination, as if she were some brightly colored but gigantic insect poised to crawl up his leg. "You are so *awful* at flattery."

She adjusted her glasses. "It's more flattery than you deserve, so you'd better take it. Listen, if these wraiths really are the Harbingers, who is their leader? What are they thinking right now? *Do* they even think, or are they mindlessly pursuing us? Or do they have some kind of plan? Will they try to outmaneuver us, the way they surrounded us and cut off the power in the shop?"

She barraged him with questions, partly to distract him from an increasingly baffled-looking Rane, partly because she desperately needed the answers.

"Could Lucretia *be* one of those wraiths?" Dru said. "After all, she did head into the netherworld."

That question finally caught Salem's attention. He chewed on the inside of his narrow cheeks for a little while, and finally shook his head. "You've been in the netherworld before." His voice was sharp with envy. "*You* didn't turn into a wraith." From the sound of it, he kind of wished she had.

"But I also don't habitually go around breaking apocalypse seals or dispossessing undead spirits. Or casting dark magic spells, unlike *some* of us." Dru pointedly looked down at his greasy-looking arm, seared by dark magic, and wished she hadn't. Her stomach turned over at the sight of it. "Ugh. Does that hurt?"

A twisted smile quirked up the corner of Salem's mouth, revealing teeth. "No. It tickles."

"Don't worry. We'll get you all fixed up." Her anger at him evaporated. The poor guy was obviously in an enormous amount of pain. Not that it wasn't entirely self-inflicted, but still. "Where was it that Lucretia said she was headed? The gleaming city? The shimmering city?"

"The Shining City," Salem said with just a tinge of yearning. "It's a mythical place supposedly overflowing with ancient mysteries and the answers to all secrets. The problem is that no one knows where it is. No one except the Harbingers."

From the driver's seat, Greyson spoke up. "We've seen it." Suddenly, he was the center of everyone's attention. He glanced at Dru. "From the causeway. Way back."

Slowly, she nodded. It seemed like so long ago that they had entered the netherworld and crossed a boundless ocean of flickering mist on a black stone causeway that stretched between portals. The netherworld sky was a nightmare of fire and shifting lights, and in the distance, a dark city skyline of glittering towers had stretched skyward.

Dru had seen the Shining City firsthand. At the time, she hadn't known what it was. Had the wraiths of the Harbingers been waiting among those shimmering towers all along?

"So glad we didn't go there then," Dru said with a shudder. "Can you imagine? What if we had taken a wrong turn and ended up in the Shining City? We would've been completely unprepared for a threat of that magnitude."

Rane let out a low whistle. "Dude, that's messed up. We would've been hosed." She reached across and poked Salem. "You should've been there, too. It was rockin'. Then *you* could be part of the whole been-to-netherworld club, like the rest of us cool kids. But no. Not you."

He glared at her with smoldering intensity. Mostly anger. But there was just a hint of satisfaction, too, as if he somehow enjoyed Rane's needling.

Rane met his forceful gaze with feigned indifference. After a long moment, she whispered, "Staring at me like that won't make me go away."

Dru's phone rang in her hand, making her jump. It was Opal again.

Hopefully it was Opal, she thought, and not Feral again. Emotions were already running high enough inside this car. She didn't need to throw any more sparks into this particular powder keg. So this time, she pointedly did not put the call on speaker. She answered carefully. "Hell . . . ooo?"

"Honey." Definitely Opal. And definitely perturbed. "Where are you right now?"

"Heading to Salem's place." Dru looked out the window at an unfamiliar row of buildings, some of them boarded up, streaking past in the darkness. "And we're taking the scenic route?" She looked to Greyson for confirmation.

He nodded, glancing up at the rearview mirror, clearly watching for signs of pursuit.

"I don't know if you know what the shop looks like," Opal said, sounding both angry and shocked, as if someone had just spilled wine down the front of her dress, "but it looks like I'm about to go file for unemployment. You know, maybe that's not such a bad thing. There are plenty of other jobs in this world where all I have to do is show up and look good. There's no monsters. No getting blown up. You just punch out at five o'clock, collect your paycheck, and go home. Speaking of which, is my paycheck still on your desk?"

Fear surged inside Dru. "No, do not go inside! There could be another wraith lurking in there, or something even nastier. We can't risk it."

"There's cops, is what there are. So many police cars out front, I can't even count. And fire trucks left and right. So many big hunky firefighters, you wouldn't even believe. Make you go cross-eyed just trying to look at them all."

"Is anything on fire?"

"No. But they are definitely checking the place out." From the sound of it, Opal was doing her own checking out, too. "Ladders and lights flashing and everything. Whole street is lit up like Times Square." Official-sounding radios squawked in the background, and a heavy truck beeped as it backed up. "You remember how I was always telling you how we need more publicity for the shop? How we need to get on the news or whatever? Well, now's our chance. 'Local New Age shop explodes. Film at 11.'"

Dru took her glasses off and rubbed her tired eyes. "Not exactly the kind of publicity I was hoping for."

"Oh, it's not?" Opal said with false sweetness. "Tell me about it. All I did was go to the store, and I had to come back to this."

In the back seat, Rane and Salem were already discussing anti-wraith tactics.

"Let's try to trap those bad boys again," Rane said.

"Let's not," Salem said. "Obviously, the wraiths have figured out how to avoid the traps, for the most part. Even if they haven't, those circles are of questionable value. Much better to divide and conquer. I can take them one-on-one easily."

"Easily?" Rane's skepticism was obvious. "I'm already going to start calling you Lefty."

Dru put her glasses back on and hunched down low, cupping her hand around the phone. She spoke softly. "Listen, this is serious. Salem's injured pretty badly."

Opal's breath drew in sharply. "What happened?"

"He cast some kind of dark magic spell I've never seen before. The backlash burned his arm pretty good. He's in a lot of pain."

Opal made a disapproving sound that was about ten percent sympathy and ninety percent that's-what-you-get-for-playing-with-fire. "Do you know how to help him?"

"Not yet. Not until he comes clean with me about his spell. It's Rane I'm really worried about. A wraith almost drained her. She's alive, but she's pretty out of it."

"Good thing she regenerates so fast," Opal said.

Dru hesitated. "Actually, that's what worries me. Her psyche could be completely out of alignment, and if she heals that way, it could leave her permanently damaged. We have to set her right, or her powers could suffer."

"That poor girl." Opal sniffed. "Of course, me, I've never had powers, so now we can commiserate. What do you need to heal her?"

Dru blew out a long breath, thinking things through. "I'll need a good solid hematite crystal, for starters. Make that red hematite, to help cleanse her blood. Probably help to bolster that with heliotrope, too." Heliotrope was just a fancy name for bloodstone, which was a combination of red hematite and green jasper. Rane clearly needed all the healing stones she could get. "Also plenty of sulfur to absorb any negative potential left behind by the wraith. Some fossilized wood would be good. And green agate to make sure we don't miss any hidden problems."

"Sounds a little bit like I should be making a list," Opal said dryly. "You do realize that all of those crystals are inside the shop, where you just explicitly said I should never go."

"Well, I didn't say *never*, exactly. After all, if there are already fire-fighters in there . . ."

"Uh huh. Why do I get the feeling I'm going to spend the rest of the night answering all kinds of uncomfortable questions?"

"At least they'll be asked by a hunky firefighter. Right?"

"Mmm. There is that." Opal sounded unsure.

"Please. We got hit really hard. We used up all of our moon dust, and now we don't have any way to physically fight those things. Rane is down and out. Salem is barely holding on. All we can do is try to outrun the wraiths until we figure out a plan."

Opal didn't say anything for a long moment. A siren whooped and blipped somewhere behind her. Dru recognized the deserted warehouses marching past Hellbringer's windows and realized with a start that they were almost to Salem's place. Greyson turned off the cracked road, and their headlights swept across the graffiti-covered building with its smashed-out windows.

"We're here," Dru said apprehensively. "I'm going to grab whatever I can, as fast as I can, and then we'll get back on the road. We have to keep moving, so those things don't catch up."

"All right," Opal said softly. "Red hematite, bloodstone, all the rest. I'll find it. Don't know how I'll get it to you, but . . ."

Dru's heart swelled. She knew Opal would never let her down. "We'll figure it out. Just stay safe."

"It's you I'm worried about, honey."

Dru hung up, trying not to dwell on the fact that Opal was right to worry. Even more danger could be waiting just around the corner.

21

HARD HAT AREA

Opal considered herself to be an extremely persuasive person even under the worst possible circumstances. After all, not just anyone could boss around unruly sorcerers, cajole favors out of ancient animal spirits, or make a believer out of even the most hardened skeptic. When she told people what they needed to think and believe, generally they listened to her, with Dru being a notable exception.

But no matter what approach she tried with the tall and lean-bodied police officers who were cordoning off the sidewalk, she was denied entry to the Crystal Connection. They just folded their arms and shook their heads. Straight-up honesty didn't work with them. Neither did sweet talking, flirting, demanding, or even crying. Nothing she said moved them in the least. She was told, in no uncertain terms, that she had to stay on the outside of the strip of yellow plastic tape that repeated CAUTION - CAUTION - CAUTION all the way across the demolished front of the building.

She crossed the street in a huff and climbed back into Ruiz's van, slamming the door. "Well, that's it. I don't know how Dru is going to save Rane and Salem now. We can't get in there."

Ruiz frowned. "That's terrible. Rane is like the life of the party. And Salem is a good guy, too."

"Nuh uh, he is not. But we have to save him anyway. Somehow." Opal idly watched through the windshield as Mr. Chen from the liquor store next door gave a statement to the police. He pointed up at the Crystal Connection sign, hanging sideways. The cop glanced up and nodded, taking notes.

Behind the seats, Feral shifted in the gloom. He was a little too comfortable being naked back there. "We need to get out of here."

"Not yet. First, we need to get those crystals." Opal resisted the urge to turn around and get a good look at him.

Ruiz brightened up. "You know what we need? A distraction. Yeah."

"Yes." Opal snapped her fingers. This time, she did turn around, but only so she could look Feral in the eye. "You need to go out there, get their attention, and draw them off so we can get inside."

Feral frowned and shook his head in a sharp no. "I don't turn into a wolf when I'm downtown. Last thing I need is Animal Control on my ass. Again."

"No, I mean by being naked. You should run around like a crazy person, draw them off. They would chase you."

He gave her the same look the cops outside did, and just folded his arms across his broad, bare chest.

Opal flung up her hands in frustration. "What else are we going to do?"

Ruiz took a deep breath and blew it out, then gave his head a little shake. "Okay," he said, with a surprising amount of finality. "Okay." He nodded to himself and started the van.

Opal gave him a suspicious look. "Okay, what? I don't like the sound of that 'okay.'"

A bright smile split his face, lighting up the interior of the worn-out van. "You know I got mad skills, right? Don't worry, baby, I got a plan to get us in there. This is gonna work, I promise."

Before Opal could tell him exactly how much the sound of that worried her, he hopped out of the van and shut the door behind him, leaving her speechless. A moment later, he opened up one of the van's side doors from the outside, coming face to face with Feral, who was still totally naked.

"Whoa." Ruiz put up a meaty hand to ward off what he was seeing, and then turned to dig through the thick pile of jackets and coveralls hanging from a hook behind the door. He held out a pair of khaki pants with big square pockets. "Here. Try these on."

Feral's muscles flexed as he worked his way into the pants. A little voice inside Opal told her that she shouldn't watch. She ignored that voice.

Feral zipped up. His feet and calves stuck out the bottom of the legs, and the fabric was stretched tight. "Little short in the inseam."

"Uh huh." Ruiz gave him a sour look, then pulled on a reflective yellow vest and a well-used hard hat. He shut the door with unnecessary force and climbed back into the driver's seat again.

"Ruiz, what on earth are you doing?" Opal asked.

"Going to work, baby." He flipped a pair of toggle switches. Yellow flashing lights sprang to life on the corners of the van's roof, adding just a little bit more chaos to the red and blue lights already bouncing off the street around them.

Spinning the wheel, he executed a perfect three-point turn and drove the long van around the corner and down the alley behind the shop. Long before they got there, though, a police officer appeared out of the flashing lights and waved them back urgently.

Opal hunched down a little lower in the seat. "Turn around! Last thing I want to do is spend the night in jail. Unless you're planning on bailing us out, we need to go back."

"Oh, you think I'm going to miss out on all the action? No way, babe. Watch this." He parked the van with the engine running and hopped out, returning the cop's wave as if it were a professional greeting.

Plainly annoyed at being misunderstood, the cop strode toward them, talking into the radio on his shoulder.

Quickly, Ruiz opened another door and heaved out a heavy stack of tall orange construction cones, dirty from years of use. One by one, he dropped them off across the width of the alley, blocking it off. Then he busied himself with unhooking a giant orange fiberglass ladder from the van's roof rack.

The cop, still talking into his shoulder radio, paused and glanced toward the other end of the alley, as a fire truck backed up on the street outside. He gave Ruiz another suspicious glare.

In the side-view mirror, Opal watched Ruiz climb halfway up the back of the van, giving the cop a wave that clearly said, "Thanks, I got this."

Apparently, it was enough for the cop, who obviously had other things to attend to. He turned and headed back into the flashing lights surrounding the front of the shop.

Ruiz leaned out from the side of the van, craning his head around to make sure the coast was clear. Then he climbed down, hopped in, and drove the rest of the way to the shop's tiny back parking lot. It really wasn't much more than three parking spaces right off the alley, but the van with all its flashing lights managed to block off the area while at the same time looking completely official about it.

Seeing Ruiz in action like that made Opal's heart melt, just a little bit. She leaned across the tool-filled space between the seats and kissed him, good and proper.

When she pulled back, he looked so amazed that he had to hold onto his hard hat. "What was that for?"

"Honey, you know I love a strong man in uniform." With a wink, she climbed out of the van and sneaked into the shop through the alley door.

The back room of the shop looked completely normal. As normal as things ever got around there, at any rate. The lights were on. The circle painted around Dru's workbench was smudged and broken. The paint had shriveled and browned, as if it had been exposed to extreme heat, or some kind of magical spell. No monsters anywhere.

The shelves were crammed with musty stacks of ancient books of all sizes, along with a few rolled-up maps and even some clay tablets. In the corner hung bundles of rare and bizarre-looking herbs. A just-opened cardboard box of creepy porcelain doll heads filled up one of the ugly plaid armchairs. Business as usual.

The firefighters had already tromped through here, leaving dirty boot-shaped footprints everywhere, and the door that led upstairs to Dru's apartment was ajar. Opal leaned her ear close to the gap and listened to make sure no one was up there.

"We're all alone back here." Feral's deep voice boomed behind her, making her jump.

"Don't sneak up on me like that!" she hissed.

He jerked his chin toward the front of the shop, where all the squawking radios and flashing lights were focused. "Party's all up front. We're gonna be fine. What are we looking for again?"

"Keep your voice down. And where's Ruiz?"

"Out back on his ladder, keeping a lookout. Still making like he's one of the Village People." He sounded unimpressed.

"I'll have you know I happen to like the Village People. You just keep an eye out for trouble. Not just cops. Anything. Specially if it looks like a ghost that wants to suck out your soul." She was satisfied by the worried look that crossed his features. He looked back over both shoulders, but they really were alone. At least for the moment.

She made Feral put those big tattooed muscles of his to work, moving cardboard trays full of rocks so she could get to what Dru needed. It didn't take Opal long to find everything, considering that she had just finished taking an exhaustive inventory that week, something she hated almost as much as soul-sucking undead creatures. Maybe even more.

She was hoping, by some miracle, to find more lunar meteorites, so she could grind up some more moon dust. But they were among the rarest rocks on Earth. The chances of another one miraculously turning up, even in a collection as large as this, were effectively zero.

She stepped up on a chair and scanned the shelves full of books to see if any curious-looking rocks had been tucked away as paperweights, which occasionally happened. No rocks turned up, but she did find a tiny leather-bound book tied shut with coarse twine. It must have fallen behind the other books and lain there for years, impossible to find without standing on a chair and reaching way back. She would have ignored it, except that there was a yellowed slip of paper tucked into the twine that said "Tristram" in her own handwriting.

The name caught her attention immediately. Tristram was the mad sorcerer who had written about trapping dispossessed souls.

Curious, Opal brushed the dust off the book and took it over to Dru's workbench to clip off the twine. As she leafed through its crackling brown pages, she found a chapter about confronting "outsider" spirits. After the usual admissions not to approach spirits or speak to them directly, there was one line in particular that caught her eye:

They come from beyond our world, and lo, their weakness is likewise that which comes from beyond our world.

"Such as moon dust, for example," she said out loud, thinking hard. That line hinted at a much bigger idea, she was sure of it.

Feral just looked confused. He hefted the cardboard box full of rocks. "Where you want this?"

"Just hold on." She waved her fingers at him, still distracted by the book. No wonder Dru always had that preoccupied look on her face. She was busy thinking in six different directions at once.

Opal kept turning the dry brown pages and scanning through the text. Several pages on, she found a drawing of eerie, mist-like forms, presumably some sort of outsiders or dispossessed spirits, being struck down by meteors plummeting from the sky. Again, it said, *Their weakness is that which comes from beyond our world.*

Still hefting the box, Feral came around to stand behind her, reading over her shoulder. He smelled like pine needles and sweat, but not necessarily in a bad way. Still, she stepped away from him.

"You have to call down meteors on these things, or what?" Feral said.

No sorcerer she knew had that kind of power. Then it occurred to her that Feral probably didn't understand the magnitude of anyone else's powers. By his own account, he had only recently become a sorcerer. He was still figuring out what was possible and what wasn't.

Well, for one thing, him getting any closer to her was impossible, but he hadn't caught on to that fact yet. Opal was about to say as much when she finally figured out a solution. It hit her like disco lights spinning to life in a dark nightclub. She was so excited, she almost broke out dancing.

Feral mirrored her bright smile, apparently thinking it had something to do with him. Fine, she could let him think that, as long as he kept carrying that heavy box of rocks for her.

She dug through a nearby shelf and handed him a heavy chunk of gray metallic stone riddled with scintillating amber-yellow crystals. "Pallasite," she sang out.

"Palace what?"

"It's a meteorite, honey. An extraterrestrial rock with some olivine crystals stuck in a whole bunch of nickel and iron. Tristram says we need something that comes from beyond our world. He didn't say it *had* to be from the moon."

Feral gave her a vague smile. "Whatever you say."

"Just follow along and bring that box. I've got to find us some coesite. And stishovite. Those are from meteors, too." She was about to say more when she remembered her paycheck was still sitting on Dru's desk. She darted back, found the little envelope with her name on it, and folded it up with a little sigh of satisfaction. "Next chance we get, I am definitely going to have a good long talk with that girl about the size of this paycheck. Because as you can see, I make this job look *good.*"

22

BEHIND THESE WALLS

Greyson left Hellbringer running, and they all climbed up the ladder to Salem's place by the glare of the headlights. "Dude," Rane panted when she heaved herself over the top, obviously in pain, "this ladder thing is *so* over. Your next place needs an elevator. Seriously."

"You okay?" Dru said, knowing she wasn't. The woman had not only lost a hard fight, she had also nearly had the soul sucked out of her body. "Here. Lean on me."

Dru didn't actually expect Rane to lean on her, considering how fiercely independent the woman usually was. Besides, at six feet tall, Rane was practically twice Dru's size. So it came as a bit of a shock when all of that lean sweaty muscle sagged against her at once, nearly pile-driving her into the tar-covered roof. Luckily, Greyson stepped in and put Rane's other arm around his shoulders. Dru, legs wobbling, gasped at the effort of trying not to be flattened like a human panini.

Salem held open his door for them using his good arm, and together they hobbled inside. The dark, cavernous space was lit here and there by tiny pools of light that hid more clutter and antiques than they revealed. Curiously, the place didn't look that much different than it had the night before, when they'd fled from the first wraith. Despite its size, it still felt claustrophobic to Dru.

"Okay, I don't know how fast the wraiths will catch up, but we can't stay long," Dru announced, wishing she still had Tristram's wraith-detecting device. "Let's grab anything we need and get out of here."

Salem tugged a ratty-looking cardboard box full of cell phones halfway off a shelf, and dug through it until he found one that turned on. Holding it in his good hand, he typed out a text with his thumb.

Greyson eyed the box curiously. "Got enough phones in there?"

Salem's gaze slid over to Rane. "With her around? Not necessarily." By way of explanation, he raised his voice. "Buttercup? Where's your phone?"

Rane gasped in pain as she eased down into an antique chair, making its wooden legs creak. "Dunno. Don't care. Lost it in the fight."

"Ah," Salem said in mock surprise. He stepped up behind her and held another phone over her shoulder. She took it without comment. Then he turned and slipped away into the shadows.

"Stay here and keep an eye on her?" Dru asked Greyson, dropping her purse and the unwieldy apocalypse scroll next to Rane for safekeeping. When Greyson nodded, Dru launched herself after Salem, determined not to lose him in this maze. He knew his way through the semidarkness easily, but she had to follow the jutting silhouette of his top hat.

"Salem!" She had to hurry to catch up with him, since he hobbled along with surprising swiftness. "Let me see your arm. This is serious."

"Serious, is it? You're a sharp one, aren't you?" He didn't even glance her way. "Lucky for me, I can always depend on you to point out the blatantly obvious." He grabbed a lantern off of a dusty side table. A few limping strides later, he held it up to a shelf crammed with jars and bottles of hand-labeled powders and potions. He pointedly stood in Dru's way so that she couldn't get a good look at the shelf.

"What spell did you cast that did that to you?" Dru asked. "That's the best place to start. Then we can figure out what went wrong."

"I didn't cast it *wrong*." He slammed the lantern down on a nearby table and started digging through the shelf. "It was a calculated risk. And it did the job, didn't it? I saved all of you." He shoved the jars and bottles aside, one by one, with increasing ferocity. They clanked together until Dru was afraid they would break before he found whatever he was looking for.

Dru resisted the urge to lecture Salem about the dangers of dark magic, and the backlash those forbidden spells could create. In the end, if he only lost his arm, he would get off lucky. Some of those spells were rumored to cost you your life. Even your soul.

Instead, she focused on trying to help, even if she was forced to speak to his back. "If you can just tell me the name of the spell, or at least the sorcerer who composed it—"

"I don't *know* the names. And neither do you." He gave her a dangerous glare over his shoulder. "You're too wholesome and bubbly for what I do."

She adjusted her glasses and folded her arms. "I want to help you," she said simply. "The sooner you get better, the sooner Rane will stop worrying about you." That was a bit of a stretch, because Rane hardly ever worried about anything, even matters of life and death. But in the grander scheme of things, it was true enough.

Bringing Rane into this finally forced Salem to relent. With a put-upon sigh, he finally turned around. "Fine. If it would get you to stop pestering me. Have a look." He leaned down and laid his icky-looking arm across the table in front of her.

The light of the lantern fell across the glistening, overcooked-looking skin. It resembled nothing so much as a hot dog that had been blistered over a campfire, then dropped into the cold ashes to shrivel and congeal. The sight of it threatened to bring up Dru's lunch, and she had to turn her head away.

Salem seemed to derive some sort of perverse satisfaction from that. "Look at my arm," he ordered.

"Fine." She swallowed and adjusted her glasses. Steeling herself, she peered closely at his arm. "But would it kill you to say the magic word?"

His voice rose. "If I *knew* what magic words to say, you wouldn't be *here*, in my sanctuary, pestering me with your—"

"*Salem.*" She looked over the top of her glasses at him. "The magic word is *please.*"

His lips twitched as if he wanted to speak, but nothing came out. Eventually, he just turned away, leaving his grisly arm sitting motionless on the tabletop. But his body language softened, as if Dru had somehow established a kind of equilibrium that allowed him to relax.

As long as she remained analytical and thought of the arm as merely another magical problem to be solved, she could bear to look at it. She just couldn't think about who it was attached to.

As far as she could tell just from looking, his arm wasn't actually burned, not in the traditional sense. But his problem had the potential to become much bigger. The dark magic had transformed him somehow, so that his arm had become something other than human. Left unchecked, the effect could eventually spread throughout the rest of his body, until he truly became a monster. She didn't know how long he had. But he certainly needed magical intervention as soon as possible.

The question was, what exactly would set things right? The wrong approach could send him into a downward spiral.

She felt useless without her crystals, and there was no telling when or where Opal would come through with the rocks she needed. "It would be helpful if I had some green agate."

"Sorry, fresh out," Salem snapped.

"Me too." She thought about the crystals she had stashed in her purse, but none of them would really help with a problem this exotic. "Do you have *any* crystals around? I know I've sold you plenty."

He started to make a sarcastic retort, then changed his mind. The muscles in his face worked, as if being helpful required an enormous effort. "Red zincite." He brushed past her and pulled open an antique chest of drawers, digging one-handed through the drawer until he came up with a spiky red crystal that looked like a pile of transparent plastic cocktail toothpicks.

She vaguely recalled selling him that crystal at the beginning of the summer, but it wouldn't do any good here. "Not unless you've been hypnotized, or you're having trouble doing math in your head." As his expression turned angry, she added, "I always have to use that calculator app on my phone. Did you know it can calculate dates, too?"

He frowned. After a slight hesitation, he said, "What about a yellow carnotite crystal?"

Dru remembered that one vividly. Salem had asked for it specifically, and she'd had to special order it from a tall, smelly prospector who worked deep in the mountains and insisted she sign a four-page liability waiver. That was because carnotite was a dusty, lemon-yellow crystal that also happened to be somewhat radioactive. To hear Opal tell it, it was a colossal threat to public safety. She had refused to come anywhere near it. Dru had been forced to store it in a lead-lined bucket in the closet until Salem had finally shown up to pay for it.

Dru shook her head. "No, as far as I know, carnotite can be used for scrying spells, but supposedly you can't see anything within living memory. Maybe if you were an Egyptian mummy, it would be helpful. But today? Not so much."

Salem drummed the fingers of his good hand, scowling at Dru as if this situation were somehow all her fault.

"You have to have *some* other kind of crystal around here, Salem." Dru looked around at the cluttered darkness. "Looks like you've got everything else."

With a start, Salem snapped his fingers and silently led Dru around a corner to a workbench of sorts. On the wall above was tacked a topographical map of a mountain range, along with a row of newspaper clippings from the 1920s. The headlines screamed about tourists going missing at a hot springs resort. Below, several creepy-looking experiments were well underway on the workbench.

In one, a thin line of viscous, honey-like liquid slowly dripped into a large petri dish, flowing over an ancient clay tablet covered in esoteric magical symbols. But no crystals.

Next to that, a cubical glass case gave her a queasy look at a swarm of black half-inch-long grubs clustered around a lumpy object that Dru fervently hoped wasn't an animal skull. Truly disgusting, and also not a crystal.

Salem led her to the far end of the bench, where a glass terrarium was covered on three sides with black paper. Inside, a tiny forest of pale, spiny plants grew under a black light that made their double rows of spikes look like gleaming teeth. In the center of the bramble sat a brick-sized crystal composed of clusters of sharp angles. It glowed an electric blue color. Dru recognized it immediately by the way it fluoresced under the ultraviolet light.

"Fluorite! Oh, good. That could really help you, depending on what color it is." She pointed at the plants that surrounded the crystal. "I'm not even going to ask what you're doing with those."

"Good."

She gave him a sour look. "What the heck are they, anyway? Venus flytraps, or something like that?"

"Sure. In the way that an alligator is something like a gecko."

"I see. And what do you feed them? Raw meat?" she joked.

His lips pressed together. "Not raw."

It took her a moment to realize he was serious. "These aren't natural plants, are they? You've used magic to create some sort of mutant shrubbery. Geez Louise. Is that really a good use of your time?"

"Careful, that rock is a little on the heavy side," he said flatly. "You'll need to use both hands to lift it out."

Having second thoughts, Dru took the lantern and held it close to the terrarium, shining the light in through the glass. The visible light overpowered the ultraviolet, revealing that the fluorite was actually a rich grass-green color, transparent like a pile of Jell-O cubes. The corners where the angles of the crystal met included other minerals, some rust-brown, some white and chalky. But other than that, the crystal itself looked largely pure.

"Green fluorite is perfect for soaking up negative energies and cleansing away contamination. Which you obviously have plenty of."

Salem clearly wasn't interested in hearing the details. He lifted up the lid of the terrarium, releasing a sharp deep-woods mustiness, and waited expectantly.

When it came right down to it, reaching both hands into a dark terrarium full of weird carnivorous plants wasn't exactly Dru's favorite plan. But her supply of other options was severely limited at the moment.

With no small amount of trepidation, she gingerly reached into the terrarium. She kept her hands close together, anxious to avoid any of the spiky plants. When she finally reached the big crystal, it was cold to the touch, despite its electric blue glow. Ever so carefully, she lifted it straight up, only barely brushing against the spiky plants. Their little jaws snapped shut, but none of them caught her fingers. She lifted out the fluorite crystal without incident and breathed a sigh of relief.

Away from the black light, the crystal reverted to its normal transparent green. "You know, Charles Darwin called the Venus flytrap one of the most wonderful plants in the world. Guess he never had to worry about counting his fingers afterward." She glanced at Salem's disgusting hand. "Speaking of which, come on."

He bristled at following her, but she still led him back to the chairs where Rane and Greyson waited. At their approach, Rane abruptly broke off talking to Greyson and looked up.

"Dude, your arm still looks like baby back ribs."

"And with that, yet another menu item is permanently closed to me." Salem gingerly lowered himself into the chair next to Rane and stretched out his injured arm on the armrest. He looked at Dru expectantly.

"Okeydokey. Let's see what we can do." Dru sat cross-legged on the floor next to him, with the translucent green crystal between them. She held one palm open an inch above Salem's arm, careful not to touch his skin and pick up any of his contamination. She draped her other hand over the top of the green fluorite crystal, letting her fingers form a cage.

Greyson caught her eye. The expression on his face silently asked whether she wanted his help. She subtly shook her head no. As much as Greyson's inner power could boost her crystal abilities, she wouldn't risk transferring any of Salem's contamination to Greyson. Both men had already had far too much contact with the dark side. Connecting them would be like offering herself as a human lightning rod for dark magic.

No, she would help Salem, but she wouldn't endanger Greyson to do it.

Calming her breathing, she focused on synchronizing her energy with the crystal in front of her. It took longer than usual, since the events of the night had left her rattled. But when she finally got in sync, she blotted out the rest of the world and tapped into the flow of the crystal.

Its purifying power tingled against the tips of each of her fingers. Brisk, clear, refreshing vitality raced up her arm, as if she had plunged it deep into a clear mountain stream. It surrounded her, drawing a startled gasp from her lips. Like a sudden gust of wind, it flowed down her other arm and radiated from her palm. She spread out her fingers, feeling the invisible flow of energy tickle her skin as it streamed out of her.

Though her eyes were closed, she could sense Salem stiffen in the chair. His breathing hitched, and she heard the faintest pained groan escape from the back of his throat. At first, that alarmed her, because nothing about this was meant to hurt.

Then she realized that Salem was completely unaccustomed to healing energies. He spent practically every waking hour immersed in magical research, some of it leading him to the darkest corners of sorcery. All of the negativity that he constantly swam in was the opposite of healthy, and it doubtless left invisible scars in his psyche.

Even Dru had been startled at first by the bracing chill of the fluorite's purifying energies. She couldn't even imagine what Salem was experiencing. He probably felt like he had plunged through the surface of a frozen lake.

As steadily as she could, Dru moved her palm slowly up and down the length of Salem's afflicted forearm, trusting in the pressure of the purifying energy to keep her from actually making contact with his skin. After a minute, the process became easier, and she could feel Salem finally start to relax under her care. Another minute after that, she knew she had done all she could do.

Slowly, she released the crystal and opened her eyes. Salem's skin still looked somewhat scorched and reptilian, but the intensity had faded, now more like an angry sunburn. It wasn't a total cure, but the results were far better than she expected.

Even more gratifying than that was the shocked look on Salem's face, as if he'd suddenly had his world turned completely upside down. That was good for him, too, she figured.

Rane peered at Salem's arm with a mixture of disgust and fascination. "Got anything stronger?"

Dru shook her head. "It'll have to heal naturally from here. Just wait and give it a chance to rest."

"That's all you've got for me?" Salem demanded. "Just wait?"

"Well. Maybe put some aloe on it." Dru stood up too fast, and her vision blanked into golden sparkles, momentarily blinding her. As she swayed, Greyson gently took her shoulders and guided her into one of Salem's antique chairs.

Although she loved his closeness and attention, she still resisted. "No. I'll be all right. We have to get back on the road. We can't risk staying here any longer."

"You're right," he said in her ear. "But if you don't rest for a minute first, I'm going to have to carry you out of here."

"Wouldn't be so bad, would it?" Gratefully, she sank back into the dusty old chair, feeling exhausted. She pulled her glasses off and pinched the bridge of her nose, as if that would somehow relieve the crushing pressure that bore down on her. "We have to find a hiding place for the scroll. Someplace the wraiths can't reach it."

With her foot, Rane dragged a chair screeching across the floor so that she could prop up her giant running shoes on its arm. She crossed her legs and sighed. "No problemo. These spooks go *poof* in the daylight, right? So all we have to do is keep outrunning them until dawn. Problem solved."

"Until tomorrow night. And the next night after that." Dru shook her head. "They'll be back. Again and again. Night after night. They'll never give up. They'll chase after us forever, until they get the scroll. And when they do, they'll finally get the one thing they've always been after. Doomsday."

23
THE THINGS WE HIDE

With an effort, Dru pushed away her gloomy thoughts and stood up. "It's not safe here. We need to keep moving." She tried not to let on how exhausted she was, but she couldn't hide it. "Until we can figure out what to do with the scroll. Maybe we can destroy it?"

"Good luck with that." Salem remained seated, experimentally flexing the fingers of his corrupted arm. "The apocalypse scroll is eternal. It can't be destroyed."

"Says you," Rane said.

"Oh, of course." He sighed theatrically. "Darling, what would I *possibly* know about it?"

Exasperated, Dru threw up her hands. "Well, fine. Then we have to find a place to hide it. Permanently. Where no one can ever get to it again. My guess is wherever it came from originally. Of course, only the Harbingers know that."

"I already told you. The Shining City." Salem's voice lacked its usual edge. He sounded almost like he was having a normal conversation. As normal as conversations got for him, anyway. "Only it wasn't the Harbingers who found it originally. It was Decimus the Accursed."

Dru was already taking a step toward the exit, but the calm certainty in Salem's voice brought her up short. "The ancient Roman sorcerer? How do you know that?" she said. "That can't be right. I've never heard that."

Salem finally peered up at her from under the brim of his top hat. "Shockingly, the world is chock-full of things *you've* never heard of."

"Like sea-salt black licorice," Rane blurted, as if she was trying to guess the answer to a trivia question. "Bet you never heard of that. Or wasabi-flavored Kit Kats."

"What?" Dru involuntarily made a face. "Wasabi Kit Kats? That's not really a thing."

"Sure as hell is. Green. Spicy. Big in Japan. Got you some for your birthday, but I had to try them first, and there weren't that many. Sorry." She didn't look sorry. "Needed the carbs anyway."

"That's okay. Really."

"But hey, you should try that Salsagheti that Ruiz brought back from Mexico. That stuff will mess up your taste buds, for real."

Dru didn't dare ask what Salsagheti was. She turned back to Salem. "How do you know Decimus the Accursed ever had the scroll?"

"Why else do you think his enemies blew up Pompeii? They killed him—along with the entire city, because why do things halfway?—before he could bring on doomsday. After that, the scroll was lost for two thousand years, until our hippie friends the Harbingers finally got their greedy little hands on it." Salem leisurely got out of his chair. His long black coat rippled as he turned to face Dru with all the swagger and presence of a master sorcerer. Despite his currently shabby state, he looked truly dangerous. "And now you know what I know. You're welcome."

Dru took a moment to digest that information. She pushed her glasses back up her nose. "If that's true, which I'll assume it is—"

Salem rolled his eyes. "Brilliant deduction."

"—then we have to learn how Decimus got the apocalypse scroll originally. More than that, we need to learn *where* he got it from. If we can put the scroll back where it belongs, we can put a stop to all of this." A sudden surge of hope filled her, like a warm ray of sunshine bursting through a cold, gloomy sky. "Return the scroll to its resting place, and we can stop doomsday for good."

"*Exactly.*" Salem sounded as if he'd been waiting the longest time for her to reach that conclusion.

Dru took a breath to say more, but Salem had gone so quiet and still that he kind of creeped her out. His lips parted slowly, as if anticipating her next words. As if he wanted to say them with her. His eyeliner-darkened eyes shone hungrily in the golden lamplight.

She refused to play his head games. With an uncomfortable sigh, she folded her arms and inclined her head to stare over the top of her glasses at him. "Salem, obviously you want to tell me something. Just say whatever it is. Just tell me the truth."

Without a word, he feigned innocence.

She wasn't buying it for a second. She drilled him with her no-nonsense stare, honed to a needle-sharp point after years of hearing half-baked conspiracy theories from her sorcerer customers. "Tell me how Decimus found the apocalypse scroll in the first place. And more importantly, where did he get it from, exactly? If we're going to survive this, we need to know everything you know."

One corner of his thin lips curled up. "There isn't enough time in the world for that."

"There will be a lot *less* time in this world if you keep these things to yourself."

His eyes twitched. He glanced at Rane, then back at Dru.

Rane snorted. "Dude, he has no idea."

From the angry flush that crept up Salem's face, Dru knew that Rane was right. For once, there was an answer that Salem actually didn't have. Stranger things had happened.

With a sigh, Salem turned to the brick wall just behind them and raised his hands, spidery fingers twisted to cast a spell. But before he did, he looked over his shoulder at Dru with flinty eyes. "Remember, I don't *have* to show this to you. I *choose* to."

Facing the wall again, he widened his stance and cast a spell. His fingers kneaded the air, and a hazy white radiance surrounded him.

Dru wanted to take a step back, but Rane's arm clamped down. She leaned closer and whispered in Dru's ear. "Salsagheti. It's like sweet candy spaghetti. Covered in salsa."

Not for the first time that night, Dru's stomach flopped over.

"Like spicy Twizzlers," Rane added.

"Got it, thanks. Really didn't need to know that."

"Yummers in your tummers."

"Uh-uh. I don't think so."

On the brick wall was an old, creased black-and-white poster bearing

a five-sided pentagram and the name THE SISTERS OF MERCY. It fluttered in an invisible wind and sailed away. The bricks in the blank wall
behind it shifted. One after another, they broke loose with tiny bursts of
powdered mortar. In moments, a gap the size of a window was revealed.

It *was* a window, Dru realized. It looked like it had been bricked over
when the adjacent building was built. Now, the hollow behind it served
as a convenient hiding spot for all sorts of small magical-looking artifacts
and old leather-bound books.

One of Greyson's eyebrows went up. "You guys have got to stop hiding
stuff behind posters."

But Dru's attention was immediately captured by the books, some of
which looked hauntingly familiar. *Formulaes Apocrypha. The Prophecies of
Paloma. Codex Eternus. The Scripture of Ephraim.*

That last book in particular was so dark and dangerous that it made
the breath catch in her throat. "That's one of the Wicked Scriptures. It
used to belong to the Harbingers. Salem, what the Faulkner are you doing
with *that?*"

"Bought it at an estate auction," he said slyly.

"So they're from the Harbinger's mansion in the desert. You've had
them for a while." She squinted at the other dusty old books. Some of them
looked vaguely familiar, and she realized that several of them were one-
of-a-kind titles that she'd thought she'd misplaced years before. "Wait a
minute. Are some of these from my shop? How did you get these?"

"The details aren't important."

Her jaw dropped open in indignation. "Did you *steal* those from me?"

He made air quotes with his fingers. "'Stealing' is a strong word,
darling. You know how we sorcerers are. One might say I put it to a better
use."

Rane jabbed a finger at the secret hiding space. "How come you never
told me about this?"

Salem spared her only a glance, and said nothing.

Dru leaned closer to Rane. "Because you would have told me about it."

"Damn straight, dude. I tell you everything, don't I?"

Dru unwillingly recalled some of the more anguish-inducing conversations she'd had with Rane over the years. A brief flurry of too-much-information moments flickered through her brain:

Rane in front of the cash register, unzipping her spandex shirt: *Dude, you got your magnifying glass? 'Cause you need to take a look at this rash.*

Rane at the candy bowl, pointing as Dru chewed on a sweet: *Hey, that one's nasty. I know. I just spit it out.*

Rane after gobbling down a feast of Japanese takeout, loudly exhaling noxious breath in her face: *Dude, I ate that whole boat. Tell me if I smell fishy.*

Rane, sweaty from a run along the river, tugging up at the waistband of her pink shorts: *Yeah, ran out of underwear today. Thing is, Salem's underwear keeps riding up on me.*

With a shudder, Dru snapped back to the present. Awkwardly, she said, "Yes. Sharing has absolutely never been a problem for you."

"You know it. Share because you care." Rane held out her fist. Hesitantly, Dru bumped it.

Salem's twitchy fingers fluttered across the shelf until one ragged-edged book shot out into his hand with a puff of dust. He turned and presented it to Dru with a flourish, unduly proud of this particular possession. She realized why after she puzzled out the elaborate gold leaf script on the front cover, now flaked and pitted from age. It spelled out two archaic words that made her blood run cold.

Katabasis Decimus.

Rane leaned over her shoulder and frowned. "The hell does that mean?"

Dru cleared her throat. "*Katabasis* is the story of a descent into the netherworld. You know, like Odysseus or Hercules. Is this what I think it is?" She looked at Salem for confirmation. "Is this about Decimus finding the scroll?"

He nodded smugly.

Dru was astonished that such a thing existed, and even more astonished that Salem had it. The only thing that didn't surprise her was that he had kept it secret all this time. The implications were overwhelming. If this book revealed how Decimus came to possess the scroll, then it stood to reason she could find a way to reverse the process and put the scroll back. Then, this entire nightmare would finally end.

"We need to take this with us." With a sweep of her arm, Dru indicated all of the books in the hiding space. "We're taking all of this."

"Hmm. Let me think about that." Salem laid a finger along his cheek, then slowly lowered it to point at Dru. "How about . . . *No.* The books in there are ancient. Too fragile for any kind of rough treatment."

Rane flipped her hair back. "Hey. Dru is too fragile for this kind of treatment, too. But you don't hear her complaining about it."

"Um." Dru wasn't sure how to take that. "Thanks?"

Salem's lips twisted into a snarky frown, and he drew in a breath to speak.

Greyson stopped him with a big outstretched hand. "Listen. Like it or not, those wraiths are on their way down here right now. That means we have a serious problem. You want to fix it? Bring this stuff. Don't leave any tools sitting in the toolbox."

Salem's eyes narrowed. "Does everything with you always come back to cars?"

"It does when that car parked outside is your only ride out before the wraiths get here," Greyson said steadily. "Unless you want to get left behind, I suggest you pack up those books. Right now."

Salem obviously thought hard about that, and then his face lit with a wicked smile. "Fine. *You* get to carry the cursed ones."

"I'm already cursed. Let's do this." Greyson stepped up to the hiding space and reached toward it.

Behind his back, Salem said to Dru, "I'm starting to like your half-demon boyfriend." He held his thumb and finger an inch apart. "Just a teensy little bit."

Greyson paused and half-turned, as if a distant noise had caught his attention. "They're almost here," he growled.

She didn't have to ask who he meant. She knew.

The wraiths.

24

DON'T SCRY FOR ME

Dru's heart was pounding hard as they scrambled back into Hellbringer and roared away into the night in a blast of exhaust and howling rubber. Outside the demon car's windows, the ghostly fronts of dark warehouses streaked past in the darkness. Their rows of tall loading doors were blacked out in deep shadows, like a chorus of mouths open in silent screams. Dru scrutinized every passing building, dreading another ambush. The wraiths had caught them off guard once already, and that had been nearly fatal. She watched the night carefully.

The only sound inside the car was the constant growl of Hellbringer's big engine. "Best bet is if we head out of town," Greyson said into the tense silence. "Get us somewhere where we have more room to maneuver. Those things can move through walls. But we can't. We need to make sure we don't get boxed in."

Dru nodded, resisting the urge to add the word *'again'* to that thought. She kept looking back into the darkness behind them, expecting the horde of ravenous wraiths to come sailing up behind them, eyes burning like hot embers, hungry for their souls.

Rane caught her eye and silently raised her empty hands. The frustrated expression on her face was clear. *I can't do anything.*

Any other sorcerer Dru had ever met would have been absolutely crushed by such a defeat. But Rane looked simply angry and determined, as if this was just one more obstacle in her path to be overcome. Dru took some small comfort in the fact that her friend was just as tough mentally as she was physically.

Dru smiled as reassuringly as she could. *I know.* She would find a way to heal Rane. She had to. With Rane left powerless like this, they were doomed.

Sitting beside Rane in the back seat, Salem licked his thumb and paged through the ancient book on Decimus, obviously looking for a specific passage. When he found it, he handed the surprisingly heavy book to Dru. "Read this part. Don't worry, it's in English, so you won't have to strain yourself."

Dru ignored the barb and took the book from him. By the light of her cell phone, she studied its aged pages. The uneven sheets of parchment appeared to have been cut apart and sewn into a book long after it was written. The musty leather binding was so dry and cracked that she feared it would fall apart in her hands. She suspected this wasn't even the first binding that had wrapped around these pages. Everything was carefully hand-lettered in ink that the centuries had faded to the color of old wood. In some places, the parchment was so thin that the handwriting showed through on the other side of the page.

It was written in English, all right, but it was Old English, which still required quite a bit of mental translation on Dru's part. The grammar was closer to German than to modern English. The book described Decimus and his ruthless hunt to claim the apocalypse scroll—and with it, solidify his powerful grip over the entire world. Definitely not a nice guy. Then again, he wasn't known as Decimus the Delightful.

The anonymous author of the book claimed that he or she had personally observed Decimus, referred to here as Decimus the Damned, descend through a cave into the netherworld. The author even claimed that within the netherworld, Decimus had found a gate that led down to Tartarus, a lake of fire so deep in the abyss that hardly any mortal beings had ever set foot there.

To bolster this far-fetched account, the author of the *Katabasis* cited other works of antiquity that Dru had mostly never even heard of. The quotations were set apart from the main text by double diples (>>), which were early precursors of modern quotation marks.

Dru pointed them out to Salem. "I think this book is a fake."

Salem couldn't have looked more shocked if she had ripped off his top hat and beaten him with it. Which she had actually considered doing, from time to time.

Awkwardly, she held up the book so that he could see it over the seat. "See here? That's a double diple, which was invented by Rufinus of Aquileia in the fifth century. The thing is, Decimus died in the destruction of Pompeii, in the first century, before anything like quotation marks were invented. Since this book was written at least four hundred years *after* he died, it can't possibly be a firsthand account like it claims to be."

In the driver's seat, Greyson checked the mirrors. "Can a sorcerer live that long?"

From the back seat, Rane said, "Who *wants* to?"

"No. Not that I've ever heard of." Dru gave Salem a searching look. "How old are you, anyway? Exactly?"

"Please. I think you're getting your wires crossed. There's a simpler explanation for this book. Our anonymous fifth-century sorcerer used a particularly potent scrying spell to look back in time and find out exactly what Mr. Accursed was up to. And then they just wrote it all down."

"*That's* your simpler explanation? At best, this could be a copy of an earlier work. Heavily annotated and embellished."

Salem's half-crazed eyes grew even larger, revealing the entirety of their bloodshot whites. "Just. Keep. Reading."

Dru held his crazed gaze, wondering what sort of secret communication was passing between them, because Salem obviously thought he was sending her a message, even though he wasn't.

Puzzled, Dru faced front again and flipped through the pages, skimming over the Old English as quickly as she could. The bizarre grammar was starting to give her a headache, as sentences that started out meaning one thing ended up meaning the complete opposite.

If the book had really been a blow-by-blow account of how Decimus entered the netherworld and found the apocalypse scroll, then it would have been incredibly valuable to Dru. Because then she would have a chance to reverse-engineer everything Decimus had done. And the world would be safe again.

But nothing was that easy. The book noticeably lacked the crucial knowledge she needed. It didn't explain how Decimus had found the scroll, or where. The book just dwelled at length on how terrible it would be if any of the seven seals were broken. As if she didn't already know that.

As Hellbringer left the golden-lighted towers of the Denver skyline behind and shot out of town into the stillness of the dry plains, Dru grew more and more frustrated with the book. She was about to toss it aside in frustration, until she flipped to the very end and saw what was on the last few pages. Her jaw dropped open.

The pages were filled with cryptic magical signs. She immediately recognized it as sorcio, the language of sorcery. The very first symbol was an elongated hexagon, meaning *crystalos*.

It was a crystal magic spell.

Her pulse quickened as she flipped the pages back and forth, mentally switching between Old English and the esoteric language of sorcery. She puzzled out that it was a scrying spell, which enabled the caster to see events that had occurred centuries before. Apparently, the author had been telling the truth about witnessing Decimus descend into the netherworld.

There was a chance maybe Dru could do the same, if she could find the right crystal.

That was a challenge, though, because the spell called for a crystal that was largely unknown at the time. The author described it as a cursed yellow crystal that bloomed in sandstone like a field of dusty yellow flowers. Handling it too much was said to bring disease and death. So it was definitely toxic, possibly even radioactive.

Dru scratched her head, mentally sorting through dozens of possible crystals, until she remembered the carnotite crystal she had once special-ordered for Salem. Carnotite was a strange yellow crystal formed by trickles of water that millions of years ago had seeped through petrified trees and fossils, dissolving uranium from the surrounding sandstone. It matched the description. Had Salem somehow figured out, from this secret book, how to cast a scrying spell to peer into the distant past? How had he done it? And more importantly, what did he see?

She looked back over her shoulder to where he sat in the gloom of the back seat. From the glum look on his face, she suddenly knew, without a doubt, that he had tried to cast the spell himself—and failed miserably. It wasn't any surprise, considering that he wasn't a crystal sorcerer.

But she was. And the moment she had helped him with his corrupted arm, she had seen the shock on his face. As if he had never before considered just how powerful her crystal magic could be. He'd seen her cast magic plenty of times before. But that was the first time she had cast a spell that directly benefited him.

For once, she had truly impressed him. And that was why he had shown her this book, so that he could convince her to cast this scrying spell for him. That explained why he hadn't come right out and asked. She could only imagine how much of a blow it was to Salem's fragile ego to face the fact that she was, in this particular case at least, a more powerful sorcerer than he was.

A tiny, deep-down wicked part of her wanted to voice that fact. After suffering so much condescension and aggravation from him over the years, she wanted to hold this over him, even just for a moment.

But just one look at his defeated expression told her that he had come to the same conclusion. He knew what she was thinking. He was at her mercy.

If their situations were reversed, she had no doubt that he would put her in her place. But she decided to take the higher ground instead.

"So . . . there seems to be a crystal spell in the back of this book," she said with as much innocence as she could muster.

Rane and Greyson traded looks.

"Oh, is there?" Salem said carefully, sitting up straight. "And what do you think about this particular spell that you've discovered?"

Dru savored this tiny victory for just a moment longer, but she had to get back to business. She sighed. "Pretty sure I could cast it, if I had the right crystal. But I don't."

The relief that flooded his features would have been embarrassing to watch, if it weren't so amusing. "I thought you would never ask." He reached into the inside pocket of his voluminous black coat and pulled out a scratched gray metal box the size of a hip flask. She recognized it from his hiding space behind the poster. Carefully, he undid the tiny brass latches along the side and opened the box.

"Oh. Well, lookee here." In Salem's hands, radiant against the dull lead box, was the yellow carnotite crystal. His eyes glittered. "Where do you want to cast the spell?"

* * *

To do her magic, Dru needed a quiet, safe location. Her shop was usually the best place, when it wasn't blown to pieces. This far outside the city, in the middle of nowhere, nothing looked promising.

Greyson turned Hellbringer off the two-lane state highway onto a rough rural road that led through a thick aspen grove. Past that, dry hay fields spread out on either side, silver and ghostly in the moonlight. In the distance, the only sign of habitation was the dark hulk of an old barn that leaned dangerously to one side. Some bit of metal or broken glass flashed against Hellbringer's headlights.

Rane leaned up against the back of Greyson's seat, alert and watchful. "Get us closer, dude. Me and Salem will go check it out, make sure nothing's hinky in there."

"I have my spyglass," Salem said. "I can see it from here."

"Screw that." She pounded on the back of Greyson's seat. "Let me out."

While Salem argued with her, Greyson looked a question at Dru.

"I just have to be out of the car and not moving. So, this is fine," she said, although she wasn't really sure about it at all. Trying to cast a millennia-old crystal spell for the first time, out of the back of a moldy fifth-century manuscript, using a radioactive crystal, on the side of the road. What could possibly go wrong?

She took a deep breath and blew it out. "How far away are the wraiths?"

He pulled over, set the parking brake, and shut off the engine. "Tough to say. They're still following us. I can sense them back there." He winced, as if a sudden muscle cramp had just seized up the back of his neck. "Just don't go too far from the car."

Dru got out on stiff legs and tilted the seat forward so that Salem could climb out of the back. Rane, smiling crookedly, practically dragged him toward the abandoned barn, despite his protests. Then she whispered in his ear, and from that point on they moved in uncanny silence, slipping away into the night, perfectly in sync. Dru wondered how many times the two of them had worked together to fight different kinds of supernatural evil.

"They make a good team," Greyson said, coming over to her side of the car. "Too bad they're always trying to kill each other."

"I hope they make it," Dru said.

"To the barn?"

"Just in general." Dru looked around at the unimpressive hay field, realizing with a grimace that it was probably full of bugs and field mice, and who knew what else. With Hellbringer's engine off, the night around them was alive with the sounds of insects whirring, crickets chirping, and wind feathering through the grass, bringing the fresh scent of green things growing.

Greyson's boots scuffed on the gravel as he left the side of the road and swished through the tall grass. As if sensing her discomfort, he held out his hand to her. "It's okay. Come on."

She took his strong hand, drawing confidence from his presence, and stepped up onto the grass. It came up to her knees. She held up Salem's heavy little lead box in her other hand. "This is far enough. I need to sit down to do this."

Without a word, Greyson stripped off his leather jacket. He laid it down at her feet and spread it out like a picnic blanket, motioning for her to sit.

"No, I can't—"

"Yes, you can. We don't have much time." Greyson pulled her close, and suddenly she felt overwhelmed by his presence. His eyes burned red in the night, much brighter than the stars twinkling overhead. Then she was kissing him, pulling him to her, holding him tight.

She was weak in the knees when she finally pulled away. She looked up into his eyes and tried to find some words to express what she felt. Everything was happening so fast. The wraiths. The scroll. The shop being destroyed. Again.

She didn't want to cast this spell. She didn't want to run for her life anymore. She just wanted to be with Greyson. Here, now, beneath the stars. She wanted the rest of the world to just stop hurtling toward oblivion, just for one night. Was that too much to ask?

She opened her mouth to say all of these things, and her phone chimed in her pocket, destroying the moment. Suddenly, she didn't notice the stars or the quiet breeze or the warmth of Greyson's strong chest anymore. Now there was only the ugly metal box in her hand and the fact that the clock was ticking. The wraiths would catch up if they stayed here too long.

"Well, at least we have cell signal." She checked her phone. It was a text from Rane.

Barn is empty. U R good to go.

She showed it to Greyson, who nodded grimly. "Are you ready?" he said.

She wasn't, but she nodded anyway. With a nervous sigh, she opened Salem's box.

25

OF ROMAN DESCENT

K neeling on Greyson's jacket, Dru did her best to block out the world around her and focus on her breathing. She slowed it down, concentrating on the sensation of the cool country air traveling in through her flared nostrils, filling her lungs, and then flowing out through her gently parted lips.

Against her will, her mind filled to overflowing with anxieties. The wraiths chasing them. Rane losing her powers. Salem corrupted by dark magic. Her shop reduced to rubble. She couldn't simply ignore any of those worries. She could only acknowledge them and then mentally set them on a shelf to deal with later. Right now, her mind had to be completely clear and sharp. She couldn't afford any distractions.

Although she'd been using crystals for years, it was only since she'd met Greyson that her abilities had truly risen to the levels of a genuine sorceress. The more adept she grew, the more careful she had to be about staying steady and poised as she called up her inner magic. As her spells grew ever more powerful, the margin of error shrank until it was razor thin. She couldn't afford to take a misstep and end up like Salem. Or worse.

That was particularly true with this new spell. The energies involved were both incredibly powerful and pinpoint specific. Unlike most of her crystal magic, which used combinations of crystals to balance and harmonize various magical energies, this spell depended entirely on the chunk of carnotite sitting on the grass in front of her.

The problem was that it wasn't actually a single crystal but rather a cluster of tiny canary yellow crystals, thousands of them, all crusted into a triangular piece of sandstone. Most of the crystals were no larger than a grain of sand, and some were as small as dust. Her success or failure would depend entirely on how she modulated her magical power over thousands of individual crystals at once.

No pressure or anything.

She flexed both hands wide open, stretching out her fingers. She could almost hear the magic humming through the tiny crystals, a blur of white noise punctuated by sharp cracks, like the first threatening strikes of icy cold hailstones during a rolling thunderstorm.

The last thing she really wanted to do was touch the carnotite, and not only because she was afraid of casting this spell. Carnotite was radioactive. Not enough to kill, but enough to give her the creeps. In the mountains, it was commonly mined as uranium ore.

As slowly as she could, Dru reached toward the carnotite. The closer she got, the louder its energies grew in her mind, until it practically roared inside her skull. The moment her index fingers made contact with either side of the dry, cold rock, her magic poured into it. A wave of vertigo washed over her as the carnotite splintered her soul in thousands of different directions at once. Each thin sliver of energy reflected and broke apart over and over again, pulling her consciousness out of her body and scattering it through the mists of time.

Part of her wanted to scream out loud with the sheer animal terror of losing her own sense of self. She felt like she was falling, and she couldn't stop it. She couldn't feel her own body. She had no idea which way was up or down. As she teetered on the edge of losing her mind completely, she used all of her strength to clamp down and focus on where she wanted the magic to take her.

The Shining City.

She had seen it only once, seemingly long ago, but its memory was indelible. Scintillating towers soared up out of the eerie fog of the netherworld, like the monuments of some long-vanished age. As she thought of it, it materialized before her, as if she was actually there.

Her mind raced through the netherworld, crisscrossing long causeways built of dark stones bound together with luminous magic. The Shining City grew brighter as it towered over her, blinding her. She had the fleeting impression that she was seeing it not as it currently was but as it had existed for thousands of years. The centuries blurred together before her. She was losing her sense of time.

Decimus, she thought. She had to find a way to zero in on the evil sorcerer's journey to the Shining City. It would help if she had some possession that had belonged to him, so she could focus on that. She had once owned his amulet, although it was long gone. She tried to picture it in her mind. It had a heavy gold chain with thick, squared-off links. It was the size of her palm, built up of golden rings inscribed with magical glyphs that surrounded a single eyeball-sized painite gemstone the color of dried blood. Being powerfully evil, it had always left a particularly sour taste in her mouth. She concentrated on recalling that sensation.

The glare around her flickered, leaving her nauseous, and then came into sharp focus on the amulet. Suddenly, she could see it hanging in front of her, every detail exactly as she remembered it. She could practically reach out and grab it. Except that it hung at the open collar of a sun-bleached tunic, swaying with the gait of the man who wore it.

Decimus the Accursed.

She had always thought of the evil sorcerer as a bent and twisted old man, with a long gray beard and gnarled fingers. But as it turned out, Decimus the Accursed was exactly the opposite of what she had imagined.

He strode alone through the blinding glare of the Shining City, marching through the netherworld like a conqueror. His every movement radiated strength and capability. His eyes were deep-set and dark, his nose hawkish, his broad chin bracketing a fierce frown.

Instead of the long flowing robes Dru had imagined, Decimus was dressed for battle. In a Roman sort of way.

Over his knee-length tunic, he wore banded iron armor that encased his torso and shoulders. Each strip of articulated metal was engraved with magical protective sigils. His helmet was chased with polished bronze, with flaps that protected the back of his neck and the sides of his scowling face. He carried a tall rectangular shield and a long spear. An earthenware vessel was slung over both shoulders on a length of rope, like a backpack.

Dru knew he couldn't possibly be here, now, since he had died nearly two thousand years before. He seemed almost real enough to touch, although he continuously swam in and out of focus, disappearing occasionally into the blinding glare.

A colossal archway rose overhead, peaked at the top, a crack of darkness in the eternal light. With purposeful strides, Decimus marched through and was swallowed up. Only his amulet glowed softly, lighting the way.

Dru followed his descent deep into a chasm of raw black rock. It could have taken hours or even weeks. She had lost all sense of time. It grew hotter as he descended, because he glistened with sweat as he discarded clothing and armor. But he never gave up the strange clay vessel strung across his back, nor did he ever open it to take a drink.

A ruddy dawn emerged in the distance, along an invisible horizon that split the endless blackness. Dru lost track of Decimus then, overwhelmed by visions of a world of black rock and fiery torment. In this desolate place, everything burned and seethed. The smoking rock underfoot splintered and fell away into pools of lava that flashed like liquid gold and rubies.

Tartarus. The deepest abyss of torment.

Dodging among plumes of fire, winged demons came to roost on ribbons of dark rock that jutted up from the hungry flames. Plumes of white heat burst up from the lava, twisting into more of the diabolical creatures. Newly formed skeletal arms clawed blindly at the eternal darkness of the dead sky overhead. Their eyes burned red, and their snapping jaws dripped with liquid fire.

To Dru, all of it happened in an eerie silence from which she could hear only the rasp of her own awed breaths. She wanted to look away, but she couldn't help but watch endless legions of demons spawned while others were consumed by the eternal fires of Tartarus.

In the scorching heat, Decimus labored across the broken land until he reached the bare slope of a black mountain. He trudged onward, step by heavy step, until he had reached the desolate mountain peak. There, with a wolfish grin, he raised his hands and cast an elaborate spell.

In a blinding flash, the mountain peak before him turned red-hot, then gold, then white as the summer sun. Ponderously, it collapsed in on itself, leaving a seething crater of lava. Heat waves shimmered around

Decimus as the mountain peak sank away, leaving a smoking pit that gaped down into the center of the underworld.

Only then did he shrug off the clay vessel he carried on his back. It was an amphora, a traditional Roman vessel with a body the shape of a wasp's stinger, and two long handles stretching up on opposite sides. Decimus's amulet crackled with magic. His hands rippled with flickering blue flames, which licked the surface of the clay amphora until it cracked open.

A sickly curl of mist unspooled through the cracks, snaking across the ground as if heavier than the air around it. Gradually, it coalesced into a serpentine shape with a definite head and blazing red eyes. The cloud of mist coiled and shifted, suggesting a canine head, then bat wings, then a scorpion tail.

Decimus hadn't come here alone, Dru realized. He'd been carrying a captive demon with him the whole time.

As the demon tried to slip away, Decimus abruptly pinned it in place with crackling streams of power from his hands. The thing writhed beneath his spell. He shouted at it, the same words over and over again, but Dru couldn't make them out. She held her breath, waiting to see what would happen next.

Decimus didn't release the demon until it caught fire. But rather than harming the demon, the flames only made it even more powerful. It was now a mass of writhing, living fire. With unsettling calm, it gathered itself up and stood on four long legs. Its long tail swished sparks and smoke. A powerful neck loomed over Decimus, terminating in an equine head. The demon unmistakably became a horse composed of red-hot fire.

It reared up on its back legs. Sparks flew from its hooves, and gouts of flame shot from its nostrils.

Decimus pointed to the seething pit where the peak of the mountain had once stood. Rippling with heat, the demon turned and galloped toward it, leaving behind a trail of burning U-shaped hoof prints.

When it reached the edge of the precipice, it didn't hesitate. It leaped into the fiery abyss and vanished.

With the demon horse gone, Dru expected Decimus to finally turn and retreat from the heat. But instead he squatted down and coldly regarded the pit, an expectant look on his cruel face. Dru wasn't sure what he was waiting for, but she soon found out.

The demon horse emerged from the depths, leaping up out of the flames as easily as jumping over a fence. Trailing sparks and smoke, it trotted up to Decimus, carrying a gleaming object in its teeth. With a start, Dru realized what it was.

The apocalypse scroll.

It looked just as ancient then as it did now. Wrinkled brown parchment, spiked silver tips, and seven wax seals as red as blood. The demon lowered its massive head and dropped the scroll into Decimus's greedy outstretched hands. His gloating face lit with a wicked grin.

The muscles of his face tensed. He sensed danger. He cast about, then turned and looked directly at Dru.

According to everything she knew, it was impossible for him to see her, but he did.

Immediately, he turned and snapped out a command to the demon horse. She was close enough to read his lips, but she could make out only the last word.

Infernotoris.

She knew that name. Knew what it meant. With a wrenching gasp, Dru broke the spell. She lurched to her feet in fear, stumbled backward, and fell into the grass. Greyson caught her before she hit the ground.

"Easy, easy." Greyson whispered reassurances in her ear. "You were out for a long time."

She wasn't listening. A few yards away, at the side of the road, the hulking black shape of Hellbringer gleamed silently against the darkness of the night. Its angular black wing stood high in back, like a blade. In its pointed nose, twin yellow parking lights burned like the eyes of a hungry carnivore, watching her. As if it wanted to pounce. Run her over. Crush her. Feed on her soul.

Out of sheer panic, she fought against Greyson, trying to get away. "It was a demon. Decimus was helped by a demon," Dru choked out, the words running into one another. "It obeyed him."

On arms and legs still half-asleep from her trance, she tried to scramble away from the possessed car until her back was pressed up against a rough wooden fence post. She tried to picture the demon horse trapped in the car, the burning-hot spirit bound into the cold steel by sorcery and agony.

Greyson stayed with her. "What's going on? You're not making any sense. Talk to me."

She tried to calm down, but she couldn't. "The demon that brought Decimus the apocalypse scroll, he called it by name." Her voice quavered with exhaustion and fear. It wouldn't stay steady. "He called it *Infernotoris.*"

Greyson frowned. "That sounds familiar."

She finally tore her gaze away from the car and looked up at Greyson. "That's because *Infernotoris* means . . . *Hellbringer.*"

26

EVIL RIDES WITH YOU

At the sound of its true name, *Infernotoris*, the black demon car rumbled to life. Dru didn't take her wide eyes off it as she grabbed Greyson's hand and stood up on shaky legs. She felt like she couldn't catch her breath. Even just looking at Hellbringer now gave her the creeps. She knew the car was badly behaved, but she had no idea it was evil enough to act as an accomplice to doomsday.

At that moment, Rane and Salem emerged from the darkness, coming down the country road from the direction of the empty barn, holding hands. Rane's cheeks were flushed. Salem's hair was messed up, and his top hat was on slightly crooked.

"Cool. We ready?" Rane's grin was bright. "Did the spell work? What'd you find out?"

Dru's gaze tracked from Rane to Salem, who was conspicuously occupied with picking bits of hay off his long jacket. His silk shirt was buttoned crooked. He didn't meet anyone's gaze.

"Um." Dru cleared her throat and adjusted her glasses, unsure what to say.

"We can talk about it on the road." Greyson guided Dru toward Hellbringer. "Come on. Let's go."

"No!" She dug in her heels. "No. That car is evil, and—"

"That car is part of me." Greyson came around to stand before her. The stubble along his dark jaw was just a smudge in the moonlight, beneath the burning intensity of his red eyes. "We're connected. Deeply. Hellbringer is not going to betray you. I know this."

She wanted to believe him, desperately, but she couldn't. The sight of that demonic coiling mist in the netherworld was indelibly burned into her brain, threatening her with images of gnashing teeth, leathery wings, and burning hooves. That was Hellbringer's true form, a shape-changing demonic creature, not this sleek black muscle car.

"All this time I've been trying to convince myself that Hellbringer is on our side. That we can trust him." Her voice trembled. "But everyone has been warning me. Deep inside, Hellbringer really is a demon. He is a force of destruction. He was there at the very beginning. It was Hellbringer who gave Decimus the apocalypse scroll. I can't believe I never realized it before. Doomsday has been on its way for two thousand years now, and *it's all Hellbringer's fault.*"

Rane looked shocked. Salem shot her an *I-told-you-so* look.

"Dru, look at me," Greyson said.

Instead, Dru backed away, blinking back tears. "I can't. I can't do this."

The feeling of betrayal stabbed her so deeply that she felt like she couldn't breathe. Despite the broad moonlit fields and crisp night air around her, echoing with the hushing chirps of crickets, she felt like she was in some kind of prison. She felt like the world was trying to grind the life out of her. Crush her beneath a fate she couldn't avoid. She marched away down the country road, away from the bloodred taillights and the stink of exhaust.

Greyson followed her, reaching for her. "Dru . . ."

"All this time, I've been fighting to save Hellbringer. To earn his trust. To bring him out of the darkness and onto our side, to help us *save* the world. Instead of *destroying* it. But why?" Her voice cracked. "I should have known all along. That car is a demon. Always has been. Always will be. But that's not the worst part."

She kept walking, waiting for Greyson to ask about the worst part. But he just quietly matched her pace. Without a word, he radiated a silent strength that she desperately craved, and yet at the same time she feared to depend on it too much. Because it could be taken away from her in a heartbeat, the same way her trust in Hellbringer had just been destroyed.

She stopped and studied the dark, cracked pavement at her feet.

Greyson stopped in front of her. He said nothing.

"The worst part is," she said, "I don't know what I'd do without him."

Greyson's leather jacket creaked as he folded his arms. His voice was a quiet rumble in his chest. "Are we talking about the car? Or me?"

She tried to will away the burning tears. He had spoken a scary kind of truth that she did not want to talk about, the kind that cut right down to her soul. But she knew it was coming, and she couldn't avoid it.

"You don't know if you can trust me." He stated it as a flat fact, not an accusation. "Because I'm cursed. I'm part demon. Your friends tell you that I could turn on you. And you wonder if they're right."

She wanted to deny it, but she couldn't. Not exactly. "I think you're a good person. I know it."

"But," he said.

"But sometimes I have to wonder. When I see things like I just saw, Hellbringer handing over the apocalypse scroll to the most evil sorcerer in the world. How can I trust that speed demon ever again? How can you?"

Greyson turned his rugged face to look out across the empty fields. "I know Hellbringer. He's changed. I've sensed it happening."

She watched him carefully, wondering what exactly was going on behind those burning red eyes.

He turned those eyes toward her again, and the heat inside them made her melt just a little bit. "I've changed, too. Because of you."

She shook her head. "No, I haven't done—"

"Yes. You have." He wrapped his strong hands around her arms. "You don't give yourself enough credit for the difference you make. You don't realize just how much good you actually do."

A hard lump formed in her throat.

"Before I met you," he said, "I felt like the world was an awful place. Full of people who were just out for themselves. But now I know that's not true." His words came out slowly, as if he had trouble finding the right thing to say. But as he spoke, she could hear the certainty in his voice. "Hellbringer is a demon. Always has been, always will be, like you said. But even demons can change. For the better. Because of you. I know that for a fact." He took a deep breath, and his chest swelled. He let it out slowly. "Maybe I deserve to be cursed, to be part demon. Maybe I don't.

But either way, this is how things are. If I have to fight to keep Hellbringer on our side, I will. And if I have to fight to earn your trust, I will." He leaned closer, and she could feel his warm breath on her cheek. "Every day, you remind me that some things are worth fighting for."

She kissed him hard then, and held him tight, wanting to drink in everything about him until she lost all sense of time or place. The rest of the world faded away, taking all of her worries and doubts with it. There was only the two of them together, and it felt like it could go on that way forever.

She finally broke away to catch her breath. But she still clung to him, feeling his strength, recognizing the truth down deep inside that whispered they belonged together. Greyson and Hellbringer were a package deal, inseparable. And if she believed in him—which she did, completely—then she could believe in Hellbringer, too.

As Greyson held her, she looked past him to the slitted red taillights of the demon car, and suddenly realized the full implications of what she'd seen in Tartarus. She pulled away from Greyson's embrace just enough to look up into his serious expression. "Hellbringer knows where the apocalypse scroll came from."

He nodded as he absorbed her words. She could almost see the gears turning in his head. "So that means . . ."

She headed for the car, leading him by the hand. "Hellbringer knows where we need to go to put the scroll *back*."

* * *

Hellbringer's engine let out a steady purr as the demon car carried them, endlessly fleeing from the wraiths that were somewhere back there in the night. As they drove, Dru turned around in the front passenger seat and told Rane and Salem everything she'd seen through the scrying spell. By the time she was done, Salem stared furiously at nothing, puzzling over her words, his hands steepled before him.

Beside him in the back seat, Rane just looked perplexed. She chewed on her lip. "That doesn't make any sense. I mean, like they put on fish?"

"What?" Dru's brain struggled to make the connection, and utterly failed. "I don't . . . What?"

"Tartar sauce." Rane made a face. "I don't get it."

"No, no. I said we have to *get to* Tartarus."

"All of us?"

"Well, that's the idea. I don't think we have any choice."

Rane resolutely shook her head side to side. "No way, dude. Nobody gets to tartar me."

"No, no. That's not what—"

"Probably good for your skin though. Oh, my God, I want fish and chips so bad." Rane made lip-smacking sounds.

Dru's phone rang. It was Opal. With a sigh, Dru held up one finger, signaling for Rane to just stay silent for one minute. No matter how soon she got the crystals to cure Rane, it couldn't be soon enough. "Opal. Are you okay? Were you able to get the crystals we need?"

"About time you finally got reception," Opal's voice crackled in her ear. "Where are you right now, anyway?"

Dru glanced over at Greyson, whose gaze cut up to the rearview mirror. "About three hours outside of Denver," he said.

"Ugh," Opal said. "I'm not driving out that far."

"This is really important," Dru said. "I need one more thing. My green vivianite crystal."

Opal's put-upon sigh turned wary. "Why? That's for opening a portal to the netherworld."

"Exactly. I have a solution to our problem."

Opal made an unpleasant noise. "Which one? I've lost count."

"About what to do with the apocalypse scroll."

"Oh, *that* one."

Dru idly nudged the scroll with her toe, which was currently sitting on Hellbringer's black carpeted floor, between her feet. She found it strange that an artifact so powerful, so highly sought after, was so small and old, and rather smelly, too. "All this time, we've been thinking that the Harbingers found the scroll. But they weren't the first. It was actually Decimus. He found the Shining City, and descended all the way down to Tartarus. And with the help of . . ." She glanced nervously around the shadowy interior of the car, and out along the long hood onto the dark road ahead. "With the help of *a demon*, he got the scroll, and that's what started this whole doomsday thing, thousands of years ago. But we can undo that! We can put the scroll back where it belongs. All we need to do is get away from these wraiths, get everyone fixed up, and then find a portal to the netherworld."

"Oh. Is that all? Piece of cake, then." Opal's sarcasm practically oozed through the phone.

"Well, I didn't say it would be *easy*."

Opal was silent for a long moment. "So that's your plan? How exactly are you going to put the scroll back without getting burned to a crisp or having your soul devoured? You do realize that Tartarus is not only full of red-hot lava, it's also chock full of demons. And you're a mortal being, which makes you basically demon kibbles. You're going to, what, knock politely? Wear a disguise? Try to talk an infinite legion of freaky, hungry-ass demons into *ignoring* a tasty treat like you?"

"Umm . . ." Dru pursed her lips, thinking hard. "The details on the last part of the plan are still a little hazy. But hey, Decimus did it, so—"

"Oh, I see. You and him, you're all pretty much on the same level. World-class sorcerers, masters of the fate of the universe. You know, I remember the good old days when you *weren't* too big for your britches. You've been hanging out with Salem all night, haven't you? Honey, you need to stop taking advice from anyone who never sees the light of day. Probably all that vitamin D deficiency is making him delusional."

Dru shook her head. "That's not what's happening here."

"Mmm-hmm. Did it ever occur to you to wonder how, exactly, the Harbingers ended up floating around in the dark as dispossessed wraiths?"

"Well, you know, I just sort of figured . . ." Dru's voice trailed off. She hadn't actually figured that part out yet. She glanced nervously back at Salem, who was still doing his frowning, finger-steepling thing.

"Honey. Let me tell you something," Opal said. "The Harbingers did all of this to themselves. Those people may have been super-powerful, but that wasn't enough for them. Because no matter how much power you have, it's never enough. To get more, they made deals with *demons* to do their dirty work. *Deee*-monnns. You hear me? You can't try to do what they did. You can't. It will destroy you. No one comes back normal from that."

Her words stung, because they were true. "Well. Being normal is overrated, anyway."

"You know what I mean."

Dru wanted so badly to tell Opal that she was all wrong. But was she?

Dru knew that she had survived all of this apocalyptic mayhem so far partly because of her half-demon boyfriend and his demon-possessed car. So on the surface, it did seem like she was headed down the same dark path as the Harbingers. Just like them, she had made her own arrangements with demons. But she knew in her heart that her situation was different. She wasn't power-hungry or corrupt. She was trying to save the world.

Then again, the Harbingers had insisted they were trying to save the world from itself. They had said all of the same things. Dru knew there was a difference between them, but it was hazy and indistinct, and that troubled her. Was this exactly the sort of thinking that had darkened the Harbingers' souls until they became bodiless undead creatures of the night?

Was she doomed to end up the same way? The thought terrified her. But the hard fact was that right now, she didn't have any other options, and time was running out. They couldn't keep fleeing forever.

Dru tried to swallow down the hard lump of fear in her throat, but it stayed stubbornly put. "We have to do this. We will find a way."

"Even if . . . ?" Opal didn't finish the thought out loud. From the heartbreak in her voice, Dru knew what she was thinking: *Even if she ended up like the Harbingers.*

"No matter what," Dru said, hating how small and fragile her voice sounded, and especially hating that she knew everyone else in the car could hear that. With an effort, she cleared her throat and forced a strength into her voice that she didn't truly feel. "Like it or not, we have the scroll now. And we have to find a way to end this. At any cost." She didn't turn to look at any of the others. She couldn't bear to meet their gazes. "In the meantime, Rane really, *really* needs to get herself back in balance." Dru resisted adding, *Before she drives me out of my mind.* "We need those crystals from the shop."

"Honey, I've got all that. And something even better." Pride swelled in her voice. "Did some research of my own, and I found stones that'll give you a fighting chance against the wraiths. Not moon rocks, but other rocks from outside this world. According to Tristram, anyway, any kind of meteorite will do."

A ray of hope lit Dru from within. Meteoric rocks were few and far between, and those containing crystals were even rarer. But if she had a crystal, maybe she could energize it enough to fight back against the wraiths. She thought fast, trying to think of meteoric crystals. "Do we have any olivine crystals? Maybe some pallasite?"

"Way ahead of you. I also found you a piece of coesite and a nice big hunk of stishovite, too. Well, I say 'nice' because of the size, not the looks. These rocks are ugly as all get-out. But most meteorites are."

"Opal, you're a genius."

"Don't have to tell me that. I know it. Problem is, we don't have much. Three rocks, total. Two of them are pretty small. But the big one is a pallasite specimen full of olivine crystals."

"I'll take it. Anything is better than nothing. What worries me is that those wraiths are still back there somewhere, still following us. I just don't know how to meet up with you and get those rocks from you. We can't turn around and come back, or we'll lead them straight back to you."

"Don't you worry about that. I've got someone here who owes me a great big favor," Opal said cryptically. The phone rustled as she pressed it against the fabric of her shirt. "You ready for this, sweetie?"

27

IMMORTAL CRAVINGS

This late at night, this far from the highway, the dingy off-brand gas station was the only source of light on the flat, dry plains. As the wind ruffled across fields of moonlit grass, Hellbringer sat at the edge of the buzzing fluorescent lights, exhaust pinging with residual heat. But even with the engine off, the black demon car was poised to explode into motion. Its sharp nose pointed back toward the desolate road, like an arrowhead notched and ready to fire into the night.

At the back of the car, Dru had the trunk lid open under the towering spoiler. Bent down, she rooted through the pile of forbidden books Salem had dumped in there with the spare tire and bumper jack. By the light of her phone, she flipped through crackling pages of ancient magic, desperately trying to find a spell that would help her locate a portal to the netherworld.

So far, she'd had zero luck. And it was increasingly difficult to avoid lingering over the darker passages in the books. Her morbid curiosity kept drawing her toward secrets she didn't really want to learn.

The handwritten pages whispered to her in the timeless language of sorcery, promising to give her everything she wanted, offering bargains no sane person would accept. Goose bumps rose on her arms just from glancing at the pages.

She felt dirty even touching these books, which was saying quite a bit after the disturbing restroom experience she'd just had inside the gas station. Leafing through the books was even worse. While some of them had actually belonged to her years ago—before Salem had surreptitiously "borrowed" them—she'd never so much as cracked them open before. Even back then, before she had faced the end of the world, she'd been too scared to look at their pages.

Now they might be her only hope.

A foot scuffed on the gravel scattered across the blacktop, making her jump. She almost let out a little scream before she realized it was Greyson. When he saw the look on her face, his forehead wrinkled in worry. "You okay?"

Her hands balled into fists of their own accord. She had to take a moment to compose herself before she spoke in an urgent whisper. "Where's Rane?"

He jerked his thumb toward the restroom that would live on forever in Dru's nightmares. "Salem's guarding the door."

"Yeah, the latch is broken. Don't want anyone busting in there."

Greyson grimaced. "I think he's there more to keep her from busting out."

Dru nodded, not really listening as she glared at the unhelpful books. She chewed on a fingernail.

Greyson realized what she was doing and suddenly looked even more worried. "Thought you said those books are forbidden."

"They are. For a very good reason. Plenty of reasons, actually." She took one last look at the page she was on, finally admitting it was useless. She shut the book with a harsh crackle and a puff of dust. For a moment, she just stood there, staring at nothing, breathing hard as she tried to accept what she'd feared all along.

Slowly, she turned to face Greyson, unwilling to tell him the truth. But she had to. "In order to get the scroll to Tartarus, we have to open a portal to the netherworld. The problem is, we've blown up every portal we've ever used. We have to find a new one. But I don't know how."

She wasn't sure what kind of response she expected from him, but Greyson didn't move a muscle. If anything, he grew more still, as if he had been somehow carved out of the night. Only his red eyes reacted, growing harder and tighter at the corners.

"You'll think of something," he said finally. "You already asked Opal for a green vivianite crystal."

"Sure, I can use that to *open* a portal. But first I have to *locate* one." Dru jerked a frustrated hand at the open trunk of the car. "I thought maybe, just maybe, there would be some helpful tip in these books. But everything in there is dark, and gross, and devious, and I'm not even sure I believe half of it. And I can't get back to the shop to do research. And we don't have any time. And there's no one to call. We have nothing. All we can do is keep running."

He stood unmoved, looking back at her with a certainty and confidence that she didn't share. "We'll find a way."

"*How?*" It came out as a bark, louder and harsher than she intended. Pent-up frustration burned inside Dru. "I've been turning it over and over in my head, trying to find a way. There are supposedly portals scattered all throughout the mountains, but I don't know where they are. It's not like there's a map." She realized with a start that it was her old friend Titus who had told her about the portals in the mountains. She felt a pang of regret when she remembered the terrible fate he had suffered. That led to a darker train of thoughts about all of the sorcerers she knew who had suffered and met horrible ends, and that dragged her toward despair. There was no hope. For them. For anyone. For the world.

"Hey," Greyson said, putting a big hand on her shoulder. He stepped closer, until she could feel the heat coming off his body. His presence brought a welcome reassurance she hadn't even realized she needed. It shook her loose of those dark thoughts.

But even as she looked up into the chiseled angles of his face, her attention kept wandering back to the open trunk. The books in there, packed full of secrets, kept tugging at the edges of her consciousness. Like a crowd whispering her name. It made her feel like someone important. Someone powerful. They promised her exactly what she wanted most.

All at once, she realized what the dark books were doing, and she stepped back, hands flying to cover her ears. "*Gaah!*" She saw Greyson's worried look, and rushed to reassure him. "Not you! It's not you. It's these stupid dark magic books, trying to get inside my head." She reached over and slammed the trunk lid with a steely finality. Her hands, all on their own, made nervous shooing-away motions. "*Bleeargh.* Those things are nasty. No wonder Salem keeps them bricked inside a wall."

Greyson regarded the shut trunk with one raised eyebrow. "Good. Glad it's not my breath."

"No, your breath is . . ." She took his arm and tried to finish that sentence in some way that wasn't the opposite of romantic. "Your breath is . . ." Inwardly, she cringed. How did you compliment a guy on his breath not being stinky?

Just when she decided the only way out was to just go ahead and kiss him, she was interrupted by a swirl of shadows that gathered together in the parking lot. The air quivered, and with a breath of wind, Ember was there.

Instead of her usual heavy, formless black coat, she wore a rich dark-red Victorian coat with intricate embroidery and twin rows of heavy brass buttons. She had changed, and it wasn't just her outfit. Instead of slouching down, she stood straighter and prouder than Dru had ever seen. And for the first time Dru could ever remember, Ember flashed her a smile. That was a shock.

But Dru was happy to see the thick cardboard tray she carried in both hands. It was loaded down with different-colored crystals that sparkled and shimmered beneath the harsh fluorescent lights of the gas station parking lot.

Ember glanced over both shoulders and nodded slightly to herself, as if confirming something she already knew. She pushed the tray toward Dru. "Here. These are for you."

Interestingly, Ember did not ask where Salem was. Or Rane. Considering the history between them—notably that Ember had a serious romantic fixation on Salem, and Rane accordingly wanted to commit bodily harm to Ember—it seemed highly unlikely that she wouldn't at least ask.

Meaning that she already knew they were inside the convenience store. Meaning that Ember hadn't teleported here straight from seeing Opal, but instead had probably first shown up out there in the darkness somewhere, beyond the edge of the light, and watched them until Rane went inside.

That creeped Dru out a little. She couldn't really blame Ember, a sorceress with few friends and many enemies. It made sense to check things out before arriving somewhere blindly.

But still. Creepy.

"Thank you so much," Dru said, meaning it, as she moved to take the heavy tray of rocks.

At that exact moment, the glass doors of the convenience store burst open and Rane lurched out. Her arms were laden with bulging plastic grocery sacks. Shiny bags of potato chips, boxes of snack cakes, and long spicy meat sticks stuck out in all directions. "Oh my God, I haven't had Ring Dings since high school!" she shouted, spewing chunks of brown devil's food cake and white creamy filling from her stuffed cheeks.

Salem followed behind her, frowning at what looked like a chocolate-covered hockey puck. He held it out at arm's length and studied it with almost scientific curiosity.

Both of them saw Ember and stopped.

Ember made longing doe eyes at Salem, but her expression instantly transformed into wide-eyed fear as she saw the crazed look frozen on Rane's face.

With a rustle, Rane dropped her bags to the ground, freeing up her fists.

Ember shrank back a step, still holding the tray, and visibly swallowed.

Dru stepped in to take the crystals, as much to keep them safe as to head off any impending violence. Rane had a habit of breaking everything around her, and Dru absolutely couldn't afford to let these crystals get damaged in the slightest.

Rane marched right up, still chewing furiously on the Ring Ding stuffed in her mouth.

"Wait," Salem called after her, but everyone ignored him.

Dru smiled as brightly as she could manage. "Thank you, Ember! For bringing these beautiful crystals! Also, they are incredibly useful!" She pulled the crystals out of the line of fire. Some of them rolled and sparkled in the light, catching Rane's attention. She stopped and stared, transfixed. Still chewing.

Dru gave Ember a meaningful look and a nod. *Go now. While you still can.*

Ember nodded and stepped back, touching the lapels of her long coat, preparing to teleport away to safety. But Rane's long, muscular arm shot out and wrapped around her neck, yanking her close. Ember let out a muffled squeak.

"You brought these crystals? For me?" Gasping with wonder, Rane drank in the sight of the rocks. She pulled Ember even closer, spewing tiny crumbs of devil's food cake as she spoke. "Can't believe it. That is *so* cool. I love you, dude." She nuzzled Ember affectionately.

Dru's jaw dropped open. She glanced from Ember's terrified expression to Salem's shocked look. Greyson just folded his arms and watched, slightly amused.

"Yes. Of course. I hope you feel better soon. *Uhh.*" Grimacing, Ember strained to extricate herself, but Rane's grip was like iron. "I'm sure you want—*uhh*—for Dru to cure you now. I wish you good fortune."

"Thanks, dude." Rane pulled until they were pressed cheek to cheek, and whispered. "You mess around with my guy, I will crush you. Like a bug."

Ember paled.

Rane kissed her on the cheek. "Otherwise? I love you, dude." She released Ember, who staggered back and held up her hands in surrender.

"Alrighty, then!" Dru said, much louder than absolutely necessary. "Everybody in the car. We've been here too long already. The wraiths are undoubtedly on their way, and we still have to find a portal to the netherworld. Which hopefully won't be impossible." She couldn't keep the bitterness out of her voice. "Come on."

"Wait." Ember edged back. She studied Dru for a moment, as if making a difficult decision, then spoke directly to Salem for the first time. "You have to tell her."

Dru didn't know what was coming next, but she had a bad feeling about it. "Have to tell me what?"

Rane roused herself from staring at the sparkling rocks and turned on Salem. "Yeah! What the hell?" She glanced back at Dru. "Wait, what?"

Dru gave her a reassuring look and shook her head, indicating the need for silence.

Salem just frowned deeply. No one spoke for a moment.

Ember cleared her throat. "About the hot spring."

"Hot spring?" Dru's alarmed gaze ticked back and forth between Salem and Ember, filled with horrible visions of the two sorcerers skinny-dipping in a bubbling, steaming mountain spring. She could only pray that the ferocity of her gaze could somehow squeeze an explanation out of them before Rane inevitably came to the same conclusion and committed grievous harm on Ember. Dru glanced nervously at Rane, who apparently hadn't caught up just yet, and cleared her throat. "Let's not talk about any of that. Time to go."

Salem let out a heavy sigh, then stuffed the Ring Ding in his mouth. His drawn cheeks bulged out as he chewed. "Hmm," he mumbled, looking pleasantly astonished at the taste. "Surprise, surprise." He pointed at Rane's groceries and motioned for Greyson to put them in the car. "Should take us probably three hours to get there. Maybe less, if we can count on our unholy driver here."

With obvious annoyance, Greyson snatched up the bags. "What makes you think I'll take you there?"

"Well." Salem carefully sucked melted chocolate off of his fingertip. "For one thing, there's a portal to the netherworld. What more do you want?"

28

THE DARK UNKNOWN

Just under two hours later, Hellbringer labored to climb up through the cold thin air of the Rocky Mountains. The winding dirt fire road was barely suitable for four-wheel-drive trucks, much less an old rear-wheel-drive street machine with barely any ground clearance. Rocks constantly banged inside the wheel wells and pinged off the underside of the car.

Dru had long since traded places with Salem, and now he hung out the open passenger window, stretching his sparkling fingers into the night. As he made spidery flicking motions, the jagged boulders jutting up from the road ahead sank down into the dirt or else lumbered aside, clearing the way for the low-slung demon car.

Greyson sat hunched over the steering wheel, gripping it tight. The moon was hidden behind a nearby mountain peak, so that outside the twin cones of their headlights, the surrounding slope was pitch-black. "I don't like this," he growled. "We're moving too slow. The wraiths are gaining on us. I can feel it."

Salem spared him only a brief, unhinged glance. "Has it occurred to you that we wouldn't have this problem if you'd had the foresight to bond with a demon-possessed *truck?*"

In the back seat, Rane held out an open box to Dru. "Want some Devil Dogs?"

"Again, no. Thank you."

"Fruit Doodles? They're Yankee-Doodle de-licious."

"Oh, my God. No."

This whole time, Rane had alternated between stuffing her face with junk food and chatting about every random thing that popped into her sugar-addled brain. Dru, exhausted by trying to keep up, finally tuned her out and instead focused on sorting through the heavy cardboard tray of rocks that threatened to crush her lap with every bump. By the light of her phone, she slid the crystals around the gritty cardboard, planning out the magic spell she would use to heal Rane and finally undo the damage wrought by the wraith.

And, not to put too fine of a point on it, finally make her shut up.

Opal had sent them a sizable chunk of hematite, as cloudy red as if it had been poured from the bottom of an old wine bottle, and shaped very much like a heart. Not like a cute Valentine's Day heart, but an actual human heart, which was more than a little macabre. Next to that was a polished bloodstone, streaked with complicated swirls of green, red, and tan that reminded her of the clouds of some gas giant planet as seen from space.

Opal had also thrown in a glittering pyramid of quartz, a golden fragment of iron pyrite, and a doorknob-sized chunk of fossilized wood. Plus Dru's jagged-edged green vivianite crystal, which she was glad to see again. But she wouldn't need that until they actually reached the portal.

If there even *was* a portal. Salem had been wrong or deliberately evasive plenty of times before, and she wasn't one hundred percent sure she could start trusting him now.

Dru picked up the heart-shaped red hematite and turned it over in her hands, shining the phone's light through it, looking for flaws. It was so well formed that Dru could already feel the subtle healing vibrations coming off of it in invisible waves. As always, Opal had the perfect eye for choosing crystals.

Dru gave Rane a sympathetic look. "You're being really cool about this, you know?"

Rane finished off the box and crumpled it. "Cool about what?"

"About losing your powers. I mean, personally, I think I would be freaking out right about now."

Rane's throat worked, as if unable to swallow down the last crumbs of the Fruit Doodles. "I'm not freaking out."

"I know. You're cool as a cucumber. Which is really impressive, considering."

Rane's nostrils flared. Her unblinking eyes bulged out, and her substantially sized hands started to shake. "I'm not freaking out about losing my powers. Why would I be freaking out?"

Uh oh. Dru patted her arm reassuringly. "No, oh, no. You're going to be fine. I promise. Don't freak out."

"I lost my powers." Rane's nostrils flared. "I can't do anything. I'm useless."

"No, no! You'll be all right. Really. We'll fix you up."

Rane's chin and lips trembled, and her breath came hard and raspy. "I am not freaking out!" she yelled.

"No, you're not!" Dru couldn't match Rane's volume, but she tried. "You're not freaking out! You're cool!"

Rane pressed her fists against the sides of her head. "I know! I am cool!"

"You're going to be fine!"

"Totally fine!" Rane's knees tried to curl up into a fetal position, but she was too big. There wasn't enough room in the back seat. In frustration, she wadded up the Fruit Doodles package into a crinkly fist-sized missile, and hurled it at Salem hard enough to smack his hat off the top of his head.

"Hey!" He fumbled to grab it before it flew out the open window. "What was that for?"

"This is all your fault." Rane unfurled her long body and sniffed the air, until she started to look dangerously nauseous. "Dude. Do you smell that?"

Dru's nose wrinkled of its own accord as a horrible stench filled the car. It was like someone had scrambled up an omelette out of an entire truckload of rotten eggs, then dumped it into an open sewer and forgot to put the lid back on.

Rane pinched her nose. "Oh, my God. Salem! Did you cut one loose?"

He sighed. "We're almost to the hot spring, Buttercup. That's just how the water smells."

Still holding her nose, Rane made a face. "No freakin' *way.*"

Unable to take the stench, Dru pinched her own nostrils shut too. "What *is* that? No water on earth smells that bad."

Salem smirked. "That's because it's not *from* Earth, darling."

"Whatever, dude," Rane said. "That's the last time I'm letting *you* eat a whole box of Ring Dings."

But as it turned out, Salem was right. They turned off the dirt fire road onto a gentle grassy slope, navigating by headlights around altitude-stunted pine trees until a swirling column of steam rose up ahead.

The hot spring was a churning pool of cloudy water at least thirty feet across, and almost perfectly round. Bubbles constantly frothed the surface, releasing foul-smelling gases. Marble-sized clusters of black, white, and green minerals bobbed in the shallows.

The natural pool bubbled in the center of a bleached-white halo of mineral-crusted rocks of all sizes. Some were as big as boulders, some as fine as sand, and all were worn smooth by the elements. No plants grew there, not even a single blade of grass. The water-rounded rocks were completely crusted with chalky minerals, making the pool and the whiteness surrounding it look like the mountainside had a vast eyeball, and it was open wide in terror.

Greyson left the headlights on when he shut off the engine, and the crushing silence that descended on them was broken only by the burbling of the boiling pool.

Salem got out and indicated the hot spring with a sweep of his pale hands. "Beautiful, isn't it? And also deliciously refreshing, if you're thirsty."

Dru made a face. "Good to know. Next time, I'll bring some loose leaf tea. And nose plugs." Dru got out of the car and set her heavy tray of crystals on Hellbringer's warm hood.

Foul-smelling steam curled in the headlight beams. On the far side of the pool were squat shapes that looked like long, carved stones. Dru adjusted her glasses and squinted until she could make out a fragmented ring of simple, squared-off benches sitting in the open, under the stars. Whether they had been broken by human hands or the harsh mountain weather, she couldn't tell from here.

"Doesn't look like any portal I've ever seen," Greyson said, leaning against Hellbringer's roof with his arms folded.

"Yeah," Rane chimed in. "For one thing, it's full of water."

Salem gave Greyson a sour look. "And you're the portal expert, I take it."

Greyson didn't budge. "Believe I've seen more netherworld portals than you have. And like she said, none of them were wet."

With an exaggerated display of patience, Salem produced an antique brass spyglass from an inner pocket of his black coat. With a quick snap, he extended it to its full length and held it out to Greyson. "Here. Put a big, fat demon eyeball on it and see for yourself."

Greyson gave the brass spyglass a long, suspicious look, and then took it. He raised it to his eye and frowned for a long moment. "Looks to me like . . . water."

"Oh, give me that." Salem reached out a long arm and snatched it back. "You're doing it wrong."

"You can't look through a telescope *wrong*."

"Apparently, *you* can." Salem stepped out of the headlight beams and into the darkness to take Rane's hand in his. His eyes glinted chips of reflected light. "Those wraiths must know by now what we're up to. They won't waste any time getting here. Better get a move on."

"Damn straight." Rane yanked his top hat off and bent to kiss him on the forehead. Then she shoved his hat back on crooked and turned to Dru as he struggled to right it. "You ready, cowgirl?"

Dru led Rane over to one of the cold, smooth stone benches at the edge of the light and set down the cardboard tray of crystals. Salem followed a step behind and watched as Dru carefully selected the crystals she needed.

Feeling the pressure of his gaze, she glanced up at him. "Do you mind?"

"Not at all." He settled down on an adjacent bench, still staring. "Carry on."

Stifling a tired sigh, Dru did her best to ignore him and handed Rane the chunk of fossilized wood.

She hefted it. "What do I do with this?"

"Nothing yet. It's just to give me a base reading. Get a good grip on it."

The tendons in Rane's hand flexed, and the muscles in her bare arm bulged out.

"Maybe not quite *that* good of a grip." Dru took a swirled green blade of agate, full of branching green markings that looked like plant leaves, and ran it all over Rane's body. She started at the fossilized wood and systematically moved up one arm and down the other, staying about an inch above her skin. The whole time, she concentrated on the green agate, straining to pick up any changes in its vibration. She spoke softly. "Moss agate helps nurture new growth, so I usually recommend it in the later stages of the healing process, as the body and soul grow to meet future challenges. But with you, I have to get ahead of the curve, because you always heal so darn fast."

"Vitamins," Rane answered simply. "Protein. Complex carbs. Hey, that tickles."

"Sorry." As Dru charged up the crystal, it grew more sensitive in her fingers, until it became an extension of her senses. She could feel Rane's heartbeat, the slow and steady intake of breath, the tension in her muscles as she shifted on the hard bench. This level of intimacy would have been awkward with anyone else, but she'd been through so much with Rane, it felt for a moment like the two of them were connected on a level beyond words.

Dru deliberately waited until she had checked everything else before she moved up to Rane's neck, where the wraith's cold, bony fingers had choked her. As the moss-colored agate traveled slowly up over her throat, it jumped in Dru's grip, and she gasped. She had braced herself against what she would find, but the damage was much more severe than she expected. Although the angry bruises were nearly gone from her skin, the invisible psychic wounds went much deeper. Jagged tatters of Rane's energy lay raw and exposed. When Dru found them, they convulsed in every direction, nearly knocking the agate out of Dru's fingers.

"*Ow.*" Rane winced.

Salem twitched. "Watch what you're doing."

Dru scowled at him. "I didn't even touch her."

"Are you sure you're qualified for this?" he said.

Dru pointed back toward Hellbringer. "If you can't stay out of this, go wait in the car."

Salem glowered at her. He didn't get up, but at least he remained quiet.

Taking a deep breath, Dru turned back to Rane. "Okay, I have to warn you, it looks like the wraith did a lot of damage to your psyche."

"No kidding?" Rane snapped.

"Yeah." Dru probed gently with the agate, not liking what she found. "Here's the bad part about healing superfast like you do. Your soul has tried to patch itself back together again, which ordinarily would be a good thing. But everything that healed improperly has to be re-broken to make you whole again." Dru gritted her teeth in sympathy. "I think this might get a little rough."

Rane let out a long sigh, and Dru could feel her warm breath against the night. "*Pshh*, yeah, right. Nothing you ever do is rough. You're the best. Like a little kitten. With superpowers."

"Oh, well. I wish *everybody* had that kind of faith in me." Dru couldn't help but glare at Salem, but apparently he didn't notice. She put the agate back into the cardboard tray and took out the smooth cylinder of swirled green-and-red bloodstone. Folding her fingers over it, she felt its cool heaviness start to warm in her palm.

Meanwhile, she picked up the heavy heart-shaped chunk of red hematite in her other hand. Mentally, she attuned herself to it until she felt comfortable with its entire crystalline structure. She had been preparing herself for this moment during the long drive. Now she finally started to charge up the crystal, and she was ready for the primordial red force that pulsed in its depths.

As the spring bubbled nearby, Dru suddenly remembered the map and newspaper clippings she'd seen above Salem's workbench. She turned to Salem. "This is the location you had marked on your map, isn't it? Where those tourists disappeared back in the 1920s."

He smiled faintly. "Not just the 1920s. They'd been disappearing every so often since settlers first found this place in the 1890s and tried to turn it into a health resort. Saps. The native tribe that originally lived in the area told them the pool was dangerous, but did they listen? Of course not. And as a consequence, I imagine some unfortunate health-seekers found themselves accidentally sucked into the netherworld. I'm sure that didn't work out well for them."

Dru suppressed a shudder at that thought.

But Salem didn't even bat an eye. "By the way, there are some collapsed buildings back that way." He waved vaguely into the darkness. "Nothing left but timbers and a rusted wood stove. Pretty boring, actually. The interesting part is the pool, which serves as a portal to the netherworld. Hence, the general creepiness surrounding us."

"Creepiness," Rane repeated. She stared in fascination at the hematite pulsing brighter and brighter in Dru's hands.

Dru could only shake her head at Salem. "Why do you never tell anybody about these things when you discover them?"

He leaned closer. "Because then it wouldn't be a *discovery*, would it?"

She felt her blood start to boil. "You're impossible, you really are. The carnotite crystal. The map to this hot spring. All this time you've had the scroll, you've been trying to find a way to send it back to the netherworld. Just like I've been trying to do. Why do you always hold out on me? We've been on the same team all along. Why don't you just tell me what—"

He stopped her with an upraised finger. "You're still relatively new to the whole sorcerer thing, so I'm going to give you a hall pass just this one time. But for the future, remember this. Sorcerers don't have *teams*. Teams imply messy concepts. Cooperation, shared enemies, trust. In magic, these things are slippery. They shift and change. Constantly."

"Not for me, they don't. I trust my friends. That never changes."

He actually looked sad for her, and then his suspicious gaze slid down the length of Hellbringer's sleek, menacing body. "Sooner or later, darling, that's going to get you killed."

Dru bit off her reply. She opened up her other hand to reveal the bloodstone she had warmed up in her palm. Tiny pinpricks of light bloomed inside it, surprisingly bright. Her anger at Salem was making her lose control over her energy flow. Before she could slow it down, the hematite in her other hand started to flash like an old-fashioned police gumball light.

Dru had meant to ease Rane gently into the uncomfortable healing process. But the finger-length bloodstone sparkled with hot golden lights, driven by Dru's temper, and the hematite pulsed bright red. Magic coursed through the crystals and sparked against Rane's wounded psyche much sooner and harsher than Dru intended.

A silent pop of light flared out around them, as if a camera flash had gone off. Rane's whole body went rigid. Every muscle stood out in the flare of light, circling her biceps with deep shadows, highlighting the crevices of her abs, hollowing out her cheeks. The petrified wood exploded in her tight fist, littering the ground with fragments, and she pitched backward off the bench as if she'd been kicked off by a mule.

Salem yelled in surprise and kneeled at her side.

"Rane!" Dru set down the crystals, now dark and cold, and rushed to her other side. A haze of tiny sparks swirled in the air around them, winking out one by one. She smelled burned hair. "Oh, my God, I'm so sorry!"

Rane coughed hard, again and again, blasting Dru with the foul odors of frosted cupcakes, salt and vinegar potato chips, and processed extra-spicy meat sticks. Dru gagged.

Still gasping for breath, Rane raised her fistful of petrified wood fragments and stared at it, going slowly cross-eyed. With a straining groan, she tightened her knuckles even harder, and all at once her hand turned a rich, striated brown. The effect spread down her arm and across her body, until Rane had completely transformed into petrified wood.

"It's working," Salem whispered. Then it became a shout. "It's working!"

"Rane!" Dru was afraid to touch her. "Are you okay? Talk to me."

Rane grinned, showing teeth that looked like wine corks. "Rock and roll, dude."

"*Heads up!*" Greyson shouted in alarm, and pointed out across the mountainside. The moon had finally risen above the peak. Silvery light spilled down, burnishing the silhouettes of the pine trees with platinum highlights and turning the grassy slope pewter gray.

In the far distance, an eerie brilliance streaked toward them. Then another, and another, spread far apart. Six widely spaced ghostly forms flew just above the mountainside, heading straight for them like heat-seeking missiles.

The wraiths of the Harbingers.

Rane rolled to her feet, stone fists bunched. "All *right*. Let's get it on!"

"No! This is no time to fight!" A cold shiver of fear ran through Dru. "Come on!"

"No way, D! I just got my mojo back! It's payback time."

"Everyone," Greyson barked, opening the car door, *"get in."*

Dru grabbed the cardboard tray of crystals. "Listen to me. We can't stand here and fight. We need to get the scroll into the netherworld. *Right now.*"

Salem smiled slightly. "You go. We'll cover you."

"Oh, for Pete's sake, Salem. Since when do you want to leave the fate of the world in my hands?"

He looked troubled by that thought. To Rane, he said. "She has a point. Into the car, Buttercup."

With an inarticulate growl of anger, Rane turned and ran with the rest of them back to Hellbringer.

Greyson slid behind the wheel. "Ready?" He turned the key, and Hellbringer rumbled to life.

After Rane and Salem got into the back, Dru flipped the front passenger seat back into place and got in. "Can somebody explain to me why this car was built with four seats but only *two* doors?" She wedged the cardboard tray down around her feet, wincing as the crystals all clattered together. She found the angular vivianite crystal and willed it to come to life. Its murky green depths twinkled, like sunlight playing through weed-choked water. Mentally, she summoned up the complex magical glyphs needed to open a portal to the netherworld.

The sea-green light of her vivianite crystal lit the car's interior with an unearthly underwater flicker. She poured in everything she had left after healing Rane, and was rewarded with a jolt of power that flowed through her entire body. Magic flared around the round rim of the boiling pool, then stirred up its depths, growing so intense that the light poured out across the mountainside.

"Go!" Salem yelled. "Go, go!"

Greyson looked to Dru.

She nodded.

Engine bellowing like a prehistoric creature, Hellbringer shot down the slope toward the bright pool. The spinning tires clawed for purchase first in the soft grass, then across the bleached-white pebbles, as the speed demon accelerated toward the blazing portal.

The wraiths swooped after them, ghostly bodies rippling in the night. But Dru blotted them out of her mind, focusing all of her attention on opening the blinding white portal to the netherworld. The moment Hellbringer passed through, she intended to snap it shut, trapping the wraiths here on Earth. Then, at last, they would be free of their pursuers.

She had only a second to worry that there was some kind of terrible miscalculation in her plan before Hellbringer plunged nose-first into the pool. But instead of splashing into a wave of churning water, she was hit by an icy blast of wind. It howled in through the open window, nipping at her skin, tugging at her clothes, swirling her hair.

The intense white light blew out everything else, blinding her. It shined through her skin, into her soul, crackling through her with an electrical sizzle that made her teeth ache. She wanted to call out to the others, but a vast rumble drowned out all sounds, so deep and reverberating that it shook her rib cage. Gravity whirled around her, yanking her back and forth in the seat.

Then they were through. The blinding light died away to a dark sky rippling with twisting colors, slashed through by the smoking trails of massive shooting stars. Below the horizon lay nothing but an ocean of eerie mist that rose and fell in undulating waves. They were no longer on Earth.

Instantly, she willed the portal to close behind her. The bone-shaking rumble stopped, unmasking the aggressive growl of Hellbringer's engine. The demon car drove along a narrow, elevated stone road, mere yards above the cloud ocean. It was a causeway, made of black cobblestones held together by magic that burned like molten steel just poured from the forge.

For a moment, Dru thought they were safe. Then she turned around to look behind them.

29
THE SHINING CITY

Hellbringer's headlights burned searing holes in the darkness. The speed demon roared down the causeway, only seconds ahead of the wraiths. The undead creatures had slipped through the portal after them, and now they swooped after the demon car in a ragged V-shaped formation, their ghostly bodies rippling with speed.

There was no escape, Dru realized. Not even here in the netherworld.

The dark sky overhead pulsed with mysterious ethereal lights that flared and faded away, cut through by fiery meteors that trailed oily smoke as they fell. In the far distance, shimmering needles jutted up from the eerie mist along the horizon, and Dru's breath caught in her throat at the sight.

The Shining City.

She recognized it instantly. This was the same strange city skyline she had first gazed at with Greyson, when he had carried her across the causeway in his strong arms. She remembered wondering how an entire city could possibly exist inside the netherworld, and pondering how it had come to be there in the first place. She still didn't know.

Back then, she had largely confined her magical activities to the safety of the shop. Since that day, she had explored so many things, discovered so much, and grown in power until she had become a sorceress in her own right. Yet now, somehow, she had even more questions than ever.

Hellbringer knew the way to the Shining City—that much was clear. The demon car roared down the open straightaways and growled around the corners, speeding down narrow pathways that were meant for foot travel. Every so often, a causeway would end at a mostly flat mesa of black stone. The tires bounced over the uneven rock, and bigger bumps banged the suspension, and then Hellbringer nosed onto the next cobblestone causeway and accelerated once more. The deserted magical roadway stretched out endlessly before them, suspending them over the churning mist of the netherworld.

At every turn, the wraiths followed right behind them. Their piercing eyes smoldered in the shadowy hollows of their eye sockets. Their hungry mouths gaped open, like a silent chorus of the dead. Yet their ravenous faces still retained a cunning intelligence that was unsettling to see. As they flew along just above the surface of the causeway, they swooped and swirled around one another, a chaotic tangle of flickering bodies and grasping fingers. Dru could only pray Hellbringer could outrun them.

The causeways became narrower as they went on, and Dru gripped the armrest so hard it made her fingers ache. She was afraid to lean out the window and look down. The rough edge of the cobblestones ended just inches outside the tires, and below that was nothing but eternal darkness.

These causeways had been built and expanded over the centuries by various ancient sorcerers, each with their own dreams of power. Some sought to carry out secret dark magic experiments in the highly charged environment of the netherworld. Others hid their treasures and secrets here, where no mortal being was ever likely to uncover them. And still others used the netherworld as a shortcut to traverse vast distances across the globe. A short trip down a single causeway could translate into hundreds or even thousands of miles of distance in the mortal world. Dru had once found that out the hard way.

Pushing those thoughts aside, she forced herself to turn around and look out through the back window, where the view of the causeway behind them was framed by Hellbringer's tall back wing.

In the back seat, Rane had become human again. She and Salem watched the wraiths intently, planning their next move. Their voices barely carried over the combined thunder of the engine and rumble of the rough road surface punishing the tires.

"We're not losing them." Rane's voice was high and tight with either fear of the undead or excitement at the prospect of battle. Probably both.

"At the same time, they're not gaining on us either. Not yet." Salem's cool tone sounded forced. "But sooner or later this demon ride will hit a dead end. If I can get out of the car now and get a straight shot at them, I can pick them off, one by one."

"They're ducking and weaving too much." Rane traced a finger through the air. "Tough to get a bead on one until it comes right at you. How about this: you focus on holding them back, and let them come at me one at a time. I'll pound them into next week. Dru got more space rocks. It'll work."

Salem swayed as they rounded a tight turn, and then he placed the long, slender fingers of one hand on her muscled arm. "Maybe let's avoid the direct approach this time, Buttercup."

"No. I've had enough of all this running around. You know what time it is?" She waited a moment for him to respond, but he didn't. "It's time to *kick ass*."

He just sighed.

She scowled at him. "Don't give me that. You didn't have your soul half yanked out through your neck." The car rattled and shook. "It's payback time. And I'm going to make these bitches pay through the nose."

He shook his head. "They aren't mindless creatures, love. They may be undead, but they are the dispossessed souls of sorcerers. Demented, obviously, but still sorcerers. Notice they aren't lighting us up with their spells right now. Either they're conserving their energy, or they're herding us somewhere." In the gloom of the darkened car, his black-lined eyes twitched, making him look even more crazed than usual. "They have a plan for us."

Rane cracked her knuckles. "Yeah, well. Everybody's got a plan. Until they get punched in the face."

"I have an idea," Dru offered.

Both of them turned toward her, swaying with the motion of the car. Rane's face seethed with anger, but it wasn't directed at Dru. She couldn't say the same for Salem, whose sharp eyes glared out from under the brim of his top hat.

Dru held onto the seat back for support as they swung through another curve. "We know that these wraiths are actually the Harbingers, removed from their bodies, right? Well, in the Harbingers' writings, they made several references to the Shining City. They never described exactly what it was, or where it came from, only that they intended it to be their refuge from doomsday. This was supposed to be their luxurious home base of operations and refuge while the mortal world burned down. When the apocalypse was over, their plan was that they would emerge to shape a brand-new world in their image. They thought they were going to be able to accomplish this pretty much right away, in 1969. They didn't realize it would take fifty years to break all the seals."

"Not *all* the seals." Salem's eyes narrowed dangerously. "There is still one left. For the moment."

Dru shook her head. It was always so hard to avoid starting a fight with Salem. "My point is, I bet the Harbingers thought they could just hang out here in the netherworld until the time came, like this was their own secret clubhouse. And you know, that makes a spooky kind of sense. In centuries past, ancient sorcerers opened portals to the netherworld so that they could come here and hide their most precious artifacts. Some of them built fortresses here. Conducted magical experiments that would be impossible to attempt in the mortal world. So you know, there's this history of sorcerers coming here to the netherworld. Briefly. But the important distinction is that once they were done here, they went home again before something rose up from the mists and devoured their souls. They didn't try to *stay* here, long term."

"Wham, bam," Rane said. "In and out."

"Exactly. According to the demon hunter Nicolai Stanislaus, humans can't survive in the netherworld forever. It's toxic here. Over time, it corrupts you. It slowly drains the life essence out of you," Dru said. "Lucretia told me that the other Harbingers were here in the Shining City, waiting for her. Maybe for decades. And if that's true, and they stayed here that long, then maybe that's how they became dispossessed. As time went by, their bodies eventually shriveled up, or just broke down. Eventually, they would have had to leave their bodies behind. They became these ravenous wraiths."

Rane looked chilled at the thought.

Salem's eyelids fluttered in annoyance. "All very fascinating, I'm sure. But we're in a bit of a time crunch right now. So let's skip ahead to your big idea."

Dru forced herself to look at the cluster of ethereal creatures swarming up the causeway behind them. Gleaming eyes burned holes through the darkness. "If we can find their bodies, we may be able to cast a spell to reverse the dispossession. I don't know what you call that. Un-dispossession? Repossession? Just plain old possession?" Dru tapped the back of the seat with a fingernail, thinking. "Anyway, if we can trap the Harbingers in their decrepit bodies, that should stop them dead. Or at least slow them down long enough for us to get away and take the scroll to Tartarus."

Rane made a face that was halfway between disgust and fascination. "Think their bodies are all mummified and gross by now?"

"Probably, yes."

Rane thought hard. "So then, they'll be like . . . undead zombie mummy sorcerers."

"Um . . ." Dru tried to visualize that. It didn't paint a pretty picture. "I guess?"

"Cool." Rane grinned like a hungry shark. "Means when I get done kicking their asses, they *stay* kicked."

Dru nodded. The logic was a little dubious, but it did make a satisfying kind of sense.

Salem flapped his hands as if shooing away a fly. "This is all immaterial at the moment."

"So are they." Dru pointed out the back window. "That's exactly the problem."

"Oh, ho ho," he snapped. "Regardless of the logistical problems with this brilliant scheme of yours, has it occurred to you just how vast and enormous the Shining City really is? How do you intend to find their moldering old bones in all of that?" He pointed past her, through the windshield.

Dru faced front again and gasped.

At these insane speeds, Hellbringer had covered at least ten miles while they'd been talking, maybe more. Now, the Shining City rose up before them in all of its glory, taller and more majestic than anything she had imagined. As far as she could see in either direction, countless towers jutted into the fiery sky, some of them branching off at angles, others curved into graceful arches. They were built like nothing Dru had ever seen before.

Facets and sharp angles glittered in a hundred different jewel tones. It was impossible to tell whether they were transparent, or whether they reflected the unearthly light of the netherworld, or both. Together, they formed a dazzling alien-looking metropolis that dominated the meteor-streaked skyline.

The black stone causeway beneath their tires, mortared by red-hot magic, shot arrow-straight through the city. Hellbringer roared onward through the mass of crystalline towers. Dru could only gape as the Shining City swallowed them up in its brilliance.

All this time, she had assumed that the city was a contemporary of Alexandria or the first settlers of ancient Damascus, or perhaps it was even older. Mesopotamian, maybe. There were countless old legends about cities such as Uruk, Eridu, or Ur that had been abandoned thousands of years ago and lost beneath the sands of time. She'd stayed up all night studying exotic mysteries like the vanished city of Ubar or the long-lost Iram of the Pillars, which no one had ever managed to find again, despite centuries of searching.

Some renowned scholars of the occult, including Valery Lafayette and Blake the Younger, had theorized that cities like Iram hadn't simply been buried in the desert or fallen victim to the elements, but instead had been wholly transported into the netherworld. After all, there were plenty of wild tales about mad sorcerers building towers or fortresses in this ghostly realm for their own purposes. Why not suck in an entire city and make it your own, if you had the power to do so?

But those stories never carried much weight with Dru. Even someone as formidable as Decimus the Accursed didn't have that kind of might. So the origins of the Shining City remained a mystery.

But now, looking out the window at the mirror-like walls flashing past, a hundred different colors shimmering at once, Dru knew without a doubt that this city was something else entirely. It wasn't a stone-block metropolis spirited away by some ancient sorcerer. It was far older and weirder than that. This was a city that wasn't built by human hands.

So who had made it, then? Demons? Angels, if there really were such a thing? Some long-vanished and never-discovered race far more powerful than mortal humans?

Absently, Dru pushed her glasses back up her nose as she stared wide-eyed up at the impossibly beautiful architecture soaring overhead. At their dizzying heights, the spires of the impossibly tall towers flickered with reflected light from the crazed skies above. They also flashed with their own inner power, like the silent flickers of heat lightning on a hot summer night. She felt sure that the city was not dead after all, but merely dreaming, waiting to be woken up again when the time came.

In her giddiness at being in the center of such an astonishing discovery, she momentarily forgot everything else around her. Her heart beat faster, until her arms and legs tingled with excitement. Every fiber of her being wanted to get out of the car and go explore this wondrous mystery. She could spend a lifetime here, delving into its secrets. As the breathtaking crystalline city swept past in all its slumbering glory, she had to clap her hand over her mouth to keep from laughing out loud.

Then Hellbringer made an abrupt right turn on screaming tires, and she was thrown against Greyson's broad shoulder. He caught her effortlessly and spared her a tight grin, no doubt picking up on the childlike wonder written all over her face. "Buckle in," he warned her. "Hellbringer is taking us down."

She wanted to ask when, where, and how, exactly. But then the answer loomed up before her in the form of a towering archway that jutted up from the heart of the unearthly city. The two towers that formed it were too brilliant to look at directly, but they gradually curved toward each other and joined at a distant point, easily a hundred feet overhead.

She realized with a jolt that it bore an uncanny resemblance to the archway that the Harbingers had built behind their desert mansion back in 1969. Only this one was much taller, much narrower, much more alien in proportions. And where the desert archway had been dark, carved stone filled with bright light, this portal was its exact opposite: brilliant crystalline stone holding pitch darkness.

This was the opening Dru had witnessed with her scrying spell. This was where Decimus the Accursed had made his descent into Tartarus, so that he could steal the apocalypse scroll and set the world on the path to utter destruction.

As Hellbringer hurtled toward the unholy gloom, Dru had only seconds to reach down to the carpeted floor at her feet and blindly find the scroll. As her fingers closed over its unnaturally cold curl of raspy parchment, Hellbringer plunged them into a darkness even deeper than the netherworld itself.

The last thing she thought before they entered the portal was that in all of human history, only a handful of mortals like her had descended this far of their own free will, and fewer still had returned to tell the tale. But for Hellbringer, this meant coming home for the first time, back to the lawless fiery pit of the abyss that had spawned him. How would that affect the speed demon, being back among his own kind—and what would that mean for his passengers?

30

UNDER A HOLLOW SKY

Dru clutched the scroll tight to her chest as Hellbringer screamed downhill into the darkness. The unrelenting descent made her stomach try to crawl up into her throat. Rough black rock rose high on either side, disappearing beyond the reach of the headlights, reflecting the roar of the engine so hard that its echo drummed into Dru's bones. But the demon car didn't slow down. If anything, it sped up as it hurtled down into the depths.

Salem leaned forward from the back seat, gripping Dru's shoulder with his wiry fingers. "We have a problem!" he shouted over the thudding noise of the exhaust. "Where are the wraiths?"

Dru looked back. The spear of light marking the archway rapidly shrank into the distance. Everything else around them was impenetrable darkness.

"We must have lost them," Dru said, wondering why she didn't feel more relieved. "The wraiths must not be willing to follow us down here."

Salem's eyeliner-ringed eyes looked haunted. "No. Those are the Harbingers. They're willing to do *anything*."

He was right, Dru realized. Something was terribly wrong.

She peered out through the darkened windows, trying to look in all directions at once. Somewhere from above came a flicker of light, so faint and distant that she wouldn't have noticed it if she hadn't been looking for it. It danced like a bolt of lightning, but there was something about the quality of the light itself that she recognized immediately.

It was a magic spell.

All this time, the wraiths had chased them, and never once had any of them cast a spell. Not even here, in the netherworld, when they had been right behind Hellbringer. At first, she had theorized that they couldn't use their magic here in the netherworld. But that wasn't true at all, she realized. Instead, they had been holding off until they could spring a trap.

An icy spike of fear drove through her as she realized what that meant. She grabbed Greyson's arm. "Stop the car! *Now!*"

Greyson always checked with Dru before he did anything drastic. Usually just a silent glance, waiting for her to nod or shake her head. The level of trust he placed in her was humbling, in a way, and one of the things that she had grown to love about him. It really felt like the two of them operated as an inseparable team. But this time, Greyson didn't so much as glance her way. There was no time.

Instantly, he slammed on the brakes.

The tires howled in protest, a heart-stopping shriek that clawed at Dru's eardrums. Hellbringer's long nose dove down toward the ground, as if the car was bowing. Everything inside, including her, catapulted toward the windshield. Rane grabbed her shoulders. Dru had forgotten her seat belt, and only Rane's catlike reflexes and unbreakable grip kept her safely pinned in the seat. Greyson, meanwhile, caught Salem as he pitched over the seats between them and nearly face-planted into the dashboard.

The speed demon only grudgingly slowed to a halt, swishing back and forth on screaming tires. The inside of the car filled with the scorched smell of overheated brakes and the throat-coating stench of melted rubber. Thick white tire smoke drifted through the headlight beams.

When at last they came to a full stop, Salem glared up at her from the vicinity of her knees, his hair tangled over his face. "That's a little bit *dramatic*, don't you think?"

Before Dru could answer, a deep rumble shook everything. The terrifying sound of falling rocks tumbling and cracking against one another. By the time Dru realized it what it was, Salem was already trying to shove her out of the car.

"Out, out, *out!*" he yelled, pushing at her. His skinny arms were remarkably strong.

As he started climbing across her lap, she pushed the door open and got out. The air was dry and unnaturally hot, thick with choking fumes, and it shuddered with the weight of unseen boulders plummeting down from above. Dru gaped up at the flickering outlines of the wraiths high above them, swooping and swarming through the chasm. Flashes of magic—arcs of lightning, streams of multicolored fire, whirlwinds of sparks—blasted loose an avalanche of falling rocks.

The wraiths were using their magic to bring down a rock slide. The ground trembled beneath Dru's feet with the impact of each falling boulder as it hit the ground ahead of Hellbringer. The demon car—and all of them inside it—would have been crushed if Greyson hadn't stopped in time.

Salem scrambled out of the car on his hands and knees. Instantly, he was on his feet. His fingers swept spidery patterns through the air as he strode around in front of the car and across the headlight beams. An ethereal haze surrounded his body, noticeably purer than the eerie glow of the wraiths.

Ahead, rolling clouds of rock dust were blown away by the invisible force of his magic, creating hollow tunnels in thin air. At the hazy limits of Hellbringer's headlights, dark rock boulders the size of wrecked cars crashed against one another and clattered down, threatening to block the only entrance to Tartarus.

But the angle of their descent changed abruptly as Salem swept his hands side to side, buffeting them with magic. They tumbled like asteroids colliding in deep space.

For a heart-stopping instant, Dru's mind flashed back to the horrible moment when Salem had once stood at the foot of a mountain, facing down an oncoming avalanche. Back then, he had been unable to stop the falling rocks completely, and they had buried him so deeply Dru had been sure he was dead. She couldn't bear to watch that happen again.

But this time was different. This time, Salem wasn't standing in the kill zone right beneath the falling rocks, and he wasn't trying to stop them, exactly. Instead, he swept them left and right as they fell, left and right, piling them up on the sides, leaving a pathway open through the center. He steered one particularly large slab into the middle, forming a crude capstone on top. Suddenly, he had built an archway of his own, and the rest of the rock slide proceeded to pile up atop it harmlessly.

Rane got out of the car and touched the bare steel of the door latch mechanism. Her entire body turned into shining steel, as if she'd been dipped in quicksilver. She pointed past Salem and gave a metallic shout over the thunderous roar of the falling rocks. "D! He made a tunnel!"

"I see it!" Dru pushed her glasses up her nose. "That guy must be really good at Tetris."

"Dude, you have no idea."

Above, the wraiths had obviously figured out what Salem was doing. With a chorus of bloodcurdling screeches, they swooped down to attack.

The wraiths intended to trap them here in this chasm, Dru realized, and drain their souls one by one. Worse, Dru had delivered the apocalypse scroll right to them. Practically laid it at their feet. All they had to do was come down here to collect it.

Sinuous green fireballs and jagged bolts flew from the wraiths' skeletal hands. Salem sidestepped and deflected them with a rippling blast of force, but he was horribly outnumbered.

"I gotta help him!" Rane pointed a metal finger at the cardboard tray sitting on the floor in front of the passenger seat, and the crystals that were scattered on the carpet around it. "Find me those space rocks! I'm going to crush them into powder and go all Armageddon on these jack-wads."

"Hang on!" Dru bent and searched around the dirty carpet for the small pieces of coesite and stishovite, but everything had been thrown in random directions by the emergency stop. She found the glittering pyramid of quartz and the shiny fragment of pyrite. But she couldn't find the rocks that she desperately needed. "Son of a Bieber! Where are they?"

Greyson leaned over from the driver's seat, where he held onto the apocalypse scroll. An unspoken question formed on his face.

She tried to describe what she was looking for. "The space rocks. Two brown, lumpy things, look a little melted. Kind of shaped like an Almond Joy."

For an agonizing moment, neither of them found anything. Then he reached beneath his seat and came up with a chunk of gray metallic stone. The tiny yellow crystals embedded in it flickered like yellow caution lights in the glow from the dashboard. "How about this?"

Dru was about to say no, but she suddenly had a better idea. "Perfect!" She snatched it from him and turned to hold it out to Rane. "This is pallasite."

Rane looked confused. "The crystals?"

"No, the crystals in it are olivine." Dru waved her other hand at Rane's even more puzzled expression. "That's not important right now! What's important is the rock itself." Dru tapped the stone's rough outer edge. "Pallasite is basically a chunk of meteorite, high in nickel and iron, and it's extraterrestrial. The book said the wraiths can only be harmed by a rock that comes from beyond our world. You can transform into this." In her excitement, Dru practically shoved it in Rane's face. *"Be the rock!"*

When Rane finally understood, a predatory grin split her face. She clamped her steel fingers over the pallasite with a metallic clank. A darker, rougher texture swept across her skin as she transformed into meteoric nickel and iron, making her look like she'd been chiseled out of an asteroid.

A shrieking wraith swooped down toward them like a fiery comet with outstretched fingers and a black cavern of a mouth. The air in front of it shimmered as it prepared to unleash a spell.

With long, fast strides that rang like a church bell, Rane charged the wraith and swung a bulging fist made of solid meteoric iron. The wraith was so intent on casting its spell at Dru that it didn't seem to consider Rane a threat. It raised its skeletal hands high, crackling with magic, just as Rane's fist connected with its face.

With a sound like a wave crashing on a rocky beach, the screeching wraith broke apart into pinpoints of light and swaths of eerie mist. It scattered in pieces—arms, head, ribcage—and all of them turned toward Rane as if they were part of a whole body. Its fingers clawed with electric blue swirls of magic. They erupted into deadly jets of sizzling gas-blue flame.

But Dru was already holding out the sharp-edged chunk of metallic pallasite in both hands. She charged it with as much energy as she could manage, and immediately found herself on unfamiliar ground. The rock was older than the Earth itself, and the crystals inside it felt like nothing she had ever connected with before. Having originated in deep space, the pallasite gave off the most exotic vibrations she had ever experienced. They felt raw and hostile, yet at the same time incredibly powerful.

The little yellow peridot crystals embedded in the pallasite suddenly flared to life, releasing her energy as stabbing beams of blinding yellow light, all of them aimed in random directions. Several of them shot through the wraith's jets of blue flame, refracting them like a prism so that they missed Rane completely.

The wraith's dismembered parts snaked in between the yellow beams. The clawed hands raised to attack again.

But Rane didn't give the wraith a chance to recover. Now she was a living weapon, forged from head to toe out of the wraith's only weakness, and she exploited that to full effect. She threw a flurry of punches, jabs, and kicks at the severed portions of the wraith, individually pounding its arms, torso, and head into sparkling particles of mist. They kept swirling around and trying to reform into a whole being once more, but Rane pressed the attack relentlessly.

Salem, though, wasn't faring as well. His invisible barriers barely held off the attacks of wraiths on three sides, while two more creatures streaked down toward him from above. "Little help here!" he yelled.

As Rane pivoted and charged to his rescue, Dru focused on the pallasite crystal in her hands. It was so alien that it was almost impossible to control, but she aimed its berserk yellow beams the best she could.

They shot out in all directions, stabbing through the darkness, slashing across the shimmering bodies of the wraiths. Geysers of hissing golden sparks burst out where they hit, drawing bone-chilling wails from the wraiths.

Momentarily distracted, their attention shifted to Dru, and a jolt of fear shot through her as all those pairs of burning, ghostly eyes turned her way.

Salem pounced on the momentary opportunity, and immediately swept his invisible force across them, turning their spells against each other before they could use them against Dru. The incompatible spells crossed one another, and shuddering explosions pounded the air overhead.

Meanwhile, Dru wrestled with her pallasite crystal. It behaved unlike any other crystal she had ever used, and the results were frighteningly unstable. The more she charged it up, the more unpredictable it became. Its vibrations grew greater and more dangerous, making the rock tremble in her hands. She tried to tamp it down, but instead it bucked against her, as if desperate to escape her grasp. It nearly knocked her flat on her back.

She didn't see the wispy wraith hovering above her until it was too late. It was the same wraith Dru had first encountered in the darkness at Salem's place, and it sent a flurry of shadow tentacles spiraling toward her.

Most of them were struck by the random yellow beams of energy streaming from the wildly kicking meteorite. Those severed tentacles atomized into smoke with a harsh crackle. But one of them made it through and struck the pallasite hard, tearing it from Dru's grasp.

It soared up into the air, going dark the moment it left her touch. Dru hoped against hope that Salem would catch it with his magic and return it to her, but he was busy fighting for his life, with Rane at his back.

Dru stared in horror as the pallasite crashed to the ground and smashed into a hundred tumbling fragments.

A deliriously optimistic part of her brain insisted that maybe she could salvage it. Maybe there was some small piece of the pallasite she could scoop up and use to continue the fight. But she knew in her heart that the crystal was done for. And so was she, if she stuck around.

Hellbringer pulled up and the passenger door swung open right beside her. "Get in!" Greyson called to her.

"But, but, the crystal—"

His red eyes blazed. His right hand, holding the apocalypse scroll, rested on the gearshift knob. The vibration of the rumbling engine made the silver tines at the ends of the scroll glint in the dashboard lights. He lifted it and pointed at the archway Salem had built for them. *"Get in!"*

Dru immediately turned and looked for Rane. She was fighting back-to-back against the wraiths, holding her ground, but just barely. She was only a dozen yards away, but the distance between them swarmed with ghostly wraiths and fiery spells. There was no way for Dru to reach her. No way to help her.

Any moment, the wraiths would turn away from Rane and go after the scroll. Dru would lose the only opportunity she had to take it through the archway and down to Tartarus, and end this nightmare forever. But going now would mean leaving Rane and Salem to fight the wraiths alone.

Rane looked over at Dru, and the two of them locked gazes. Dru could see that Rane had reached the same grim conclusion.

"Come on!" Dru yelled, frantically waving for her to come back.

Rane just shook her head. A savage grin lit her face as she punched another wraith to smoky pieces. "Go! We'll hold them here!"

"No!" Tears burned in Dru's eyes as she beckoned with both arms. Leaving one of her best friends behind, in so much danger, was simply not an option. Dru refused to accept it. "Come on!"

From the car, Greyson yelled, "Dru! We only have one shot at this!"

Wraiths came at Rane from opposite sides. At the last second, one of them snapped its skull-like head in Greyson's direction, as if suddenly noticing he held the scroll. Unearthly light rippled across its ghostly body as it turned toward them, preparing to attack.

Rane dodged around the other wraith and caught the skull-headed wraith with a high kick, severing one of its long arms and earning a hateful screech from it.

"Go!" Rane shouted furiously. "Go, go *go!*"

The longer Dru stood there, the slimmer their chances became. Every cell in her body wanted to stay and help Rane fight, but without the pallasite crystal, there was nothing she could do.

Numb, she sank into the passenger seat.

The door slammed. Hellbringer charged into motion.

Dru turned to look behind them, trying to catch one last glimpse of Rane. But just then Hellbringer shot into the crude rock archway. They squeezed through an opening so tight the side mirror bent in half with a bang, dragging sparks off the rock.

They shot onward through the darkness, descending even farther than Dru thought possible. Far ahead, a hellish red light stirred before them. It prodded Dru's deepest instinctive fears, those that shied away from the images of searing pain and certain death brought by fire.

They had reached Tartarus.

31

HELL TO PAY

The torturous journey that had taken Decimus the Accursed agonizing days to complete now flew by beneath Hellbringer's tires at breakneck speeds. The sleek black demon car sliced across a wasteland the color of dried blood, blasting up a dark cloud of dust that hung suspended in the foul air behind, marking their long passage across a dead realm where few mortals had ever dared to tread—and fewer still had ever returned alive.

For the most part, Tartarus was as flat and dark as an old cast-iron skillet, and it felt about as searing hot. The only light came from jagged gulches that cut across the ground here and there, freely flowing with hot lava. The molten rock spurted crimson and gold, and every shade in between, wavering under ripples of superheated air. Clouds of incandescent gas blasted skyward, spraying red-hot droplets of lava in all directions.

The bloodred sky pressed down low overhead, full of endless swirls of smoke. They appeared to coalesce into vast agonized faces the size of cities, twisted into wordless screams that melted away as quickly as they formed. In the distance, smaller specks moved with lazy deliberation, resembling flocks of birds. But Dru knew they weren't birds, not here in the deepest realms of the abyss.

She held the unnaturally cold scroll tight against her chest, but it gave her no relief from the fear that clutched her. Everything around her—the sky, the light, the air itself—felt so incredibly *wrong*. It made her feel delirious, itchy, and uncomfortable inside her own skin. Deep down inside, every instinct told her that she should never have come here, that she needed to turn around and flee, and never look back.

But she had no choice. They had to keep going.

As Hellbringer altered course to avoid a lava-filled ravine, Dru broke out in a clammy sweat, as much from the oppressive heat as from fear. She bent closer to the dashboard, scrutinizing the rows of chrome-ringed analog gauges and silver rocker switches. "It's so *hot* in here. How do you turn on the air conditioning in this thing?"

"Air conditioning?" Despite the danger pressing in on all sides, Greyson's red eyes crinkled at the corners with amusement. "This is a muscle car."

"And? So?" Dru tugged at her low collar, desperately trying to flap some air through it. It didn't work. "I'm pretty sure muscle cars are allowed to have air conditioning."

"Not back in 1969."

"Oh. Great. Because sweating is more macho. That's an interesting design philosophy."

"Hey, let me show you a trick. See these?" Greyson reached forward and turned the chrome window crank, rolling down his window to let in a blast of oven-hot air. "See? So much better." He smiled, but the tension behind it was obvious. She could tell from the way he gripped the steering wheel tight, the way he glanced in all directions, alert for danger. His great-looking smile was just meant to try to lessen her fear.

It didn't work, but she decided to play along anyway. "Oh, very funny." Dru had to raise her voice to be heard above the high-speed wind howling into the car. She rolled her window open too, gagging on the foul air of Tartarus. She could barely breathe it. It stripped every last drop of moisture out of her throat, replacing it with soot and ash.

She struggled to open the little triangular vent window in front of the main window, but when she finally got it, she was pleasantly surprised that it directed a slightly faster stream of air right across her lap. It didn't cool her off much.

Hellbringer changed directions again, giving a wide berth to a churning pool of lava the size of a baseball stadium. Dru had to turn her face away from the scorching heat. Ahead of them, the ground rose toward a lone mountain peak, truncated at the top, and Dru immediately recognized it from her vision of Decimus's journey.

She pointed. "That's it! That's where we need to bring the scroll." A surge of optimism rose up inside her. At last, after all this struggle, their objective was finally in sight. Dru allowed herself to dare to believe they actually had a chance to survive this.

Greyson nodded with satisfaction. "Good. We need to get Hellbringer out of this place. The sooner we can, the—*whoa!*" He swung the wheel as a helicopter-sized presence burst up from the lava pool and flapped directly into their path on blazing leathery wings, trailing droplets of molten fire. Its newly formed skeletal body burned with white heat, convulsing as it struggled to fly.

Dru braced herself against the dashboard as Greyson whipped them around the burning creature. Hellbringer's tires howled in protest, and they lurched into a diagonal skid. The beating wings swept over them, inches above Hellbringer's long hood, and the thing turned a skull-like face to snap hungrily at Dru with lava-dripping jaws. The heat radiating from its knife-like teeth scorched her face.

Then it was gone from the open window as Hellbringer streaked past. With a jolt, Greyson pulled them out of the skid and downshifted, sending them hurtling away from the creature and toward the mountain.

"Dru!" He reached for her.

"I'm okay." She gave his hand a brief squeeze and let him return it to the gearshift. Her heart hammered in her chest as she checked to make sure all of her body parts were still attached. Reassured, she turned around and leaned her head out of the car, into the wind-stream. Behind them, the flapping creature struggled to lift itself into the twisted sky. It watched them go with a creepy intelligence.

Dru shivered. "Congratulations. It's a bouncing baby demon. How charming."

Greyson's forehead wrinkled deeply with worry. And maybe a little confusion.

"Tartarus is where demons are spawned," Dru explained. "Apparently, they're born hungry. And they love to feed on the mortal souls of people like you and me. So, they're looking at us like Hellbringer's delivering them a pizza."

His troubled gaze dropped to the dashboard, and Dru could practically read his thoughts.

"Yeah . . ." she said slowly. "On the inside, Hellbringer is one of those things. Sorry."

Greyson's jaw set in a hard line. "That explains why he seems so . . . conflicted."

"About taking us to the mountain?"

"About being here at all."

Despite her raging fear of burning to death in the fires of Tartarus and having her soul devoured by bloodthirsty demons, a small part of Dru lit up with scientific curiosity. "When you say that Hellbringer is conflicted, do you mean that you're picking up on those sensations? Or that Hellbringer is actually behaving strangely? And, follow-up question, are you yourself experiencing any strange conflicting feelings?"

Greyson shook his head, but Dru couldn't tell whether he really wasn't sure, or whether he just didn't want to talk about it. He steered them up over a gentle rise edged by a steep cliff. The tires grumbled on the uneven rock. "Now is not a good time for follow-up questions."

Dru was about to firmly disagree, but the words died in her throat as a congregation of demons soared over the ridgeline, blotting out the tortured sky with fiery wings and sinuous tails. She had never seen so much pure evil in one place.

She shrank down into the seat, trying to make herself invisible. "Oh, what I wouldn't give for a good solid galena crystal right about now." She mentally kicked herself for not bringing any, though she had to wonder if it could even exist in this realm of such intense demonic power. The moment she tried to power it up, it might explode in her hand. It might even act as a beacon, drawing the attention of every demon for miles.

Greyson peered upward as the demons winged overhead and passed by, heading for the far horizon. "I think Hellbringer is keeping us safe. At least for the moment."

Dru nodded to herself, although she wasn't entirely sure she bought into Greyson's explanation. In a strange way, this was a homecoming for the speed demon. This forsaken place was the hellish abyss where Hellbringer had been spawned in the first place. It probably knew some of the other demons around here. That was a chilling thought, despite the volcanic heat pressing in on them.

Hellbringer climbed steadily up the black rock mountainside. Soon, the way became too steep to head directly toward the summit, and Greyson steered them on a long ever-rising spiral toward the top. Aside from occasional ridges and crevices where the rock had expanded or broken over time, the surface was unnaturally smooth. It looked less like the snow-capped peaks of the Rocky Mountains she was familiar with, and more like some kind of vast black iron plate that had been pounded up from below to form a towering cone.

As the rise became steeper, Hellbringer's huge engine strained, and the tires scrabbled for purchase on the smooth slope. The car tilted farther and farther to the right, until Dru was leaning over toward Greyson just to remain upright. She glanced hopefully past him toward the top of the mountain, but it was still so far away.

Out the open window on her right, the volcanic plain stretched out far below, crisscrossed with lava flows and dotted with flaring pools of light. Thickening smoke obscured it in the distance, but it didn't stave off the vertigo that threatened to steal Dru's breath away.

With a pitiful wail, the back tires slipped. Dru's stomach lurched as they slid sideways. They dropped only a few feet, but it was enough to send a spike of pure animal terror shooting through Dru's veins. She clutched at Greyson's arm, suddenly filled with terrifying visions of falling out the open passenger-side window and plummeting to her death.

She struggled to catch her breath. "Stop. Stop the car. We have to walk from here. Or climb."

Grimly, he nodded, clearly not liking the idea. "I think you're right." He parked Hellbringer on the steeply tilted slope and shut off the engine. The ghost of its rumble kept on reverberating in her ears, even though now the loudest sound was the hot wind sweeping down the mountain-side, clawing at her hair and pulling at her dry skin.

She tried to figure out how she was going to get out of the car without falling, and found herself clutching at Greyson's arm again. She swallowed.

"Hang on," he said. "We'll get out my side."

To her surprise, he didn't even open the door. With a grunt, he heaved himself up onto the seat and climbed out the window. Then he reached back in for her. "Come on."

Clutching the apocalypse scroll tightly, she took his outstretched hand. With considerably more difficulty, she climbed out beside him and stood unsteadily on the slope. The wind picked up again, snatching at her clothes and hair, and especially at the scroll, as if it was trying to pluck the artifact from her grasp.

She tried not to think about how dangerous the scroll was, and instead focus on getting to the top. She took a deep breath, squared her shoulders, and also made sure her glasses were firmly in place. Because the last thing she wanted to do was drop them and end up stumbling around blindly on top of a fiery mountain in Hell.

"Ready?" Greyson said.

Dru nodded and started up the steep slope. The rock wasn't quite as slick as she had feared, but it definitely didn't offer an overabundance of grip to her non-hiking shoes.

She had made it only a dozen steps when a high-pitched scream rose up from somewhere far below. It hit the very top edge of Dru's hearing and climbed beyond it, from a whistle to a wail, and as sharp and piercing as shattering glass. She looked out over the vast volcanic plain, searching out the source of the sound.

Far below, in the shadows at the base of the mountain, a deeper darkness gathered. Shadowy forms, shrunken to tiny black dots by distance, massed in a canyon between two tall ridges. Dru rubbed her glasses on her shirt to clean them and looked again, squinting into the distance. Tiny pinpoints of light burned in the darkness, and Dru had to squint to make out what they were.

When she finally saw, she wished she hadn't. Those dots were glowing eyes. A horde of demons gathered at the base of the mountain.

The shrill call came again. Greyson grimaced, as if the sound were a hundred times louder. "No," he muttered, shaking his head as if trying to clear it. "Don't do it."

She wanted to ask him what he meant, but he wasn't talking to her. He was talking to Hellbringer.

The call came a third time, and Dru realized what was happening only when Hellbringer's engine thundered to life. The speed demon's kin were calling him home.

Greyson's eyes flared even brighter red. He strode downhill toward Hellbringer with his palm outstretched in a universal gesture. "STOP!" he commanded, in a voice with so much force behind it that Dru felt it as much as she heard it.

She had seen him command Hellbringer and other speed demons before, compelling them to obey his orders by the sheer force of his will. But this time, things were different. Either the tortured landscape of Tartarus somehow negated his power, or the call of the other demons was too strong for Hellbringer to resist. Its back tires suddenly spun out peals of white smoke, and the speed demon launched into motion.

Greyson charged after the car, arms pumping. At the last moment, he leaped, barely catching the chrome door handle.

Dru watched, hand clasped over her mouth in horror, as the speed demon hurtled headlong down the mountain slope, dragging Greyson alongside. Just when she feared he would be crushed, he managed to pull himself up, and he climbed headfirst in through the open window.

But Hellbringer didn't so much as slow down. It streaked down the mountainside toward its demon brethren, until it plunged into shadow and vanished, taking Greyson with it. All that was left behind was the fading roar of its engine, and soon even that dwindled away to nothing.

Dru stood alone on the mountainside, gripping the apocalypse scroll tight. She couldn't fight off the overwhelming pain of betrayal that cut her to the core. This wasn't the first time Hellbringer had taken Greyson away from her. But the awful realization dawned on her that this might finally be the last time she ever saw either of them.

It was her own fault, she realized. She had trusted Hellbringer, even here in the abyss, when she should have realized the danger. Hellbringer wasn't human. It wasn't even really a car. At its heart, it was a diabolical demon. She had tried everything she could to bring it over to the side of good, to earn its respect and gain its help in saving the world. But in the end, Hellbringer had to choose its own path, no matter how much trust she placed in the speed demon.

Salem's words came back to haunt her: *Sooner or later, darling, that's going to get you killed.*

And the worst part was that she wasn't the only one. What about Salem and Rane? What about Greyson? How could any of them survive this awful place, with Hellbringer now turned against them?

Rather than let those dark thoughts crush her, she focused on the present. She had exactly one job to do. Bring the apocalypse scroll to the top, throw it back into the pit where it belonged, and save the world. In the end, her own life wasn't the most important thing. Everyone and everything else depended on her right now. She wouldn't stop until she had made sure that doomsday was over, once and for all.

She turned and climbed up the steep slope. It wasn't far in terms of absolute distance, but the going was rough. Here at the top, the mountain was buckled and cracked by Decimus's magic. She had to wedge her feet in footholds, one at a time, and clamber over the broken rocks. Athletic pursuits were not her strong point, and never was this more painfully clear than right here.

If it weren't for the scroll, at least she would have had two hands to work with, but she didn't dare loosen up her grip. She wasn't about to come this far and accidentally drop the scroll, sending it bouncing down the mountainside to lodge in some anonymous crevice between rocks.

She kept climbing. Legs burning, lungs on fire, arms shaking, Dru finally squeezed between the rocks that ringed the top of the dead volcano. As the wind tugged at her hair, she stepped out into the open, feet crunching on broken fragments of black stone. The wide, jagged rim of the crater yawned open before her, big enough to swallow a city block. Inside, all was dead and cold and dark.

But between her and the edge of the crater loomed a dark apparition.

Seeing it, Dru backed up a step, but there was nowhere she could go. There was no way to escape the wraith.

In one fluid motion, it swung around to face her and stretched out a cadaverous arm toward the scroll. For the first time, it spoke.

"Give it to me."

32

SOUL OF SIN AND STEEL

Greyson wasn't sure which scared him more: leaving Dru all alone in the middle of Hell, or finding himself dragged toward a horde of diabolic creatures by a rampaging speed demon. Fighting the twin forces of speed and gravity, he hauled himself arm-over-arm in through the open window and slid unceremoniously into the driver's seat. Once he was out of the worst of the wind, he tried to catch his breath. But there was no time.

Hellbringer charged down the slope toward the waiting horde of demons like a wild horse rejoining its herd. But the creatures—an ever-shifting mob of bat wings, jutting horns, sinuous necks, and shining claws—looked up at them with nothing but ravenous malice. A hundred hungry jaws awaited them, each one drooling fire.

Up until now, Greyson had thought that Hellbringer was protecting him and Dru from these other demons. Clearly, the car had other plans.

Greyson grabbed the steering wheel, but it wouldn't turn. He put his boots on the clutch and brake pedals, but they were solid as rock beneath his feet. Summoning up all of his power and fury, he shouted a command: "STOP!"

But Hellbringer ignored him, which had never happened before. His was only one lone voice, drowned out by the evil legions of Tartarus. He was powerless to stop the speed demon or even change its course.

Greyson swore under his breath as he fought the controls, but it was no use. Hellbringer was dead set on rejoining his demonic brethren. Greyson could feel it on a gut level. The connection between him and the car ran far deeper than any words could express. He could sense the raging frustration shaking the steering wheel. He could practically taste the hollow longing that drove the speed demon onward, almost as intensely as if he felt those emotions burning inside himself.

Since Hellbringer had first been spawned in these fiery pits, the speed demon had spent millennia running free through the flames of the abyss. The only purpose to his existence was to one day join the Four Horsemen of the Apocalypse and ride out across the world at the end of days, delivering fire and destruction everywhere he went. But until that fateful day, Hellbringer had been at liberty to roam at will.

That freewheeling existence had come to a crashing end when mortal human sorcerers had captured Hellbringer and forced him to obey. With tangles of sorcery and searing pain, he had been wrenched out of his own world and bound into this cold, rolling Detroit steel.

For half a century after that, the demon had been imprisoned in a dark garage, unable to run free. Unable to return home. Unable to do anything but sit and wait for what must have felt like an eternity. Until Greyson had unwittingly freed him and set him loose upon the mortal world. But that cold world, despite its winding roads and open air, was nothing like the fiery, limitless horizon of Tartarus.

Now, after everything they had been through, Greyson had finally brought Hellbringer back to familiar ground. The demon in the car rejoiced. This was everything he had ever wanted. To finally go home, where he belonged.

But one look through the dirt-smeared windshield told Greyson a different story. Those weren't welcoming looks he was seeing in the snarling, hissing demon horde ahead of them. He saw nothing but malice. Anger. Hunger. Evil. Plunging headfirst into that crowd of demons would mean certain death.

Greyson hunched over the steering wheel. "Listen to me. Those things don't want you back. They want to tear you apart."

Hellbringer didn't slow down. With the beating of great leathery wings, several of the demons flapped their way up into the air. Maybe to get a better look at this new arrival. Or maybe they were racing to see who would get to take the first bite out of the car. And its driver.

"You might think you're one of them. And maybe you used to be. But not now. Not anymore." Greyson gripped the steering wheel in frustration. "Listen. I'm telling you the truth."

But then he remembered, distantly, what Dru had once told him about demons. They weren't like human beings, and they didn't believe in the concept of truth. They believed only in the reasons for the things they did, or the things they didn't do. Truth wasn't an objective thing to them, but a sliding perspective that changed depending on what they wanted to hear.

Was that how Hellbringer still viewed the world? Or had the demon car spent enough time around Dru and the rest of them to change its ways?

Hellbringer had certainly changed Greyson's life, and not always for the better. Greyson had been born with magical potential, but no powers of his own. As an *arcana rasa*, his own magic had been dangerously susceptible to being imprinted by the strongest influence around him. And when that influence turned out to be Hellbringer, Greyson had acquired powers with a distinctly demonic taint.

For the longest time, Greyson had believed he was cursed to destroy the world. But ever since Dru had first kissed him and connected her magic with his, his destiny had been forever changed. And now he knew that he himself had changed for the better. He had used his own demonic powers to help save the world. More than once. And somehow his own grim fatalism had been replaced with the bright light of hope.

If he could change, did that mean Hellbringer could change as well? Or was the speed demon doomed to go wild in Tartarus and forget all about the human world he had once inhabited?

Greyson honestly didn't know which way Hellbringer was drawn. In an existence that spanned thousands of years, the events of this past summer were barely even the blink of an eye. The idea that a fundamentally evil being could change that quickly was too much to hope for.

But it was the only hope Greyson had.

"Don't do this," he growled.

But Hellbringer ignored him and drove straight on, into the dark horde of demons.

The wall of evil creatures parted like a black writhing sea, surrounding them on all sides with unspeakable monsters. Slitted, hateful glares shot their way. Red-hot jaws chomped, spraying droplets of fire. The first claw flashed out, dragging sparks along the side of Hellbringer's fender.

Hellbringer slowed, and Greyson could feel the hot confusion rising through the dashboard like a wash of heated air. More claws struck out, gouging the paint, shaking the car.

A dark reptilian head snaked in through the open driver's window and snapped at Greyson's face. He pulled back out of the way, possible only because of the lack of headrests in the car, and threw a left hook that caught the thing just below its blazing eye socket, burning his knuckles. He didn't have enough leverage to put a ton of force into the blow, but at least it kept him from getting his face bitten off.

He worked the window crank, raising the glass and pinning the demon's big head. It roared in rage, blasting a stream of foul, sooty breath into the car. It struggled, slashing long claws against the door with a squeal of tearing metal. The window glass cracked, but it held.

Greyson had almost forgotten that he had his boots pressed hard against the pedals. But in Hellbringer's confusion over being attacked, the pedals released their rock-solid hold and his feet suddenly plunged straight to the floor.

Avoiding the snapping jaws in front of him, Greyson pulled the shift lever across and shoved it up into first gear. He fed the enormous Hemi engine all the gas it could handle, unleashed the clutch, and launched Hellbringer in a howl of burning rubber.

The long black car squatted back on its haunches and plunged deeper into the demon horde. Inhuman bodies bounced off the fenders, rolled up the long hood, and thudded over the low roof.

For a few precious seconds at least, Greyson had control back, and he used that to maximum effect. He watched for startled demons ahead flapping skyward and steered into the void they left on the ground, weaving his way through the rapidly thinning horde.

The demon trapped in the door roared and snapped at him, spraying him with burning saliva, or perhaps venom. But he couldn't even reach up to swipe it off his cheek or risk getting his hand bitten off.

On the left, a rocky outcropping rose up, and beyond it bloomed an inferno of burning gas. Greyson steered toward it, silently hoping that flying lava didn't rain down on them at the exact wrong moment.

As the outcropping flashed past, he nudged the wheel just inches to the left, slamming the trapped demon's reptilian body against the rock. The bone-crushing impact ripped the creature off the side of the car. The demon roared, and the window exploded outward in a deafening blast of broken glass.

Then they were free, and the howling horde was close behind them, in hot pursuit. Pinned in on one side by jagged rocks, and on the other by a raging river of red-hot lava, Greyson took the only escape available to them, the smoking black volcanic plain ahead.

The stench of burning rubber filled the cabin, and Greyson leaned his head out into the wind far enough to see that the tires were on fire. The hot black ground was crisscrossed by bright cracks that burned like embers. They were driving across a thin solid crust that floated on top of a lake of molten fire. If they broke through the surface, he would be killed instantly.

Hellbringer's powers of regeneration were able to replenish the tires as fast as they burned away, but only barely. With an icy crystalline sound, the driver's window regenerated, growing back into its frame like frost on a frigid day. Greyson pulled his head back inside and looked around for other escape routes, but there were none.

Just when he thought things couldn't get any worse, a thunderous roar rose up ahead. The horizon darkened as demons crowded over the next rise. Hundreds of them. Perhaps more. Beating wings rose up into the sky like thunder clouds. There was no way through.

Greyson yanked the emergency brake and spun the wheel, sending Hellbringer power-sliding around to face back the way they had come. As the tires howled around in a long arc, the thin rock crust broke away, exposing twin arcs of red-hot lava.

The demon horde they had just run from was slowly catching up, trapping them. Hellbringer stopped, engine revving, in the center of a rapidly shrinking circle of open ground.

Greyson pressed down the clutch and gripped the shift ball tight in his fist. "Listen to me," he growled through clenched teeth. "You still think you're one of them? Think you're still a full-blooded demon, like all the rest? Think again. You're not. Not anymore. Now you don't have any more in common with those things than I do. You've changed. I know it. I believe it."

He listened to the anguished roar of the engine as Hellbringer fought to get them moving again. But now that Greyson had control, he kept the clutch pedal pinned to the floor, refusing to let it bite.

"You can't go home again. Too much has changed." Greyson watched the ravenous horde rushing closer. There was only one way out of this, and that meant he had to have absolute commitment from Hellbringer. No hesitation. No doubt. He needed the speed demon to become an extension of him again, to work alongside him with split-second teamwork. Failing that, they wouldn't survive.

As the howling demons closed in around them, the engine raced, until the vibrations shook the car.

"Who do you want to be, buddy?" Greyson flexed his fingers on the shift knob. "One of them? Or one of us?"

33

THE DARKNESS WITHIN US

Dru watched with a fascinated kind of horror as the apparition shimmered and solidified, becoming more detailed in much the same way the world came into focus every time she put on her glasses. The looming, bent figure with protruding white eyes and a halo of floating silver hair slowly changed, becoming more recognizably human.

Although Dru could still see right through his ghostly, luminescent form, he became a person at last. He was tall, dressed in an open-collared shirt and jacket. A mane of long white hair fell to his shoulders, flowing in an invisible breeze. Widely spaced, piercing eyes glared down at her from underneath bushy eyebrows. His long, gaunt face became even more drawn as he looked down his hooked nose at her. Slowly, without moving his feet, he drifted closer.

With a shock of recognition, Dru suddenly realized who he was. She had seen him only in grainy black-and-white photos from the late 1960s, standing outside his desert mansion with his followers, all of them making arcane symbols with their hands. He was the leader of the Harbingers. The most dangerous sorcerer of the twentieth century. He looked much older than he did in his photos. But it was clearly him.

His name had been on the back of the photo she had found in the desert, written in faded ballpoint pen.

"Severin," she breathed.

His chin lifted regally. He looked mildly impressed.

"Lucretia told me there was another crystal sorceress." Severin's unearthly voice reverberated through the air, coming from every direction at once. It shook in the hollow of Dru's chest and slithered from every crevice, only slowly dying away into a million little echoes.

"Really? And how is Lucretia these days?" she said, as if they were discussing an old mutual acquaintance, not an evil sorceress who had tried to destroy the world with a colossal earthquake.

Severin flicked a dismissive hand. *"She's gone now."*

"What does that mean, exactly? Is she dead? Missing? Exiled?" Dru shuffled her feet, inching closer to the edge of the crater, though it was still distressingly far away. "Did you guys kick her out of the clubhouse and take away her Harbingers membership card?"

Severin's expression was unreadable. *"She was always the outsider. Always kept one foot in the mortal world. She was never truly one of us, in her heart. Such a pity, to see her driven by so much rage, and not by righteousness. She didn't have the vision to create the future. Or the dedication to wait for it."*

"Gee, that's too bad." Dru risked another half-step closer to the crater. There was a chance she could hurl the scroll down into its depths from here, but an even greater chance that Severin would simply fly over and pluck it out of the air. She had to get close enough that she didn't give him that chance. "Of course, there's another explanation for why you guys never quite got along."

Severin said nothing, as if waiting for her to go on.

She inched a little bit closer to the pit. "Have you considered that maybe she knew moving to the Shining City was a colossally bad idea? You guys wanted it to be your ultimate sorcerer digs, your big, sparkly fortress of solitude. But no living human being can permanently relocate to the netherworld. Over time, it sucks the life essence out of you. It withers you up until you lose your body and become dispossessed. As I assume you've figured out by now."

"Now we are free of mortal concerns."

Another step closer to the crater. "Yeah, well, how's that working out for you? So far, you yourself have not broken a single seal on this scroll. Other people did all the work. Because you guys did this whole doomsday thing all wrong."

Severin floated back half a pace, straightening up haughtily. *"Your ignorance is dangerous, child. You don't understand. We will create a new world."*

"Oh, really? Think so? Tell me if this sounds familiar." Dru pushed her glasses back up her nose and deliberately stepped closer to the wraith, which also brought her closer to the crater's edge. "After you guys found the apocalypse scroll, you summoned up four speed demons as offerings for the Four Horsemen of the Apocalypse. And then you just sat around in your shiny metropolis waiting for the world to end. But it didn't. For fifty years, nothing happened. Do you know why?"

Severin's ghostly fists bunched at his sides, but he said nothing.

Dru's throat went dry. She didn't know how far she could provoke him before he would lash out at her. When he did, she would have absolutely nothing to defend herself with. She just had to make it to the edge of the crater before that happened. And the best way to do that was to keep him off balance. The moment he started to believe he was running the show again, she was as good as dead.

She just had to get the scroll into the crater. Put it back where it belonged. Undo the damage that had started with Decimus, two thousand years before. So simple, and yet so impossible.

She swallowed and took another step. "Why did nothing happen? Because you left those speed demons locked up in your desert mansion. They couldn't find their Horsemen." At that, Dru thought of Greyson and all of the pain he'd been through. He'd never done anything wrong, never asked to be part of this. Then again, neither had she. But now, she had to finish this. "It wasn't until Hellbringer and the others finally got loose that things started to happen again. So really, your great, big master plan only really got rolling because some bored bureaucrat in the government of New Mexico finally got around to auctioning off all of your junk to the public. You know what's actually kind of funny about that?"

Dru's knees shook as she took another step. She was so close now, almost close enough to throw the scroll, but not quite.

She struggled to keep her voice level and project a confidence she didn't have. "The funny thing is, back when you guys were alive, and doing all those protests in the 1960s, you kept saying the government was going to destroy the world. And guess what?" She took another step. "You were right. Accidentally. But that still counts."

Severin puffed up with rage, which was so terrifying that Dru had to avert her gaze. *"You foolish girl."*

"You know we don't actually use the word 'girl' like that anymore, right?" She moved to take one last step, when Severin barked out a harsh command that stopped her cold.

"STOP!" His voice crashed all around her, like a force of nature, a voice so powerful and enraged it could almost crack through solid rock.

She froze.

His hair fluttered in an invisible breeze as he drifted to within an arm's reach of her. *"The only reason you still exist is because of my admiration for you."*

That was unexpected. Carefully, Dru leaned back and blinked up at him, wondering what he meant.

"You have potential far beyond anything Lucretia ever dreamed. Her anger left her broken. But you can be so much more. If you are not afraid to set yourself free."

"Oh." She had to swallow to keep her voice from squeaking, acutely aware of the fact that he could kill her with just a touch. "What's there to be afraid of?"

"Hmm. I know you condemn me. Because you focus only on the destruction ahead, and you can't see beyond that. But you must understand, the old world is a prison. Like it or not, there is only one way to free yourself for the new world."

She stared up into his ghostly face, studying the regal features that rippled and wavered as if they were underwater. His countenance hinted at madness, but also an incredible intelligence. She wondered how much of that was pure, cold calculation, and how much of a capacity he still had to reason and think.

"You know, who doesn't want a better world? Right? But what's wrong with making it the old-fashioned way? Through hard work. Kindness. Good deeds. An open mind. You don't have to throw it all out and destroy the world to make a better one."

"Your way is just a dream. It doesn't work. It has never worked."

"Or." She held up one finger. "Or, maybe it just requires trying harder. Maybe, you've been out of your own body for too long. If you could just remember what it's like to be human, to have all of those hopes and dreams, and the willpower to create a brighter future—"

"*Ha!*" He let out a low, slow chuckle that reverberated around the rocks circling the crater and made Dru's skin crawl. "*It is* you *who can't remember what it's like to be a normal person. Without any magical powers. Hopeless. Insignificant. Useless. You've tasted the wine of sorcery, and you've become so drunk with your own power that you fail to seize the opportunity to do something truly great. Something no one has ever done before. You can help make a new world. You can make a world the way it should be.*"

Dru utterly disagreed with the idea of trying to create a new world, but his comment about magical powers struck a nerve. Sometimes, she did wonder whether she had lost touch with the normal world.

As if he could see that sliver of doubt in her, Severin pounded on it until it felt like it would crack her open. "*You're eager to say that you can make the world a better place. But can you? We tried that. Even us, the greatest sorcerers in the world, couldn't make a lasting difference. We couldn't put an end to war. Poverty. Nuclear proliferation. Deforestation. Pollution. Can you?*" His voice echoed to silence before he spoke again, and this time it came out softer, almost human. "*Look at your world today. Half a century later, what has changed?*"

She stared out across the vast emptiness of the dark crater. She was close enough that she could hurl the scroll in from here. But the moment she drew her arm back, Severin would doubtless grab the scroll from her.

Unless.

Unless instead of throwing it, she carried it down into the crater herself. Just a few swift strides, and she could leap out over the edge.

She could see it in her mind's eye: her feet pounding across the rocks, reaching the edge, and pushing off. It would be so unthinkable, and yet so easy. And when she finally hit the bottom, bringing the scroll home, the world would be safe.

"*Answer me.*" Severin's voice boomed out. "*What has changed?*"

She blinked back stinging tears, trying to summon up the strength she needed.

"*I'll tell you. Nothing has changed. It's all the same.*" He sounded disgusted. *"The old world is a rotting corpse, holding back the spirit of possibility. If you truly want a better world, you need to free it. Just as your body is a prison for your soul. Do you know why I chose to become dispossessed? Why we all did?"*

That threw Dru. She thought they had become wraiths by accident. "Chose?"

"To be free," he whispered. *"To be* free."

Dru swallowed. The very idea of choosing to become a wraith was horrible beyond words.

"Give up the prison of your flesh. Here, now. Join me and create a new world of limitless possibilities."

It took all of Dru's willpower to quell the shaking inside her. But when she could trust herself to speak, she squared her shoulders and turned to face him. "We can never give up on the world. Because if we give up, then we all end up like you. Without anything left. Without our humanity. Without hope." She wondered if he could see what she was about to do. "I choose hope."

A strange look crossed his ghostly face, and she only realized too late what it was. Fear.

She turned to begin her run for the crater, and at that moment the rest of the wraiths flew up over the rocks on all sides. She glanced left and right, shifting her weight from one foot to the other, but there was nowhere to go. She was surrounded.

She tried to dodge around Severin, but he reached out one ghostly arm and seized her by the throat with icy fingers.

34

ALL THAT'S LEFT IS YOU

Severin's shimmering fingers tightened around Dru's throat, wintry and sharp. As his cold touch drained away the essence of her spirit, she felt like she'd been plunged headfirst into a mountain river. The burning pain of his grip made the blood roar in her ears. Each heartbeat thudded and slowed until her hands and feet felt frostbitten.

Dru gasped. Her knees finally gave out, and she sagged to the ground. As Severin reached for the scroll with his other hand, she deliberately fell face-down on top of it, covering it with her body so that he couldn't reach it.

Severin hovered over her back, still gripping her neck tight. *"You know this is futile,"* he hissed in her ear. *"You will only delay the inevitable. For fifty years, I have waited for this moment. Stalling me another minute won't change anything."*

With her free hand, she swiped uselessly at him. Her fingers went right through his incorporeal form as if he wasn't there.

Darkness pounded at the edges of Dru's vision, but she refused to give up the scroll. Shaking, she wondered if this was exactly how Rane had felt right before she lost consciousness. The pain was so intense that it robbed her of her breath. It stole almost every rational thought.

She knew there had to be some way out of this, if she could only clear her mind and think it through. But there was no time. And her strength was fading too fast.

She had to get moving. If she stayed put, Severin would drain everything away from her. And when she was finally dead, he would get the scroll anyway. Obviously, he had reached the same conclusion, because he leaned over her, waiting for her to die.

His grip on her throat made it nearly impossible to think, though she had to try. There had to be a way. But what chance did she have, without even a single crystal to use? She was helpless, unable to use the only magical power she had. She was as good as dead.

Even Rane hadn't been able to stand against an onslaught like this. And Rane was the toughest fighter Dru had ever met.

But somewhere in the midst of her tortured thoughts, Dru realized a crucial difference between her and her friend. All of Rane's magical power was directed outward: fighting, running, crushing her opponents with sheer physical power. In contrast, Dru's power was all directed inward. She had spent her entire life trying to channel her own inner magic into crystals. Her strength came from controlling her energy in the midst of the strange and sometimes unstable vibrations of crystals.

The wraith's grip on her was far more painful than the drain of any crystal she had ever touched. But aside from the order of magnitude, it wasn't fundamentally all that different. Her only chance to fight him off depended entirely on the same skills she'd honed with her crystal magic.

Before she could give in to the terror that threatened to paralyze her, she gathered every last shred of inner strength. With as much bravery as she could muster, she mentally pushed back against the icy cold fingers. They tightened their grip, making it impossible to breathe. Her pulse thundered in her ears. The black spots pounding at the edges of her vision grew into a dark tunnel, robbing the desolate wasteland in front of her of what little color it had.

Steeling her nerve, she reached down into her very core and brought up her last reserves of magic. She put it all on the line, knowing that Severin's icy fingers were draining it away as fast as she summoned it up. In a minute, at the most, she would be dead.

But she had no choice. There was no Plan B. It was all or nothing.

With a groan of pure animal pain, Dru reached forward with her free hand and dragged herself a few inches closer to the edge of the crater. Then a little more. It wasn't much, but all the same, a renewed flicker of hope burned inside her. If she could just reach the edge before it was too late . . .

"Think of the world you're trying to save." Severin's echoing voice slithered

through her tears, filling her with dread. *"Rife with disease, starvation, open warfare. Is that what you want, for eternity? Nothing has changed since my time. Nothing will change in yours."*

Dru tried not to listen. Tried to block him out. She knew the world itself was depending on her. But it was difficult to visualize what that really meant. She tried to picture the world, and came up with only hazy images of the planet as it was visible from space. Sweeping vistas of foreign lands she'd seen only on a screen. Anonymous crowds of people. None of that fired her up enough to overcome the pain of having her soul drained out of her body, bit by painful bit.

As the wraiths circled around her like crows around a dying animal, she wondered what had happened to Rane and Salem. Were they still alive? Had the wraiths merely slipped past them to come here? Or had her friends' bodies been left lying behind in the long, dark tunnel down to Tartarus?

And what about Greyson? Had he somehow escaped from this abyss, despite Hellbringer's betrayal? Or had he been overwhelmed by a ravenous horde of demons, each one eager to devour his soul?

Would she ever see any of them again? Or were they all gone now? Had they sacrificed themselves to give her this moment, this one single chance? Had they bought her enough time?

That thought finally pushed her onward. She couldn't let their sacrifices be in vain. She had to honor what they had done. She had to take this one chance they had bravely given her, and make them proud. She couldn't let her friends down.

"The world is doomed. Let it go," Severin whispered in her ear. *"Nothing has changed. Nothing ever will."*

But Dru forced him out of her thoughts. She crawled on her belly, ignoring the rocks that jabbed at her, the fissures in the broken ground that clutched at her failing body. Despite the pain, she willed herself to keep going, even as Severin's grip drained her, until almost nothing was left.

Inch by painful inch, she crawled onward toward the jagged edge of the crater. She refused to give up. Refused to stop.

Just when she felt she could go no further, she reached out one bleeding hand and found nothing but empty air in front of her. A whistling wind plucked at her hair, tingled her numb skin.

Trembling, she lifted up her head.

She had reached the lip of the crater. Below, the vast pit descended into darkness, a gaping hole with sheer sides and no visible bottom. Dru, unable to breathe, blinked at the golden sparks of light dancing in her vision, and realized that they weren't just hallucinations. They were real. Somewhere far below, tiny motes of light blinked and winked back up at her.

As she faded away, she wondered what those strangely beautiful lights were. Could they be souls trapped in eternal torment? Or something else entirely? Even now, on the brink of death, her curiosity wouldn't let go.

This was it, she realized. This was the moment. Her time was up.

She shifted the weight of her shivering body and slowly pulled out the length of the scroll. Its silver tips winked in the light of the fiery skies.

Looming over her back, Severin cackled in triumph and reached for the scroll.

She pushed out her last breath in a whisper: *"This* is . . . what's . . . *changed."* And with her last bit of strength, she hurled the apocalypse scroll down into the abyss, back where it belonged.

It tumbled as it fell, end over end. The silver spikes at its tips glinted in the bloody light from above. As it shrank away into the darkness, the edge of the stained tan parchment flapped, held fast by the last of the seven red seals, the only one unbroken.

Severin's gloating laugh turned into a deafening roar of rage. He released Dru and dove after the scroll, his ghostly body leaving behind a luminous trail. Shrieking in unison, the other wraiths streaked after him, spiraling down into the dark heart of the abyss toward the dwindling scroll.

The moment the bony fingers left her neck, Dru dragged in a ragged breath and coughed. Her entire body spasmed, starved of not only oxygen but also the vital essence of magic that made her who she was. Shaking and gasping, she rolled over onto her side, flooded with remorse.

She had brought the scroll back here to Tartarus, and cast it into the pit, but it wasn't enough. Severin had almost reached it. His shadowy arms reached out toward it. The other wraiths were right behind him.

Clearly, they would catch the scroll before it hit the bottom. She had failed.

Then all at once, the tiny motes of light below flared brighter.

No, not brighter, she realized. *Closer.*

They weren't tiny at all. Just farther away than she had imagined. Each one was a flying demon, soaring upward from the depths on beating wings of fire. And there were hundreds of them. An unholy legion.

The tight knot of luminous wraiths split apart, each one streaking in a different direction, desperately trying to escape the demons. But there were too many of them. The dispossessed Harbingers weren't human anymore, Dru realized, but they were still human souls. And the demons were ravenous.

One by one, the wraiths were caught and devoured by the demons, sometimes by two and three at a time. Their frozen souls disappeared into fiery jaws with pitiful shrieks that echoed up from the depths. Severin was the last to go, and his tortured bellow of rage pierced Dru's ears. Then, in an instant, he was gone forever.

Meanwhile, the scroll continued its tumbling plunge until it was lost from sight, far below the carnage. Long moments later, a blinding light blossomed in the depths. It started as no more than a pinpoint and quickly grew into a swirling inferno.

Lava raged up from the depths, refilling the mountain Decimus had emptied out thousands of years before. A blast of foul, scorching heat shot up, blasting Dru back from the edge. She rolled away from the roaring fires, scrabbling to catch herself on trembling hands and knees.

It occurred to her that being here, at the top of an erupting volcano, was probably the worst possible place to be. She struggled to climb down though the rocks, but her legs failed her. She fell and tumbled painfully down the smooth slope below. The going was easier here, below the rocks, but she still had miles to go, and her strength was gone.

She lay on her back on the trembling ground, unable to move any further. The air grew hotter. Her breath burned in her lungs. The rumbling volcano was almost ready to burst.

She tried to take cold comfort from the fact that she had done the right thing. Two thousand years after the fact, the apocalypse scroll was finally back where it belonged. She had saved the world. Not bad for a day's work.

But still, not dying here would make the day even better.

A thin, strange noise cut through the deafening rumble of the volcano. It was actually two steady high notes in one, and it droned on endlessly. If anything, it grew louder. Dru struggled to place the odd sound until she realized it was a car horn.

She took a ragged breath and managed to turn her pounding head. To her amazement, a red-orange plume of flame burned its way across the tortured landscape, like a land-bound meteor. It shot across the lava that cracked open the dark ground, shot past pools of magma that burst with incandescent gases, and streaked directly toward her. A black, angular shape burned at the head of the flames.

It was Hellbringer.

Raging fire roared off every inch of the demon car, flagging out behind it in long blazing tongues, spewing volumes of greasy black smoke. Red-hot plumes of churned-up lava shot out behind its tires as it cut a searing double-track across the scorched ground.

Tears spilled down Dru's face, drying instantly in the hot wind as Hellbringer roared up the slope toward her. As it grew closer, she could make out the claw marks that savaged the car's lean body from every angle, exposing shimmering ripples of raw metal.

Behind the cracked and blackened windshield was Greyson. She'd never been happier to see him.

She must have passed out for a moment, because the next thing she knew, she could sense Greyson leaning over her, calling her name. But she was too exhausted to open her eyes. She struggled even to breathe.

He leaned close and whispered in her ear. His words cut right through the rumble of the volcano and stirred her soul. "There was a time I was lost. I had become a monster. And you brought me back."

She managed to open her eyes and look up into his stubbled, soot-streaked face.

"I love you," he said.

She wanted to tell him that she loved him too, and that right then, he was the best thing she had ever seen. She didn't have the strength to speak.

But she didn't have to. Gently, Greyson kissed her cracked lips. At his touch, she felt his magical power flow back into her like a cool rain falling upon a thirsty desert. As an *arcana rasa*, Greyson's magical potential had always been closely paired to hers. But where it had once sustained her spells, it now sustained her life.

As his energy flowed into her, her entire body tingled. The tiny spark of life inside her was rekindled before it could be snuffed out forever. Sensation came roaring back across her skin, too much to bear. She gasped, and it was as if she had relearned how to breathe. She couldn't stop trembling, and despite the searing heat, she shivered.

Greyson gathered her up and carried her to Hellbringer. She was only barely aware of the door closing and him sitting in the creaking seat beside her. Everything shook as the mountain trembled, and then the volcano erupted in a blinding roar of fire and smoke.

Hellbringer charged down the mountainside at blistering speeds, as house-sized boulders hurtled down around them and tumbled across the blackened landscape. Demons fled before them in all directions, either panicked or exuberant, or both. The deafening eruption went on for an eternity. It was too much for Dru to take.

Darkness engulfed her. But it felt like only a moment later when she was jolted awake by the door opening again. Rane was shaking her awake.

"We did it, cowgirl!" Rane shouted excitedly. "We did it!" Behind her, even Salem looked impressed.

Then they were driving uphill again, as Salem pushed aside fallen rocks to make way. Dru slipped in and out of consciousness. She was vaguely aware of holding onto Greyson's hand as he drove them out of Tartarus into the peaceful shimmering lights of the Shining City.

This alien place, which was once threatening and creepy, now shone down through the windshield with a glittering promise of so much more to come. For the first time, Dru felt like doomsday was finally over, and her whole life stretched out before her.

"We can't stay here long," she whispered, thinking of the ill-fated Harbingers gradually losing their bodies to the allure of this netherworld metropolis.

"We won't," Greyson promised, squeezing her hand. "We're going home."

35

ALL IN A DOOMSDAY'S WORK

*T*hree weeks later . . .

The half-empty potion bottle sat dejectedly on the front counter of Dru's shop, its wire-bound cap slightly crooked. Inside the unlabeled blue glass, a dark oily liquid emitted tiny, slowly rising bubbles. Dru patiently folded her hands on the front counter and put on her best customer service smile. "Well, the reason the potion didn't work is because you're not supposed to rub it into your skin. You're supposed to *drink* it."

Ember made a face, and her piercings flashed in the morning sunlight. "I am not drinking that. It smells like feet."

"Well, that's what it's *for*, so if you really want to—"

"No. Give me another potion," Ember snapped. "Not this one. I need something that works."

Dru delicately cleared her throat and half-turned to lift an open palm before the racks of potions behind her. "As you can see, I have a whole wall full of potions. You're welcome to buy as many as you want and see if any of them work for you. Or, I could help narrow it down for you if you will just tell me what you're looking for." She tried to keep the exasperation out of her voice. The whole sorcerer tradition of secrecy had long ago lost its rock-star mystique for Dru. Now it was just plain annoying.

She badly needed coffee, and their machine was broken. Greyson had run out for some, but for now she had to fend off her latest irate customer without the benefit of caffeine. With an effort, she put on a smile and added, "You know I would love to help you. With . . . whatever it is you're trying to do."

Ember scowled and glanced over both shoulders, even though they were alone at the moment. Her dark-lined eyes roamed around as she navigated her own lengthy internal decision-making process. Finally, she leaned closer and said in a low voice, "I am tracking a creature in the high country."

"A monster? In the mountains?" That immediately perked Dru up. "What kind?"

Ember looked distressed. "I do not know. That is the problem. No one has seen it yet. It arrived during a thunderstorm, a severe one, and it's been eating livestock."

"What kind? Cows? Sheep? . . . Llamas?"

Ember pondered that for a moment. "It seems to prefer ostriches."

"Ostriches. Hmm." Dru nodded encouragingly. And waited. When no further explanation was forthcoming, Dru finally added, "Well, there's a lot of potential historical precedent. We've had ostrich farms in Colorado for more than a hundred years. Mostly for feathers."

"I do not believe the creature is interested in feathers. It picks clean the bones." She made a face.

"All right. How about this: does it leave any tracks?"

Ember hesitated. "Yes."

". . . And?"

"The footprints are *very* weird." She pronounced this new information with gravity, as if it explained everything. She looked at Dru expectantly, waiting for an answer.

"Okeydokey then. That narrows it down. Let me just go in back and consult my Big Book of Ostrich-Munching Weirdos. See if anything turns up."

"Yes, do that." Apparently, the sarcasm was entirely lost on Ember. "How long will this take?"

Dru sighed, wondering for the thousandth time why she still loved running this shop. As she looked around, she realized what it was that she cared about most. Not the stuff itself—the crystals, the potions, the books, and everything else—but the incredible opportunities they offered. The chance to fight back against evil, keep the world safe, and solve the deepest magical mysteries in history. That was what she really loved.

The customers? Not so much.

Just then, Opal hustled up from the back room. She was closely followed by the muscle-bound Feral, who was wearing shorts and a tank top only because Dru had printed out a brand-new NO-SHIRT-NO-SHOES-NO-SERVICE sign, which now also bore "NO PANTS" in Opal's handwriting.

"All I'm saying is, you know you're a beautiful woman," Feral said as innocently as he could manage, strutting into the room behind her.

"I know I am. And I also know that my boyfriend is standing outside with a whole truckload of power tools." Her voice took on a dangerously sweet edge. "And he's not afraid to use them on *any* problem that's bothering me."

Feral looked wounded. But not much. Besides, he was distracted by discovering Ember's presence, and he gave her an appreciative up-and-down glance that she warmly returned. Just as quickly, she turned aloof, as if she hadn't even noticed him.

Dru looked from Ember to Feral and back again, sensing a solution to her latest problem. "Ember, did you know that Feral here is an expert on tracking down creatures in the high country?"

Ember looked at him again, this time with interest. "Oh, really?"

"Hel-*lo* there," Feral said with a blinding white smile. He held out his hand. "I'm Feral. And she's right. I can help you find anything you want." His tone made it crystal clear that he wasn't just talking about monsters.

As they chatted, Dru motioned for Opal to join her on the sidewalk out front, where Ruiz and Salem stood side by side, frowning up at the newly repaired façade surrounding the front of the building.

As the door shut behind them, Dru took one last glance back at Ember, trying to read her body language. "I get the feeling she might be playing hard to get."

Opal made a rude noise. "Not *that* hard to get." She turned around to follow Ruiz's gaze to the newly painted sign that read, "*Dru & Opal's Crystal Connection.*"

"I thought my name was going to be bigger," Opal pointed out.

"It *is* bigger," Dru said. "You have twenty-five percent more letters in your name than I do. Sixty-seven percent, if you count the apostrophe S."

Opal flapped her fingers. "Yeah, but I saw what it was supposed to look like. It was supposed to look a lot bigger."

Ruiz hiked up his crowded tool belt and looked thoughtful. "It's cause it's so high up, baby. Your name's at the top of the sign, so it's like, it's farther away. It's a perspective thing. Because of the angle. It's all in the geometry."

Salem gave him a sidelong look from underneath the brim of his top hat.

"But look, see." Ruiz stepped back a few paces and held up his thumbs and fingers to frame the sign in his vision. He grinned wider. "Your name's up on top! That's what counts."

Opal didn't look completely convinced. She tottered over to him on sparkling purple stiletto heels with gold fringe and turned to peer upward. "You think, driving by, people are going to see the sign?"

"Oh, yeah. They're gonna see the sign. Look at that." He leaned closer to her, holding up his fingers for her to see.

Salem rolled his eyes and turned to Dru. "This has been oodles of fun," he said acidly. "Really. And a worthwhile use of my powers, all of this carpentry et cetera. Putting your shop all back together for you yet again."

"Well, I know. And that's why I want to thank you. For everything. I really do." Dru carefully avoided pointing out that it was his magic that had, in fact, destroyed her shop in the first place. "You know, we've been through all these crazy things together, and I just want to take a moment to tell you that I have an amazing amount of respect for your powers. And your skills. And your teamwork. There's no one else like you." She had rehearsed that little speech over and over again in her head, but she was still surprised to discover that she meant every word. "You're a great sorcerer, Salem."

He couldn't have looked more shocked if she had slapped him. He scrutinized her face as if searching for the slightest flaw in her sincerity, and when he found none, his head gave an angry little twitch. Dru couldn't help but smile when she realized that she might have just blown Salem's mind.

"And you're . . . You're . . ." His mouth worked, but nothing came out. His squinting gaze bounced all around, settling on everything except her. "You, darling, are . . ." His fingers twitched at his sides. "Surprisingly, you *can* be a real asset."

"Aww, thanks." As backhanded of a compliment as that was, Dru could see how painful it was for Salem to say anything nice. She almost wanted to give him a hug.

Almost. But even she had limits.

Fast footsteps pounded up the alley and Rane rounded the corner, puffing, in a matching hot pink sports bra and shorts, with brand-new black running shoes. Breathing hard, sweat pouring down her body, she threw one arm around Salem and checked her vitals on her wrist monitor. "*Hehhh. Hehhh,*" she panted. "Hey, sweetie." She yanked him closer and planted a kiss on his cheek.

When she released him, he looked a little shaken, but considerably less sour than usual. Still avoiding eye contact, he pulled out his car keys, which dangled from a shiny brass skull key fob. "Time to go."

"Oh. Yeah. He has to go home and check on his *experiments,*" Rane explained to Dru, her tone making clear exactly how important they really weren't. Then she turned back to Salem. "Hey, did you talk to Greyson about your problem?"

"No, he's not here," Salem snapped. "Let's be off. Now."

Dru gave Salem a close, clinical look. "Are you feeling okay? What kind of problem do you have?"

"Not *me,*" Salem growled. "It's a problem with the hearse. But it's not important right now."

Rane grinned. "It's the springs in back. They're going bad. They get all squeaky when we start bouncing. They're like, *eee-*ee, *eee-*ee, *eee-*ee." She made a rhythmic up-and-down motion with her hand.

It wasn't until Salem began to blush around the edges that Dru realized exactly what kind of motion Rane was talking about. But she pretended not to understand. "Huh. That's weird. But I wouldn't worry. It's probably nothing."

"No, it's definitely a problem," Rane insisted. "Totally distracting."

"Well, maybe Greyson can check it out. Sometime." She waved it off, desperate to end the conversation before it got even more awkward. "Later. When you're not busy."

"Oh, it's definitely when we're getting busy—"

"Alrighty, then. Anyway—"

"And when I say *busy*, I mean—"

"Yes," Dru said firmly. "I get it."

"Boom chicka wow wow." Rane gave her an exaggerated wink. "Know what I mean?"

Salem bristled. "Yes. Even *she* can get the picture at this point."

"Yeah," Dru said flatly, folding her arms. "Even me. I strive to be amazing." She'd been *so* close to actually getting a real compliment out of Salem for once. But now he had, unfortunately, gone back to his normal snarky self. Some things never changed.

Rane hugged her, despite Dru's attempts to escape getting coated in someone else's sweat, and then she led Salem around back to the parking space behind the shop. Ruiz tagged along with them, to get more tools out of his van.

Dru found herself alone with Opal, surveying the freshly restored shop with a sigh of satisfaction. "It's been forever since things have gotten back to normal."

"Forever and a doomsday," Opal muttered. "Besides, you call this normal? Any of this?" She waved her gold jewelry-decked hands around to encompass the shop, and the city, and probably the entire world.

"Well. Normal for *us*."

A peal of thunder rolled down the street, despite the clear blue sky. But it wasn't actual thunder—it was the rumble of a demon-powered Hemi engine. Hellbringer pulled up in front of the shop, a sinister wedge of pitch blackness in the golden morning sunlight. Even after the car slunk to a stop and the roaring exhaust went silent, the speed demon looked ready to launch into motion at the slightest provocation.

She had come to accept that although she might never completely trust Hellbringer, it would always be on her side. Especially with Greyson around to keep it in line. At its heart, Hellbringer was still a demon, and it always would be. But that didn't mean it was doomed to be diabolically evil. It may have started out that way, but when the time came, it had finally set itself apart from its fiendish brethren and come back to save her life. If there was one thing she had learned from her journey into the abyss and back, it was that even demons could choose their own destiny.

As she contemplated that, Greyson climbed out, sunglasses flashing in the sunlight. Without preamble, he set a cardboard tray full of coffee cups on the roof of the car.

"Now, that coffee right there is the best thing I've seen all day," Opal said gladly. "Next time, you just need to teach that man to bring us some donuts, too."

Greyson disappeared into the car again and emerged with a wide, flat donut box from Yummy's.

Opal turned to look at Dru with newfound respect. "It's true. You are a real sorceress." Her phone rang with a blast of C+C Music Factory and she tapped it with a perfectly manicured finger. "It's a beautiful day at *Dru and Opal's Crystal Connection*. How may I help you? . . . The big cluster of amethyst? Probably. UPS should've been here already."

She headed inside, and Dru sauntered toward Greyson, almost deliriously happy at the sound of the newly reinstalled front door bell chiming open behind her.

"Hey there," she said when she reached the curb.

Greyson shut Hellbringer's door. "Hey." Before she could say more, he swept her into his strong arms and gave her a kiss that made her forget for a moment about everything else. The shop. The wraiths. The apocalypse scroll. Even the fact that the world was safe once more. At that moment in time, all that mattered was that he was there with her, so close that she could feel his heart beating faster.

When she finally broke away, breathless, she found herself staring up into his blue eyes. There was so much strength there, and love, and for once, peace. She could happily get lost in those eyes. They slowly crinkled around the edges as he smiled down at her.

"What?" he finally asked.

"I don't know. With all the danger that's been around us, sometimes

I forget what you look like without those red, glowing eyes." She traced the stubble along his jaw with one finger. "You do look better, by the way, with your natural baby blues. Just to clarify."

"Hmm. Good." He shook his head, ever so slightly. "I guess that's because, for once, it's *not* the end of the world as we know it."

She smiled widely. "And I feel fine." With that, she kissed him again, and held on tight.

THE END